Eye of the

Eye of the Storm

GEORGINA BROWN

BLACK
lace

Black Lace novels are sexual fantasies.
In real life, make sure you practise safe sex.

First published in 1995 by
Black Lace
332 Ladbroke Grove
London
W10 5AH

Typeset by CentraCet Limited, Cambridge
Printed and bound by Mackays of Chatham

ISBN 0 352 33044 9

Chapter One

'And now to bed,' he said, his lips warm against her ear.

She didn't answer – not in words. She sort of murmured as his fingers dug into the burgundy velvet of her short dress where it filled outwards over her pert behind. Tonight she'd worn no panties, hoping just the vague scent of her naked pubes would fire his imagination. But much to her frustration, he didn't seem to have noticed.

She rubbed her body against him, swaying as she did so. His body remained rigid, firm. It's amost as though nothing is expected of him in return, she thought.

She swallowed her disappointment. She would try harder, rub her burning flesh against him more intensely, bombard him with all the physical language she could. Only then would he react and take her. But in his own way: never in hers.

Her flesh was burning and familiar sensations stirred like a whirlpool deep inside. Powerful urges threatened to overwhelm her, yet she controlled them, just as he expected her to. Sadly, even after knowing Julian for six months, her true potential had not yet been reached.

'Thanks for a great evening,' she said to him. She smiled with warmth and longing, and muffled his response with her lips. She promised herself this would be the last time she would see him, but she'd been telling herself that for a while now. It would take a truly momentous happening to push him from her life. In the absence of anything more erotic, he had become a habit.

She also had a lot to be thankful for. This flat she shared with him – on those occasions he was home – was a big improvement on her single bedsit, which was all she could afford when she'd first come to London. Comfort was something she had to consider, though materialism as such had never been one of her hang-ups.

Burying her misgivings as she had before, she kicked her shoes to one side, then stood on tiptoe to kiss him, savouring the moment of closeness, of slowly rising passion. His lips tasted of wine and food. His cock was still soft against her, but she could work on that, given time. But time in this relationship was slowly running out, and that was a crying shame.

'Told you it did good food. Wine was a little warm perhaps,' he said, between kisses. A whiff of expensive aftershave and absolute maleness assaulted her nostrils. In that moment, she felt she could devour him whole.

How faddy, she thought to herself, and how trivial, talking about food at a time like this. But she said nothing. Food and drink were out of her mind. It was his body she wanted – badly!

'Trust you to notice that.' She drooled against his ear, her voice pouring like thick brandy. She nibbled the soft fleshy lobes and ran her tongue around the firmer contours. As though pre-empting his penetration of her, she poked the tip of her tongue into his ear. He groaned at first, then he spoke.

'Didn't you?'

'No. Of course not.' She sighed. 'I was far too busy noticing you.' Her soft words and half-closed eyes were convincing him.' She wondered if she was not truly convinced herself, then cast the thought aside. It would wait: she would wait. But what for?

2

Judging by the warm sweep of his hands down over her back and the sudden stirring of his hardening sex against the softness of her belly, her sentiments had hit the right spot. Inwardly she congratulated herself.

Soon his penis would grow harder and stir from its nest of tangled hair. With long fingers she would stir it even more, ply it with every little trick she could think of that would be both glorious to her and acceptable to him.

From his shoulders, she ran her hands down over his chest. Even through his shirt she could feel the firm contours of his chest muscles. She ran her hands further and felt his stomach tighten beneath her touch. Leisurely but purposefully, her hands fell further until they rested on the hardening lump that pulsated against his zip. She swallowed deep murmurs of ecstasy and closed her eyes, her dark lashes softly caressing her cheek. Soon she would have him. Soon – too soon perhaps – he would be inside her.

Lips, teeth, then lips again, rapidly in succession, his breathing, her breathing, snatched in hurried gasps wherever they could be. There was heat in their kisses, their caresses, their bodies. Then he pulled away – just as he had so many times before. Toni wanted to scream. Instead, she just smiled sweetly, the sugar of her smile hiding the surge of frustration. Instinctively, she knew what was to come and asked herself the same question she had asked herself many times before. How could someone as beautiful as him be so controlled, so much a slave to routine. She guessed what he was going to say even before he said it.

'Comfort, my darling Antonia. Let's have some comfort.'

Her eyes met his with assent, though the sparkle betrayed a question rather than desire. No matter. She just couldn't help it. Must it be the bed again? Why not the sofa, the rug, or even the kitchen table? She'd even open her legs for it across the cooker or in the sink just for some variety. But Julian was formal in everything, even to the point of calling her Antonia. No one called her that, not even her mother, and *she'd* chosen the name.

She controlled her sigh, unwilling to upset him. Rarely had he swerved away from the same format, the same position, the same bloody *bed*! When he had, it had been at her suggestion, and then only undertaken begrudgingly. When had this started to happen, she wondered? But she already knew the answer. He had always been like this: she had just been blinded by his sheer good looks, his masculine beauty.

A party had occurred in some luxury apartment in Kensington or Knightsbridge: the guests had obviously been selected for their rare good looks and sheer sexuality. Beautiful looks had rubbed shoulders with beautiful clothes.

She remembered wearing a green silk dress to that party, and that was *all* she had worn except for her shoes. It had caressed her body rather than dressed it. Her skin had been more bronze than it was now and her hair had tumbled like sun-kissed mercury to her waist. Green suited her. It complemented her hair; it matched her eyes.

The room had been warm, and the double doors had opened on to a wide balcony. Outside, she had found him there all alone. He'd been eyeing the city lights rather than the dazzling delights attending the party. Somehow that had attracted her – his solitude, his apartness. On top of that, his looks were breathtaking.

He was all man, animal, desirable. His hair was dark, though tinged with a whisper of grey at his temples. Rugged was easily the best way to describe his face, velvet his eyes. His chin was split with a deep dimple like a ripe peach.

If she hadn't touched his flesh and known it was warm and alive, she could almost have been convinced that his firm neck and hard body were sculpted from marble. Not white marble – cold, unyielding and reminiscent of the British Museum – but golden and undulating with hints of beige like the type used as flooring in a Floren-tine villa.

From the loins of that superbly structured body, his cock rose, strong, proud, demanding her as if by right. And she yielded. Right from the start, she had yielded, falling for him as easily as she would tumble downstairs.

The velvet dress fell in a soft mound around her ankles. The cream satin underwear (without the knick-ers), the sheer stockings and crisply frilled suspender belt followed before she slid between the cool sheets of the bed.

With just a sheet covering her nudity, yet outlining her curves, she watched him, her legs gently moving one against the other as if to contain the warm wetness that surged in between them. Her smile stayed fixed, hiding the frustration inside and choking the words of impatience that loitered in her throat.

As each item of clothing was carefully removed, he placed it on a hanger, re-buttoned it, then returned it to its proper place in the wardrobe, brushed with a firm hand, studied by a stern eye for any wisp of cotton, any glint of fluff.

She held back her exasperation. When they'd first met, she'd been amused by his fastidious neatness. Now it only irritated her. Was she really getting bored? Had their relationship run its course? Not quite, she told herself, not yet – at least, not tonight.

Her eyes slid to the clutch of coal-black pubic hair from which his cock jerked like a drum major's baton.

Behind her hand she smiled. He was standing in front of the mirror, viewing himself sideways. The ritual was unaltered. Was it purely to reassure himself, or just to impress her? She could never quite tell.

He bent his arms, fists above his head, and struck a classic pose, flexing his biceps. She wasn't fooled. Eyelids half-lowered, she could see his eyes were fixed on his pulsating penis. Julian was proud of his body. Sometimes she felt he admired his own body more than he did hers. It could almost be said that he had more of an inclination to make love to his own body than to hers.

She tossed her head and her critical thoughts shattered, but not completely of course. They were still there, piling up in the corners of her mind, and even now they were gradually reforming. Soon, they would be whole again. Her patience wavered.

'Are you coming to bed, darling?' she murmured enticingly, her velvet words hiding her growing impatience. 'I'm wide and wet and longing to feel it in me.'

She had an urge to add 'Never mind admiring it, how about doing something with it instead?' But Julian didn't like that sort of humour. It had a deflating effect on his intentions and she didn't want to forgo such a fitting end to a lovely evening. Like his clothes, his personal appearance, and his hygiene in general, sex was a precise science – to be applied and undertaken in as orderly a fashion as possible.

'Right there, darling,' he answered, his right hand stroking his purple-veined protrusion which responded by delivering a mere spit of salt-laden juice from its throbbing head.

At last, he pulled back the covers and got in beside her.

Despite the familiarity of it all, she began to move as the warmth of his body met hers. She couldn't help but respond. His flesh felt hot compared with the coldness of the cotton sheets beneath her. There was a comfort in it and obvious arousal.

She murmured with pleasure as his hands stroked her breasts, his fingers teased and rolled her nipples as his lips and teeth nibbled at her ears, her neck, her throat. Her stomach tightened as she felt the hard probing of his penis against her, hot and slightly sticky with the gob of juice.

She raised one leg, then slid one hand from his ribs

and over his stomach. Her fingers curled around the velvet softness of his throbbing tool. He gasped as she did it, and she moaned, thrusting her hips towards it. There was so much she could do with it if he'd let her. But he didn't.

With Julian, it was a case of touch, not taste. Oral sex was something he did not approve of. She'd tried it once, clamping her mouth over him in such a way that he could not escape. He'd been angry afterwards and had left without kissing her goodbye or stating exactly when he would be back. She let it go, though it left her dissatisfied. If this was all he wanted, then this was all he got.

'Darling,' he murmured against her ear. A given signal, as usual. She sighed and grimaced rather than smiled. He ignored it.

She tried not to feel used as she rolled over on to her back like a performing dog. Turning back her moist lips with her own fingers, she guided him in.

Despite her feelings of frustration, she couldn't help but squeal with delight as her muscles gripped the iron-hard invader. Her pelvis began to move in rhythm, slowing when he did, quickening when he quickened.

She closed her eyes, concentrating on her movements, rising to meet him at just the right time, the time when his pelvic bone pounded against her aching clitoris, sharpening her determination to gain her orgasm, to not be left unsatisfied.

In murmured breath, she stated her final release, her nails digging only slightly into his shoulders.

'Please, Toni . . .'

'Sorry, darling.'

Breathless, her ecstasy slightly blunted by his reminder, she lessened her grip. Julian didn't like blemishes on his skin. Julian liked to take care of himself.

He raised himself up off her. Another signal. She gritted her teeth, turned over, then got up on to her knees. Running her hand down over her belly and between her legs, she yet again guided him in.

He shoved hard, his balls slapping against her inner thighs. His nails dug into her rounded buttocks, his thumbs constantly smoothing at the dividing crease.

She braced her hands, knowing the tempo would now increase. Her breasts swung back and forth like half-full beanbags as he slammed harder. In the mirror that furnished the wall at the side of their bed, she glimpsed the picture they represented. She on all fours, tits swinging, he slamming backwards and forwards, hands clutching her flesh, head thrown back, mouth open as he screamed his final spurt like a man in pain.

In turn, they both went to the bathroom. Both washed before going back to bed.

Unnecessary, she thought to herself, welcoming the stickiness and smell that sex left her with. But Julian did not look at things that way. Julian was more than urbane: he was fastidious.

His arm around her, she snuggled down for sleep. She should be grateful, she told herself. Good job, nice flat, nice guy – *and* he paid half the rent. What more could she want?

She pushed the question to the back of her mind, pressed her buttocks against the soft nest of hair and flesh in the crook of his body, but did not sleep. She had a question and wanted an answer. 'When will I see you again?'

He paused as if checking a mental diary.

'Seventeenth, I think.'

Two and a half weeks, she thought, and suddenly felt empty. Two and a half weeks of waiting like a trapped bird in a well-upholstered cage.

'They certainly keep you busy,' she murmured, biting her lip to stop herself from shouting what she was really feeling.

8

'They certainly do. Not a spare moment to myself. Except when I'm with you, my darling.'

He kissed her shoulder and she murmured with pleasure. With that one act, he had pushed her fears and doubts to the back of her mind. She had a lot to be thankful for. She had affection, if a humdrum and very infrequent sex life. She should be satisifed with her life and her sex, but if she was really honest with herself, she was not. Somewhere there were greater heights she could ascend, though that somewhere (or a someone) was as yet unknown to her.

In the morning he was gone. A whole day at work. A whole day to look forward to a lonely night and many more of them in the following two and a half weeks. Her life was sliding by.

Fidelity was something Julian had not asked of her, so occasionally she had taken the opportunity to seduce or be seduced. There had been many lovers, yet somehow still there was something missing. Adventure, she told herself one night after the young black guy she had just seduced had left and gone home. Adventure – that's what I could do with.

But adventure would have to wait. She was still with Julian and the habit was hard to break.

Work was even more boring than her personal life. In fact, it was a lot more boring.

'What's on for tonight, then?' asked Audrey, legal executive from commercial leasing.

'Lean Cuisine for one. Julian won't be back for a fortnight.' She thought about the eight-inch rubber replica she'd bought from a city sex shop, but didn't tell Audrey *that* was her entertainment for the evening.

'Find yourself another fella.'

'Easier said than done,' Toni sighed.

And here she was, staring at the cold red and white packet, the microwave gaping open-mouthed at her foolishness. Was she stupid, or was she stupid? She was stupid: Stupid and sex-starved. Then the doorbell rang.

9

The woman who stood there was a stranger. Her hands were clasped tightly together, and there was an accusing look in her eyes.

'Yes?'

The woman blinked nervously.

'I'm looking for a Miss Yardley.'

Instinctively, Toni knew something was wrong. Who was this woman with dark hair, but greying at the temples?

Self-consciously, Toni raised one hand to her own hair which was red and reached almost to her waist.

'Can I help you?' she asked. It had occurred to her that the woman must be looking for someone and had rung her bell to ask directions. That was no longer an option: the woman had used her name.

Something about the woman's expression caused a knot to form in her stomach. Perhaps it was the accusing stare of the brown eyes or the way she fidgeted with the clasp of her handbag.

'I've come to tell you to stay away from my husband.'

'What?'

'You've been seeing my husband,' the woman went on. 'I've come to warn you off.' Her voice was very steady – almost a monotone. The words sounded well-rehearsed, as though she'd said the same thing many times before to other young women.

Toni laughed nervously. 'There must be some mistake!'

'Julian,' the woman said. 'Julian Bartholomew. I have proof.'

With trembling fingers she undid the clasp of her handbag. Toni stared, her mouth open as the woman pulled out what looked like a credit card receipt and a hotel bill. She waved it before her face.

The bill heading was familiar. She recognised the name of the hotel, and remembered the occasion. It was a special treat for her birthday. One night in a plush hotel. It was all he had had time for. Work, he had said;

10

he was married to his work. Not to a woman – or so she had thought.

Carefully, she took the piece of paper. 'He never told me.' Her voice faded as her eyes took in the familiar details. She was aware of weakness in her legs.

The woman sighed. 'He never does. Never has.'

'Look,' Toni said, her voice quivering with emotion, 'perhaps you'd like to come inside and discuss it.'

She stood back from the door. Her legs felt like jelly. The woman shook her head. 'No. I've got to get back for the children. You know how it is. Youth club, cubs and things.'

Toni *didn't* know how it was. Never had known. All she had known was Julian's body. This woman calling unannounced made her feel as if she was standing under a shower and had turned on the cold tap by mistake. She took a deep breath.

'Have you told him that you know?' Toni asked her.

'Not yet. He'll be back from off the rig by next week. Knowing his routine, he'll probably drop off here first. Perhaps *you'd* like to tell him.'

'Rig?' Toni raised her eyebrows. Her life and her man were breaking in bits by the minute and she was telling herself she should have known, did it really matter, etc., etc. The list was endless.

'Oil rig,' explained the woman. 'He works on an oil rig.' She paused and a softness came to her eyes. 'Poor dear,' she said in a pitying voice. 'He didn't tell you the truth about that either.' She shook her head and tutted.

Tony felt as cold as ice. She also felt a fool. This woman with peppery grey hair was feeling sorry for her!

'Might as well tell you then,' the woman went on. 'He's an inspection manager; goes round inspecting oil rigs in the North Sea. Well-paid, of course; that's why he can afford you. Though I don't blame you. You're not the first and you won't be the last. The trouble with my husband is he does like women to admire him. I'm quite used to trotting along behind him and telling his women friends just what the true situation is. It's become almost a matter of routine. By the way, what *did* he tell you he was?'

Toni swallowed guiltily. She was also embarrased but unable to lie. 'An airline pilot.'

'That's convenient.' The woman sighed and shook her head. 'I can't blame you, my dear. You weren't to know. He's not really much of a catch anyway – in bed or out. You must have noticed. Helps his ego to build himself up a bit. I'd have left him long ago, but ... well, it's the children.'

Once the woman had gone, Toni thought about what she'd just been told. 'Swine! Swine! Swine!' she screamed, then shut her eyes and counted to ten, though twenty would have been better.

She had needed an excuse to opt out of this relationship, but what had happened this evening had not exactly been what she had envisaged.

It was a shock, and one that took some getting over. She was also in need of being consoled, but there was no one around to console her. She was alone; even so, she might be able to enjoy a little light relief to help her over this.

She discarded her clothes, lay naked on the bed and, running her hands down over her body, imagined she was being unfaithful with a new lover. That's what she wanted to do: be unfaithful, be sexual, be herself and enjoy sex in the widest possible sense without any recourse to a humdrum relationship like the one she was just escaping from.

Somehow her own ministrations were an improvement on his. She rubbed her hands over her nipples, pulled and prodded at them between finger and thumb and felt the velvety softness of them, then the silkiness of her skin.

She moaned, lost in her own pleasure as she had been on so many other lonely nights. Her legs opened as she ran her hand over her belly and allowed a finger to

12

divide the moist passage beneath the crisp golden hair of her pubic lips. Her fingers travelled further and her clitoris escaped its folds and rose to meet them; with her fingertips, she teased the neat bud to burst into flower. She moaned, her hips gently heaving, legs folding over her own hand. Her fingers travelled on, then dived into the pool of hot juice that seeped from her body.

As her desire mounted, she reached for the eight-inch replica and switched it on.

Her tongue licked at it as though it were made of warm flesh and blood and not hard latex. She prodded at the head, let the tip of her tongue explore the tiny hole that would emit a salty ambrosia if it had been the real thing. But this was rubber: it was big, it was hard, and it most certainly was not real.

With her hands, she made it travel. Its head kissed at her breasts, and circled them before wandering down over her stomach, prodding at her navel.

She ran it along her warm slit, nudging at her opening clitoris before she switched it on and led it unprotesting to her aching vagina.

Slowly, she pushed it in, relishing each inch it travelled, its vibrations sending tremors of delight through her.

With one free hand, she tweaked at her nipples; with the other she pushed the pretend penis right in so its pleasures spread upwards and made her body quiver in ecstasy.

She left it to do its work, its outer appendages gyrating in gentle waves against her bud of passion and her sensitive perinaeum.

Both hands caressed and rolled her breasts. Her nipples stood proud, aching for the touch of a man's fingers but finding only her own. But it was good. She moaned as her passion mounted: Julian was obliterated from her thoughts. This was her lover; her own personal lover who took care of her when there was no one else around.

Her body moved more rapidly, in time with her rising

13

orgasm. Her back arched, and her hips followed as if it were a man she was enjoying, not a mere toy.

Within a matter of minutes, she cried her release as tidal waves of vibrating orgasm shook her body, her hips jerking against the effect of the length of rubber buried so deeply within her.

For now, she was satisfied, but tomorrow she vowed to throw the thing away. From then on, she wanted only the real thing, and lots of it. Sex was for her to enjoy. The brakes were off and she intended to enjoy the high-speed excursion.

The next morning, she rubbished his suits. Serrated dressmaking scissors produced the best effect on his silk shirts, their long sleeves chopped short. His shoes presented more of a challenge, but she coped with them too, eventually. Carefully – almost lovingly – she superglued each pair, sole to sole. The crowning touch was to place the rainbow trout she'd bought yesterday in his underwear drawer, along with the contents of three baked bean tins.

According to his wife, unaware of their meeting, he would come here first. She walked from room to room inspecting her handiwork: the hole in the television set he'd bought last year, the smashed crystal glasses trampled into the thick carpets, the foam stuffing emerging from the slashed chairs, and the life-size drawing on the bedroom mirror – an inconsequential outline of a man with an even more inconsequential appendage.

She picked up her suitcase, threw the key on the table – the flat was in his name – and closed the door.

From the bus station she made two telephone calls. The first was to Dodmans, Dearing and Pratt, Solicitors, telling them to stuff their job.

She bought herself a yachting magazine and a cup of coffee, and sat down in the red plastic cafeteria.

She opened the magazine at the classifieds page, and

found the heading, 'CREW WANTED. NO EXPERIENCE NECESSARY'.

Her heart leapt in her chest. It was just what she was looking for. She did have experience, though it had been three years since her last sailing stint. Sailing, and a sea breeze, she thought, might blow away the shame and anger that threatened to swallow her whole.

Her finger landed on the advertisement that was printed on shiny paper.

For a moment, she was distracted as a small boy ran a bright-red toy racing car along the edge of her table as he went by. She glanced up at his big blue eyes at the same time as her pen ringed the number. Then she tucked the magazine under one arm and, with her free hand, dragged her suitcase to the nearest phone.

The voice on the other end was polite and precise, but slightly distant. He wanted to know her name, her age, and what experience she'd had. She told him.

He paused, and for a moment she thought the line had gone dead. 'Antonia,' he repeated. 'What a coincidence.'

He then asked her what she looked like. She told him. 'I'm tall; around five feet eight inches. I'm good-looking, so I've been told. And I've got red hair and green eyes.' She forced herself to sound confident that her description was accurate. Men had told her she was good-looking; so had some women. It had to be true.

'Red hair and green eyes. Wait there.' A strange quality came into the voice. Muted mutters erupted in the background as if he were talking to someone else. When he spoke again, his voice was dark brown and sounded warmer, more interested.

'I'm pleased to hear it,' he said. 'Tell me, do you wear your hair long?'

'Very long,' she answered, and wondered what the devil her looks had to do with the job of sailing a yacht.

'That's good,' said the voice, 'very good.' He sounded as though he was trying to visualise her. 'You sound as though you are everything we require. Your looks and your name are an added bonus. Now tell me,' he asked with a hint of nervousness, 'what are you looking for? What exactly are *you* expecting to get from a job like this?'

Toni hesitated. What was it she was looking for? 'Adventure! I want uninhibited adventure!' she exclaimed with an enthusiasm that suprised her.

'And you are very experienced?'

'Yes. I am.'

'Would you hold the line for a moment?'

She said she would, and tried to make out what was being said in the background. Whoever it was he spoke to then replied, though what the words were she could not discern.

'Have you any money on you, cheque book or credit card?' the voice asked.

'Yes.'

'Good. Madame Salvatore will grant you an interview. If you'd like to get a flight to Rome Airport, one of our couriers will pick you up there. Bring a receipt for the flight and we will reimburse you. Should you not be suitable for the position offered, we will ensure you have a return flight home.'

'Rome?' she whispered. She frowned and glanced briefly at the ad she thought she'd circled.

'Yes,' the voice answered. 'Rome. One of our couriers will meet you there. You will then board Madame Salvatore's private plane and be brought here to the island. This is where the yacht is anchored. Should you be accepted, it will be your workplace for most of the time in Madame Salvatore's employ. Is all that clear?'

'Yes.' she whispered. 'Rome. When do I have to get this flight?'

'Now. You sound as if you are everything Madame Salvatore is looking for. She needs you now.'

Something in the way he said it made her hesitate before replying. The 'we' had turned to 'she' and the

16

need for her services more personal than professional. But she made her mind up quickly.

'Fine. Rome Airport. How will I recognise this courier?'

'Give me your name.'

'Antonia Yardley.'

'Book your flight right now and phone me back with the flight number and time of arrival.'

'Yes. Yes, I will,' she answered, unable to believe her luck.

He gave her the number and she scribbled it at the top of the magazine that she still gripped in her hand. 'I look forward to hearing from you shortly then, Miss Yardley. Good day to you.'

'Good day,' said Toni, and she put the phone down. Then she blushed. How rude he must have thought her. She'd sounded like an idiot and now she felt like one. It had never been her intention to leave the country. Her intention had been to have a few weeks in the Solent, the English Channel, and perhaps the coast of Brittany. Now it appeared the Mediterranean was on the cards. However did I make that mistake? she asked herself.

She glanced down at the classified advertisement and the telephone number she had circled. Then she covered her mouth with her fingers. She had circled the right advertisement, but the wrong telephone number. 'CREW WANTED', it said all right. 'EXPERIENCED CREW ONLY ON PRIVATE YACHT FOR PRIVATE PARTIES REQUIRED BY VERY PRIVATE MAN. MUST BE RED-HEAD WITH GREEN EYES.'

The fingers against her mouth loosened and her heart skipped a beat. The Mediterranean. Sun, sea and all the things that went with it. Perhaps, inadvertently, she had made the right choice. Outwardly she smiled, and inwardly she thanked the little boy and his noisy racing car. Adventure was what she wanted, and adventure she might very well get.

17

Who was the man? she wondered. This private man with a private yacht mentioned in the advertisement? The man on the other end of the telephone had referred to a Madame Salvatore. Who was she?

It was no use asking questions that could not be answered. She had made her mind up and that was it. She was going.

A flight. She had to get a flight.

In no time at all she had booked a seat on a charter to Rome. Two hours before boarding, she rang the number back and told the man she had spoken to earlier what time she would be arriving at Rome Airport.

It was just a bus ride to Heathrow, where she spilled out along with the eager package-deal crowd into the Departures lounge. After the necessary queuing, she sat down, no longer hampered by the heavy suitcase which was, by now, rumbling its way through Baggage Handling to be loaded on the flight out.

With a second cup of airport coffee set before her, she glanced down again at the number and address of the advertisement asking for sailing crews. The one for Southampton was immediately above the one she had committed herself to.

What the hell! Providence, she decided, had intervened. What did she have to lose?

Chapter Two

'Did you dream of her again last night?'

Philippe Salvatore opened his eyes and met those of the blonde-haired Andrea. She was kneeling between his naked thighs. Her oiled shoulders rubbed against his thighs and glistened in the sunlight. Beyond her head, he could just see the rise of her naked behind which was as tanned as her shoulders.

She kept her eyes fixed on him while awaiting his answer. Her tongue licked long and deliciously at the softness of his scrotal sac. In response, his penis quivered and tapped lightly against her forehead and tangled in her hair.

'I slept well last night,' he replied.

He had slept well, but he had also dreamed. Somehow, he didn't want to tell her that. It was his dream, his constant delight.

Before reclosing his eyes, he turned his head and looked out through a gap in the dark clusters of waving palms and bright purple bougainvillaea which bordered the wide expanse of the sun terrace. He barely noticed them. Through narrowed eyes and dark lashes, he gazed through a gap between them at that part of the sea where blue turned to jade-green.

When he closed his eyes, it was her eyes he saw – the girl in his dreams who had eyes the colour of the sea and hair as red as the setting sun.

More in response to his imaginings than to Andrea's deliberations between his thighs, his body tingled with a delicious, almost otherworldly excitement.

In his dream they did everything: he did everything to her, and she to him.

She was tall, lithe and lovely. What inhibitions she might have had seemed to have been lost somewhere like heavy baggage: unnecessary. Burdensome.

But there was also a nightmare part to his dream. Last night, in the corners of his mind, he had opened a secret cupboard. And there she was, just as he had left her from the night before. Instead of suits and jackets hanging from the metal rail, there was just her. She was lying on the floor, arms and legs stretched upwards. Chains were attached to the convenient eyelets on her anklets and bracelets. Her body lay flat. Her limbs were stretched towards the overhead bar.

Trembling, he bent down beside her. She could not see him. The hood prevented that. It was made of leather and only had an opening for her nose. A metal stud fastened the eye-pieces shut, and a zip the mouth.

He saw her shiver from the draught that came through the open door. Despite not being able to see or hear him, she knew he was there.

He wanted to release her, wanted to kill whoever had done this to her.

He tried to tell her that, but she didn't seem to be interested. He couldn't understand that. He had to touch her, had to make her understand.

She shivered again when his hands covered her breasts. Beneath his palms, her nipples hardened and her flesh grew warm.

'I didn't mean for this to happen,' he told her. 'This is Conway's doing. Not mine. It couldn't be mine.'

But she didn't answer. Languidly, her body rippled like a wave.

She was, he suddenly realised, enjoying what was happening to her, and that disturbed him. Conway had done this, and yet, like her, he could not resist.

In his dream, he kept his hand on one breast, then ran his other down over her belly to a golden cluster of hair that sat like spun silk between her thighs. His finger delved deeper and he felt her growing moistness, the cluster of flesh that clung like petals around the heart of her passion. Further, his finger travelled until it reached her hidden portal which was moist, warm and definitely waiting for him.

He plunged his finger into the humid opening, revelling in his power, the delight that he was enjoying and she was enjoying.

Now his own ardour was out of control. Flesh was around his flesh, warm lips sucking, tongue demanding that he spill his essence, and setting his senses on fire. He felt his semen rising, surging upwards like hot lava.

But how could she be doing this? he asked himself. The zip across the mask was tightly shut! How could she be sucking on him like this?

Wakefulness began to override his dream. He was only reliving it, and in reliving it he could make his own rules, blend fact with fantasy.

In his dream, he looked at her face. The mask was gone. Her red hair was spread out around her like a fiery halo, and her eyes were as green and as deep as the sea. Her mouth, warm and wide and sensuous, was clamped firmly around his throbbing tool. Their heat and orgasm reached their peak.

Cries of ecstasy burst from him as he climaxed into the willing mouth of Andrea who was real and still kneeling between his legs.

Andrea had golden hair, not red, he reminded himself. And her eyes were blue, not green. Only when he had adjusted to this did he open his own eyes.

21

'Thank you, my dear. Clean me up now.'

He didn't tell her he had a lunchtime date and wanted to be fresh and on time. It was not for her to know. It was for her to obey.

'But what about me?' she asked with more than a hint of childish petulance. 'How about *my* satisfaction?'

She was now standing between his legs, and was naked, her flesh bronzed. The blonde hair that adorned her head and pointed like an arrow between her thighs, was almost white. Each hand cupped a breast, while her thumbs flicked lightly at her nipples. Then she ran one hand down over her belly to dive between her open legs.

Philippe sighed. He had no inclination to do her any favours. Despite his own climax, the residue of his dream was still with him.

'Entertain me,' he ordered. 'Let me see you do it to yourself.' He eased himself up on to the blue and gold silk pillows of the sun-lounger. 'Stand here.' He pointed to a spot next to the head of the lounger.

Smiling, and as willing as ever to please, Andrea did as she was ordered. She thrust her hips forward slightly so the rise of her pubic mound was less than a foot from Philippe's face.

He leaned his head on one hand and watched as Andrea began to circle her fingertips over her thrusting mound and pulsating clitoris. With her other hand, she cupped one rounded breast, and smiled as she manipulated its nipple between finger and thumb.

From among her tangle of pubic hair, Philippe could see her red-painted fingernails slowly dividing her downy cleft, the pubic hair shining like silver thread. Pink and glistening, her clitoris peeped out from between her lips.

Philippe stayed his hand. He was enjoying this private show, completely uninhibited and performed for his eyes only. While she gyrated and groaned from her own ministrations, he concentrated on studying her satin thighs and silken divide, the tanned skin relieved only by her red fingernails and her golden curls and her slash of pink flesh.

Her fingers disappeared. Only her thumbnail remained in view.

She moaned as her own fingers invaded her vagina, and her hips swayed while her thumb flicked in the same tempo on her swollen clitoris.

He did not look at the hand that encompassed her breast. Instead, he watched with quiet fascination as she jerked, and jerked again; her movements coupled with anguished moans as her pleasure and performance came to its unavoidable end.

'Did you enjoy that?' she asked him, then bent and kissed his forehead, his nose, his mouth. Her hair fell like a thick curtain about them. Her breasts hung invitingly before his mouth. They remained unkissed, untouched, and she looked disappointed.

'It was a commendable performance, my dear. Now, please. Clean me up.'

Seemingly grateful for his praise, she smiled, and on high-heeled mules of cork and suede the colour of crushed strawberries, she sauntered to a half-circle of blue Delft tiles that looked like a fountain, but was in fact a useful outdoor sink.

It was shaped very much like a fountain. Glossy green leaves fell from planters around and above it. In the centre, two dolphins cast from weathered bronze stood almost on their heads.

Bending from the waist so that Philippe might get the full benefit of her rounded behind and the cluster of hair that peeped through her legs, she pressed one of the dolphins. A rush of warm water filled the blue china bowl she held beneath it. The bowl was a very dark blue, and the lemon, floating around in the water, was very yellow.

Just as she had before, she knelt between his open legs. She put the bowl on the floor in front of her, then bent down, buttocks high in the air, and sucked at the lemon-scented water. In her hands she held a towel.

With her mouth full of water, she straightened, took his penis in her mouth and let the water run down it so it trickled through his pubic hair and over his balls. She caught the residue with the towel. Three times she did this until the whole area was sufficiently wet. Only then did she apply the soap.

Working with leisurely precision, she lathered his now inert member, spread the sweetly scented suds throughout his pubic hair, over his sac and in the creases at the top of his legs.

With great concentration and quickening breath she worked, hoping, just for once, that he would regain his earlier hardness and force her into any position he cared for just so that she could feel his organ inside her body again; any area except her mouth.

This time, he kept his eyes open. He was watching her, perhaps with a hint of impatience, a yearning for her ministrations to be over so that he could leave. His diary was, of course, none of her concern, but he knew she longed to be party to more of his waking life, if not his dreams.

She repeated her dipping in the bowl and filling her mouth with water. This time, she used the water to wash the suds away. The towel completed the job. Lovingly, almost with unholy worship, she wiped his resting member, his heavy sac and the dark cluster of curls that surrounded his manhood like a thick forest.

At last she was finished, and he got himself up from the lazy angle he'd lain in since breakfast. She took the opportunity to ease her curiosity and the sense of failed anguish she felt inside.

'You didn't answer my question, Philippe.' She said it as sweetly as she could.

He stretched his arms above his head and looked at her sideways. The hair beneath his arms was as dark as that on his head. Taut muscles quivered beneath bronzed skin as he stretched. He had no spare fat. No spare thoughts either.

'About my dream?' he said without smiling.

'Yes. You always dream the same one. You told me so.'

'Then why bother to ask me if you already know the answer?'

'I just wanted to know. I wanted to help you forget about her. And I can. You know I can.' She flung herself at his feet, placed her hands on his thighs and gently kissed his glistening glans.

Philippe looked down at her. Andrea refused to see the contempt in his eyes, refused to believe that a man could be dominated by a dream.

His face relaxed, but not in a kindly way. 'She needs to be beaten from my mind, my soul.' Lightly, he buried his fingers in her glossy hair and smiled. His fingers tightened so that they tangled rather than caressed her tresses.

'Will you help me beat her from my mind, Andrea?'

'Yes,' she whispered. She looked adoringly up at him despite his grip on her hair which was bringing tears to her eyes. 'Yes. Yes, I will!'

Philippe smiled cruelly and looked at the sea before casting his eyes around the white stone of the Italianate parapet. 'Bend over the wall – just there,' he said, pointing to where a gap in the foliage framed the eddying blues and greens of the swelling sea beyond.

She started to rise. His hand held her down. 'I don't want you to walk there. I want you to crawl.'

Her hesitation was brief. Andrea would do anything for this man, even play second fiddle to a woman in a dream: a woman who was real, yet not real; in the past, yet also in the present. She did as he ordered, her breasts swinging gently as she crawled on all fours across the warm tiles of the terrace. When she came to the parapet, she got up and folded herself over the rough stonework. Her bottom was raised high, her torso hung low. The softness of her belly was pressed against the abrasiveness of the warm, white stone. Her breasts hung over the other side, and her hands grasped the carved uprights below them.

'Open your legs a little wider.'

She obeyed his order. The sun was warm on her behind. Her face was warmer, curtained, and therefore insulated by her hair.

Philippe frowned at the expanse of round and suntanned bottom upturned so pleasantly and beautifully for his delight. In the not-too-distant past, he would have felt an intense desire to part those pearlike orbs and push his rod into her tightest sanctuary. First, he would have moistened its length in her pussy. But he did not feel like that, and it wasn't just because of his earlier climax. Virility was no problem. What he felt was vexation. Born of that vexation was a chilling desire to humiliate and, in that capacity, Andrea was a willing subject.

'Open your cheeks,' he said. 'Let me see your little hole.'

Balancing herself over the parapet, Andrea reached behind her and did as he asked. Her long red nails scraped her flesh as she held her cheeks apart. The puckered opening of her anus was in full view, slightly pink and slightly silver.

Her stomach muscles tensed. So did her behind. Would he make use of it? she asked herself. Just the thought of it made her tremble with apprehension, but also with excitement. How she wished that he would do that. Anything but use her mouth again. She knew from experience it was not likely.

To the side of her, she heard the snapping of a branch.

Behind her, Philippe tore off most of the leaves leaving a clutch of three or four at the end. He eyed the leaves appreciatively, and felt their leathery softness across his palm. He turned to Andrea.

'Open yourself wider.'

Andrea pulled her buttocks as far apart as she could.

'That's better.' Philippe trailed the cluster of leaves down the narrow cleft and gently tickled them against her smallest orifice. Instinctively, her buttocks clenched. 'Keep them open,' he said and tapped the leafy switch against each one.

Biting her lip, and with the heat in her pussy matching her face, Andrea obliged, ready and willing for whatever he might bestow upon her.

She heard the swish of the supple branch before it landed on her flesh. When it did, she yelped. He had scored a direct hit on her open divide. The sting lasted for the briefest of moments before it became a tingle and the juice of her vagina ran and clung like seed pearls from the silver strands of her pubic hair.

Three times more he did this and had her half-sobbing, half-moaning with ecstasy. Through narrowed eyes, she looked out through her glossy mane to the glowing green of the sea. She removed her hands from her behind and clung to the parapet, suddenly afraid she would fall.

'What a hot little cleft,' said Philippe as he ran his fingers down through her divide to check her response to his treatment. 'Now,' he added, 'let me make your flesh hotter, and redder. So red that it will resemble a sunset, that beautiful moment when the sun sinks blood red into the sea.'

Andrea braced herself. The first blow covered both cheeks. The switch was long enough for that. Like her cleft, her behind stung at first before the sting became a tingle, before pain became pleasure.

As the intensity and the heat of her flesh increased, Andrea shifted position, her behind undulating beneath the raining blows. In that way, those parts that had not felt the sting of the supple branch eased the pressure on those that had received more than their fair share.

The blows ceased and Andrea herself eased the pressure of her teeth on her lips. Her bottom was on fire, yet not painful. It was unbruised, uncut. It only tingled with what it had received and with what, hopefully, might yet be to come.

Philippe ran one hand over her hot and colourful cheeks.

'Now,' he said very thoughtfully, to himself rather than to her. 'It is a most beautiful colour. Gloriously red, just as the sea is gloriously green.'

At the touch of his hand, she moaned with pleasure and tilted her behind just that little bit more. Perhaps, she thought, if such an angle was perfected, he would take her – whichever hole, it did not matter.

Philippe's gaze alternated between her red bottom and the sea. He was silent, and his dream was still in his mind.

Misinterpreting his silence as renewed arousal, Andrea turned over without his bidding. She lay on her back across the parapet, arms down behind her, legs wide open. 'Philippe, adorable Philippe. Take me now. I'm wet, ready for you. Please.'

Something in his look made her stop her pleading. He stared at her silvery pubes, then ran his eyes up over her body to her face. There was amazement in his face. His mouth hung open slightly and his eyes looked at her uncomprehendingly as though he hadn't expected her to be there, as though he were expecting someone else.

'Philippe?'

She wriggled her hips.

Philippe flung the switch to the ground. 'I have to go,' he said in a low, rich voice. 'I have business to attend to.'

Red-faced, Andrea raised herself up. Open-mouthed, she stared after him. Amazement turned to a dark scowl.

'Damn you,' she muttered in a voice as dark as her expression. 'Damn you and your green-eyed redhead! I'll get even with you, Philippe Salvatore, you and your bloody redhead!'

He did not hear her. But Emira did. Andrea might have been aware of Philippe's dreams, but could not know the reason for them. Emira knew his torment, knew the whys and wherefores of the whole scenario. Andrea could not know that, could never know that. All she could feel was her own jealousy, and that, thought Emira, might be at odds with the plans of others.

Emira did not linger. Under the instructions of Philippe's mother, Venetia Salvatore, there was a plane to be met at Rome Airport. Providence, Emira had decided, was perhaps lending a hand. It had been a spur of the moment thing when Antonia Yardley had phoned up and offered her services. A new and pretty crew member would have been good enough at any time; one that sounded as if she exactly matched the woman in Philippe's dreams was a bonus. But then, Emira had not met her yet. If she fitted the bill, she would be brought back to the island and Philippe's yacht. If she did not, she would be given the price of an airline ticket and told the position had already been filled.

Antonia Yardley, Emira hoped, would turn Philippe Salvatore's recurring dreams into a recurring reality. Hopefully, this young woman would reunite brother with brother – just as Venetia intended.

Chapter Three

*I*n Rome, the sky was grey and slanting rain drummed against the steamy windows that enclosed the warmth of the airport Arrivals lounge. Today, Italy, that supposedly warm, inviting place full of sunshine, was sticky, a little off-colour and very noisy.

Through the double doors that opened and closed between her and the Eternal City, Antonia Yardley caught the whiff of petrol fumes, and heard the honking of a thousand car horns, the animated shouts of baggage handlers, taxi drivers and irate mammas with screaming children. Rome, she decided, held no attraction for her. Too busy, too noisy and very wet.

Once her baggage was safely beside her, she eyed the bustling crowd for the promised courier. It seemed a pointless task really, considering he would know her name and had a vague description of what she looked like. She, on the other hand, would not know him.

The fact that she was waiting and looked as though she was waiting deterred those who believed she might be lost and alone and therefore easy pickings. All the same, it did not deter the admiring glances or the suggestive words that a few more determined souls threw her way.

So she waited patiently and passed the time thinking first about Julian, his good looks and his wife. She also thought about his inhibitions: the way he automatically adopted the missionary position, and always in bed.

The inhibitions were not hers, she was sure of that. Much as she had loved him, she had also harboured a yearning for more adventurous sex, and more exciting places in which to have it.

Everything that had happened, like his wife coming to see her, had happened for a reason. She convinced herself of that. It only needed the merest spark from a kindred spirit for her to prove it.

Then she thought about adventure. This was the first step to a new life, and she would allow nothing to spoil it, including regretful memories.

Thinking made time fly. Before long a message in English came over the loud-speaker that told her to go to the Inland Carriers desk. Coat over one arm, suitcase handle digging into her fingers and her shoulder sloping to one side, she did as requested.

Beneath the sign for Inland Carriers, was a very tall woman wearing a very smart navy uniform. She was rangy, her shoulders broad, her hips narrow. Her skin was as brown as a conker, her eyes and hair very dark. She was beautiful in a strangely exotic way: her nose straight and slightly hooked, her cheekbones high as though carved from solid mahogany. Full and sensuous lips, the kind only seen on the most rare and prized African carvings, smiled politely at her. Her eyes seemed suddenly to dance as though they had just been waiting for the right moment, the right note.

She held out her hand, palm white, skin glistening. Toni took it. It was cool, soft yet oddly firm.

'Antonia Yardley? My name is Emira. I work for the Salvatore family. I will be taking you to Mister Salvatore's private island and his yacht, *Sea Witch*. We will be travelling in the Salvatore's private jet. Your interview will take place promptly. It is now one o'clock. Can I suggest we proceed without delay?'

Toni looked at the woman in surprise. Back in England, the voice that had asked her about her hair, her eyes and her experience had been dark brown and, she had believed, definitely masculine. Not for a moment had she expected it to belong to a woman.

She barely had time to smile, and only vaguely managed to confirm that she was indeed Antonia Yardley who had been sailing yachts since she was about twelve years old. Emira left her breathless. Without asking if she needed help, Emira took her case from her aching fingers, lifting it as though it only held a quarter of the clothes that bulged against its sides.

'Come along, please,' she said in a no-nonsense way. 'I have a take-off slot already booked. I must not miss it.'

Abruptly, she turned and marched off. Toni followed, half-running, half-skipping to keep up with her.

The Lear jet was emblazoned on the outside with a snaking S in a vibrant red script. Once inside, Emira ushered Toni to a seat. 'I think this one will suit you. You don't mind sitting by the window, do you?' Emira smiled without showing her teeth as she asked.

'No, not at all,' Tony was filling up with excitement. She was also aware that Emira seemed more relaxed than she had been at first, as if the jet was an oasis amid the hustle and bustle of the rain-soaked city.

'Unless *you* want to sit here,' she added. 'I don't mind sitting elsewhere.' She smiled herself, thinking her offer might help her gain Emira's friendship. Loneliness was something she no longer wanted to experience, regardless of any man. Friends were something that had been sadly lacking in the last few months.

Emira still smiled in that Mona Lisa way, though her eyes flashed with amusement. 'I do not think so,' she said, her voice as thick as old honey and tinged with an

32

accent Toni couldn't quite place. 'Somebody has got to fly this bloody thing!'

'You're the pilot?' Suddenly Toni felt a fool, but then, how was she to know that this incredibly sophisticated woman who moved with outstanding grace could also fly a modern jet. 'I'm sorry. I didn't realise.'

'Do not be.'

As she spoke, Emira leaned over her and her long fingers reached out to check her seatbelt. A mix of heady perfumes escaped from her hair and her flesh as she came close. Toni breathed in the rich mixture, aware of the fragrance of her hair near her face, her anointed body near her own. Something tangible about that smell would not go away. It loitered in Toni's mind like half-remembered memories, and spread eerie tremors of excitement throughout her body. What was there in this woman's perfume that could arouse such feelings more commonly reserved for a man?

She was aware of a tightening in her stomach muscles and a tingling in that moist valley at the top of her thighs. Such feelings, such erotic tremblings, quelled any resistance to what happened next.

Almost casually, Emira's long fingers, with their red-painted nails, strayed across her vision to her breasts. She watched, mesmerised, unable to do anything. The fingers, flexible beyond belief, traced the curving outline of her flesh through the crispness of her cotton tunic blouse. This, she knew, was no accidental touch.

Emira's lips moved inexplicably as though she were hungry and contemplating eating something. They opened and she spoke. 'You have firm bosoms. They are a very good shape. I would like bosoms like that. It is so unfair that I do not have them.' She said it very thoughtfully, turning her head to one side as though contemplating swapping what she had for those of her passenger. Her very dark eyelashes swept across her high cheekbones. Toni felt the warmth of her breath, the sweet honeydew freshness of it coupled with the perfume and

33

that special something else that aroused rather than repelled her.

It was a strange feeling to watch Emira's face and feel her fingers running over her breasts. There was admiration in her eyes, even desire. Toni's own breathing increased and she half-closed her eyes. A small moan escaped her throat, but she did manage to speak and remind herself that this was a woman.

'Thank you. That's very kind of you to say so.' She said it all in a rushed breath.

'See,' said Emira suddenly. 'Feel your own breast, then feel mine.'

Aroused feelings replaced any inhibition Toni might previously have felt. At first, her own hand moving inside her own blouse and covering her own breast felt uncannily alien. But the feeling did not last. Her flesh felt pleasant beneath her fingertips – like satin. And cool, firm, perfectly formed. How strange it felt, and how exciting that her hand covered one breast, and Emira's covered the other.

She looked into Emira's big, dark eyes, studying the beautiful face that was so squarely cut, so sharply defined, yet so incredibly beautiful. Black liner edged the dark eyes, a blush of rose rouge adorned the strong cheekbones, and lipstick the colour of ripe plums coated the plush richness of her lips. She saw a pink tongue flick out from between those lips. Almost as if she'd been willed to do so, she found herself imitating the same action.

'Now,' said Emira, 'feel my breast.'

Slowly, Toni unfurled her fingers, reached out her hand, and felt the hard thrust of Emira's breast through the clean-cut lines of her jacket. The jacket itself had a cool sharpness about it. The style and cut looked to be nothing less than Armani.

Toni's own hand was still on her own breast. So was one of Emira's. There was a contrast between the feel of

34

each woman's breast: Toni's was firm, Emira's had a hardness about it she could not describe.

For a moment, her fingers hesitated as she considered the difference.

'What's the matter?' asked Emira. 'Haven't you ever seen or felt transplants before?'

Surprised by her open declaration, Toni stared, then shook her head. 'No,' she said, and tried to smile. 'I haven't.'

With a widening smile and the unbuttoning of her jacket and silk blouse, Emira firmly guided Toni's hand inside the lace that spanned her breasts.

Toni gasped as her fingertips gently touched the firm brown flesh. She shivered, wanted more; not just because she was curious, but because she was aroused.

'It feels – very good,' she said. Thoughtfully, she paused as she searched for the right words. 'Quite incredible.'

Emira's smile was big and brazen. 'Do you mean it?' she asked in that nut-brown voice of hers.

'Honestly,' replied Toni. 'I mean it. I'm sure there's nothing else like them.'

Suddenly, Emira threw back her head and laughed long and loud. She only stopped when she saw Toni staring at her Adam's apple which was cruising rapidly up and down her throat.

A little perturbed by Emira's laugh, Toni concentrated on Emira's bosom. With the hardening of Emira's nipple between her finger and thumb, a wetness invaded Toni's thighs and any words she might have wanted to say seemed to stick in her throat.

Emira's own hand eclipsed the breast that was not covered. Now each of them held one of their own breasts, and one of each other's.

Emira's nipples stood purple and proud from between one set of white fingers, and one set of dark brown. The top few buttons on Toni's shirt were undone, and her

35

own nipples showed pink from between a matching set of fingers.

'Does that feel good?' Emira asked.

'Very good,' Toni replied. 'Very good indeed.'

'Taste them,' said Emira. 'Go on. Taste them.'

It might have been an order or it might have been an invitation, but whatever it was, the sensations running through Toni's body urged her to respond. 'I've never done this before,' she said softly. But her eyes were fixed on Emira's nipples, and her mouth was open and moving forwards.

'Then now is the time to try it,' said Emira. Her teeth flashed like polished ivory against the deep purple of her lips.

'I will,' murmured Toni. 'I most certainly will.'

Memories of London fell away from her the moment that her lips encompassed the rose-like nubs. She sucked the first one into her mouth as her other hand moved to Emira's twin breast.

As she sucked and nibbled, her own arousal was heightened, invigorated by the heady scents of Emira's body: that odd mix of exotic perfumes, and that intangible something that was there, smelt, yet not quite recognised.

Dark lashes closed over her own green eyes. Red hair escaped from the black velvet band that held it at the nape of her neck. In her mind, she was falling, flying away from everything, from Rome and from herself. She was stepping into uncharted territory, and, so far, she was enjoying the experience.

'That's it, my darling Antonia. Keep sucking my breasts. Play with them for all you are worth, and I will make you remember this moment, this first time.'

Engrossed in the feel of the breasts against her face, in her hands, and in her mouth, Toni was only vaguely aware of the fingers unfastening her waistband, of the sound of her zip being undone. She felt the long fingers slide down inside her white lace underwear, felt the nails catch in her pubic hair as they travelled further and divided her lips.

She opened her legs, and moaned in gratitude as Emira's fingers slid over and around her most passionate bud and its surrounding petals of sensitive flesh. Slippery with juices, her sex opened wider to accommodate the advancing fingers that slid onwards to her most secret portal. They slid in, and as they did so, Emira's other hand held Toni's head more tightly against the hard round breasts.

Toni was smothered by them, enveloped in their warmth and their scent. Her tongue explored the silky skin, her teeth nibbled the hard nipples. Her own breath was hot and quick against the dark flesh, and her moans were lost in ecstasy as Emira's fingers withdrew from her vagina and concentrated on her swollen clitoris.

At first, each of Emira's fingers tapped at it before just finger and thumb tightened, rolled, tapped, touched and dug. She could not move from where she was. Her head was held tight against Emira's breasts. Yet she did not want to move. She was lost in her own ecstasy, her new adventure.

Soon, her thighs trembled. Her hips rose, again and again and again, until she was bucking hard against the hand and the knowing fingers. Holding it firmly in her hand, Toni held Emira's breast tightly against her mouth. She gripped the other breast with her free hand until spasm upon spasm of climax washed over her in diminishing waves. One wave of sensation followed another, until the latter spasms were nothing more than mere echoes of the first, the second and the third.

Emira was smiling when at last Toni opened her eyes. She smiled back, and knew her eyes must be sparkling. A new awareness made her flesh tingle. Something had erupted deep inside: it had been dormant, but now it had come to the surface. She was beginning a new chapter in her life, a more lively one than the episodes that had gone before.

'That was incredible,' she said breathlessly as she tossed her wild hair away from her face. 'I never knew it could be like that with a woman. I've never done anything like it before.'

There was a hint of mockery in Emira's smile that Toni could not understand, so she ignored it. 'Well, you have now, my darling,' said Emira, before kissing her on the lips. They tasted like honey. Her smell dominated Toni's senses and she could not help but respond. She felt grateful, and she had a need for more exploration. More adventure. She sighed and ran her hands down Emira's body. To her surprise, Emira caught her hands before they got below waist-level. 'Later,' she said in a strangely conspirational tone. 'There is time for that later.'

Toni frowned at the tightness of Emira's hands around her wrists. She clenched her fists and tried not to sound childish as she spoke. 'I thought you might need it too.'

'Not as much as you evidently did,' Emira returned as she stroked Toni's Titian-red hair away from her face. 'Care to tell me about it?'

It hadn't occurred to Toni to tell anyone about it, certainly not until she had had time to completely banish Julian and her own stupidity to the past. After all, it was early days yet and time would make things easier and make her feel less stupid.

But there was something in Emira's eyes and the soft, deepness of her voice that gave her comfort and trust. So she told her. 'What an idiot I was,' said Toni, when she'd finished recounting her sad tale. 'What a stupid little cow!'

'Yes,' said Emira, with a laugh. 'Yes. You certainly were. But now,' she said, her long fingers caressing Toni's face, 'everything will be different. There will be adventure, Antonia Yardley. There will be many adventures and new experiences before your time here is through.'

Again, she caressed Toni's hair, and as she did so, pulled the velvet band from her head so that her hair fell to her shoulders. As one hand slid the band into the pocket of her jacket, Emira refastened the pearl buttons of her own so white, so silky shirt.

'I hope there will be. I really do,' murmured Toni, her voice sparkling like her eyes.

Emira looked into those eyes that were so green and so bright. She reached out and touched the hair that was as red as sunset. Antonia Yardley was everything she had said she was, and that was enormously pleasing.

Emira stood up and ran her hands over her own breasts and down over her stomach. With a wry and secret look on her face, she patted her palm against her crotch and murmured something that Toni could not catch. Then she went, and before long, the hustle and bustle, rain and honking car horns of Rome were behind them and the plane was slicing through the clouds.

Soon the marbled grey of the sky turned to clear blue. From the window, Toni looked down on the sea which looked no more than a reflection of the sky. Sunlight kissed her face as the plane banked and turned towards the island of the mysterious Madame and Mister Salvatore.

From where she was, it appeared that his island was really a group of islands; four or five in fact. They were small, with only five miles or so between each one. They were yellow, except for dotted greenery and the sprawling expanse of whiteness which she assumed to be buildings.

She pushed her breasts back inside her shirt that had started out so crisp and was now slightly crumpled. Thoughtfully, she ran her own hand over her golden-haired sex and briefly touched her clitoris with the tip of one finger. It was still tingling from her recent climax. Soon, it would lose that last tingle, and again it would be as ready for adventure and new experiences as she was.

As though it were a hidden treasure, she smiled down at her crotch, did up her zip, and waited to land on Philippe Salvatore's private island.

Chapter Four

*T*hey landed at Melita's private airport where a car awaited them. The car was black, sleek as a panther, shiny as a newly minted coin. It had cost big money, Toni thought to herself, and spoke money being as much a statement as a mode of transport.

Silent and as solid as a colossus, the driver held open the car door for her. He was a thick-set man with broad shoulders and a shaved head, a gold ring in one ear and a scar down his right cheek. His skin was the colour of cast bronze. Although it glistened with sweat, he still had the appearance of being made of metal.

Intrigued, Toni eyed him. Like Emira, he was unusual, even exotic. She thanked him before she slid into the back seat of the car, then let her eyes run downwards from his immobile face and over his wide chest and thick thighs. His whole body seemed to be bulging in protest against the cut of his white jacket and the pencil-sharp seams of his linen trousers. Her look was provocative. She knew it was, and felt a delicious thrill that she could get away with looking at him like that.

Julian would not have approved. But Julian was behind her. She was in a new place with, hopefully, a new job in the offing and, if recent experiences were anything to go by, she could indulge herself.

Anyway, the man gave no indication that he had heard her speak or seen her brazen gaze. He did not blink. Did not move. But just for a moment, she fancied his eyes had stayed with her. It was brief, half-imagined perhaps, but she thought she saw a glint in his eyes and a swelling in his trousers. Both disappeared once Emira came into view.

Now higher in the cloudless sky, the sun was getting hotter. The car smelt of warm leather, and she could feel it through her clothes.

Emira's shadow cooled her body as she slid in beside her.

'Welcome to Melita.'

There was sincere warmth in Emira's voice, and even more in the lips that kissed her cheek. Her smile was wide and obviously welcoming.

Toni responded with reciprocal warmth and an excited smile. 'I'm glad to be here. Very glad.' She meant it. She really did. She carried on expressing what she truly felt. 'I was trapped, and now I'm free.' She filled her lungs with the sea-fresh air that wafted into the car, and looked out at the passing white and yellow of the landscape, the odd clutch of greenery, the black-clothed men working in the fields. Her hair blew freely around her face. 'I will never allow myself to be trapped again,' she said in a voice that rose little above a whisper. 'Never!'

Because she was looking out of the window, she didn't see Emira's frown, couldn't know how Emira was trying to discern exactly what she meant by 'trap'. She only saw the passing scene, the blue sky, the patches of gold sunlight and black shadows thrown by square houses and conical trees. Emira was interested in this young woman, not just because she was beautiful, but also because of what she might achieve.

She reached out and gently touched Toni's shoulder. 'Let me see your breasts again.'

Surprised from her daydreaming and sightseeing, Toni turned to look at her. Just doing that reawakened the sublime sensations she had experienced earlier. What was it about Emira's looks, her presence, and that more subtle scent beneath the expensively glorious perfume she wore?

For a moment, Toni did not answer, though her lips were half-open, and her breathing quickened as her mind and body responded. But that something she sensed in Emira got through to her and took her over. With slow deliberation, and still not quite knowing why she did it, she undid the top buttons of her shirt.

Without waiting for further invitation, Emira's fingers slid up beneath Toni's shirt and caused her breath to flutter in her throat. Not with uncertainty; more with apprehension. Eyes glinting beneath half-closed lids, she moaned as she lay against the warmth of the car seat.

Like a woman drowning, a certain light-headedness erased any inhibitions she might have felt about what this woman was doing. Instead of protesting, she moaned and shivered as the advancing fingers ran over her skin and gently caressed the lower outline of her right breast.

Her breasts were firm and stood proud of their own accord. It was rare for her to wear a bra and, even when she did, it was worn more as a pretty lace garnish than for necessity. As a result of Emira's earlier caresses, her nipples strained outwards pressing against the crisp cotton she was wearing. Once they were exposed, they grew to even more fruitful proportions.

Toni was all desire, all listless feelings of wanting to drown in the touch of Emira's hands. But her attention was suddenly drawn to the black eyes watching her via the car's rear-view mirror. The driver was of necessity paying attention to the road. But he was also watching her.

'But what about him?' asked Toni. She nodded in the

direction of the broad-shouldered man who sat on the other side of a sheet of clear glass.

'Does it worry you?' asked Emira, her eyebrows arching high on her forehead, her voice flowing in a long and sluggish way.

Toni's green eyes met Emira's bitter chocolate ones. In one way, she thought, they were a mirror image of each other. Both women had eyes that looked as though they were outlined in black, as though some artist had decided to accentuate the feature. Such eyes could haunt a man's dreams, could follow you round a room. That was where all similarity ended: Emira was the reflection in a dark mirror, Toni's was that in a lighter one.

Toni looked from Emira's dark eyes to the jet-black ones of the man driving. Poor man, she thought. He could only give her body *some* of his attention. Emira gave all of hers.

'No. It doesn't worry me,' she said. Serenely, she smiled as she pulled her shirt away from her breasts. To tease him more, she arched her back away from the warmth of the seat so that her breasts thrust forward before Emira's hands covered them.

'Let him look,' breathed Toni, her green eyes half-closed and her breath quickening, 'Let him see what he can't have.'

She writhed and moaned and closed her eyes completely as Emira's fingers squeezed and tapped at her nipples. Her palms covered, then cupped her breasts as if assessing their worth.

All the time, she was aware of the driver watching, his face immobile, his eyes darting like a panther's. She enjoyed that, enjoyed the feeling of power it gave her; the power to tantalise, to tease. There was an other-worldliness about this whole episode, almost as though she were standing apart from it and the exploring fingers were cool and arousing on someone else's body and not her own. It was like she was only watching, but unlike him she could feel the thrill of sexual desire emanate from those fingers.

Emira kissed each swollen nipple before bringing her face close to Toni's own, her breath mingling with hers, hot and rapidly intense.

'Are you enjoying this, my darling? Are you enjoying what I am doing to you? Do you like Emilio watching what I am doing to you?'

'Yee-es.' Her reply was a long hush of a drawn-out sigh, as much half-said as her eyes were half-closed. Like them, she was only partly aware of the outer world, yet slave to the inner world.

The long fingers of the hand that had caressed her breasts now cupped her face. Despite the heat, Emira's fingers were still cool, smooth yet strong.

As the gap between their lips lessened, their breath mingled, a sweet and spicy perfume in the air between them. Eyes met eyes. Emira's lips met hers and the warm wetness of her tongue stabbed against Toni's teeth.

Unable to resist, she gave it entry, sucked on it, and raised her own to meet it. Emira took hold of her hands, raised them and spread her arms along the back of the car seat. Her fingers tightened around her wrists and her lips pressed more firmly, more determinedly on Toni's mouth.

Then Emira's lips left hers, but her face was still close, her breath still sweetly near. She smiled and her teeth flashed white. 'My dear,' she said in that deep-sea voice. 'You did say you wanted adventure, and in the service of Madame Salvatore and your duties for her son, it is adventure you shall have. This,' she said, nodding towards the driver, 'is your first adventure. By virtue of this first adventure, you will gain entry to many more. Tread where you have not been before, my dear Antonia, enjoy what you have never tasted. The sweet fruits of your own sexuality will wither and wilt if you leave them hanging on the tree. Pluck that sexuality. Lick, nibble and bite it; eat it whole until you are satiated, until your appetite is in tune with its many flavours, its many diversities.'

'Yee-es.' Toni's reply was as lost on her breath as before. Her eyes sparkled like jade and the world and her surroundings seemed to disappear as she looked into Emira's eyes. In those eyes, she felt she was melting.

Was it the smell of this strange woman, or was it her honeyed words that made her feel she was swimming in the warmest of waters and could only go on, go forward and believe everything she said? The question was unanswerable, but the heat of her own arousal was hot in her veins yet tingling like dry ice all over her body.

A fire burned in her loins. Her legs opened in response. She could do no more than obey. No, not obey – go with the flow; enter the adventure.

Beyond control, her breasts rose and fell as her ardour and breathing quickened. Her flesh tingled in response to the exploring fingers. Emira's touch was languorous, her fingers soft and cool.

Toni glanced towards the eyes of the driver. He was still watching intently, his eyes glowing with excitement. In that split second, she felt desire and power all rolled into one. She wanted this man who watched to respond to her body, yet not touch it. She wanted him to desire, to feel his pulse quickening, his cock hardening as he drove and watched, but did not have. Just as Emira had suggested, she was entering adventure, truly savouring the first bite of the apple. She was enjoying, and this man was watching.

And how deliciously did Emira play with her breasts, the path of her fingers leaving tingles of anticipation in their wake.

Toni closed her eyes and savoured the rapture, the sheer ecstasy of her sensations. When she opened them, Emira's gaze was fixed on the breasts she was kneading beneath the firmness of her soft palms.

Her own desires put words in her mouth, on her tongue. 'Kiss them,' she pleaded. 'Please kiss them.'

Emira's eyes met hers before she licked her generous lips, opened her mouth, then bent her head.

Toni moaned long and deep, her eyes closing as she savoured the effect of the long tongue that flicked over each hard nipple. Moans of pleasure deepened as the licking ceased and her nipples were sucked into Emira's generous mouth. She flexed her fingers, wanting to hug Emira to her. But her wrists were held tightly against the back of the seat. Emira was in control, and Toni was enjoying it.

Dark hair brushed roughly against her collar-bone, its smell sweet, its texture as black and soft as velvet. But it was her warm lips and tongue that made Toni moan. Her nipples stretched to the point of pain as Emira sucked each of them into her mouth in turn. With her teeth, she held them there, nibbling them at their root and tip whilst her tongue probed and circled again and again and again, until Toni felt she could scream.

All the time, when driving allowed, the man whose skin glistened like metal eyed the action in his mirrors. But he was forgotten. This pleasure of being done to – of being watched – was Toni's alone. Her breasts ached from Emira's treatment of them. Her sex was damp again, but this time there was to be no satisfaction.

The car came to a standstill, and Emira kissed her breasts one last time before she released them and her wrists and sat bolt upright.

'We are here,' she said in a brisk and businesslike fashion, and reached for the car door.

'That's a shame. A little more time would have been very useful,' said Toni as she re-buttoned her blouse. Emira's hand covered hers. 'Adventure, Toni. Remember, you have come here for adventure, for more bites of the fruit of passion. You have plenty of time for more. Plenty of days to enjoy many new experiences, many new adventures.

Toni slid across the seat after her.

The sun was bright yellow amidst a clear blue sky.

47

The air was warm, and feeling its warmth on her body gave birth to sensations she could not describe. She was happy, and that was enough.

Full of new confidence, she slid across the car seat. The driver held the car door open; as she got out, she glanced up at his face.

He did not return her glance. He looked beyond her, over her head to some point near the rocky headland where white-crested waves smashed against jagged rocks. She smiled smugly to herself. This, she decided, was fun. For once, she had enjoyed herself at the expense of a man. It made a very nice change.

The sun hit her body and her eyes. Even though it was only spring, its warmth gave a taste of what was to come. She squinted and looked about her. This was the private quay where Mister Salvatore kept his yacht. From the quay, white marble steps rose to an expansive sun terrace on which she could just see the tips of waving palms, the legs of tables and sun loungers. The perfume of spring flowers mingled with the smell of the sea. She heard the splash of someone diving into a pool and the rattle and clink of ice against glass. Beyond the terrace were the white balconies and façade of the main house; a villa in true Mediterranean style, shining white as a wedding cake in the sun, its balconies shaded and facing seawards. Just like them, she turned her gaze to the water.

Bobbing gently at anchor, the water throwing diamonds of moving sunlight against its sides, a yacht was moored. This was the yacht she had come to crew. Its sheer symmetry of design and pure elegance took her breath away. She could not help but be impressed.

Sea Witch was ketch-rigged and eighty feet or more from stem to stern. Her whiteness shone like glass in the climbing warmth of the sun, and her rigging tinkled like bells in the soft breeze that blew up from the Sahara.

Admiring the trim lines of the long, white yacht, Emira reminded Toni why she was there.

'Come. You need to freshen up and rest before your interview with Madame Salvatore.'

'Will I have time?' she asked, after glancing at her watch. It was almost three and she was impatient. 'When will I meet Mister Salvatore?'

'Your interview will be soon enough. First, I will evaluate you myself. Only when I am satisfied that you are suitable will you meet Madame Salvatore, and only when she is satisfied, will you meet her son.'

Toni was not concerned about who was interviewing her. She was here, the sun was bright, and nothing, she decided, absolutely nothing, could stop her now.

She followed Emira aboard the waiting yacht.

The whiteness of the hull dazzled. Above her, the tall main mast seemed almost to be piercing the blue pool of sky.

Palm sweating, Toni placed her hand on the side-rail, and put her foot on the first riser of the green-carpeted gangway. Once one step was taken, it was easy to take two.

'What about my luggage?' she called out, and turned back to the quay. Her eyes met those of the man who had driven them to this place. The driver, who had his back turned to her, was handing her luggage to two young men with blonde hair, bronze skin and uniforms that were white and smacked of navy smartness and navy discipline.

Politely, and in perfect time one with the other, they turned and smiled at her. 'After you,' said one.

She thanked them, smiled at them both, and both smiled back. She saw admiration in their eyes, a desire to please, but also a desire to savour.

Not only were these young men worth more than a second look, but the way they were dressed caused her to stare longer than she should have; she tripped over a piece of anchor chain. Only Emira's quick action saved her from falling. Emira's hands were strong. Her smile was almost mocking.

'Easy does it, my dear Antonia,' she said with a knowing look towards the bronze young men. 'All appetites must be controlled, even the most hungry. One bite at a time, my sweet lady, one bite at a time.'

It was noticeable that Emira's voice was deeper than it had been earlier. Even then it had been deep enough. Something about its sound echoed the smell that Toni had found so intriguing when they had first come close. Like a vague memory or a tune half-forgotten, it ran around in her head. It was memorable, but not recognisable. She filed it away for future reference.

On board, Emira turned and waited for Toni and the two young men to come to her side.

'Antonia. This is Mark. This is Martin.'

The two young men nodded and smiled. 'Pleased to meet you,' they each said. 'Welcome aboard.'

Toni's breasts rose with her sigh of pleasure, and her hair caught in the breeze as she responded. 'Nice to be here,' she said, and meant it.

'Take Antonia to her cabin. She has a need.' said Emira, her lush lips smiling suggestively. 'Make sure that need is fulfilled – within reason.'

Various interpretations of what Emira was implying ran through Toni's mind. Dare she hope at what their duties might be?

The two young men, who now held only Toni's coat and over-stuffed suitcase, saluted smartly.

While Emira went on to list what the young men's duties would be once they had taken care of Toni's needs, Toni herself took the opportunity to study her fellow crew mates.

Their smiles were wide, teeth white, their skin a well-weathered bronze. Their blonde hair curled over the crisp neat collars of their white shirts. The effect of their appearance was vaguely naval and tropical, except that, as this was a sailing yacht and agility was needed, they wore white trousers made of some stretchy material which accentuated the muscles of their thighs and calves.

It also accentuated the rising bulges that pressed against the square naval flap where trouser flies would normally be. Their deck shoes were white too. The only relief to the whiteness was the red insignia of the snaking 'S' on the epaulettes of their shirts, the gold trim in two stripes along them, and the brass buttons that ran from the deep 'V' of their open necks to the gold-braided belts around their waists.

The whiteness of their uniforms and the tawny healthiness of their skins was further relieved by the gold bands around their wrists and matching chokers around their necks which drew attention to their handsome faces. A few links of loose chain hung from the glistening bands and nestled in the groove of their collarbones. A few also fell from their bracelets and tinkled like laughter when they moved.

There was no mistaking what the bracelets and necklets were made of. They could only be gold.

'And this,' Emira went on, 'is Marie. Marie is French.'

Marie had blue eyes and tawny brown hair and was dressed the same way as the two young men.

Marie, although seemingly offhand, greeted her. She had pouting lips and a heart-shaped face. Like her lips, her breasts thrust forward in perfect spheres beneath the crisp cotton of her shirt which was identical to those the men were wearing. Toni was aware of the girl dropping her eyes to her own breasts which Emira had so admired. The glance was brief, and the ensuing smile of welcome, or perhaps of adoration, was for Emira rather than for her.

'Emira. Welcome back.'

Emira kissed the girl. Toni would never have expected herself to feel jealous in such a circumstance, but she did. However, she told herself, this was no time to feel like that. Emira was the first person she had met. Granted, the tall, dark African had made a tremendous impression on her, but she was still the first. There

51

would be more, so her jealousy must by nature be short-lived.

'I am glad to be back, but I am very tired, my darlings,' Emira was saying. 'I will go and take a bath and then lie down. I will see you all later.'

Marie smiled after her. 'Yes, Emira. Have a good rest. I will see you later.'

Her smile was gone when she turned back to Toni. That odd tinge of jealousy Toni had felt when Emira had kissed the French girl was nothing compared to what she saw in Marie's eyes. Judging by that look, Marie's jealousy was likely to be far more intense, far more lethal than her own.

Within just a few minutes of boarding, she knew instinctively that she had made an enemy.

'Follow me,' Marie snapped.

Silently, Toni followed.

Below decks was cool and dark compared to the brilliance of the sunshine outside. For a moment, she had trouble seeing until the sunspots before her eyes had disappeared.

She followed Marie, whose body was tanned and whose buttocks slapped gently together like two fully grown mangoes. She wore white pants similar to those the men were wearing and, like them, their closely fitting lines left nothing to the imagination.

'This,' she said at last, as she came to a halt beside a bulkhead door, 'is your berth.'

'Who am I sharing with?' she asked Marie. Toni was fully aware that on these sort of assignments, sharing was often the norm.

'No one. Unless you wish to, or unless someone wants to share with you. Mark and Martin will take care of your needs.'

Marie turned her back and marched away, leaving Toni to enter the cabin, followed by Mark and Martin.

Their presence and what they might have to offer were enough to dispel any insecurities Marie might have instilled in her. What they might have to offer was very much on her mind.

Even before she turned to face the two young men, an enticing and very masculine smell filled the whole cabin. It was an intoxicating mixture reminiscent of sea spray and indelible youth.

Mark put her luggage down, and Martin followed.

'Don't worry about Marie,' said blue-eyed Martin. 'She's a bitch, but can't help it.'

'So I noticed.'

'Welcome aboard *Sea Witch* anyway,' said Mark, whose eyes were brown. His smile was still bright, his teeth as white as his uniform. They were both handsome and almost a mirror image of each other except for their eyes.

Toni looked from Mark to Martin. She felt like a child in a sweet shop. Toffee fudge or coffee cream. What a choice!

'Do you need any help unpacking?'

There was something in the way Martin said it that made her hesitate. She smiled at them and to herself. 'Well, three pairs of hands are better than one.'

Martin looked pleased at her answer. So did Mark. They exchanged looks with each other, then looked back at her. There was devilment in their eyes, sensuality on their lips. 'We hoped you might say that.'

The way their eyes explored her body and the change in their breathing was most definitely sending her a message. She was intrigued, but also keen to know that she was interpreting that message correctly.

'Just a moment,' she said, raising her palm forwards to stay their advance. She needed to be sure of what they had in mind, and had another very pressing need that ached between her legs. 'As I understand it, you are to take care of my needs – all my needs. Is that correct?'

Brown eyes looked to blue and back again to her. Their mouths smiled, their teeth sparkled. 'That's exactly right,' said Mark.

'Exactly,' echoed Martin.

'But we will help you unpack first,' said Mark.

'Be my guest.'

The door closed and the porthole was opened. A breeze carried in a hint of salt and fish and the screams of circling gulls.

No time was wasted in unpacking, though both Martin and Mark did take some time to lovingly finger her more beautiful bras, pants, stockings and lacy suspender belts before they put them carefully away.

She let her silk wrap fall like a wave on to her bed in a shock of azure blue. 'I'd like to take a shower now,' she pronounced, and raised her fingers to her shirt front.

'We'd like to help you.'

Just the sound of their voices and the look in their eyes was enough to make her tingle. She tried to speak, yet only little jerky noises escaped from her mouth. She made an effort to form them into words. 'I thought you might,' she said. Then she smiled. Slowly she began to unbutton her blouse. Again her breasts were free to the air and to someone else's sight. She let the blouse fall to the floor and tossed her fiery hair. She kept her head tilted backwards so that she could continue to feel her hair brushing against the small of her back. As she wetted her lips and made them glisten, she narrowed her eyes.

Ripples of pleasure made her body tingle. She tingled even more when she saw the tightening of their jaws, the glint in their eyes and the growing bulges in their trousers. Slowly, for their pleasure and her own, she cupped her breasts, and fingered her well-used and, by now, bright red nipples.

Martin and Mark did not wait for her to say anything else. Martin reached out and began to unfasten her faded but high-quality jeans. Mark went behind her and helped Martin pull them down to her ankles.

They ran their hands down over her hips, her thighs, her knees, her calves.

Above them, she moaned, reached down to touch the head in front of her and the head behind.

'No. Leave us to service you, to take care of your needs. Put your hands on your head. Relax,' ordered Martin.

'Leave it to us,' added Mark. 'We'll take care of you.'

Hesitantly, then decidedly, Toni did as ordered. Tremors of nagging desire began to re-stir throughout her body. In the mirror opposite, she saw herself, graceful arms raised, hands on head, breasts proudly thrusting forward. Her eyes sparkled, her mouth was slightly open, alive to quickening breath and quickening pulse.

Like a rich, red veil, her hair framed her creamy flesh. She was beautiful, an epitome of autumn, a fire goddess whose hair was of flame and whose eyes were made of emeralds. Classic and Grecian, she thought to herself, sure of her beauty, her free-roaming sexuality.

But all the time, she could almost hear the pounding of her heart as two pairs of obviously male and powerful hands ran over her naked thighs, down her legs, and pulled off her jeans from around her ankles and her sandals from her feet.

She blinked, seeing the pinkness of her face in the mirror, and fingers other than her own hitching into the band of her underwear and pulling them slowly down over her hips.

Like a burst of flowers, her pubic hairs sprouted into view.

She felt a pair of hands run down over her behind and take each perfect orb in hand, divide them and run thumbs down in her most secret crease.

In the mirror she watched Martin's thumbs play over her pubic hair as his fingers pulled her knickers down further. Without urging, she opened her legs a little wider and gasped in sweet delight as his thumbs returned to pull aside her lips. She heard him gasp as her budding clitoris sprang from in between them.

Just as she had hoped – in fact, what she had always

55

dreamed Julian would do – Martin dropped to his knees and pressed his mouth against her pussy.

His lips were firm and demanding. His tongue was wet, strong and gratifying. With strident flicks and probings, he divided those willing lips and licked her growing bud with loving abandonment. She moved slightly. Her legs opened more to give him that bit of extra room to manoeuvre so his tongue could journey more easily through the silky hair and the velvety folds of her labia.

So light and so gentle was his touch, she wanted to expose her rosebud to his tongue even more than if he had been forceful.

She moaned as she undulated against his mouth, burying his nose in her nest of hair. Behind her, she felt her buttocks being opened wider by forceful fingers and thumbs. Another tongue ran slow and wet down her glossy cleft and prodded at her tightest orifice.

Her first instinct was to clench her buttocks together. She resisted the urge, and caught the gasp of surprise in her throat. This tongue was not violent in its quest to enter the puckered opening of her anus: it was tentative, speculative even, as though it were politely asking whether she would accept his intrusion.

All tenseness in her buttocks vanished, and the sliding tongue invaded further. All virginity that area might have held dear was untouched no more.

The reflection in the mirror beckoned her eyes to look, to behold what was happening to her. There in its glassy gaze she could see herself, see these golden-haired men, one at the front, and one at the back, probing into her.

Like slaves, they knelt before and behind her. In the mirror, her body glistened and trembled with pleasure as she wove her pelvis forward to one man, and back to the other. It was hard not to moan, not to respond to their pleasure-giving. In time, that sweeping crescendo of orgasm would envelop her as if eating her whole. She let it rise, waited for it to take her. With the clearest detail, she imagined their hardness invading her hair-covered cleft, dividing it like the prow of a boat slicing through a wave.

Her orgasm was unrestrained and washed over her in a torrid and unstoppable wave. She moaned, writhing on the twin tongues that wrenched this climax from her. Through narrowed eyes, she saw herself come. Rapturous and undulating against these twin worshippers, she rode as though riding the waves.

Her hands were still on her head. She moved like a tree in a gale until the storm had passed, her climax over. The young men who had knelt around her thighs now got to their feet.

'It's time for your shower,' said Martin. Gently, he kissed her cheek.

Mark did the same before going to switch it on.

Toni, with breathless anticipation, eyed Martin's crotch for any sign of a rampant member rising against his so white trousers. There was none.

How could he be that controlled? she asked herself.

The question could not go unanswered. 'What about you? Don't you want to come, too?'

Martin smiled at her as though she were nothing more than a child. 'It's not part of my timetable for today.'

Mark joined him, and sorrowfully shook his head. 'Nor mine.'

Aware that her cheeks were turning pink, Toni looked from one to the other. Was she reading what they were saying correctly? 'Do you mean to say that you were ordered to do that? To bring me to climax, but not to climax yourself?'

There was no attempt to lie and spare her blushes. It was Mark who answered. 'We were. And a very nice task it was, too.'

'It was just to make sure that you really were suited to seek adventure. Emira ordered us to do it. Some people say it, but don't really mean it. They only think they do.

You, I can see – we both can see – really *are* ready for adventure.'

Toni was speechless and still as pink-faced as before. On top of that, her mouth hung open. But she rallied. If the happening in the car with Emira was one adventure, and this was another, what others were in the offing, and would they all be just as pleasant, just as exciting?

It was Mark who spoke again, giving her what sounded like orders, but no clues. 'You'll be sent for later,' he said. 'Madame Salvatore wishes to see you personally. She wishes to explain the rules. Emira will come for you, tell you what to wear, what to expect.'

'But I thought I had to satisfy Emira's evaluation first?' she said.

Mark shrugged. There was a smile on his lips, almost, she thought, as though he was having a joke at her expense. 'I don't know anything about that. Ask Emira. Emira knows all the little secrets around here.'

She shrugged it off. Perhaps Emira didn't tell everybody everything.

'Your shower is ready for you now,' Martin added. 'You haven't got much time. We'll be sailing shortly. Your help up top would be appreciated. Wear your own clothes for now – until your employment is confirmed.'

'Right.' Her voice faded into disappointment as they opened the door to leave.

They left her there, though she had half-expected them to stay and help her wash and wipe herself dry. The door closed, she was alone, and the shower was running. Water is a precious commodity on any boat, so she did not let it go to waste.

The water washed away the smell of sex and male bodies, but it did nothing to quell her curiosity. It also did nothing to assuage the lingering sexual demand in her loins. Although recently satisfied, it was smouldering like a dormant volcano and would readily spring back to life given the right circumstances.

* * *

58

Andrea had left the pool in time to see the new arrival go aboard Philippe's favourite possession. *Sea Witch* was his pride and joy. She was like a woman to him, a love affair he could never quite get over, even though she could be cruel and cantankerous.

Andrea had once argued with him about his obsession with the boat. He gave it, she told him, more attention than he gave her. That was when he had told her about the woman he had named her after, the woman who still haunted his dreams, who had divided him and his brother. And yet, he told her, he couldn't even say whether she was real or not. Sometimes he thought he saw her, in a crowd for the briefest of moments, or in the sea. Mostly in the sea. He saw her eyes in the sea, he'd told her, saw her hair in the redness of sunset. So far, he hadn't found her or anyone who looked remotely like her. For that, she had been thankful. What was it to her that this memory kept brother from brother? She preferred things to remain unchanged.

With a towel draped before her naked body, she reached for the iced lime-water one of the servants had poured for her. She sipped. The ice was cool against her lips, the liquid refreshing in her throat. She tingled, feeling vibrant with health and sexuality. Then she saw the new arrival a little closer than before. Her fingers tightened around the glass. The ice cube stuck in her throat and the promised coolness disappeared. She reddened in anger. She was also afraid.

'Damn you, Emira. And damn you, Venetia Salvatore!'

Chapter Five

*B*y the time Toni got up on deck, they had left the more narrow confines of the island harbour and quay behind. The engine which had brought them safely away from the shore had been cut. Sails, broad and white, cracked like whips above her as they were unfurled and took the wind against the bright blue of the sky. She smiled at them as if they were old friends and smelt the same salt breeze that filled the canvas. With her hand, she shaded her eyes and watched white silhouettes of seagulls dip and weave above and beyond the mast. Ahead, the prow of *Sea Witch* cut through the blue and green of the waves. White foam sprayed outwards and over the blue and the green.

'Antonia.'

She turned. It was Emira who called her. Emira was standing next to Mark – or was it Martin? It was difficult to tell at this distance as she could not see the colour of his eyes, the only feature that distinguished one from the other.

But her concentration did not linger on the young man who, with his brother, had so gratified her needs in the private confines of her cabin.

This time, it was Emira who took her breath away.

Emira wore a tunic and trousers in deep plum silk. They had an Oriental look about them; the sort of things you might expect men to wear in Delhi or Bombay and then only in white. Her sandals were gold. So was the band of metal zigzags that held her hair in a high pony-tail which cascaded like black rain to her shoulders. Toni noticed that, like Mark, Martin and Marie, Emira also wore gold wristbands and a gold hoop around her neck.

In Emira's company, she felt positively unkempt. My God, even the black woman's nails were unchipped, bright red and highly polished. How did she do it?

Toni smoothed her hands over her navy T-shirt and her neat white shorts which she had previously thought looked suitably smart and nautical. Now they seemed mundane, definitely bottom drawer.

'Mark,' said Emira, 'let Antonia take the helm.'

With a curt nod and a warm smile, Mark moved to one side before Emira ordered him up front to assist Martin. Not that Martin looked as though he needed any assistance. There was no winding of winches or pulling of sheets and ropes by hand on *Sea Witch*. All her sails were automatically operated with the use of powered gear and hydraulics. Emira, Toni guessed, wanted to speak to her alone.

She didn't mind that. She was grateful to be able to concentrate on the helm rather than on her appearance. With eager hands and genuine admiration, she reached out to take the wheel. It was wooden, fashioned more in the style of an ancient brig, than one found on a modern yacht. But it was decidedly opulent, its wood warm to look at and just as warm to touch.

She glanced at the gauge which read the wind direc-tion, flicked the wheel to let wind out of the sails, then flicked it again to take it back up and increase speed. The depth gauge she ignored. One look at the sea itself was enough to tell her that the waters this far out from land were deep and, anyway, a course had been set on the third gauge and that was the one she'd be steering to.

After making sure of her position and the accuracy of her compass, she turned to Emira. 'As you can see, I am perfectly capable of handling this boat. I trust my skills are adequate for the job in hand.'

The wind was blowing full on to Emira's face. She narrowed her eyes against it and the flying spray.

'It is not only your yachting skills that are required. There are other things, too. More specialised things that are unique to some and completely absent in others.'

Toni tossed the hair away from her face and thought about the answer Emira had given her. She also thought about the scene down below in the cabin and how spontaneous her reaction had been to Martin and Mark. Even when they had told her afterwards that they had been ordered to satisfy her, it took nothing away from the delight she had experienced. Curious to know more about the specialist skills that were required, she changed tack of the boat and her enquiries. 'I thought I was to have an interview.'

The sails cracked and Emira ducked as the boom swung before she answered. 'You are, my dear Antonia,' she said, in that dark, dusky voice before she straightened up.

Toni pressed on. 'I thought it was to be this afternoon.'

'It will be. Soon, very soon.'

Emira came close. 'Call this a preliminary examination,' she said as her dark, soft hand covered hers. Her teeth flashed as she smiled. 'Yes,' she said again, 'a preliminary examination.'

Toni licked her lips, but did not answer. Emira's fingers were caressing her bent knuckles and gripping fingers.

'You have very strong hands,' Emira said.

Toni glanced at her and saw something in her eyes that she would normally only see in those of a man. Again, she detected that unusual smell of perfume and

62

something more alluring, more demanding. She tingled, and took her time to speak. When she did, her voice was as hushed as the surf, as fluid as the wind.

'They need to be,' Toni said, sure of her knowledge of general seamanship. 'The wind and the sea have no respect for weakness. There is no room for mistakes.'

Emira came closer. Toni swallowed as she felt Emira's warm breath against her neck and her fingers on her arm. Now that exquisite and unique smell, that only Emira seemed to own, was strong in her nostrils and in her head. It confused and even frightened her. Despite the shape and the clothes of this woman, Toni's body was responding to her as though she were a man. Between her legs, a moistness had erupted and was already spreading.

Emira's lips kissed her skin. Her tongue flicked provocatively at her ear lobes.

Questions invaded Toni's mind and her knuckles whitened as she fought to maintain her course and not let either the surging sea or Emira's distracting ways destroy her concentration.

How can this be happening? she asked herself, but knew no answer. Her breasts rose and fell with the heaving and tumbling of the waves and the soft caresses of Emira's long fingers and probing tongue. How wet and warm her breath was. How sweet her fingers and her closeness.

When Emira spoke, her voice seemed to flow into her head and through her body. 'I understand that,' she said. 'I also understand that the need to concentrate on your skill is paramount.' Emira paused. Toni looked at her sidelong, saw the great dark eyes like midnight pools eyeing her speculatively, her broad lips smiling without her teeth showing through.

'It is.' It was all she could say. Despite the coolness of the breeze, her body was hot, and her sex even hotter. She was aroused, and sensed that Emira was also.

But the fingers continued to glide over her bare arms,

her clothed body. Sweet and low, Emira's voice poured into her ear. 'How strong is your concentration, my sweet Antonia? Strong enough to withstand the most exquisite of distractions? The most powerful of worldly urges?'

As she spoke, Emira's body curved against hers. Her legs twined around her thighs. Emira raised her leg, and bent her knee so that it nudged against the deep 'V' between Toni's legs.

Toni gasped, but did not swerve from her course or take her eyes from the far horizon. It was difficult to find the words to say, but she found what she could. She opened her mouth. 'I don't . . .' Again, it was all she could say. Whatever else she might have uttered was lost in her throat. Emira moved position. She stood behind her now, and her body was close and warm. Her breasts were hard against Toni's back. Toni gasped as the dampness of Emira's breath caressed the nape of her neck. She tingled at the close proximity of this person: no longer could she term her 'woman'; she was a person, a body desirous and desired, regardless of gender. Slowly, the hands that had caressed her arms now ran down her back, thumbs following spine, palms flat, fingers pressed into muscles. She shivered, arched her back, and made her arms rigid.

Concentrate, she told herself as she clenched her jaw. Concentrate!

Withstanding the urge to close her eyes, she moaned and let the sensations wash over her. Her hands and arms tensed as Emira's hands left her back and followed the lines of her ribs before rising and covering her breasts. She gasped, her own hands tightening on the wheel as Emira's fingers did delicious things with her nipples. Independent of her mind, her nipples thrust forward with rebellious abandon.

It was wild. It was incredible to think it, but she had this crazy notion that her body was breaking into different sections, one bit going one way, and one another.

She rode the battle, the storm that was going on inside her, and just when she thought she would crumble, a light laugh sounded against her ear.

'You are doing very well, my darling Antonia,' said Emira. 'Better than I ever would have expected. At least, I hope that is the case. I hope my attentions are giving you more delight than you have ever known.'

Instantly, Toni knew what was expected of her. Independence in body and in mind – an adventure in itself. She found her voice and the strength to respond.

'Of course I am. How could it be otherwise?' She was aware of her voice being as rushed as her breath. 'Your attentions are deliciously arousing. But I must not be distracted by what you do. However, I will enjoy them.'

Now it was Emira's turn to be surprised. Toni still stared ahead, but could sense the hesitance that told her Emira was thinking on it and considering what to do next.

Emira's body pressed more tightly against her back. That in itself was arousing enough. But there would obviously be more. There had to be more, and there was. Toni's stomach muscles tightened as Emira's fingers pulled her T-shirt from the waistband of her shorts. With outstretched arms, her hands still firmly on the wheel, she could do nothing as Emira rolled the cotton upwards and over her breasts. Once they were free and cooled by the breeze, Emira neatly tucked the roll of material under her armpits.

The touch of the breeze was gentle on her naked breasts, barely perceptible, yet incredibly delightful. Her flesh tingled and her nipples expanded beneath its feathery touch.

Toni, still standing and guiding the yacht, moaned and shifted position. There was a dull ache between her legs, a reminder both of her encounter with Mark and Martin, and a new ache acquired as a result of Emira's hands and the touch of the breeze on her breasts.

'How does it feel?' Emira asked.

'Very good.' She could say no more. It was incredibly hard to steer this long and graceful yacht, and at the same time enjoy the sensations which were spreading like a cool veil over her body. Yet despite the responsibility for steering *Sea Witch*, she wanted to enjoy those feelings. Inhibition and adherence to strict guidelines had once been part of her life. It was no more. She had made her decision to enjoy, to explore, and she had every intention of doing just that.

Emira's hands caressed the past away as they fondled her breasts. Dark thumbs flicked consistently at her pink nipples.

'Delicious,' Toni moaned. It felt good to describe how she was feeling – almost as though by describing her reactions she was taking the pressure off her reeling senses.

'And this?' said Emira. Toni's concentration wavered for just a moment as Emira supported her breasts with her pink palms, then with spread fingers, squeezed until a cry escaped Toni's throat. She winced, then winced again as fingers and thumbs pinched at her nipples. But this time, she did not cry out. Neither did she lose her concentration nor any volume of sensation. She was still in control, yet highly aroused.

'Martin!' Emira called out suddenly.

Martin deftly made his way along to where they were, his uniform damp and clinging after a sudden spray had caught him when they had heeled to a starboard tack.

Clinging like a second skin to his body, his wet clothes emphasised his body and the bulge in his trousers.

Toni's glance was brief, but enough to send her pulses racing. Why hadn't she had the benefit of his member back in her cabin? Just the thought that she had been denied that enviable pleasure annoyed her. What else, she wondered, would he be ordered to do? And what a shame he could not follow *his* urges and help her assuage her own.

The excitement, already aroused in her by Emira's

experienced fingers, intensified. Before her eyes, she saw one long finger point at Martin. No order was given, no word was spoken.

On bended knees, Martin squeezed between her and the wheel.

She gasped with surprise as her shorts were undone. Warm, gentle hands and swift fingers slid them down over her thighs. From breasts to ankles, she was bare. A man's hands were clasped over buttocks, and his lips were kissing her naked mons. But she could not look at him and would not move. She was still at the wheel of the boat, still responsible for the safety of the craft and those aboard it.

But she had to ride this! It wasn't just the job and the fear of failure that made her determined to get through it. It was something in her that responded to the challenge of dividing the coolness of her mind from the heat of her body.

Instinctively, her thigh muscles tightened as she prepared herself for what was coming. The yacht heeled to port and she mewed like a kitten as Martin's thumbs held her pubic lips apart and his tongue lightly prodded her rising clitoris.

Her senses reeled, and for a moment her mind seemed to toss and rear like the sea. She fought to control it just as she would a plunging boat. It was no easy task. Martin was at her feet, and Emira at her back. As Martin licked and caused her legs to tremble, Emira's palms rolled over her jutting breasts, her fingers pulling and tweaking at her hardened nubs.

With the glint of determination in her eyes, she used every ounce of self-control she had in order to concentrate on what she was doing and to enjoy what was happening to her flesh. The glorious electricity of sweet sensuality and demanding desire flowed throughout her body. She had the best of both worlds, and suddenly she knew how to make use of them.

Just as if she were tied to that wheel, Toni held her

position, legs slightly apart, arms outstretched, her eyes fixed on the muted horizon.

Briefly, as the sensations sent her blood racing, she glanced at the gauges: it was a difficult task. For the most part, she avoided looking down at them. If she did, she could see Emira's dextrous, dark fingers kneading and pinching her breasts and nipples. Beyond them, she could see Martin's blond head. Too many glances, and she might let the wheel go, taking full advantage of Martin and the situation. But she couldn't do that. So she stayed, trapped by her need to prove to Emira that she could cope with both, that she could carry out her duties as well as enjoy the fruits of her labours.

Not once did Martin's fingers stray along to her more-than-willing vagina.

What a shame, she thought to herself. Even now, she was aware of her lush folds flowing with the sweet honey of her need. She moaned quietly, though it was still louder than the breeze.

Shimmering like floating silk, the waves before her seemed to turn to gold as her hips jerked against Martin's tongue and nose. The golden waves seemed to explode before her, the sun and the sea combining in one glorious, glistening haze as the ministrations of tongue and fingers brought her to a thunderous ecstasy.

Arms shaking, legs trembling, she still held her position, though her breasts heaved until the last of her orgasm had floated away.

Both Martin and Emira rearranged her clothes.

Martin, aware perhaps by some pre-arranged signal that his duty was at an end, left them.

'You did very well, Antonia. Very well indeed,' said Emira. 'It will stand you in very good stead for your interview.' Affectionately, Emira's hand patted her bottom. It seemed a very masculine gesture and, some-how, Toni appreciated it. All the same, it did make her wonder what form her interview would take.

There was no time to ask that question. Before them

was another island which rose like a woman's breast from out of the sea.

Emira pressed a button, and the mighty sails began to furl back into the mast and booms. She pressed another, and the engine spurted into life. 'I will take the helm,' said Emira, and gently pushed Toni aside. She looked down at her, smiled, then briefly touched her flame-red hair. 'You'd better get ready for your interview.' She paused. Her smile seemed almost dreamy, as though she were contemplating something that was very vague or very far away. She came back to reality. 'Once we are berthed, I will come for you.'

Chapter Six

S ea Witch was berthed and the waves were beating a gentle tom-tom against her sides.

Toni was in her cabin which was cool and, although not large, was well-provided with lockers and drawers. All the fitments were of highly polished teak, its richness enhanced by bright brass handles and hinges.

With an air of self-assurance, she eyed herself in the mirror that ran the full length of a locker door. She liked what she saw and considered herself ready for this mysterious interview. As with all other interviews she'd ever attended, she was wearing a sensible suit, pretty, but sensible shoes, and wore her hair fastened away from her face in a thick and highly woven plait.

Emira however, who was surprisingly courteous enough to knock before entering, was not impressed. Frowning, she looked her up and down.

'You cannot wear that,' she said, in an abrupt manner that was obviously second nature to her when she wanted something done right and quickly. She turned away from her and began to bang open various locker doors. 'What have you got in here?'

Emira's bright red nails were soon scudding over the mix of clothes Toni had brought with her.

Many colours and many outfits were hanging in that locker, some more suitable for a city in November than a Mediterranean spring or summer. But Toni had been in a hurry, one quickened by her annoyance and disappointment at the fickle Julian. Anyway, it hadn't been the tropics she'd been thinking of. It had been Southampton and Poole, hadn't it? A few quick trips around the Isle of Wight while she got her thoughts and pride together. She stood silent and a little apprehensive as she watched the tall, dark woman survey her clothes and make her selection.

'This, I think,' said Emira as, with a swirl of her own silken outfit, she handed Toni a plain white dress with a low-cut neckline and a bias-cut skirt. 'Take that suit off.' Her voice was authoritative.

Toni stifled her protests. The dress was far from formal. Emira, she decided, must have some reason for having chosen it. Perhaps it had something to do with the skills required of her.

Under Emira's watchful gaze, Toni stripped off the smart navy suit with yellow-edged lapels and stood in her underwear and stockings. The lacy underwear was also navy blue, and exceptionally pretty. With a view to being superbly professional and perfectly matched, she was also wearing navy blue stockings kept up with a navy blue suspender belt. Very nice – under navy – but definitely not under white.

'I'll have to change my underwear. It'll show through the dress.' She had started to open a drawer as she said it. What Emira said next stopped her in her tracks. 'No need for underwear. We have not got time for that. Take the underwear off. Just wear the dress.'

Aware of some urgency in Emira's voice, and a sudden heat in her body, she was pretty quick in taking off the bra, knickers, suspender belt and the fine navy stockings. Letting them fall from her fingers, she was aware that her breathing was as hurried as her movements.

What, she asked herself, would she look like in such a

diaphanous garment? It was easy to imagine. Breathtaking, almost naked. In response to that mental vision, her hand dropped to the silken russet of her pubic mound. Her fingers found a stray curl and casually twirled it through her nails. It was damp, and not *just* because the cabin was getting warmer.

'Let me help you,' said Emira.

With a sigh of regret, Toni stopped caressing her ribbon of pink flesh with the very tip of her finger. Obligingly, she raised her arms so Emira could let the dress fall over her in a silky wave. In a cool caress, it covered her, the fabric of the bodice tantalising her nipples, the skirt dropping in a swirl from her hips to mid-calf.

'Let your hair flow free,' ordered Emira, her fingers already tugging at the thick plait.

'I took a long time plaiting this,' Toni returned, with a touch of defiance which melted as she saw the look on Emira's face. What was it she saw there? What was it about the woman that made her pulse race and her pubic hairs hang heavy with moisture?

It was only a yellow scarf holding the plait at the nape of her neck, but she had thought it looked neat and presentable. Emira, however, thought otherwise. The scarf was removed, and her hair tumbled free. Obviously, Emira had her own ideas about how Toni should look in this interview.

'Don't you think this is a bit revealing?' Toni asked the question as she caught sight of her own reflection in the full-length mirror.

'I think,' said Emira, her hands flicking like fans beneath Toni's hair so that it fell in a red cascade around her face, 'you look very well. Very well indeed. And now, I have a present for you.'

Toni had seen the white kid envelope Emira had brought in with her and laid down on the bedside table, but had given it no further consideration. Now, Emira opened it and took out a gold necklet and gold bracelets

72

just like those she and the others wore. 'These are a sign that you are one of us,' said Emira, her deep-red lips parting as if she were just catching her breath. 'Let me put them on you.'

Emira's hands were soft and beautifully cool. Just the lightest touch of her fingers, and tingles of pleasure ran down Toni's spine. But she let herself be gilded – like the lily, she thought, as she caught another glimpse of herself in the mirror. White dress, red hair, green eyes and the gleam of gold around her neck and wrists. She flexed her hands and fingers. The links that hung from the wristbands tinkled like bells as though heralding her entry into a secret world.

She slipped on the pretty, flat shoes that she had been going to wear, but Emira again rummaged through her closet and took out a pair of high gold sandals that fastened around the ankles.

'Wear those until we are off the boat,' said Emira, 'then put these on.'

'If you say so,' said Toni, her imagination suddenly leaping with the sensations those shoes could generate. Even before they were on, she could imagine how they would tighten her legs, cause her bottom to thrust out against the dress, and allow her inner thighs to brush against her hidden bush.

Before leaving the cabin, she glanced one more time at the striking picture she presented. Her hair was wild, Titian red and flowing down her back. Her eyes were as green as emeralds and bright with excitement, brighter still when she saw what a picture she made in that dress, which she had never worn before without underwear.

Through its fine weave, she could distinguish the dark areolae of her breasts, the thrust of her nipples. The rise of her belly was equally distinguishable – even the hint of indentation around her navel. The dress lightly caressed the curve of her hips, and the sleekness of her thighs. Between them was a hint of shadow where the deep triangle of her pubic hair shone like pale gold through the fine silk.

Bracelets tinkling, she followed Emira along the passages. The gold around her neck and her wrists weighed heavy, but complemented the lustre of her skin, the fire of her hair.

As she followed Emira, the air-conditioning hummed, and the sound of waves gently kissing the hull echoed around her. There was something melodic about it which caused her hips to sway and the hem of her dress to swirl around her calves. Down here, all was shade, all was cool. Through smoked-glass windows, the water sent alternate patterns of sunlight and shadow which made the ceiling and walls appear to be moving, undulating as though they were as liquid as the sea itself.

Up top, things would be different.

In the heat of the afternoon, the world both on deck and on the island they had come to seemed empty. The breeze had died, leaving the air hot and heavy. The sky was scorchingly blue, the yellow rocks dazzling bright. Only the sea moved, its hushed voice lapping against the gnarled stones of the quay, and lisping against the shingle beach beyond.

There was a smell of salt, a smell of heat, no other noise except the churning of the waves. Even the seagulls had gone, leaving the sky silent and empty.

Emira too was silent as she led Toni over the hot and crumpled stones of an uneven wharf that must have been built in far-off times when Roman galleys bobbed in the sheltered bay. The water was caught between two jutting headlands which bound the bay like two embracing arms of the curving sweep of a giant horseshoe.

Toni followed Emira, aware that her flat yellow shoes were noiseless on the ground. Emira's too were quiet, although it seemed an effort for her. There was a furtiveness in the way her head turned and her eyes glanced around them; a noiseless gliding in the way she

74

moved like a cat across the quay, along and around the boundary walls of the small jetty.

To their right there was a low wall where lemon trees stood in upright battalions, the perfume of their leaves hanging like a sharp mist in the air.

To their left was open ground; tufts of newly sprouting grass, bright green at this time of year. By September, they would be dry and shrivelled.

Emira led her down a dusty track just beyond the curve of the lemon orchard, and into the shade of a group of cypress trees. Under the trees stood a car that was as sleek as Emira's body and as red as her fingernails.

'Get in. Quickly!'

Emira's voice was low, yet sharp. Toni did as she ordered. Although the car had been parked in the shade, the white leather seat was hot beneath her.

'Ouch!' Her cry did not elicit sympathy.

Emira got in beside her and placed the gold sandals in her lap. 'Endure the heat, my dear Antonia. Put these on. That'll help you get used to it.'

Even before she had finished tying the last strap around her ankle, the doors were closed and they were away. Emira turned on the air-conditioning. She cruised the straight, then took a tight bend. The trees on either side threw alternate stripes of shade and sunshine across the narrow road. Dust flew from the front wheels and flared like a muslin veil behind them.

How pert my nipples look, thought Toni to herself as she looked down at her breasts. The hard nubs prodded against the thin material as though they were trying to break through. Lush pink flesh sat around them like soft cushions. For a moment, she wished her dress was covered with pink spots instead of being plain white. At least her nudity would not be so brazen, so obvious. But her dress was white, and the material it was made from was very thin.

Why, she wondered, had Emira wanted her to dress

like this? For the first time, apprehension mingled with the knowledge that she looked beautiful.

'Where are we going?' she asked.

'To your interview,' replied Emira.

'With Mister Salvatore?'

'No, Madame Salvatore. She wants to meet you. She wishes to make sure you will suit her son. As I have already told you, many skills are required to fill this role. Appearance is also important.' Emira's eyes slipped sidelong and met those of Toni's. 'You have the looks for the job. Let us hope you have the stamina to go with it.'

Toni was confused. Never in her wildest dreams could she have imagined the things that had happened to her since coming here. At least, not in dreams she would admit to.

Many questions and longings raced round in her mind. One of her longings was to meet the mysterious Mister Salvatore rather than his mother.

How special was he? How handsome, how sexy? Curiosity made her earlier apprehension turn to fear. What if he was a monster?

Emira herself noticed that the silence was too heavy, too intense. With a sudden sharp burst of laughter, she reached forward and adjusted the controls of the air-conditioning. Originally, the rush of cold air had been circulating through various vents throughout the car. Now its blast was coming from somewhere just above Toni's feet and, like a parachute, the skirt of her dress lifted, exposing her limbs and her golden-haired sex, as the hem of her dress blew somewhere above her head.

'Wow!' she exclaimed, her hands and arms thrashing with a mix of surprise and delight as she fought to control her wildly billowing dress.

'Open your legs,' said Emira. 'Enjoy it.' She was still laughing, but only one hand was on the wheel.

As Toni wrestled with her upwards-floating skirt, she felt long fingers forcibly diving between her legs, tickling her nest of hair and gently enticing her clitoris from its

76

protective hood. She had no option but to open her legs and enjoy both the blast of cold air and Emira's experienced fingers.

The more aroused her sex became, the more she moaned, undulating against those fingers. As desire replaced effort, she gave up trying to control her skirt. Instead, she rested her hands on her shoulders and let the tremors of pleasure and her skirt billow over her head. I wonder, she thought, what anyone would think looking into the car to see a woman, bare from the waist down, legs open, head hidden by her dress? Not that it mattered. There was no one else on the island, no one else on the road. All that did matter was that Emira's ministrations were making her wet and willing yet again. But not for fingers; not even for a hotly pressed mouth and experienced tongue.

Dearly, she thought, I would like a penis this time. Something hot and throbbing inside, not fingers, not tongue – the real thing!

Emira removed her hand and adjusted the air-conditioning again. The skirt of Toni's white dress fell back around her thighs.

Toni felt a little put out. She still tingled with desire, was wet for it, ready for it and longing for sexual invasion.

'I think that was a little unfair,' she said as she looked sidelong at her companion.

Emira did not turn to look at her. She kept her eyes firmly fixed on the road ahead, as though determined to get where they were going. She smiled. It was a vaguely secretive smile, and Toni found herself wishing she was in on the secret.

She sighed and sat back in the seat looking thoughtfully at the view through the windscreen. There had been dark cypresses up until now, standing in strict and straight lines on either side of the road. In one instant, they were behind them, and there was space, the same yellow earth and the vast expanse of bright blue sky.

Just a little way ahead, across an expanse of flatness, rose a high mound of pink and grey stone put down a millennium ago in some Jurassic sea, and now proud and separate from its surrounding plain.

On top of this jagged outcrop was a square-shaped building crowned by regular castellations. Perhaps it was a citadel, or a castle.

Flesh still prickly with unrequited lust, Toni leaned forward. The building was, in fact, a tower. It was red, built of the same stone as the rock itself. Even in the garish gold of the afternoon, it was supremely red. A road ran up to it through jagged rocks that suddenly became high stone walls. Emira took that road.

'What is this place?' Toni asked, craning her neck to stare up at the high straight sides that had few windows but lots of castellations.

Emira answered. 'We call it the Red Tower. It is very old and did have another name at one time. But it was not an understandable name. It was of another language, a forgotten language. Phoenician, I think. So it is called what it is. The Red Tower. Come. We are expected.'

There was no portcullis arch to enter, no inner courtyard in which to park. The car was left outside between the tower and the high walls alongside a deep violet Rolls-Royce and two or three low-slung sports cars.

Just as she had expected, Toni responded to the effect of the high-heeled sandals. Her legs seemed longer and more taut then before, her stomach more flat, her behind more prominent. As she walked, she could feel the silkiness of her inner thighs caressing her pubic down and kissing her sweetening lips.

Even the sun could not leave her body alone. Through her dress, she felt its searing rays burning her flesh. Oh, how she wished for the gentle caress of a sea breeze, the tang of its smell and its taste. But there was none here. Inland, there was only heat and a bright blue sky.

Once inside, heat and brightness were replaced by the coolness of stone walls, stone floors, and the muted light that shone in rainbows through coloured lead-paned windows set high up in the walls. There was grandeur in this place; the silent statement of centuries, and of inherited wealth and acquired power.

Rich tapestries of silk, cotton and wool adorned the high red walls. Heavy lights of noble size and elaborate design hung from the arched ceiling. Some were made of bronze, some iron, silver or brass. All hinted at Byzantine decadence or Arabic sensuality.

Greek statues in classic pose, and classically naked, turned from white to red, blue and green beneath the light of the windows. Others of Hindu or Chinese origin drew the eye, not because of their ageless beauty, but because of the sexual perversions and contortions of the figures portrayed.

There were suits of old and ornate armour, furniture of heavy wood and dark, deep colours. Adorning the walls, the furniture and high stone shelves, were samovars of silver, shields, weapons, coats of arms and vast Turkish carpets and Flemish tapestries, all bursting in vibrant splendour.

The stone floor was polished to a high shine by centuries of many shoes, boots and bare feet. The scent of sandalwood and the tang of mingled spices hung in the air.

Once their footfalls had stopped and their echoes died, there was no sound except for their own breathing.

In the hallowed combination of centuries, sandalwood and brittle silence, Toni could not speak. It was an odd feeling, almost as though if she *did* speak, everything would break into bits: the tower, the lanterns, the statues – even herself.

Fortunately, it was the sound of someone's feet that broke the silence and the spell of another time and place. A young man was walking towards them and he was smiling.

He greeted them. He was young, and had the physique and face of some of the statues. His hair was dark and fell to his shoulders. His eyes, like hers, were green with dark eyebrows that met over his nose. His body was taut; strong yet stocky. It was also on full view, apart from his bulging member which was covered by a mauve pouch that looked to be made of softest chamois.

Toni enjoyed that view, staring, studying, taking full advantage of his near-naked appearance, the easy pose of his torso, the gleaming tan of his skin.

Thick thighs and calves, arms and shoulders, chest and back. He was handsome in the way an animal – a bull, a stag, a stallion – is handsome.

There was an aura of decadence about him, the sort of decadence reminiscent of Pan, Priapus and everything Saturnalian or Bacchanalian.

Him, thought Toni to herself, her eyes resting on the prominent bulge. I wish I could have him. The thought stirred her already escaping juices. It was Emira who spoke and cracked her fantasy. 'This way. Come on, Antonia. Stop daydreaming about what you might get, and concentrate on what you will.'

Accordingly, Toni snapped out of it, though she did wonder for a moment whether Emira had been reading her mind. She followed where he led, her gaze transfixed by the bronzed buttocks which were hard and muscular, and rolled gently one against the other above firmly curving thighs.

Given the chance, she would have reached out and cupped each globe of his behind. But again, Emira seemed to be one step ahead of her.

'In here,' she said over her shoulder.

A door opened and they went in. The room they had entered was in complete darkness. Once in, Toni could no longer see either the young man or Emira. Taken by surprise and not entirely fearless, she stepped back, felt a hand grab her by the shoulder and push her forward.

She steadied herself, fought for self-control and willed her nervous shiver to turn into tremors of excitement.

Sight was denied her. Sound was confined to her own breathing and that of her companions. Perfume reminiscent of rare and priceless body oils lay heavily on the air.

In an instant, a circle of mauvish-coloured light appeared in the heart of the darkness. Within it was a raised plinth, on which were two stone pillars as red as the tower of which they were a part. Between the pillars was a single stone block, that was of a darker red than the uprights.

It is almost like an altar, Toni thought. 'What is this?' she whispered expectantly. Weird movies about human sacrifices and ancient devil worship suddenly came to mind. She took a deep breath, resolving to keep her cool.

'Hush,' said Emira, her voice like escaping air beneath a locked door. 'Do not be afraid. Just do as you are told, and that ache you are feeling between your thighs will be satisfied. You will get the penetration you so greatly want and so richly deserve.'

Toni was going to ask her how she could know her thoughts and needs so well, but another voice spoke beyond the circle of light and out of the darkness.

'Bring her forward.' A woman's voice. The voice had no body and its suddenness startled her. She stared into the darkness that surrounded the plinth. This must obviously be Madame Salvatore, but she could see nothing. Her heart was quaking, and at first she felt fear. There was some consolation knowing that the young man who had led her in was on her left and was gently rubbing his body against hers.

Between the thin covering of her softly falling dress, her flesh began to prickle with renewed desire. Just the touch and smell of the young man was enough to turn her fears into excitement.

Even as Emira's hands and then the young man's gripped her around her wrists and elbows, she did not feel fear. Again she caught a whiff of that masculine aroma that is animal, salty, but is really pure testosterone. Apprehension did not leave her, but as desire began to take control, she let them lead her forward.

There were two steps leading up on to the plinth. She did not stumble. She felt a pride in the way she walked up those steps and stood between her companions, the stone pillars and before the stone altar.

From out of the darkness she stood in the glow of the soft mauve light. How must I look? she thought, as she remembered the diaphanous quality of her dress, her prominent nipples, her starkly obvious pubic hair. For all her dress was covering, she might just as well be naked.

She gasped as a hand, Emira's hand, reached across her breasts and gently pinched each nipple so it protruded more aggressively through her dress. The hand then cupped each one in turn as if offering the invisible voice a gift – two gifts.

'You see,' said Emira with a hint of pride. 'She has beautiful breasts. Beautiful nipples. She also has red hair . . . and green eyes.'

'Thank you, Emira. I can see that for myself.' The voice was undoubtedly that of a woman, but one who did not compromise and knew exactly what she wanted.

There was silence for a moment, as though the unseen person was using her eyes, and those eyes were appraising her.

The voice from the darkness echoed around her. 'Raise her skirt. Let me see her body.'

Hands on either side of her did as they were ordered. Her wrists were still held, although she did not really feel like protesting. The mood, the darkness, the light all contributed to the way she was feeling. Her blood was rushing through her body, her breasts were tingling. Partly as a result of the golden sandals, her sex was already juicy and willing.

Her dress was raised and the golden redness of her crotch was exposed to the scrutiny of the unseen eyes.

Just as she had with her breasts, Emira's fingers lightly

touched her pubic curls which stood proud and profuse at the cusp of her thighs.

'A true redhead,' said the voice. 'You have done well Emira. And is she as hot as the colour of her hair?'

'Yes, madam. She is,' returned Emira. 'Fate has smiled on us. She is everything you ordered.'

'Show me.'

Toni felt her wrists being released. She could have run if she'd wanted to. Heaven knows, her heart was thumping in her chest. But she didn't want to. She wanted to stay, to see what she had been chosen for.

'Would you like to take your dress off?'

It was Emira's voice. It was also a question rather than a command, yet she obeyed.

The dress was flung aside in one silken heap somewhere in the darkness. She stood naked, her only adornments were the gold necklet, the wristbands and the gold sandals that stretched her legs and exaggerated the curve of her behind.

Skin slightly silver in the pale mauve light, she stood there defiantly, eyes glowing, flesh tantalised.

The hands that had let her wrists go now held them again. They brought her hands up behind her towards the nape of her neck. Now she found out what the wristbands and the loose links were for. Both links were fastened one to the other then in turn fastened on to the back of the gold necklet.

Reacting to the arching of her back and the imposition of the high-heeled gold sandals, her breasts jutted outwards towards the direction of the voice.

Even if she hadn't been orchestrated by the restraining of her hands and the effect of the sandals, she would not let that voice browbeat her into slouching, into hunching her shoulders and feeling fear or, worse still, shame. Her body was beautiful and she knew it. Others would see it and know it too.

Her pride did not elicit the response she had sought.

'So. You are proud, my dear,' said the voice. 'I am

glad of that. I want no demure daisy here, no cold water-well. I want fire. I want obedience, but I also want an unquenchable fire to suit my purposes. I want vivacity, energy, agility. There is no obedience, no submission, without those qualities. What achievement is there in evoking submission from something that is already submissive? None at all! None at all!'

'I am not submissive,' protested Toni. 'I will not be submissive!'

The woman laughed. It was a short-lived laugh and not entirely merry. 'Should I sanction your full accept-ance into our happy band of employees, one of your tasks will be to crew my son's boat. You know how to take orders, do you not?'

'Yes. I do.'

'Are you afraid of taking orders?'

'No, I'm not.'

'Then why should you be afraid of gaining the art of being submissive in the sexual sense? Isn't submitting to someone else's pleasure all part of the act of giving pleasure? Isn't it also true that in giving pleasure we are also receiving it?'

'I'm not afraid!' returned Toni defiantly, her head a little higher and her eyes a little more fiery than before. 'And I know how to give pleasure. I also like to receive it.'

'Ah!' said the woman. 'So you say. Let us see if that is, in fact, true. Are you willing to follow orders, to see if you can submit, yet at the same time enjoy what you are told to enjoy?'

'Yes.' Her first response was hesitant. Quickly, she gathered her thoughts as the scent of the young man at her side filled her head. Briefly, she glanced in his direction. 'Yes,' she said finally. 'Yes, I am!'

'Good,' said the voice. 'Now, let us see if what Emira has told me is correct. Let us see if duty and delight are so inextricably bound up in you that you can endure and enjoy at one and the same time. Carlos!'

The last word was definitely an order.

The young man who stood at her side, and whose bottom she had followed with wide and delighted eyes, stepped into the light.

He was smiling, his eyes never leaving her own as he peeled off the small triangle of material that covered his bulging penis. As he undressed, his member sprang forward, hard, purple and gently pulsating. He kicked the discarded scrap of cloth to one side and stood proud and upright before her.

He filled her eyes, and she was aware of her breathing quickening into little eddies of hot and hushed rushes. Her mouth was open, and her tongue felt dry. Before her was something she had been wanting all day, and now, hopefully, it was being offered to her.

Carlos smiled but said nothing. Then he turned, reached both arms behind him, and lay his torso and head out flat on the dark red stone. His bottom rested on the stone, his legs did not. His knees were bent and his legs were open.

The sight of his hard body lying there like some Aztec sacrifice was enough to make any heart race, any woman's honey seep from her inner void. On top of that, his penis remained long, thick and blatantly upright as though it were staring at the ceiling. Every so often it moved; in time, it seemed, with her own rampant breath.

Toni felt hands pushing her forward until she too was on her knees between his open legs. His scent rose to her nostrils, humid, enticing. As she breathed him in, she felt Emira's fingers tangle in her flowing hair.

'Lick his sac,' she ordered, and as Toni sank lower until she was sitting on her calves, Emira firmly pushed her head to the deep and dark division between the young man's legs.

There was no question of her refusing. What with Emira's hand and her own dire need to get near to a real flesh and blood penis, there was never any question of her refusing.

Her tongue reached out and licked the fragile vein that divided the length of the warm and succulent scrotum. Beneath her touch, she felt his balls pulsate and fall to one side like gold ingots in a soft velvet purse.

Because her nose was pressed into his softness, her head became full of the smell of him, of his sex, of his obvious masculinity.

Crisp dark curls of pubic hair brushed lightly at her cheeks, and the firm solidity of his penis was heavy against her forehead.

It didn't seem to matter that Emira's hand was guiding her upwards to tackle the base of his upright stem. Even without urging, Toni's mouth would have gone there anyway. Almost worshipful, she kissed and moaned at this hot and hard rod, sucking and licking it, murmuring against it as though she were inviting it into her own moist domain.

The hairs on his legs brushed against her breasts, and she was only vaguely aware of one of Emira's hands now being on her head. The other had travelled down to her bottom and those long fingers were now dividing her anal split, teasing the tight little hole, then running onwards to her more accommodating vagina.

Warmth surrounded her face: his legs were warm, his scrotum was warm, and so was the penis that sprang so erectly from its nest of crisp, dark hair.

Behind her, she could feel Emira's fingers sliding through her plush lips and over her slippery flesh.

Gently, her breasts swung in time with the beat of her licking, sucking action. Behind her back, she flexed her fingers, wriggled briefly against the metal bands that held them to her neckband. The movement was purely exploratory. It was almost as though she wanted to prove that, despite being bound and powerless, it was *her* doing this. Her mouth was pleasuring this supine man, and dark, dextrous fingers were evoking more fluid from her willing vagina.

Gently nipping the scrotal skin that she had sucked

into her mouth, Toni closed her eyes, and murmured against his warmth.

'How is she?' asked the light but sexy female voice from the darkness.

Emira's fingers plunged in a little deeper. 'Wet, madame, very wet,' Emira replied, her voice even more deep and husky than usual.

'Do you judge her ready?'

'She is, but might I suggest she make Carlos a little more ready first?'

'Good idea. See to it. His cock gives me great pleasure on occasion, and I don't want to see it incapacitated by any rough treatment.'

Emira's fingers tightened on Toni's hair, then pulled firmly yet gently upwards.

'Take his cock in your mouth,' she ordered.

Tony went upwards on to her knees. Deftly, her tongue flicked at the bulbous head of his cock. It moved of its own accord in front of her, swaying gently before her eyes.

Seeing she was having some difficulty getting her mouth over the glistening glans, and as Toni's arms were still pinioned behind her back, Emira guided the hot member into Toni's mouth.

It was generous in length, and thick in circumference and her lips formed a perfect 'O' around it. Yet she drew it in, sucking on it as best she could from the position she was in.

'Wet it,' she heard Emira say. As much as possible she did, but still the object of her attention was only wet and slippery halfway down.

As if she had correctly assessed the problem, she felt the fingers of Emira's other hand dip into her moist well, then retreat and, before her eyes, she rubbed her own sexual fluid on to the remainder of the mighty stem. She repeated the action two or three times more until the cock was wet and slippery right the way up to Toni's lips. Soon, she tasted the juices of her own arousal.

87

'They are both ready now, madam,' said Emira, turning to the darkness as she spoke.

'Good,' said the voice. 'Put her on him.'

Regretfully, Toni let the stiff stem of flesh fall from her mouth as Emira pulled her to her feet. Firmly but gently, she pulled her backwards, and guided her as she did so. Once she was out of the way, Carlos closed his legs slightly, but only slightly. His scrotum was still in full view, and his penis still stared at the ceiling.

'Get astride him,' ordered Emira.

Toni needed little urging. Her own sex was wet, her own need to be penetrated screamed throughout her body. With all the agility of someone who is slim, firm and young, she flung her leg over him, and hovered above his ripe member. Once she was certain of her position, she lowered herself slowly so that he would slide into her more easily.

It might not have presented any problem, but Emira helped anyway. She let go of Toni's hair and placed one hand on her hip, the other one halfway up the erect penis. With careful deliberation, she brought the two together, her head just a hand-span from their union, the scent of their sex in her nostrils, her eyes absorbed with the dividing of Tony's lips as the cock entered. For a moment, her thumb gained entrance along with the penis before she took it away.

Toni closed her eyes and threw back her head as she finally drew him into her, her muscles closing around the stiff stem as she fastened him to her.

He filled her body, filled her mind and satisfied her earlier cravings.

She felt Emira's presence behind her, her hands on her shoulders. The hands pressed her firmly down on to the mighty member like a piece of wood on a nail. Their pubes met. She was impaled on him, her clitoris trembling like a vibrating bell against the hardness of his pelvic bone.

Without any urging from Emira, she began to ride the

man beneath her. Although she felt the presence of Emira, in the sweet violet light, she saw only Carlos and was lost in her own sexual abandon.

As she rode, Emira's hands came around to cup her breasts, to play in that delicious way of hers with her nipples.

She groaned, and the man beneath her groaned at the sight of her breasts being played with as though he were doing it himself. There was now no need to open her eyes, to see what was happening to her. What was happening belonged to her and her alone. *They* did not feel it; not Emira, not the voice in the darkness. Even the man beneath her could not know how she was feeling, how important it was that she was on top and he was beneath.

She would have gone on thinking that way, observing that if this was submission – her submission – then she was surely missing something somewhere.

There was a clinking sound somewhere above her, and not until Emira had pushed her forward and attached something to her neckband did she realise what was happening.

She was bending forward now, suspended above him, her breasts lightly brushing against the hard chest beneath her. She could see his eyes, could stare into them, watch his flickering lids, hear his rapid rush of breath mix with hers. Now she was within range; his hands, his fingers, replaced Emira's on her breasts.

His tongue repeatedly licked at the dryness of his lips as his fingers squeezed her nipples and his eyes enjoyed the sight of her breasts. They were round and firm when he cupped them in his palms, trapped and hidden when his hands closed tightly over them.

Her flesh shivered as Emira's hands ran down her back, and her fingers dived again into that fine crevice between her buttocks. Nothing in her body, it appeared, would be allowed to go sexually unchallenged. She moaned at the thought of it, the fires of her desire rising higher and higher. Bit by delicious bit, she felt she was being consumed.

'Is she ready for that?' asked the voice from the darkness. The voice had attained a sudden richness. Briefly Toni wondered why, though her curiosity was short-lived. She was far more interested in what she was doing than what had caused the woman's voice to alter.

'I will check, madam,' responded Emira.

Although she was half-crazy with delight, Toni tensed and cried out when Emira's finger dipped around her wet sex then nudged into her anus. Even so, she couldn't help her muscles closing around the sharp-nailed intruder and gripping it as though loath to let it go.

'She is very tight, madam.'

The alien feeling of having both holes so tightly filled was so all-enveloping that Toni could do nothing but squirm on Emira's finger and, despite herself, mumble something about it could be good, it could be so good . . .

'Ah! That is a pity,' said the voice from the shadows. 'You will need to get her used to having it used. Start her training now. But a little discipline first. Just a little so she knows about giving pleasure and taking it. Couple the discipline with the training of her anus.'

'Yes, madam.'

Toni's eyes were still closed, and her hips still jerked up and down on the juicy cock. She held her orgasm, held it until she was sure that she was nearing the end of this most unusual sex session. Curiously enough, she knew Carlos was doing the same.

'Lick and suck this,' ordered Emira.

Toni opened her eyes. The object Emira was forcing into her mouth was about five inches long and made of something resembling marble or even ivory.

Dutifully, she did as ordered, and her eyes met those of Emira. There was a new look in those eyes, a deeper, darker gleam than before. Perfume also wafted from her, yet was drowned in the stronger smell of male musk that Carlos seemed to have in plenty.

The object was indeed hard, yet it was also smooth and shaped with an obvious purpose in mind. It was phallic, yet not a penis. It was intrusive, yet irresistible. She sucked on it, lavished it with the juices of her mouth as though it were an animate object.

Once it had left her mouth, Toni resumed her dedication to enjoying what she was doing and what was happening to her.

She squealed in a delighted way as Emira's hands fondled her buttocks then pulled them gently, but firmly, apart. In an instant, she knew exactly where that five-inch device was headed. She felt trepidation, apprehension, a halting and surprised cascading of breath. Yet laced through those feelings, those reservations, was a thread of excitement, a fine frond of curiosity and unabated desire.

There was no time to brace herself, no point either. To do that, she would have to interrupt her stroke, break her rhythm and, therefore, ruin her pleasure.

Initially, a thin wail escaped her mouth as the device was slid into her smallest orifice. Once the sphincter was breached, her wail became a gasp and in turn a long drawn-out moan.

The tempo of her ride did not falter. With the device firmly embedded in her anus, and Emira's hands back on her breasts, she continued her ride. She was still suspended above him by the chain that passed through the link on her neckband. She was leaning forward with her hands still tightly fixed behind her back.

Then Emira's hands left her.

It did not matter. She was lost in her own desires, her own pleasures, hanging from the chain, poised in mid-air like a flying swan.

Emira came suddenly into view. She was standing in front of her, smiling. In one hand, she held a black rod, and from the rod hung a clutch of thin leather tails. A cat, they'd called them in days gone by. Although this one was similar to the ones they'd used aboard ship,

Toni fancied it was smaller. All the same, she knew where it was intended to go, and braced herself accordingly for what she knew was to come.

This, then, was the discipline she had been promised. Instinctively, she knew what was required of her. Her pleasure was the effect of the penis of flesh that was in her vagina, and the false one that was in her anus. Both, she knew, were for her to experience: one to enjoy, and one to endure.

Trailing the long ends of the cat down Toni's back, Emira walked along until she was level with her bucking backside. The ends of the cat trailed over that backside, and Emira nudged its hardened point against the anal device so it went in a little further than before. Toni cried out.

'Not so loud, my dear Antonia. There is far more to cry about yet. Madam wants to hear you cry, wants to know that you are enduring as well as enjoying. It is good that you do. Good for what you are here to do.'

There was no sense in the words, none that Toni could make out, anyway. She did not know of any task she was to do except to crew a sailing yacht called *Sea Witch*. What she did know was that she was expected to carry on using this man and enjoying his body even when the cat raised pink stripes across her satin skin.

The coolness of Emira's palm caressed her jerking backside before she heard the swish of the many tails and felt their kiss on her flesh.

She yelped, but not once did she falter in her stroke or disturb the rhythm of her ride on the man beneath her.

'That's it, Antonia. Ride him,' whispered Emira into her ear. 'Ride him for all you are worth. Cry out. Show madam that you feel the whip, and show her also that your passion is undiminished by its angry kiss.'

Toni didn't need telling. The twin points of ecstasy – his penis in her vagina, the device in her anus – were too irresistible to ignore.

Her back arched as slivers of sensation coursed down

92

her spine. Her eyes closed to savour it and her half-bound body continued to bounce up and down with its unending rhythm.

'Ride him.' ordered Emira. Again, and again, the cat rose and fell across her behind where the blunt end of the anal device peeped from beneath her divided cheeks.

She cried out again, though not so loudly this time. It was as though the heat the lashes had generated was as hot and as welcome as the heat in her pussy and behind.

'Louder, I want to hear her cry louder,' said the voice from the darkness.

'There is only one way to do that, madam,' said Emira, a tone of surprise lacing her dark, low voice.

'I know,' returned the voice. 'Do it.'

Stinging and tingling so her flesh felt as though it were parting from her bones, Toni groaned regretfully as the device was taken from her anus. She wriggled her bottom as if inviting it back. She had liked its intrusion, had enjoyed the twin heat of its penetration and the sting of the lash across her flesh.

'Patience, my dear,' said Emira.

Toni could not see what was happening behind her. She took it for granted that Emira would return her invading finger to her anus and recreate the same sublime sensations she had created before.

It was a sudden shock to feel hot, hard thighs against the backs of her own, and a clutch of coarse hair tickling her backside.

Was she imagining this, or was there another man behind her? Her eyes opened wide when she felt another hard object nudge at her anus. Only this object was softly covered.

But there was no other man in the room. There was only the man beneath her, and Emira.

That clinging perfume that she had tried so hard to interpret seemed to be filling her head. With it, came realisation.

'Emira!' She cried out her name, yet knew that this

could not be her name, that Emira was not a woman, that Emira had a cock, and that cock was pushing into her anus without regard to her comfort.

She cried and cried again, yet even in the midst of her most extreme discomfort, when Emira's penis filled her to the hilt at the back, and Carlos' at the front, she did not lose her tempo, did not lose the rhythm of the fantastic climax that was about to wash over her.

With frenzied cries that echoed and re-echoed round and around the room, she climaxed. Again and again, she thudded up and down on him, Emira with her, as though they were one. Her clitoris, engorged with blood, hammered against him as he himself expelled and throbbed within her.

Against her ear, she heard Emira take a breath, murmur in long and drawn-out sighs as her – no, his – climax ran up his stem and thudded against her muscles.

Deep within her, she could feel both subsiding, could sense her own body dispelling the last shiver of climax.

She was breathless, her flesh glittering with sweat, and her sex as supine and relaxed as the man who lay beneath her.

Above her, Emira swayed like the long limb of a cedar tree before sliding out.

Carlos rolled out from beneath her, but because of the fine chain that passed through the eyelet on her neck-band, Toni remained where she was, her breasts suspended above the dark red stone that also passed between her open legs.

She was breathless, a fine sheen of sweat glistening on her skin. Her sex tingled and her backside stung. Yet for all that, she was content, sure she had passed her interview, perhaps even willing to try it again.

She was also hot, and her hair clung damply to her forehead.

What next? she wondered.

The voice of the unseen woman answered her own question. 'Wet the stone,' it said.

94

'What?'

'Pee,' whispered Emira.

After the journey and her experiences, it wasn't hard to do. A shower of golden rain fell on to the stone, and something in doing that made her feel more relaxed, even more satisfied than she already was.

'Replace the device,' ordered the voice.

Again, Toni felt Emira's fingers slide the device back into her anus.

'Hold it there,' said Emira. 'Make sure it doesn't slip out or you will get another taste of Madam Whip before the night is through.'

Emira made her walk back to the car as she was, naked, her hands still bound behind her to the neck collar. Emira carried her dress over her arm. Carlos walked behind them. Toni did not, could not, turn to look at him. There seemed no need to recognise that it was him she had ridden, him she had used to satisfy her own aching need. He had been the tool; it was the result that truly mattered.

The sun had set, and the evening was full of stars and a crescent moon in its first quarter. A cool breeze was blowing in off the sea. It blew Toni's hair across her face, cooled her hot sex, and disturbed her ripe pubes.

She had so many questions running round in her head she didn't know which one to ask first. But one had been answered. Now she understood why just the scent of Emira had so disturbed and aroused her. During her hesitation, Emira answered before she could even ask.

'I like dressing in women's clothes. They are so much more chic, so much more beautiful. And I like make-up, and perfume, and I like pretty jewellery.'

Emira had stated all the things he was by listing what he liked. There was no need to say anything else. Emira was really Emir – perhaps it was a title. Emira/Emir was also a transsexual – he liked to cross-dress and probably liked sex with men as much as with women.

'And when do I meet Madame Salvatore face to face?'

'No need. Just know only that your welfare is her welfare. Nothing bad will befall you if you obey her. Nothing bad at all. She wishes only harmony.'

'What harmony? Whose harmony?'

'Everyone's!' said Emira with obvious finality. 'Now. Less chattering like a parrot. Bend over the bonnet of the car. I want to check that the device is still in place.'

The bonnet was warm beneath her breast and belly. The warmth also helped soothe her aching arms, which had been tied back for some time now.

She squirmed and yelped as Emira's fingers pried between her buttocks. 'Keep still,' he said, and smacked the flat of his hand on each cheek in turn.

She stopped squirming and let him inspect her behind.

'Good,' he said with obvious satisfaction. 'It is still there. Now, open your legs.'

Wondering what was to come next, but disinclined to disobey, Toni obliged.

Fingers again coaxed her vagina to renewed juiciness.

'She's ready.'

It was Emira who had spoken, but the penis of Carlos which entered her; they were his hands which held her hips to him, his thrusts that pressed her to the bonnet of the car.

Short, blunt cries escaped her mouth. The bonnet was warm against her face, and hard beneath her hips.

There was no point in asking him to be gentler, to be more considerate to her sexual needs. She was being used by him, just as she had used him. Now it was his turn, and although she should have felt outrage, she felt strangely grateful. When she had used him, she had lost herself so far into her own gratification, that she had forgotten he was there. Now, he was doing the same to her – almost, but not quite. He kissed and ran his hands over her back every so often before gripping her thighs.

There was sweat between his crush of thick pubic hair and the gleaming softness of her behind. The wetness of their combined juices seeped over her buttocks, through her divide and ran in warm rivulets over the bonnet of the car.

Long and slow he thrust into her, then withdrew almost to the very tip of his member before plunging back in and repeating the same process all over again. As his pace quickened, his thrusts became less considered, more abandoned to his own gathering climax.

Toni's breasts, and even her breath, felt squashed against the car. As his thrusts became more violent, more rapid, their force lifted her off her feet. Deeper and deeper, his fingers dug into her hips, holding her to his timing, his climax. When his moment came, he pulled her on to him in one hard action as though she were an item of new and tight clothing. Tightly pressed against her, he called his satisfaction to the dark indigo of the night sky.

if she had expected it to stop there, she was very much mistaken.

Emira replaced Carlos and, strangely enough, Toni welcomed his intrusion. As his penis pushed soundly into her vagina, the force of his thrusts pressed the anal device more firmly into her tight hole. At the same time as he took her, something in the warmth of his body and the touch of his hands spelt affection, consideration. Beneath his hands, she melted, was pliable, just as she'd been with Julian – only different. With Julian she had felt like a hot meal served up on a very cold plate. With Emira, she felt as though she were a box of very fine chocolates. Care had to be taken when opening the box, and that care should be followed by a languorous perusal of contents, a study of coatings and fillings before choice and method were decided. The end result was unfamiliar, reckless and deliciously sublime.

There was a way about Emira that was definitely masculine, but ultimately feminine. Emira, she surmised, had been blessed with the best qualities of both genders.

Nipples warm and pressed into the metal, and clitoris

fondled by his fingers, Toni came when Emira did. She felt his hard thighs tense against hers, sensed the journey of warm fluid up through his stem before he throbbed inside her and murmurs of ecstasy escaped from his throat.

Once Carlos had cleaned her up with a towel, Emira checked again that the anal device was still in place before unfastening her hands.

In awe, perhaps also in adoration, she looked up at him and smiled. He smiled back.

'Do I still call you Emira?' she asked him. Somehow, she already knew the answer.

He pouted, just as she thought he might do. 'I am Emira. I prefer to be called Emira,' he said, and in an uncommonly self-conscious and feminine manner, he patted his hair.

'I understand,' she replied. And she did. That was the strange thing about it. Emira could be nothing else than Emira; male by birth he might be, but in an odd and strangely intriguing way, he epitomised womanhood; added a reverence and nobility to the gender that those who owned it by natural right could not even come close to.

He did not allow her to put her dress back on. All she wore were the gold sandals.

On the journey back to the yacht, the car windows remained open, and her flesh rose in a smattering of goose bumps as the breeze chased away the heat and sweat of her exertions.

Every so often, he looked at her and smiled warmly. She smiled back, cuddled close up to him, and rested her head on his shoulder. She felt good. She felt fulfilled, and she also felt slightly in love, though, as yet, she wasn't too sure whether it was with Emira or the scenario he had introduced her to.

Once he had escorted her back to her cabin, he called on the intercom for food: freshly baked bread, bright yellow butter, thinly sliced ham and heaps of crisp salad and sweet potatoes.

Toni looked at him, wanting to ask, wanting to know . . .

As before, Emira used that sixth sense and began to disrobe. 'I know you are dying to know whether you were imagining it or not . . .'

When he was naked, she could see that Emir, who had silicone implants and preferred to be called Emira, was indeed a man.

The penis that had invaded her was black as velvet and twice as beautiful. His body was as lithe and lovely as his face. Only the breasts were a giveaway to contemporary plastic surgery and an offering to the more feminine side of his nature. They were round, pretty and perfectly formed. Toni was almost envious and said so.

'They're splendid,' she added, and looked down at her own.

'Do not be envious, my sweet,' he said in that low, husky voice of his as his fingers traced the contours of each bosom. 'Your breasts are more beautiful than mine and, of course, yours are natural.'

Pursing his lips so that his mouth resembled a close-cupped rosebud, he planted a kiss on each naked nipple.

Mouth opening and eyes closing, Toni savoured the sweet softness of those lips sucking in her willing teats. Those lips, she thought, were luxurious, like plush velvet cushions against her flesh. They were too unique to describe; they were made to give her pleasure and not to be thought about.

When his mouth at last released her, she looked down at her nipples. As red as ripe raspberries, they glistened with the juices of his mouth and looked longer, as though he had stretched them with his tongue and with his teeth. They pleased her. They looked as decadent and garish as some she'd seen painted on ancient Cretan statues; women with big breasts and bigger areolae that stared more resolutely than their eyes.

Emira's hands touched her face, fingered her hair. 'Bend over,' he said softly.

Her eyes met his and she knew he had more to give her. There was desire in her, and she could see that desire reflected in the dark pools that looked back at her.

For a moment she was reminded of Julian as she rolled over and got up on to all fours. But the moment was brief. Julian and her old humdrum existence were many miles away. She was here with this beautiful man. To him, she again presented her buttocks.

The warmth of his palms was on her buttocks, and his thumbs were dividing one cheek from the other.

She groaned with pleasure as his fingers pried into her, then with regret as he withdrew the device inserted earlier. Her regret was short-lived. As his body covered hers, the glorious warmth and combined hardness of his penis nudged at her sphincter, breached it and entered.

Like a rich concoction of dark chocolate and whipped cream, their bodies mingled.

He pushed into her, pierced her to the very core, and in that piercing, that ploughing of her most unadulterated orifice, she found herself and drew strength from her own desire.

Once their cries of climax had echoed from the warm wood of the cabin walls, they lay together, her buttocks nestling against his resting cock.

He kissed her shoulder. It was like having icing on the cake. She knew she had his affection as well as his passion.

His voice was warm and damp against her ear. 'I don't think you need that device any more,' he said.

'Neither do I,' she said, and groped behind her until her fingers touched his penis that now lay dormant against his pubic hair. 'This one suits me better,' she said, and closed her eyes.

That night, they slept together.

Through one of the high windows which was nothing much more than a slit in the ancient red stone, Venetia Salvatore had watched as the dark form of Emira and the lighter one of Carlos availed themselves of the charms of Antonia Yardley. She smiled and congratulated herself. Emira had been right about the girl's suitability. Her colouring was right, and it appeared that her sensual nature was everything she could wish for. If things went well, the girl could soothe one son and placate another.

Venetia's face, smooth despite her years, creased in a smile. She stood straight and tall, the dark intensity of her eyes stirring to a blaze. The scene below was intense enough to affect her own sensuality.

Despite the fact that her hair was as sleek and white as the flitting wing of a seagull, that she was of an age when some women forget they once had experienced passion and had known the bodies of men, Venetia remembered. Venetia had known much passion in her life and refused to relegate it to the past.

Now in her sixtieth year, she was no longer constrained by half-formed emotions, half-remembered guilts and the inexperience of youth. Nowadays, everything was in her favour. Sex and sensuality were hers for the taking in any form she wished.

She smiled and ran her graceful hands down over the pale mauve gown that covered her body but did not hide it. Just as it had always done, her body responded. It made her laugh. How well she knew her sensitive flesh, how easily she recognised its demand to receive some semblance of what the red-headed girl had received.

Behind her, the door opened, then closed in a single breathless hush.

'Madam?'

'Ah. Pietro.' She turned slowly from the window and did not even look in his direction. Her chin tilted and her body seemed to glide like her robe as she moved away from the window.

Pietro stood with his arms clasped behind his back, the muscles of his chest accentuated by his stance. Only his thigh muscles bunching under his skin and his cock rearing against its pouch gave any clue as to the apprehension and impatience he was feeling.

He was similar in colouring to Carlos, but taller, leaner. Unlike Carlos, his cock was still fresh and proud in his groin, unused since earlier that day. Pietro, who was dressed as simply and as minimally as Carlos, was there to do her bidding.

Mauve was Venetia's favourite colour. Like her softly flowing robe and the minuscule pouches of her young, male attendants, the *chaise-longue* that stood alone in the middle of the room was upholstered in mauve velvet, its cabriole legs ending in taloned feet that were gilded with gold. It had no side-rails, and one end swept up and then curved over like the neck of a swan.

She draped herself over it, let the soft folds of her wrap fall open, and her silk slippers slid to the floor.

'I require you to give me pleasure, Pietro, but give me wine first.'

Pietro was well-trained in the art of pleasing his mistress and benefactor. Without comment, he crossed the room to a long sideboard of lacquered maple. Light from a table-lamp, whose base was a naked Hercules, threw a faintly violet glow along its length. The sideboard shone as if its lacquered top was really made from silk.

An enormous silver tray with a deep and filigreed edge held crystal decanters with silver tops and spouts. Around them were long-stemmed wine-glasses, which although being of clear-cut crystal, caught the light and turned it into rainbows.

Pietro poured her wine, then brought the glass to her.

'Thank you, my dear Pietro,' Venetia said as she took the glass from him.

Over the rim of the glass, her dark eyes reflected the deep red of the wine. Her gaze flowed like water over the body of the young man who stood before her. How beautiful he was, she thought to herself, how hard and youthful his body, and how strong his erection. Like Carlos, Pietro had been hand-picked by her – in a manner of speaking. On interview, she made a point of inspecting their cocks, her fingers teasing them to full erection so she could evaluate their full length and circumference.

Yes, she had chosen well. Pietro was a superb specimen of a man, and so was Carlos. On top of that, their loyalty and their stamina had proved unquestionable.

Her elbow rested on the scroll end of the chaise, her chin in the palm of her hand. In her free hand, she held the glass. She looked at it, then spoke.

'No olives, Pietro?' She smiled secretively as she said it.

'No, madam,' returned an equally smiling Pietro, 'but I have an interesting alternative.'

Deftly, he flicked his fingers at the ties of his one and only item of clothing. Unhindered, it fell to the ground. His penis leapt forward, hard, proud and grown to full length.

Still smiling, Venetia lowered her glass and her eyes.

Taking hold of his own penis with one hand, and bending his knees slightly, Pietro dipped his manhood into the glass of red wine.

'How absolutely divine,' said Venetia. 'I have no doubt that its immersion will improve the bouquet no end.' She laughed lightly, then nodded.

Carefully, Pietro eased his penis out from the dark red burgundy, yet held it, still dripping, over the glass.

Ruby-red teardrops of wine hung from his glistening flesh.

Venetia was purposely slow in her movements. How tart, she thought, and how stinging the wine would be on his most sensitive glans. She savoured the sight of the red globules, and relished the sound of his hissing breath as he clenched his teeth. Only when she chose to do so did she open her mouth and lick the wine from his trembling stem.

She drew extra pleasure from knowing that every

muscle and nerve in Pietro's body was strained to the limit as the sting of the wine and the touch of her lips combined in a heady cocktail. In confirmation, Pietro groaned long and low above her.

How very satisfactory, she thought to herself. Then she closed her eyes and sucked thoughtfully and slowly.

The girl with the red hair was still on her mind, as were the plans she had in store for her. But for now, she filed such thoughts to one side. This was *her* time, her pleasures she was attending to, not the girl's and not her sons'.

The wine was rich on her tongue, its taste, she decided, greatly improved by the immersion of a man's pride and joy.

Pietro retreated from her mouth, and Venetia, eyes still closed, swallowed then licked her lips.

'Lovely,' she said. 'I think it was a good idea leaving that particular vintage laying down for a while – but then, everything improves if it's well-laid.'

Pietro laughed at her little joke. A little joke, a little laugh. But she appreciated it, and although she usually only gave herself the pleasure of one immersion in the wine, on this occasion, she felt that both she, and therefore he, deserved a little more.

'I'll take some more like that,' she said with a tilt of her silver-haired head and a darting delight in her velvet, brown eyes.

'More, madam? Why certainly. Anything for madam.'

The sting of the wine was apparent in his eyes, but so was the sudden surge of his heavy member.

How sweet, she thought to herself, that he pretends to submit to my will and bear the sting of the wine for me. And yet I know it is a lie. Pietro loves the unique sting of the fruit of the vine, though he will not admit it, and I do not want him to.

By choice she chose wine with an overabundance of tannin. It was tannin, she had decided, that could better sting a sensitive glans. But her 'boys' bore the wine and her foibles. Her boys enjoyed her taking them in her mouth, and such an event was a privilege – one they did not enjoy too often.

'That,' she said, 'was delicious. Now, I will drink the rest while you pleasure me.'

With an imperious gesture of her hand, she swept her wrap behind her so that the lower half of her body and her breasts were fully exposed.

In her other hand, she still held her glass of wine. She sipped gingerly at it. Her eyes remained clamped on the trim, tight buttocks of Pietro as he walked with purpose to the sideboard.

From a drawer he took a box which he brought with him and stood beside her head. He held the box open while she chose which devices she required.

She took out a double vibrator, her very favourite toy. With pleasure, she ran her hand up and down one of its lengths.

'This,' she said with a knowing smile. 'And these I think for later.'

With a gracious sweep of her hands, she placed two sets of beads to one side. Then she motioned to Pietro that she had finished with the box. Without shame, but with obvious intent, she opened her legs.

Pietro, like the good boy he was, inserted the larger dildo on the double connection into her vagina. The smaller one he inserted into her anus. She murmured as he did this, then gulped at the wine as he switched on first one, then the other.

'Delicious!' she exclaimed.

Through half-closed eyes, she watched as Pietro pulled the means of his own satisfaction from beneath the *chaise*. It was a plastic box with a hole in it. Pietro came closer as he inserted his erect member into the hole, then gasped as he turned on the switch that would suck him to distraction.

Both eddied away on their own fantasies, ably assisted

by the whirring contraptions that never complained, and never tired.

Venetia lay there, legs open, dildos whirring, while this handsome youth before her played and sucked at her breasts, ran his hands over her still firm body, and groaned at the progress of his own arousal against her ear.

Yet she was doing nothing to augment that arousal. Everything was being done to her. She was just lying there, chin in hand, sipping at her wine. Her eyes were closed as he pleasured her, as the dildos pleasured her, and as she considered just how much work she had been relieved of by the plastic box that so ably sucked at his rampant manhood.

Ah, she thought to herself, it is good to be older, to command, to enjoy without recourse to guilt or inhibition.

Philippe and Conway were still in her mind, but she deserved this little diversion, she told herself. Call it providence, call it sheer luck, but she had found what she had been looking for. The bait was in place. Now for the plan.

It was a jerking orgasm when it came, both for the elegant woman with the snow-white hair, and for the dark-haired young man who served her so well.

Before she sent him away to clean out his little plastic box and the dildos that had so sweetly climaxed her experienced pussy and well-used anus, she kept her legs open and ordered him to insert the love beads.

One set of love beads was purple and the other mauve. One strand was meant for the vagina, and one for the anus. One set was also smaller than the other, although the first bead on each half was bigger than the rest, and on the end of each was a washer the size of a bath plug with rubber spikes all around it. That was the best bit, she thought, the piece that held her openings open and cajoled piquant sensations from her erogenous flesh.

It was pleasant to feel Pietro's fingers pushing each

bead into her vagina. She especially enjoyed that final thrill when she was completely plugged and the rubber spikes pressed against her most sensitive areas, reminding her that she still had a sex drive and knew how to use it.

It was the same when he pushed the beads into her rectum, his finger just behind each one, taking care that he pushed them up as far as possible so he could get them all in. There was not as much room in that orifice as in the other.

'Ahhh!' she said at last. 'Thank you Pietro, darling. That is just beautiful, absolutely beautiful.'

'I'll just tie them together, madam, and then you will be ready for bed.'

She sighed some more, and moaned again as he passed a wide length of satin ribbon between her open legs. She eased herself away from the *chaise* as he slid a satin belt around her waist. The ribbon hooked into the belt at the back and front. Patiently, she flexed her hand and studied her fingernails whilst Pietro made a final adjustment, opening her nether lips so they folded over the ribbon rather than let the ribbon run over them. He did the same with the cheeks of her buttocks so that they protruded high and prominent over the dividing encumbrance.

'Now,' said Venetia, with a weary, yet satisfied sigh, 'I am ready for bed.'

She looked up as Carlos entered the room, and smiled. 'A job well done,' she said. 'You look as though you could do with your rest, darling. Come. Let us go to bed.'

They followed her to the immense bed that lay behind long, fringed curtains of mauve and silver muslin. Pietro stood on one side of the bed, Carlos the other. At one and the same time, they pulled back the single satin sheet and, finally divesting herself of her flimsy wrap. Venetia slid naked into the middle of the bed.

Pietro and Carlos slid in on either side of her.

Once the lights were out, there was only darkness, a sliver of light from a watching moon and the soft sound of a satisfied sigh and contented breathing.

Chapter Seven

'Gentlemen, these disagreements are getting us nowhere. The trust needs you both to sign, both to agree. It will be very difficult for me to assign these papers correctly and run the trust efficiently if you two do not come to some agreement.'

Lawyer Guido Desmato mopped a white, creased handkerchief at his sweating head which was bright, shiny and entirely without hair. Hot from his dealings with the two men before him, he had taken the unusual step of removing his jacket and setting it over the back of his chair.

It didn't help much. He was hot and getting hotter. Despite the open window that let in the scent of geraniums from the balcony and traffic fumes from the Merini Piazza beyond, circles of sweat had appeared beneath his arms. The top of his head still glistened despite his dabbing, he wiped his neck instead.

Concealing his annoyance, he eyed his clients. The two men were silent, and sat at opposite sides of the room which made Guido's task even more difficult than it already was.

One mother, two different fathers. There were similarities between the two men, but their differences were greater.

Philippe was the eldest, father Italian. Head held high, he stared down past his aquiline nose at his hands. They were very still and very rigid as though, given the chance, one would grip the other with incredible fierceness. But Philippe would not show his anger. It was there all right, but kept firmly bottled inside him.

Conway, on the other hand, languished rather than sat in his chair. His eyes appeared to be studying a bluebottle that had floated in with the scents from the open window. His hands draped over the sides of the chair in the same way his body slouched in it. Casually, he placed one foot over the knee of the other leg.

But Guido Desmato was not fooled. He could feel the tension in the air between these two; the jagged edge of a serrated fury that could tear from either into the other at any time.

'Gentlemen . . .' he began, 'come. Your mother wants you two to come to an agreement on this. It is very important to everyone – to her; especially to her.'

The thought of Venetia Salvatore and her lovely eyes and still lovely body made Guido sweat that much more. He was obliged to lick his lips as the memory of their last meeting came to mind, her bare breasts pressed against his face, her plump nipple in his mouth. But he held it back. He had to concentrate on business, the law and finance.

It was Conway who spoke first. 'Guido, I didn't want to come here. I never want to come here. Why the hell do you always insist on it?' With slow but dramatic intent, he got up and crossed to the window, staring out at the teeming mass who crossed the piazza below him. Like ants from up here, he thought, like an army of angry ants.

'Your mother . . .' Guido began.

'Is trying to get us to be friends again,' Philippe interrupted. 'And that is an impossibility.'

'But your disagreement was so long ago . . .'

'That does not matter,' said Philippe, his tone clipped

110

and precise, although tinged with an Italian accent. 'Yesterday, it might have been. But nothing has altered. Nothing has really changed.'

Verging on desperation, Guido looked from one brother to the other. Philippe, suave and breathlessly handsome as a Classical Greek – or rather Roman – statue. Dark-eyed, well-structured face and sensuous lips. He looked as though the gods had smiled on him and perhaps had taken him as one of their own. His dress reflected his wealth, his breeding. Italian good taste; silk shirt, lightweight suit – mixture of silk and angora – tie the same, shoes unmistakably Gucci.

Then there was Conway.

Unlike Philippe, Conway's hair flicked around his shoulders in lengthy curls. His eyes were blue and inherited from his Australian father. He had an earring in one ear and a full and slightly untidy moustache. Yet he too was handsome, as well-built as his brother, but more rugged and a lot more unkempt.

Instead of a business suit, Conway wore jeans, a black vest and soft suede boots. They were casual, but undoubtedly expensive. Conway had a look more reminiscent of an old Che Guevara poster.

Conway, his eyes still studying the scurry of people down in the piazza, began to whistle some unrecognisable tune. He swayed from heels to soles as he hummed it.

'Gentlemen,' said Guido again as he stuffed his handkerchief half in and half out of his pocket. 'Please, your mother asked me to . . .'

Philippe too now got to his feet. 'Guido, if I had known that . . . HE was going to be here, I would not have come. Send the papers on to me at my hotel. I am staying at the Palermo. Room 121. I have no further business here.'

Exasperated, but relieved that the meeting was disbanding, Guido nodded. 'Yes, yes, yes.' He frowned as

111

he answered and dug his fingers into the resulting furrow.

Venetia had been counting on him. And he'd been counting on his success to gain favour with her, perhaps even get her to take a closer look at the still-vigorous penis that lay curled like a viper in its nest of thick and furry pubic hair.

'Good day to you, Guido,' said Philippe. 'No doubt I will be seeing you again when my mother again asks you to arrange another of these useless meetings!'

'Ciao,' said Guido. 'Ciao.' His goodbye was lost against the closing door. He sighed and felt suddenly old and useless. He had been looking forward to achieving success. With success came Venetia. With Venetia came one of the most incredible nights of pure indulgence he could ever contemplate. Those breasts, that nest of copious hair: Venetia had it all. She was everything he had ever dreamed of, so experienced, and so exciting. Venetia would still have her toy boys, Pietro and Carlos, and all he was left with were memories. What a shame.

'Never mind, old sport!' Conway slapped him on the back. He was smiling – almost as though he had scored one over his brother. Had he? Guido didn't know for sure. Despite these two being Venetia's sons, they were a mystery to him. They were as good-looking as their mother, and their respective fathers, if Venetia's descriptions were anything to go by. But that was where any resemblance ended. They mystified him – and frightened him. They were complex, and he was simple. For once, he was glad of that.

'Tell me,' said Guido to the smiling and friendly face of Conway, 'what is it with you two? Why do you not be friends like your mother wishes, eh?'

Conway laughed and shook his head. His hair swung when he shook his head like that – like a girl. But there was nothing feminine about Conway. He was all man. A woman's man: pure macho, pure nature.

Amiably, he slapped Guido's middle-aged shoulders.

'You wouldn't understand, old sport, you wouldn't understand at all. It's a matter of honour – and of sour grapes – though no doubt my brother wouldn't see it that way. Anyway, nothing can be changed.' He paused as though he were remembering something very sweet, very precious. 'Sometimes, I wish it could be. Sometimes, I know just how he feels. Trouble is, I'm not so sure our mother entirely understands just how much the past can haunt the present.'

The lawyer coughed and sputtered something about being too old to mediate family feuds.

Conway only laughed. 'Never mind though, Guido. You've done your bit. No doubt Venetia will reward you accordingly. My mother's generous like that.'

With a laugh, he slapped Guido's back again, which only served to make him cough more.

'What about the papers? Shall I send them to you? Are you staying at a hotel?'

'No,' returned Conway, one hand already on the cut-glass knob of the heavy mahogany door. 'I'm moored in the harbour. My boat's called *Enchantress*, in case you didn't already know.'

'I know that,' Guido replied. 'Though it is still a great disappointment to me that you two do not be friends. It is very disappointing, very disappointing indeed.'

'Ciao, Guido.' Conway raised one hand before he left. He didn't look directly at the lawyer who had been handling their affairs for years. Seeing Philippe again had given rise to old memories, old passions, and those now filled his thoughts.

Conway liked to blend in with the masses and preferred to walk the cobbled alleys that led away from the piazza and down shaded side-roads to where his yacht was anchored.

Enchantress was not white and frostily new like *Sea Witch*, his brother's boat. She was made of wood that was varnished to perfection and gleamed in the sunlight. It had been more than a century since she had been built,

113

but her lines were classic, her displacement heavy and strong. She was fit to face anything, though inside her fittings were as rich and refined as the age in which she had been built.

He stepped aboard, but turned expectantly when the shuddering sound of a diesel Mercedes rattled over the uneven surface of the wharf.

A taxi stopped in the shade of a brick-built warehouse. He saw her get out, pay the driver, then smile as she walked towards him.

'Andrea. I haven't seen you in a fair while.'

Her smile widened. Like a cat, he thought, and wondered why she'd come, why she had felt the need to phone him earlier that morning and invite herself along.

'Conway, darling,' she drawled. Her voice was southern States, sweetly fruity, yet tinged with a hint of citrus.

She touched his arm, kissed him on one cheek.

He smelt her perfume which, coupled with resurrected memories, sent the blood rushing through his veins.

'You look as good as ever,' he said.

She thanked him, and he noticed that his compliment seemed to make her walk taller, smile wider. Andrea was a woman who fed on compliments like some people fed on caviar.

She had the look of a woman who knows she looks good, he thought. Her hair was twisted high on her head. Her dress was the colour of burned toffee, and her belt and sandals were of muted gold and glossy browns.

'Come on aboard then, darlin'. Let's make you feel at home.'

If he was making fun of her, she didn't bite.

Strange that, he thought to himself. To him it was obvious he had been mimicking her accent. But there you are. Nothing's ever certain.

She followed him aboard.

The boat was deserted except for the loyal and heavy-weight Emilio whom he'd asked to stay until he had got

114

back from his visit to the lawyer. He wasn't strict with his crew. They needed their time and space as much as he did.

'You can go now then Emilio, old pal. See you later.'

Emilio eyed Andrea speculatively before his face broke into smiles. 'Thanks. I'll be seeing you.'

'Come on down,' said Conway to Andrea.

He led her to what was obviously his office. With a hush, the door closed behind her. The walls were warm and rich with Oriental teak. Brass wall-lamps that might once have been oil but were now powered by the boat's generator added a golden lustre to the opulent richness of the bulkheads.

Apart from the fitted office desk and computer equipment, there was only a white leather couch and matching chair, plus a low, wooden coffee table in the middle of the room which was fixed to the floor.

'Sit down.' Conway pointed to the couch. The tone of his voice made her want to obey. It was as dark as Emira's, and entirely irresistible.

He sat himself in the swivel chair, and turned round in it so he was facing her. Before that, it had been facing the desk where a computer blinked with a harsh blue light.

His eyes were intense and very blue. His hair erupted from a widow's peak above his forehead then fell to lay in a soft mantle beyond his shoulders. A hint of gold glinted in his ear.

Andrea took a deep breath. What harm was there in using one brother so she could stay in favour with the other? None, she decided. With slow deliberation, she crossed one leg over the other; so slow that, at one stage, he must have caught a glimpse of her naked pussy.

The back hem of her dress swept the floor. She leaned back on the couch and was sure that the crease of her seated buttocks must be showing. She liked the thought

115

of that, liked to feel that perhaps such a sight would catch Conway off guard.

Even though he did not speak, she saw his lips move as though he were tasting her.

'So to what do I owe this pleasure?' he asked. 'Don't tell me it was purely to flash your pussy at me, and I'm pretty sure you're not here on my brother's account.'

Andrea was too experienced, too resolute in her mission to blush or stammer. She did not part her lips and show her teeth when she smiled. But she leaned forward slightly, uncrossed her legs, and let them open. Still smiling, she rolled up the hem of her dress. 'I don't hear you objecting to my little sideshow.'

'How could I? You asked to come here and see me. You have me at a disadvantage, my dear Andrea, yet I know your purpose is not purely sexual.'

'Perhaps.'

'No perhaps about it. What do you want in exchange?'

'What can I interest you in?'

The action that followed was as provocative as her voice. She leaned back on the couch and opened her legs wide. Her dress rolled up over her thighs so that her sex was exposed in all its golden-haired glory. The pink lushness of her moist lips smiled from between her thighs.

Conway was not unaffected by the sight. He felt his rod stiffen and rise. While considering his actions, he turned towards the computer screen and switched it off. It was purely a ruse, a brief stalling. He knew he would take her, knew she would let him. In fact, thinking about it, he had known it from the moment Andrea had phoned him that morning.

Hands folded in front of him, he looked at her face, then lowered his eyes. His gaze lingered on her breasts. He took his time before he let them wander further, until they rested on the golden delight she was so obviously offering him.

Andrea was a woman experienced in all the things

that pleasured the body. She would give herself to this man willingly in order to draw him into her plan. To keep one brother, she had to seduce the other, draw him to her. It could not help but be a pleasant task.

Moistness touched her sex as though it had been teased there by his tongue. Aware of the quickening of her own breathing, the soft rise and fall of her breasts, she shifted slightly where she sat.

A brass wall lamp protruded from just behind his head. In its bulbous base she could see a distorted view of the cabin and her half-naked body. But her flesh was tantalised. Perhaps it was just her imagination, but she felt that every hair on her body was moving of its own accord as her skin responded to his gaze.

Desire spread over her like a veil. But she was no bride; more a creature of sex, a user of it, a slave to it.

'Do you like it?' she asked.

'Yes. I do.'

'How much?'

'Very much.'

'*Show* me how much.'

'Not there,' he said. His voice was low and husky. She perceived the rise of his penis against the tightness of his jeans. 'Here.' He patted the edge of his desk above where the chair slotted in. In order to make room for her, he slid the computer back further on to the desk.

Triumphant, Andrea kicked off her high gold sandals, stood up and, after undoing her belt, let her dress glide to the floor.

She liked the look in his eyes, the way they settled on her naked nipples, the way his tongue snaked across his lips as though he could discern their flavour on his tongue.

The increasing size of the lump in the front of his jeans also betrayed the fact that he was beyond the point of no return. He would have her, or was it her having him?

Her feet bare on the thick pile of the carpet, she walked over to him, hips swaying, her golden pubes

117

thrust slightly forward. She ran her hands down over her breasts, her belly, and down her loins. With a look of sadistic pleasure, she ran her fingers further and pulled back the outer lips of her sex to expose the more glistening and precious inner lips. She noticed Conway's neck move as he gulped back his surprise. The lump in his trousers had grown. As though demanding release, his cock thrust against his zip.

In the subtle light of the cabin, her eyes met his. They were rich with colour, with intensity. His skin, tight across his high cheekbones and firm chin, was well weathered by the sun and the sea.

He slid his chair backwards so she could ease herself on the area of desk in front of him. The top of the desk was cool against her behind. As he slid the chair forward, he placed one of his hands on each of her knees and prised her legs further apart. She was open to his sight, her fingers holding her outer lips open so his view of her inner lusciousness was unhindered.

With a look of satisfaction on her face, she smiled down on his hair. For a moment, he said nothing. He looked at her sex, studied it closely. As if looking through his eyes, she imagined what he was seeing: the pinkness of her clitoris fringed by golden hair, the rich open folds of her outer labia that usually curled towards each other like folds of rich velvet, the inner labia glistening with the silver opulence of her sexual secretions.

'Yes,' he murmured into her belly, 'you have a very pretty pussy.'

She would have answered, but instead caught her breath as he slid from the chair to his knees in front of her.

His fingers replaced hers as they pulled her outer lips apart and then played pleasurably with her labia, her clitoris and her willing vagina.

Bracing her palms down on the desk so she could savour this treatment, she closed her eyes and mewed with delight. Her legs remained open wide. Even when his hair brushed against the satin softness of her inner thighs, she did not open her eyes. Instead, Andrea, being the creature she was, let her sexuality loose. No matter what her true reason for coming here, this man would appreciate doing all the things she wanted to do.

Meltdown almost came when his tongue began to trace and divide each leaf of flesh, each dewy nerve-end of desire. But that was nothing compared to her rapture when his tongue entered her vagina. This was something extraordinary, something she had not quite expected. His tongue was huge.

She opened her eyes. Almost as if he were expecting her to be looking at him, he left what he was doing and looked up at her. Without the slightest vestige of emotion or smile, he ran his tongue over his lips. Then, with great deliberation, he poked it out at her. It was enormous, virile, like a dark pink snake out looking for dinner, and she was that dinner. What was more, she wanted to be that dinner. Just the sight of it knocked the breath out of her.

As if reading her mind, he bent his head back to the task, and again, his tongue pushed at her clitoris, and all by itself folded her labia to one side as it travelled back to her wet vagina.

Lost in the intensity of her own passion, she closed her eyes again and moaned with delight. Never had she come across a tongue as strong as this. Once its prying tip had reached her open sex, it pushed inwards – slowly, sensually, inch by powerful inch. This, she decided, was a bonus she had not expected on this mission.

Deep in her throat, sweet groans of pleasure came into being and rumbled upwards. All that she had been, and experienced, broke into little fragments and blew away.

His tongue filled her. His fingers played expertly with the rest of her sex. Between one thumb and forefinger, he rolled her clitoris. His other fingers stroked, coerced and teased her pink flesh to absolute frenzy.

In time with his tongue and her breathing, her bottom began to beat a quick rhythm against the green leather desktop. Her hips rose in short spasms to meet him. The desktop was no longer cool: she had transferred her own heat to it, and now her moans and her rapidly increasing movement were bringing her to the ultimate conclusion.

His mouth now tight against her, his lips sucking her, his tongue deep inside, she cried out as shivers of absolute ecstasy radiated outwards and engulfed her body.

Again and again she cried and jerked against his mouth until she was spent. His lips still gripped her, his tongue still filled her. Not until he was absolutely sure that he had wrung ever last vestige of orgasm from her did he retreat.

When she opened her eyes, her gaze met his. His eyes were narrowed beneath his pale gold brows, almost as though he was doing his best to withhold some emotion.

He got to his feet; his face came close to hers. She lowered her eyes to the glistening moistness of her own juices around his lips, smelt the pungency of her own gender on his mouth. He kissed her and she tasted herself.

His lips left her. She was breathless, her breasts still rising and falling. He stood up before her, wildly handsome, ruggedly desirable. His face was firm and unsmiling. Andrea sensed her own attempt at control was diminishing, but there was no turning back. The chance was still there. Her plan was still there.

'Stand up,' he ordered.

She slid off the desk and did so.

'Turn round and bend over the chair,' he said. 'Put your hands on the seat of it.'

She did exactly as he asked. Her torso was lower than her behind. Without being asked, she opened her legs and tilted her bottom. Through her thighs, the wet lips of her pussy smiled enticingly at him. She eyed him over her shoulder and caught something in his eyes that she

120

had seen in Philippe's, something that made her think he was thinking of someone else rather than her.

'Well,' she said sharply. 'Are you going to be there all day?'

A frightening darkness overcame his features and just for a moment, Andrea lost her natural confidence.

'Shut up,' he said. 'And do as you're told!'

His right hand landed in a loud slap on her right cheek; his left hand did the same to the other.

She cried out, thought of leaving, then remembered why she'd come here. I can bear it, she decided, so she stayed as she was.

'Good,' said Conway, his voice like gravel. 'You want something from me, or you want me to do something for you. Fair exchange is no robbery, they say. And I want an exchange. Your backside and your body for whatever it is you want. Do you agree?'

She thought of telling him there and then what she had in mind and that, if her plan went right, he would be receiving something anyway. But she didn't. Conway was the sort of man who'd take both anyway; her *and* the green-eyed girl.

'If you insist,' she answered.

She was aware of him going over to the desk, and remembered seeing a plastic ruler lying across the data sheets. Knuckles whitening as she gripped the edge of the chair, she gritted her teeth. Philippe liked to smack her behind, and she liked him to do it. But there was something in Conway that was certainly different from his brother. His arm swung more fiercely, his blow landed more sharply.

Pain and heat mingled as the plastic ruler seared across her behind, favouring the right buttock rather than the left.

She gasped, her whole body tensing against the blow.

'And do you like that, my treacherous little minx?' Conway asked her.

It took some effort, but Andrea managed a frightened

whimper; although, in all honesty, she had a yearning to moan with delight and roll her bottom for more.

'Good,' he said. 'Now that's what I like to see. A woman who knows what she deserves. A woman who knows her place.'

Conway raised his arm again. The ruler hissed through the air, and this time reddened her left buttock.

Playing her part to the full, Andrea whimpered again and even managed to squeeze a tear from the corner of one eye. A fizz of delicious tingles congregated in her sex and spread with alarming rapidity through her loins.

'There,' said Conway with obvious satisfaction. 'See what a lovely red bottom you have.'

Andrea squeezed a few more tears from her eyes as she looked over her shoulder.

Conway was holding a mirror to her hot behind. In it, she could see twin patches of bright red seeping over her white flesh. Just below her firm posterior peeped her sex, the lips as golden as light pastry around a filling of fresh strawberries.

'You don't look very repentant,' he said.

So hypnotised had she been by the reflection of her red bottom, Andrea had forgotten to look suitably subdued, and upset. In all honesty, the sight of the redness among the white had excited rather than frightened her. Conway, she realised, did not want that.

In response, she had to goad him. 'I'm not!' She said it tartly. If he wanted to do this right and treat her really badly, it was up to him to get on with it. From experience, she knew she could take it.

She heard him put the mirror down and guessed he was coming back to her with the ruler. What she hadn't expected was the elastic bands he slipped over each of her breasts.

It was easy now to moan as the tightness of the bands constricted her flesh.

'That's better,' he said, and she sensed his satisfaction in the way he said it. 'I get the impression, you little bitch, that your bottom's hardened to more than a ruler. But it's a safe bet your titties aren't. Am I right?'

For once, Andrea bit her lip with true meaning. She couldn't answer. What he said was correct and, already, the blood was rushing to her nipples with apprehension as well as arousal.

He laughed. 'I thought so! I knew it! So, let's get on with it then. This, my dear Andrea, is all for you.'

Andrea's hands were still on the chair. The ruler came from beneath her and caught the nipples of both breasts. With a deep breath, she rode the sensation and opened her eyes wide. Surprisingly, it was not as bad as she had thought it would be. Because the blow came from below, it was tempered by gravity and, instead of great pain, there was only that tingling sort that ignited sexuality rather than subdued it.

But she had learned what Conway Patterson was like, so she squalled that he was hurting her, that he was cruel, he was torturing her.

Conway liked that. In response to the joy her words gave him, he continued his treatment of her breasts until he could see tears on her face and feel the hardness of his cock bulge tightly against his flies. Hard and hot against his zip, the time came when that erection could no longer be ignored.

Tears streaming down her face, and triumph in her eyes, Andrea sobbed as she heard the sound of discarded clothing falling to the thickly carpeted floor.

Her breasts as red as her behind, she gasped as strong hands cupped her buttocks. Warm palms pressed into her hot flesh, and firm fingers roughly prised one rounded orb away from its sister. Now the smallest orifice of her body was exposed to his gaze, his thumbs pressing either side of it.

Andrea was no stranger to what he was about to do, but it would not do to let on. 'Please don't,' she cried out. 'Please don't put it in there. Please don't hurt me!'

Mercy was a grace that Conway did not have. It was

the last thing he would give her, and she should know that.

Expectantly, she moved her hands so that, again, she was gripping the edge of the chair. Behind her, the hot moist glans of Conway's penis forced its way between her cheeks.

As with his tongue, nature had been generous to Conway Patterson. Andrea gasped as the largeness of his bulbous head prodded her buttocks apart and stretched her straining ring. With no regard for her comfort or pleasure, it nudged forward and upward into her forbidden channel.

She braced her legs, clutched at the arms of the chair and cried out. Again, as with his tongue, he took his time. Inch by inch he entered. With each measure of him, she groaned, but in ecstasy not discomfort.

Even before he had fully entered, she felt fit to burst. But she did not cry out. She continued to moan as though what he was doing was the most delicious thing in the world.

'So you want me to help you.' He said it calmly, almost as if his breathing was without exertion.

'Yes.'

'And you promise me some redhead that my mother acquired for my brother. Is that right?'

As he slammed more forcibly into her, Andrea yelped before she answered. 'Yes,' she said eventually.

'How certain are you about delivering this woman?'

This time she groaned and her knees sagged a little. 'Yes.' It was more a wail than an answer to his question.

'Then, my dear Andrea,' said Conway as he gripped tightly at her shoulders. 'we have a deal.'

His withdrawal was almost as uncomfortable as his entrance.

Andrea groaned with as much vitality as before, then gasped with gratitude as he transferred his penis to her vagina.

Her sex was full, and still he pushed inwards. Soon,

there was no more length to give her and no room if there *had* been.

With each forward thrust, she cried out as if in pain. With each retreating stroke, she sobbed pure misery. Yet, all the time, she was savouring the coarseness of his pubic hair against the sting of her behind, the ripeness of his balls, soft as eiderdown, against the silkiness of her inner thighs. She struggled, but his hands held her in place, and his fingertips dug cruelly into her flesh. As he thrust forward, he pulled her on to him; as he retreated, he pushed her away.

In time with her body, her abused and stinging breasts tapped gently one against the other and against her ribcage. Strands of hair fell around her face so that her closed eyes and her open mouth were hidden from view. She was lost to herself, but still remembered to cry and wail and sob in the right places. This man had taken more than her body; he'd enticed to the surface, then taken and used her own sexuality. She had used his tongue, delighted in its nubile delicacy. Now he was using her more than willing vagina.

How would he feel, she wondered, if he knew that even as he thrust deep within her, she was thinking of his brother, comparing the two both in size and, more importantly, technique? How, also, would he feel to know that her entreaties were false, that she enjoyed his cruel hands and even more cruel penis?

All that was happening to her would be worth it anyway. Her original plan had grown as much out of jealousy towards the newly arrived redhead as out of the hatred she felt for Venetia Salvatore.

She had come here for a purpose. Now her aims were lain aside as she enjoyed the perverted terms of Conway's compliance with her plan.

Even though she could not see him, she knew Conway's eyes must be closed and his climax near. She felt his body tensing as his orgasm travelled from hidden depths. The swiftness of his strokes increased with her breathing and his breathing. Cries of pain escaped her throat, such cries that sounded as though they had been ripped from somewhere deep inside.

Their effect on Conway was electric. With each pain-filled wail, his fingers dug into her flesh a little more intensely, a little more cruelly. She knew he was coming.

Breast tapped more urgently against partner. Body rammed more determinedly into body as his moment of release approached. Without any thought for her behind, he thrust with all his strength for one last time and left his cries in her hair.

He tensed against her, throbbed within her, then threw himself forward on to her back and gripped her aching breasts as his last tremor of climax clamped the hardness of his thighs to hers.

A moment passed. The weight on her back lessened as he slid out of her. She remained in the same position while she caught her breath, licked her salt-laden lips and opened her eyes.

'One moment,' he said, as she began to move. 'Stay like that a little longer. I want to look at you again.'

'But why?' she whimpered, determined to play her part to the end. 'Haven't you used me cruelly enough already?'

His hand gripped her head and he pushed it down into the seat of the chair so that her backside was even higher than before, her head lower. 'Stay like that,' he ordered. 'And do as I say. Open your sex with your hands. Let me see you more fully.'

Compliant and impatient to put her plan to him, she followed his instructions and ran her hands between her legs, which meant opening them wider than ever. With her fingers, she folded back the glossy folds of her labia and opened her sex to his gaze.

Silently, he studied her. It was a while till he spoke. 'I don't know your true reason for wanting to get rid of this redhead. After all, you can have any man you want. Why would you want to stay with my brother?' he said at last. 'Not that I really care. I'm guessing that my brother is neglecting you, and that you are submitting to anything he wants to do in order to keep him. So now my mother has got him a new toy to play with. Sad man, my brother. Still, his loss is my gain. Tell me whatever you want to tell me about your plan. In the meantime, give me the submission I want, and I'll give you what you want. Is that a deal?'

She tossed her head and looked at him over her shoulder.

There was a wicked look in his eyes and on his lips. In that moment, she knew her plan would be accepted, as long as she was willing to bend to his wishes. She also promised herself that the moment her part of it was completed, she would be off and back to Philippe.

Snivelling slightly, she wiped at her eyes. 'OK,' she said. 'It's a deal.'

Chapter Eight

*T*he house Philippe instructed his driver to take him to was white with pale green shutters. Only the warm red of its tiled roof showed above a high wall in one of the most select districts of the city.

The wall, too, was white, and blossoms hung over it like bunches of grapes, around which a myriad bees and butterflies buzzed and fluttered.

The whiteness would have been too stark, too brilliant if it hadn't been for the blossoms of the spreading bougainvillaea and the dark green cypresses ranged in rows behind it like phallic warriors. They provided shade and a softening to the contrast between white walls, red roof and blue sky.

The wrought-iron gates opened automatically. He was expected. The car entered, and drove over the yellow gravel to the fluted columns that ran along the frontage of the house.

Philippe did not tell his driver how long he would be. This was not the first occasion they had come to this place and, no doubt, it would not be the last.

The wide double doors opened at his approach.

'Good day, sir. It is good to see you again.'

Dressed in white shirt and loose blue trousers, for all

the world like some latter-day eunuch, the man who had opened the door bowed stiffly from the waist. With a flamboyant flourish, he waved to a door immediately opposite the one by which Philippe had just entered.

Philippe nodded, returned the 'Good day', and walked across the white marble floor which looked as if it would crack like ice at each footfall.

Another man, as big and as blue-black as the first, opened the next door.

As each door opened and closed, Philippe became more and more relaxed. His cares, like the world outside, seemed to have passed away. Here, in the cool confines of this villa, all things were possible, and all fantasies catered for.

Heads turned and smiles widened as he entered the coolness of the inner courtyard. Limbs that had been relaxing at the side of a bright blue pool now intertwined one with the other as though urging the juices of love to come creeping to their fleshy lips.

Few wore clothes. Clothes were to cover the body against cold in northern climes: here, clothes were but garnish to the goods offered and could either embellish or constrain.

Blondes, brunettes, redheads – the latter he lingered over, his eyes meeting theirs, the corners of his mouth rising, then reclining once his eyes had met theirs and he'd tasted disappointment. Some eyes were green, but not as deep nor as dark as those he remembered.

Perfumed flowers and perfumed women combined to assail his senses and arouse his sex drive. What he sought was not here, but at least he could indulge in pleasure for a while. In a darkened room, he could at least pretend . . .

'Philippe. Darling.'

Rich lips that had tasted many flavours and many men in their lifetime now kissed his cheek in sisterly welcome.

He looked down into ice-blue eyes and at a face that

had lived, and lived long, but was still strong, still sublime.

'Helga. How are you?' He took her hand and kissed it like the gentleman he was born to be and was.

'Very well,' she answered. 'And how are you?'

'Oh, well enough.'

The way he replied was as offhand as usual. His eyes, and she guessed, his thoughts, were elsewhere.

He went back to scanning the lovelies who lay so available and so naked around the glassy surface of the pool. In one way he was affected by them. What man wouldn't be? In another, he was not. What he was searching for was not there, or not in quite the form he required.

'Perry is here.' Helga dropped her voice when she said it, as though inviting some comment from him, some sign that he was pleased at that.

He stopped scanning the lush breasts, crisp pubic curls and the naked lips of those who had none. With a look of interest in his eyes, he turned to Helga whose white hair was strained back into a tight but glossy bun.

'Is she free at the moment?' he asked.

Helga nodded. 'Do you wish me to arrange things? It won't take a moment.'

Briefly, he considered saying no. But the old stirrings his meeting with Conway and Guido had resurrected would not go away. Anyway, he had dreamed of her again last night, that woman with the red hair and green eyes who had once filled his life and now filled only his dreams. No matter. Perhaps Perry would go some way to laying his own private ghosts.

He relaxed, took and drank fruit juice and watched the other girls while he waited.

Helga had instructed them on how best to keep this particular client amused, and the girls, professional from the tips of their glossy heads to their painted toenails, willingly obliged.

After they had helped him off with his clothes, he lay

130

out on a lounger, his cock already firm and rising skywards.

Not one girl there would have denied whatever he wanted of her. Wet tongues licked dry lips as their eyes raked his naked body. In wild imaginings, they cupped their own breasts and teased their juicy clits with their own hands and fingers.

Stretched out, he lay watching them almost as intently as they were watching him. They were beautiful women, every last one of them. He was a good-looking man, and he could see they thought so. Their lips smiled, their eyes smiled as they ran their hands down over their bodies, pinched their ripe nipples, and opened their legs so he could see what they were offering.

His flesh tingled as their eyes ran over him. He put himself in their place, and saw himself through their eyes.

The muscles of his shoulders were well-formed, though not over-zealous. At the chest, he was wide, though not with the solid beefiness of a heavy man. Each muscle gleamed and jostled with its neighbour. Each had shape and, from his chest, his body curved in a long and provocative sweep to his waist. From there, it rose over his hip-bones, then a little more over his thighs from where it curved down to his knees, then up again over the tightness of his calves before narrowing at his ankles.

Opposite him, and no more than four feet away, was another lounger on which a leggy blonde had also stretched out, though she was lying the opposite way round to him.

In direct line of sight, she opened her legs and displayed herself. All was white skin and pink flesh. Her quim, he could see, was completely defoliated.

Red-painted fingernails darted like small birds over her naked labia as she started to finger herself for his delight. Before his eyes, she held open her shorn lips, and deftly tapped at her clitoris which shone as though touched with dew.

131

With the fingers of her other hand, she caressed her breast and pinched a nipple.

He let his eyes wander from the glistening fingers that fondled her sex, and travel up over her body.

She had a good body, wide hips with no hint of surplus flesh. Her waist was narrow and her breasts were full and heavy with dark pink nipples. The one she was playing with was glowing slightly redder than its partner.

He studied her face.

Through half-narrowed eyes, she looked back. Her mouth was open; her tongue flicking at her top lip, then at her bottom one. It was almost, he thought, as though it were following the same tempo as her fingers.

Once his eyes were back on her sex, she mewed with delight, then squealed as she pushed her own finger into her vagina. Her mews of pleasure became groans.

As he watched, he was very aware of the rise of his own organ, its soft swaying as he took delight in watching the girl pleasure herself.

More blood rushed along his stem the more intently she murmured, the more her moans trembled in her throat.

The hand that pleasured between her legs began to move faster. Two fingers now plunged in glorious rapture into her open vagina and a stray thumb knocked at her clitoris.

With furious abandon, she gave in at last to her own fingers.

'Finito,' she said in a low and gravel-edged voice. 'Finito.'

As though she were melting before his eyes, she fell back on her lounger. Her breasts heaved, thrusting upwards like virgin hills that still trembled with the aftermath of volcanic action. He watched them rise and fall above her ribcage which grew convex above her belly. Slowly, she regained her breath and her previous languid enjoyment of just lying in the sun like a lazy lizard.

Just once, she opened her eyes, smiled at no one in particular, then rolled over and let herself fall into the pool.

Spray from the very blue pool flecked his face and stayed immobile on his chest before running down over the hardness of his body. It trickled down into his pubic hair and, with feather-like sensitivity, circled around the stem of his cock. In response, his penis swayed slightly, and a single pearl drop of semen seeped on to its crown.

Just as a pert and smiling Chinese girl opened her legs on the lounger in front of him, and pulled out a long strand of love beads, Helga reappeared. 'Everything's ready,' she said. 'Are you?'

'Yes,' he replied and got to his feet. 'I'm more than ready.'

As though in response, his length of hard, purple flesh nodded expectantly and swayed from side to side as he walked.

The room Helga led him to was cool, shady and faced the sea.

From the sea, the breeze entered and billowed the fine muslin curtain that graced the wide expanse of glass door which opened on to a balcony.

Helga took him by the hand and led him to the bed. 'Here, darling. Let me tuck you in.'

She pulled back the sheet, and just as if he were a child again, Philippe got into bed.

The pillow and sheets were cool, crisp and smelt of fresh air. Closing his eyes, he drank in their odour and fingered their texture.

Cool fingers caressed his brow and resurrected old memories, old dreams.

'So glad to have you home from school, darling,' he heard her say. 'So glad.'

School, soft sheets, a soft voice. He'd been sixteen at the time. He remembered that. Sixteen going on seventeen and thinking of university in England as per his mother's wishes.

Not only had it been a hot summer, but his own body had become hotter, fierce with new emotions and new urges.

He felt the coolness of Helga's fingers run over his neck. He savoured their softness, their coolness and, in his imaginings, he was young again and Helga was his mother.

Once she was sure he had drifted into the past, Helga left the room, just as she always did when they re-enacted this very important phase in his life – just as his mother had really done all those years ago.

He let his imaginings take him over, although his throbbing tool did not entirely release him to his dreams. It was real, very hard and very eager.

He heard the door close as Helga left the room, then heard it open again.

'Philippe. Philippe. It is me. Are you awake?'

He did not open his eyes, but he did reply. 'Yes. Yes I am.'

His voice was dreamlike, just as this moment was, just as it had always been.

As though she were of gossamer, her footsteps were light on the floor, her presence a mere shadow on the air. And yet he was very aware of her. Even now, his prick stood upright under the sheet.

He rolled over, lay on his back, but did not open his eyes.

'I watched you today, Philippe. You are so different to when I last saw you. You were still a boy, a little boy. Now, you are a big boy.'

'No,' he responded, just as he had then. 'No. I'm sixteen. I'm a man now.'

She laughed. Her laughter was as light as her presence.

'Foolish boy. Of course you're not a man. You're still a boy.'

He felt her fingers trace across his forehead, his cheeks,

his nose, his mouth. He groaned as her hand proceeded down his neck to lay flat on his chest. It was all the same, the same as it ever was.

'No. I'm a man,' he said suddenly.

As she leaned over him, his head was filled with her scent. Her hair swept like the softest of feathers over his chest as she kissed him. Warm lips, sweet lips reminiscent of many tastes, but one above all others. She tasted of woman – such a familiar taste now, but such an unfamiliar one in that time when he had first met the girl with the green eyes and red hair; but exciting, still exciting.

Her lips left him. Still he did not open his eyes.

'No,' she said. 'No. You are still a boy, Philippe, but not for much longer. The time has come for you to become a man. Your mother has sent me to you. She has given you to me as a boy. When I have finished with you, *then* you will be a man.'

How stirring those words were, how rich the memory, the taste and the touch.

A muscle knotted in his stomach as her hand ran down under the sheet and followed the sweeping hardness of his lithe and beautiful body.

'You are so beautiful, Philippe. Like a young god fit for an offering. I am that offering, Philippe. Do you want me?'

'I don't know,' he said, his voice thick with his need. 'Are you really an offering?'

In his mind she was not. In actuality, she was not, and yet his voice trembled, for he wanted it to be her, to be someone.

Running through his clutch of crisp pubic hair, her fingers thrilled him. With an expert touch, she lightly touched his upright rod, circling it, tracing imaginary lines along its length and gently tapping at his heaving glans.

He squeezed his eyes shut as she pulled back the sheet.

135

He felt her lips kissing his body, her hair brushing his chest. And he smelt her. That beautiful smell that reminded him of the sea, the beloved sea with its wild undulations, its unpredictability, its calms and its storms.

Her hand circled his cock and, gently at first, she began to pull on it, her hand sliding as she did so.

He was aware of her climbing between his open legs, the mattress dipping gently beneath her weight. Just by smelling her and feeling her presence he knew she was naked, but could not bring himself to look. If he looked, his dream would be shattered.

Brushing against his open thighs, he felt the sweep of her hair as her head burrowed between his legs. Her mouth sucked at the soft suppleness of his scrotum, and the end of her nose rubbed against his stem.

Almost choking him, a sound stuck, then erupted from his throat. It was like a half-formed word, but self-explanatory. What she was doing to him resurrected all his old memories, all his old feelings.

In a sudden moment, her mouth left him. 'Did you like that?' she asked.

'Yes. Very much. Will this make me a man?'

'No,' she replied in a voice that provoked and promised. 'But this will.'

Against the clustered nerve-ends that sat on the tip of his cock like a crown, he felt the wiry crispness of her pubic hair. Lightly, it brushed over its tingling surface before the fleshy lips of her sex sucked him in.

He gasped, just as he had gasped that very first time. 'Are you eating me?' he asked.

She laughed. 'You could say that. You could say I am eating you, chewing you up as a boy so you re-emerge as a man.'

His whole body was on fire. He felt her inner warmth and wanted more. His hips left the bed and jerked up to her, embedded him in her.

'That's it, my darling,' she moaned. 'That's it. Give me your beautiful prick. Bury it in me. More, more, more!'

As his hips jerked upwards, she rode him as she might a horse, bobbing up and down on his stalwart member that burrowed itself so willingly in her.

He could feel her hot lips thud against his pubes, the constricting of her womb around his member.

Deep within him he felt that surge of something hot and liquid. He hadn't known it well then – not so openly, not so honestly – but he knew it well now, knew how it would fire up from deep within and render him almost senseless with its echoing embers of total climax.

When it came, he cried out, just as he had then.

Once the last tremors had died away, he opened his eyes again, just as he had when he had been sixteen.

Perry smiled. 'And now, Philippe, you are a man.'

He smiled back. His desire was satisfied in all departments except one.

Perry wore a red wig, but was neither naturally red-headed nor green-eyed. She was not that golden woman whose name had been Antonia but he and his brother had called *Sea Witch* or *Enchantress*. But, for now, she was all he had.

Chapter Nine

*T*he heat of the afternoon faded into the warm darkness of a spring evening. After dinner, Toni wan-
dered on deck beneath an indigo sky that was studded
with a myriad stars and lit by a low hanging moon. It
was a sight designed by nature to excite; yet even
without it, anticipation tingled like creeping water
throughout her body.

Emira, that creature whose clothes and name were
nothing more than a shield to what he really was, had
been in her body and was still in her thoughts. Sleek and
hard as ebony, his body had lain with her, and his rod had
pushed through her slippery folds and invaded her body.

The memory of the Red Tower and the voice in the
shadows were also still with her. Lying in the hard
strength of his arms, she'd asked Emira to what purpose
Madame Salvatore had employed her.

He'd been reticent.

'Your task will gradually unfold,' he explained. 'That's
all I can say. There is no detail to it, no real pattern. In
one way, it is all down to Providence. If you suit, one
thing will undoubtedly follow another.' His voice was
as deep as the ocean, his words hushed by the closeness
of her hair.

The long, slim fingers had brushed her hair away from her eyes. His plush lips had kissed her forehead, and like a child, she had felt a great urgency to drift off into a dreamless sleep. Her own curiosity gave her determination to press further.

'She was testing me. What for? What task does she have in mind?'

The long fingers stilled in their caressing of her hair. Tension tightened the beautiful black body that lay so soft-skinned yet hard-muscled against her.

In a reciprocal action, Toni had let her hand run down between their bodies, her palm flat against the iron wall of his stomach. With enticing dexterity, she had trailed her fingers over his supine cock. It rose its silken dome beneath her touch. She snuggled closer against him. His tension lessened and his erection increased.

'You are very astute, Antonia, and you are also irresistible. I am convinced you are the one we have been searching for, but only Madame can make the decision. Soon, you will know for sure.'

It was at that point that Toni had curled her fingers around his rising stem. 'I want to do it,' she said suddenly, her fingers tightening so much that his penis pulsated hotly in her hand. 'Whatever it is, I want to do it.'

Emira's laugh was laced with a moan that was a direct reaction to the movements of Toni's fingers around his groin. 'I am very glad to hear it, Antonia. Very glad indeed. The lady will be glad too. It will help her decision. If you enjoy what you are doing in an open and full-hearted manner, it will also assist in your mission.'

His penis throbbed and swelled in her hand, ready again to do to her what he had done so well before. She let her other hand rest against the iron hardness of his chest, let her breath take in his odour, that mix of scents she had detected from the first: perfume and masculinity.

'Is this thing dangerous; repugnant?'

'I do not think you will find it so, not with your attitude to such things. I think that with your skills and capacity for sexual enjoyment, you will find the whole thing very gratifying – surprisingly so.'

He had run his fingers over the cheeks of her behind at that point. She'd started, her flesh still sensitive from the sting of the whip.

He kissed her and murmured soothing, unrecognisable words into her ear.

She moaned and thrust her body nearer to his. As she did so, his fingers invaded the moist membranes of her vagina. In response, she opened to him.

'You like that?' he'd asked.

'Ye . . . s,' she'd murmured, eyes closed as she relished the twin sensations of fingers inside her, and his warm penis nestling in her hand. 'It's delicious,' she said. 'Too delicious for words, only actions.'

Emira had let out a long breath and the warmth in his eyes seemed to cover her like a soft breeze. 'My, my. I think you really are the one Madame has been seeking.'

Toni snuggled closer. 'Will Madame be happy about that?' She stroked Emira's manhood as she spoke so that it jerked away from her, then fell back into her hand for more.

'Madame,' Emira had breathed, 'will be happier than she has been in a very long time.'

Tonight, Toni was happy too.

She was glad to be here, excited that tonight she would meet Madame Salvatore face to face. Tonight she felt good and looked good, and nothing could stop her from being everything she was required to be.

With help from Emira, she had prepared her body, her hair and what she would wear. The dress she had chosen was dark green and swept like a wave over the contours of her body and swirled around her calves. Her hair was caught up in a band so that it sat on her head in a casual and sexy way. Because it was so long, it still reached her shoulder-blades. A few stray strands blew with the breeze around her face.

The gold necklet and bracelets she wore complemented the dress, and Emira had added gold anklets whose dual purpose she guessed were identical to the other gold bands.

The breeze was cool as it swept up over her naked thighs and belly. Because her dress was so sheer, she had put on panties and bra. But again, Emira, with dark voice and darker hands, had helped her to remove them. Now, she felt almost naked beneath the obvious transparency of the dress, her sensuality heightened by the kiss of the breeze.

Tonight, the world was hers – or at least, that was how it felt. Beyond the jetty, she could see the dark form of the island that lay low upon the sea like a sleeping Buddha. In the distance, atop its one sheer height, the Red Tower stood starkly black against the deep purple of the evening sky.

The magic of the night was enhanced by the intrusion of a voice she had come to know very well. 'Madame wants to see you now.'

Emira, Marie trailing behind her, had come to fetch her. The French girl, almost it seemed in deference to Emira, did not speak, but looked down at the deck.

Toni followed them down the stairs and companionway and into the presence of Madame Salvatore.

The saloon she entered had a creamy gold carpet that matched walls of golden teak. Recessed lighting sparkled overhead from brass-banded inserts in the rich wood of the ceiling. Fat couches of gold-coloured leather lined the walls. Another sat in the middle of the room.

There were two pillars in the room, one at each end. These, Toni knew, housed the masthead fixings, though she'd never seen any decorated quite like these before. Around the top of each one, was a row of brass rings with another row halfway down, and another around the bottom. Remembering her experience in the Red

Tower, she dragged her eyes away from those and back to the woman who sat before her.

Venetia Salvatore was a woman of extraordinary beauty and breathless elegance. The woman's hair was strikingly white, like newly fallen snow.

She had the most intense brown eyes, high cheekbones and the lips of one who has savoured long and well the fruits and the fancies of life. It was impossible to put a price on the clothes she wore. The colour resembled wild violets, the weave and style a glorious mixture of shining threads interwoven to form differing tones of the same colour. The dress fell in scalloped edges to mid-calf. Her shoes matched the dress. Jewellery of silver, deep amethyst and gold shone from around her neck, her wrists, her fingers and her ears. Outstandingly eye-catching, outstandingly expensive.

Like a queen surveying her subjects, she sat in the centre of the room. Behind her stood Carlos and another like him who was just a little taller and a little leaner. Like Carlos, he wore the smallest of pouches in the softest of mauve chamois.

Briefly she glanced at Carlos, but did not have time to exchange knowing looks or lustful glances. One glance was enough to see that his member was straining against the skimpy pouch. How big it looked, and how capable of bursting through the flimsy material in one hard rush!

It took an effort for Toni to drag her eyes away from his heaving groin and back to Venetia Salvatore.

'This,' said Emira, with a sweep of one hand, 'is Madame Venetia Salvatore.'

'I see.'

It didn't seem the right thing to say, but Toni couldn't quite bring herself to say 'Pleased to meet you', or even 'Good evening'. There was no doubt in her mind that this was the woman who had stayed in the shadows when she had visited the Red Tower. This was the woman who had ordered her to endure the whip and enjoy the man that was put beneath her.

As though she was reading her thoughts, the woman smiled. 'Antonia,' she said. Toni's suspicions were confirmed. 'I am pleased to see you. Very pleased. You are everything I require, and I understand from my dear Emira that you are willing to carry out the duties I have designated you. I am very pleased indeed about that. Very pleased. Have you any questions?'

'I have,' Toni began. 'I would like to know what my duties are likely to be – the extra duties that you will require me to do.'

Like some old-time Roman emperor, Venetia Salvatore held up one hand that had many be-ringed fingers. A bracelet of gold circled her wrist like the coils of a snake.

'Not now,' she exclaimed. 'I will speak to you later on. But, for now, we will rejoice in your capacity to respond to the tasks I will be allotting you. Yesterday, I privately viewed your capacities. Today, I will proclaim them in public for everyone to see. Each day I will proclaim them while training you further in the delights of enjoyment and endurance, and all to a worthwhile climax.'

There was a tittering at her last word and hidden smiles behind flat palms.

'Enough!'

There was immediate silence. Everyone stood to rigid attention awaiting her next word, her next action.

'Emira. Marie. Prepare her.'

So mesmerised had Toni been by the woman and those eyes of velvet brown that she was hardly aware of Marie and Emira's fingers suddenly encircling her waist.

'Kneel down,' Emira ordered.

Marie and Emira's hands now on her shoulders, she was pushed down until her knees sank into the softness of the carpet. Marie and Emira still stood on either side of her.

'Are you willing to carry out the tasks I will set for you?' asked Venetia Salvatore. 'Will you obey me entirely, without question, with humility, downcast eyes and complete submission?'

143

The sound of what was required of her was enough to make her loins twitch and her answer catch in her throat. But she managed to speak. 'Yes,' she replied. 'I am.'

Her own words surprised her. One half of her wanted to rebel, and yet the other half was ready and willing to be bidden. But somehow, she knew that this submission would be different to the sort she had experienced with Julian. In this submission, she would be a willing, and indeed, enthusiastic participant. This submission would be enjoyable.

Venetia Salvatore nodded slowly, her eyes holding Toni's. 'There are rules, disciplines. Are you ready to accept these?'

Her voice drew her in, snaring her as a spider does a fly in a thick and ancient web. But she was a willing fly. She wanted to be snared, wanted to be eaten up with the fires of desire, the sweet entreaties to obedience.

'Yes,' Toni replied. 'I am.'

The sensuous lips of Venetia Salvatore smiled, and her teeth flashed white. Her eyes looked like deep pools beneath a sparkling sky. Determination and pride kept her chin high.

'Then I will outline those rules. Mutiny in any form will be thoroughly discouraged, as it is on any vessel. But your role is nebulous, to say the least. I have need of your presence which will bring different reactions from different people. During your discourse with these people, you will experience many new things. By experiencing those things, you will be doing me a great service. In time, you will know exactly what that service has been. Its nature is vague, and is invoked in just being yourself without having to do anything you do not wish to do. Do you understand that?'

'Yes, madam.'

Toni was aware she had answered almost automatically, without pause for thought or consideration. As though she were on a downhill ski-run, she was plunging headlong into this – and in so short a time. How long had it been since she had left London? When had she arrived in Rome? Days, mere days. And yet here she was now, intent on throwing herself into a situation that could be confining.

Venetia Salvatore looked incredibly pleased with the answer Toni had given her. She smiled suddenly. It was a warm smile, sincerely given, sincerely meant.

'Welcome, Antonia Yardley. Welcome to the *Sea Witch*. Welcome to the three islands of the Salvatores.'

She did not wait for her to reply. She nodded at Emira who stood on one side of her. Marie still stood on the other. They dragged her to her feet.

It was Emira who caught hold of her wrists, raised them behind her back and fastened the fine chains of the wristbands to the one that dangled from her collar.

'Enjoy,' Emira whispered in her ear, her breath wet and warm.

What few reservations she might have had melted away. Something different was happening to her. Something even more different was about to happen though she did not know what form it would take.

Silently, Emira and Marie pushed her towards one of the masthead housings. They unfastened the chain that held her hands to her neck collar, turned her to face the room and re-chained her wrists to one of the brass rings above her head. The chains that tinkled so delightfully from her anklets they fastened to rings around the other side of the pillar. Her legs were now spread wide and around it some way behind her.

They stepped back and looked at her. The room was silent, waiting for the word. But what word? What next was in store for her. She was bound to the masthead, yet she was not afraid. She was still clothed and in the company of people who looked at her as though they had seen her somewhere before, as though she was special and well worth looking at. What happened next was something she had not been prepared for.

145

Out of the corner of her eye, she saw Venetia nod to Emira and Marie.

Emira pointed to a low table of light-coloured marquetry which was heavily inlaid with mother-of-pearl. Marie walked to it and came back with a pair of scissors. Emira nodded at her, and Marie, much to Toni's astonishment, began to cut at her dress.

'What are you doing?' she cried out, hurt that a dress she loved so much could be so swiftly cut from her body.

Venetia answered, her voice resonant in the hollow confines of the saloon deck. 'You have accepted a future on board *Sea Witch*. You have accepted my future. Your past is gone. Your clothes are from your past. It is symbolic that they be cut off just like your past has been cut off and thrown behind you.'

As Toni considered what she should do, what she should say, she bit her lip. Wide-eyed, she followed the path of the shining scissors. But she held her tongue. At a given signal, the scissors snipped at the dress she'd shopped all afternoon for. But that was back in London, that was back with grey skies and Julian, and now, like him, her dress was just a memory and a pile of rags at her feet.

She was bound and naked. She clenched her buttocks as if that would cause her sex not to gape as widely as it did. But the lips of her sex were open, its fleshy nubs and folds nakedly obvious.

There was an electric expectation in the room. It hung there, unseen yet tangible. There was nothing now between her and those around her. They saw her as she really was, her bare skin, her firm and creamy flesh and the pink membranes clustered like crushed silk between her legs.

Blushing was an option that simmered somewhere beneath the first layer of Toni's skin. Naked and widely exposed as she was, she controlled the urge to do that. Her strongest urge was to close her legs against the eyes that feasted on her fiery-coloured fleece and crowd of

146

pink and very moist flesh. But that was not an option. She was bound to the masthead, hands fastened above her head, legs wide and ankles firmly chained some way around the side.

There was no sound in the room except for the hushed increase in breathing which resembled the spilling of surf upon rough sand.

Venetia was still sitting on the couch directly in front of her. She held one hand to her mouth, one finger thoughtfully tapping at her lips. Her eyes ran over Toni's body.

Half-closing her eyes, Toni writhed against her bonds, letting her hips undulate from side to side as her breasts swelled more quickly along with her breathing. Cool air kissed her naked sex and triggered the heat of desire. She was naked, she was vulnerable, yet she was also desirable and, in turn, she desired.

Venetia began to speak. 'Now, Antonia, you shall have pleasure.'

Audience or not, Toni found herself becoming aroused. In anticipation, she began to murmur low and longingly in her throat, her hips thrusting away from the hard cold column behind her. Carlos left his mistress's side and stood before her.

Conflict between her old ways and her need for this new and exciting sex was fast disappearing. Emira was right, she thought. This new and exciting sex was like a gourmet food. Once tasted and enjoyed, she couldn't help but yearn for more. Longing to feel a hot and hard body against hers, she fastened her eyes on Carlos' swelling groin. She licked her lips, and waited.

With something akin to reverence, Carlos raked his eyes down her body. They lingered on her breasts, his breath quickening as they gazed on her open labia and glistening clitoris. There was nothing to stop him taking her, and she wanted him to take her. She was all his.

He moved and covered her body, his flesh warm and hard against her. Between her crested mons and his rising prick was the mauve chamois of his pouch, his penis pushing fiercely against the soft material.

He half-closed his eyes when he lowered his head to kiss her lips. The scent of a man filled her nostrils. The salty taste of male sweat transferred from his upper lip to her own as his tongue met hers. In her mouth, one tongue circled the other, like a pair of birds wheeling in the sky. She sucked at his tongue, and he reciprocated until, breathless, they parted.

Their breathing mutually hot and rampant, they gazed at each other before he groaned and sank to his knees.

She cried out in rapture as his tongue lapped into her navel and over her belly before licking her clutch of pubic hair so it lay flat and damp against her skin.

Control ebbing away and her eyes half-closing, she gasped with delight as he flicked delicately between her open lips and gently teased her most sensitive jewel from its folded hood.

She arched her back so that her hips and pubes spasmed against him, and her buttocks slapped against the pillar behind her.

There was no sound from anyone in the room.

Venetia watched, her eyes fathomless, her lips still smiling.

Already half-delirious from her own sensations, Toni thought at first that she was seeing things, that she wasn't *really* seeing the older woman raising her skirts, couldn't *really* see the other young man going on his knees in front and between Venetia's open legs.

The view she was getting heightened her own sensations. Even from where she was, she could see that Venetia was wearing no pants, that her quim was as exposed as her own, and the young man was poking his tongue into it. Affected by what she was seeing and what she was feeling, Toni could not help but moan and gyrate against the chains that held her.

Outer labia held neatly aside by his fingers, Carlos tasted her sex with his tongue and ran its tip around each silky contour. Despite the watching eyes, or perhaps because of them, Toni begged for more, pleaded with him to put his cock where his fingers were.

Just when she thought his tongue would bring her off without his penis entering her, his tongue retreated and he began a slow ascent, licking her belly, then her ribcage and the curve of her breasts.

Through narrowed eyes, she could see the bare and taut haunches of the other young man whose head was still nestled between Venetia's thighs. Fascination gripped her. Sex filled her eyes and flooded her body. She was seeing sex, she was feeling sex – she almost felt she was drowning in it.

As Carlos' fingers did delicious things to her nipples, his tongue licked over the warm slopes above them. Still with one nipple committed to his fingers, he sucked the other into his mouth as would a hungry or greedy baby.

Toni cried out, trembling to her toes as his teeth nibbled at her flesh, plucking her nipples away from her body. Tantalised beyond belief, intoxicating sensations made her arms go rigid as he repeated the process. She hissed through clenched teeth as his bite closed on her rigid nubs, then groaned as he sucked them and soothed her to new sensual heights.

Fearing she might faint away with the sheer sensuality of it all, she opened her eyes, but there was no respite from her overwhelming desires. Sexual longing hit her with double its usual force as Venetia and the young man filled her eyes. By now, Venetia's bodice was open, and the dark areolae of her breasts were disappearing one at a time into the mouth of the much younger man. His fingers were embedded between her legs, his head tight against her breast.

Sublimely lost in her own arousal, Toni moaned in ecstasy. Without his guidance, Carlos' member slid between her pubic lips. She sighed as his hands left her breasts and ran down her back. The sigh turned to a murmur of delight as he cupped each buttock in the palm of his hands.

Steadying her and taking careful aim, he thrust his pelvis towards hers. With exultant delight, she cried out as the crown of his penis jabbed into her vagina, and the coarseness of his pubic hair bristled against her belly. She gasped, caught her breath and with wide eyes viewed the faces that watched. They were enthralled. And she was ecstatic. Closing her eyes and way beyond the point of no return, she uttered those sweet and unintelligible sounds that only come into being when the senses sweep away the rigours of conformity or the rules of society. Every sensation she had ever felt seemed to fade into insignificance beneath the onslaught of her senses. Currents of reaction ran over her skin where his flesh mets hers. The lips of her vagina curved over the throbbing member that divided her. Her succulent sex wrapped around his member as it buried itself deep inside her flesh.

Hard pubic contact coaxed her clitoris into full bloom and, with its flowering, the member that divided her sex in two, throbbed its climax as Carlos again moaned in ecstasy aganst her ear and she did the same in his.

She was spent and satisfied and, once Carlos had withdrawn, she hung as limp as a rag doll within the confines of her chains.

She saw him smile and felt the damp heat of his body as his lips kissed her.

'You are a very beautiful woman, Antonia Yardley,' he said in a heavy accented voice against her ear. 'And I would do this for you any time you like it without anyone ordering me to.'

His dark hair was damp around his face and neck, and his once proud cock now hung down his thigh.

'I will bear that in mind,' she murmured, and took the opportunity to study the man and his body anew.

There was a brightness in the darkness of his eyes, a keen glint like some magic elf or some wicked boy. Lips long and made for loving parted as she smiled. He winked at her, and in that one moment she wanted to call him back, to ask him what he was doing later and would he like to come to her bed, to join both her and Emira in a night of unparalleled sex and sensuality.

But Carlos, loyal to the last, had gone back to his mistress, who sat and surveyed all she saw like some divine goddess.

Venetia Salvatore was imperious and wealthy. She was also, Toni surmised, a sexual libertine – not exactly without morals, but very much in favour of taking sexual advantage of her prosperous age and position.

The rise and fall of Toni's breasts lessened as she caught her breath, and a fine sheen of perspiration covered her skin. And yet her flesh still tingled, as though she would have more, as though there was still more to come. Through a fringe of dark lashes, she could see the satisfaction on Venetia's face. Presumably, she too had reached a climax.

'Now,' Venetia began, as her young man refastened her bodice and rearranged her skirt. 'You have enjoyed the body I provided for you – just as you did yesterday. Now for the endurance. Now for the sublime taste of harshness against the softness of your flesh. To suit my final requirements, you must endure as well as enjoy. Your acceptance of my terms must now be proved.'

Trepidation filled her as Emira and Marie moved forward. She saw Emira pause and look almost lovingly, but not without mischief, at Venetia. Eyes met eyes. An unspoken message seemed to run between the mature woman and the dark-skinned man who did not look entirely like a man.

Emira – his saffron silk blouse clinging to his borrowed breasts, and his slinky skirt slit thigh high on one side – undid the gold rope fastenings of his silken tunic that floated to mid-thigh. His breasts, those incredibly hard, yet perfectly round implants, thrust forward. Toni had already felt their alien attraction against her body, and just to look at them was to remember how they felt. In immediate acclaim for their look and their touch, warm fluids flowed from her sex. Again, she wanted to feel them.

Despite Emira being endowed as a man by nature, his breasts seemed strangely natural. They were as shiny as burnished teak; his nipples, which protruded a good inch from the rest of the twin bosoms, were as black as midnight.

Marie at his side, Emira stepped towards Toni.

They undid her chains and rubbed her aching arms. Emira, his face a cool mix of female grace and male confidence, cupped her face in the coolness of his hands and kissed her lips long and lovingly.

Whether it was the smell of Emira or just the magic of the moment, Toni couldn't help returning her ardour. Sex was in her mouth with Emira's tongue, and against her body with the hardness of him, and in her nose with the smell of him. Emira was a beautiful enigma that was seemingly ethereal, but achingly animal.

Once the kiss was over, Emira did not release her head. Instead, he moved his hands and pressed Toni's lips to his breast that was woman, yet not woman. Demandingly, a robust nipple forced its way between Toni's lips. Emira held her head tight against his breast. Marie had linked Toni's wrist-chains back to the collar-chain. Her hands were fastened high behind her back. Even if she had protested, she could not possibly have moved.

'Suck my wonderful nipples, Antonia, and tell me how beautiful my breasts are.'

Emira sounded ecstatic, but no matter how much he might urge Toni to compliment his body, the exercise was wasted. Her mouth full with nipple, Toni could say nothing. Breast against her lips, she just murmured deep in her throat, enough to satisfy Emira and those around that she was enjoying what she was doing.

Once Emira had judged that one nipple had received

enough vigorous sucking, he forced Toni's mouth and head on to the other. Both breasts were unusually firm, but the skin soft. Toni had never been near enough to breast implants to recognise them. They had undoubtedly surprised her. Their shape was so perfect, so firm.

'Suck this one too, Antonia. Suck this one until I tell you to stop,' said Emira.

Toni, aching and wet between her thighs, did as she was told noisily and with obvious relish. Oddly enough, she was thinking of Julian, though what Emira had in common with Julian, she just couldn't imagine. Except, of course, that both called her Antonia. Somehow, it sounded more beautiful, more like a love song coming from Emira, than it ever had from Julian.

'Enough.'

It was the only word Venetia said, but Emira and Marie's response to it was immediate.

Gasping for air, Toni was released from Emira's full bosom and turned back to the masthead.

What next? she asked herself. They undid the chains that bound her ankles, then turned her round. Instead of being freed, the chains that hung from her wristbands were again fastened to the brass rings above her head. Her anklets were again fixed as they had been before so that her legs were wrapped around the masthead rather than up against it. Her bottom, she knew, stuck obscenely outward, legs and buttocks apart.

The wood that encased the mast was cool against her hot breasts and belly. She rested her head against it. It was also cool against her cheek.

'Fix her waist,' she heard Venetia say. 'Tie her fast, and reintroduce the device.'

She heard the clink of a chain and felt its coolness as Marie, and now Carlos, ran it around her waist and clicked it tightly around the other side of the masthead. Now her breasts and belly were squashed tight against the mast, and her legs were clamped around it.

She felt Emira's fingers prod and push in another

device to plug her anus. She groaned, engorged with substance.

'Enough,' said Venetia. 'Now take it out.'

The same fingers that had pushed it in now pulled it out, leaving Toni feeling oddly bereft, oddly empty.

'I think it has done its job very well, Madame,' said Emira.

'Good,' returned Venetia. 'Then I think you could insert the next size. That way, she will be that much more welcoming, that much more accommodating.'

Where Emira got the new and larger device from, Toni did not see. She only felt it as Emira parted her cheeks with one hand, and pushed the device in with the other.

She squirmed, started to protest, then remembered she had promised submission, obedience. Once in place, the device was not so bad. It filled her, reminded her that she had such an orifice, but only to the point of pleasure, not pain.

Then Emira was gone, but only for a moment.

Out of the corner of her eyes, she saw him. Their eyes met. Marie was standing holding a champagne bucket, and from the bucket poked the handle of something.

Emira's long and exotic fingers wrapped slowly and sensuously around the dark handle that had a band of gold around its very top, and pulled it from the bucket. The handle was that of a whip from which hung three separate fronds. From their feather-thin ends, water dripped like tears into the champagne bucket.

Instinctively, Toni clenched the cheeks of her behind. Wide-eyed, she gasped as Emira stepped towards her.

'The cap,' ordered Venetia.

A hat or cap was pulled over Toni's head, which covered her skull and reached to just above her nose. This was no ordinary cap; it completely obliterated her vision. She could see nothing.

'I will not gag you, Miss Yardley,' said Venetia. 'As at the Red Tower, I wish to know that you can accept discipline. I want you hear you whimper in pain or in

154

ecstasy. Not scream, mark you. Screaming is not required. If you scream, then you are no good for me. If you cry out, you will receive expenses and your flight home.'

While Venetia paused to gauge her response, Toni bit her lip and thought of London; of the mountains of leases that would be waiting for processing back in her old office, and of the word processor that was never switched off; of rainy streets, miserable nights and television meals. Then she thought of Emira's velvet cock and iron-hard breasts and the pleasure he had given her earlier. She could stand a lot more of that.

'I will accept,' she said and, trembling slightly, waited for the kiss of the whip's wet fronds.

It hissed through the air before landing on her bare rump. She tensed, bit her lip, but did not cry out.

There was a pause, as though the one who was using the whip, presumably still Emira, was waiting for instructions. 'Five,' said Venetia. 'I think five would be adequate.'

Five! Toni gulped and clenched her fingers into her palms. Could she stand it? She had to. She bit her bottom lip really hard and squeezed her eyes tight shut even though the cap prevented her from seeing anything.

Another hiss, and the muscles of her bottom clenched against the wet sting of the leather and the device that so ably filled her anus.

There was no time to think before another came. Again there was a hiss before it stung her behind. Three, four and five followed before cool hands caressed her burning cheeks.

'They are burning very nicely, Madame.' It was Emira's voice. The hands too, she guessed, belonged to him.

'Let me see.' It was Venetia. Toni knew she was nearer. She could hear the rich swish of her violet skirt and smell the sheer luxury of her perfume.

Even though it felt as though her behind was on fire,

Toni shivered with pleasure as the soft hand and agile fingers of Venetia Salvatore ran over her flesh. She moaned with pleasure rather than pain. The earlier need for climax was twitching of its own account between her legs. She wanted it again. She begged for it again. Would she get it, strung up as she now was?

It didn't matter to her who might be watching. She would have it here; have it and enjoy it.

As if in answer to a prayer, she heard the rustle of clothing as it fell to the floor.

Gently fanning out from her spine, hands that she guessed could be Carlos' or Emira's, ran down over the smooth flesh of her back. She shivered with apprehension and rising excitement. Threads of desire spun into shape and began to intertwine throughout her body as those same hands again tenderly touched each burning buttock, leaving ice where there had been fire.

Fingers that were both gentle and strong travelled to her hips and a mighty member divided her behind.

The hands that had been on her hips ran forward to form a deep 'V' beneath her navel. Her buttocks tilted slightly and, although she was restrained by the chain around her waist, she tensed herself against it and forced her own vagina towards him just that little bit more so he could take her that much better.

What joy she felt as the velvet head of his penis penetrated her moist portal. She cooed like a dove against the coolness of the masthead. It didn't matter that she could not see him. It was enough that he was in her, his mighty tool opening her body to suit his size, his shape.

Her vagina was full of him. The device in her anus echoed the delight in her sex.

As the fuzz of his pubic hair rasped against her behind, his fingers divided and tickled her pubic lips and worked her clitoris until another orgasm exploded from her loins.

Behind her mask, she was lost in her own sensations, and even though there were others in the room watching as his penis throbbed within her, it didn't matter. Her pleasure and her climax seemed a solitary thing within that darkness. Her burning bottom was a preliminary to the incredible warmth that now invaded her body.

Once he had slipped out of her, the mask was removed and her chains were unfastened.

Marie was smiling. So were Carlos and Emira. Their eyes glittered in a strange way as though they knew something she did not.

'You must thank Pietro for that,' said Venetia, her voice as serene as her expression.

Pietro. At least, thought Toni, I know his name, and I know who it was that filled me with his penis and gave me my climax.

She could see him over her shoulder, standing again at the side of his mistress whose sex life had become richer and more heady with age; a bit, thought Toni, like old wine.

Venetia Salvatore had taken her own climax from his tongue. His own climax and erection had been given to her.

Venetia must have seen her puzzled expression. 'I have not the energy I once had,' she said, her words seeming to curl from one to the other, 'so I only receive sexual climax. I do not give it. It was very useful to have you here.'

Chapter Ten

*A*ndrea put the telephone down and felt as warm as the sunlight that streamed from the terrace and through the open French doors.

Philippe had gone on to another business meeting after the one in Santa Paula. Now, he was on his way back, unaware that she had made a pact with his brother and sealed it with a lot more than a kiss.

With one silver-ringed hand, Andrea pushed the white of the billowing curtain away from her face as she went through the doors and looked out on the soft green of the sea. Her eyes narrowed – almost as if she were hating its colours, hating its consistently moving surface, its waves that curved and moved like a woman's body.

The sea came between her and Philippe; the sea and the woman who haunted his dreams and divided him from his brother. It was sad that they had quarrelled and she could understand their mother wanting to reunite them. But reuniting them would part Philippe from her. She didn't want that. She wanted to keep him, wanted to continue indulging in his games that depended so much on his dreams continuing. But Venetia, with the help of Emira, was doing everything possible to make his dreams come true.

She had to stop that happening and, with Conway's help, she might very well have a chance.

Of necessity, she had been sparing with the truth in order to enlist Conway's collusion with her plan. There was no way she would fully describe the girl with the red hair and green eyes. All she had said, was that Venetia had employed the girl for Philippe alone. That, in itself, was enough to make Conway shout down the phone at her and tell her to get her silly ass down here and let him know what she had in mind.

No, she had hedged her bets. From the way she had expressed herself, she had left Conway with the impression that what they would be doing was no more than a practical joke, another example of the tit-for-tat relationship the two brothers kept constantly on the boil.

Her eyes narrowed as she viewed the white speck of sail and yacht that could only be *Sea Witch* on her way back to home port.

Like a bird, she thought, a sweeping gull or a flying swan winging its way home. And on that yacht was the object of her practical joke, and the threat to her own position and her own security.

She let the curtain fall from her hand. She was frowning and, like a cloud going over the sun, the falling curtain hid the cause of her frown. That boat. That woman. The woman who looked so much like the one Philippe dreamed about and described in graphic detail.

She turned her back on the sea and the wide expanse of blue sky. Carelessly, she took off her dark cerise wrap and ran her hands over her body. With undisguised admiration for her own body, she studied herself in the mirror, tossed her golden hair, and rolled her firm breasts in the palms of each hand.

'I'm golden,' she said to her reflection. 'My hair's golden blonde, my body is almost golden.' She smiled, and with one pink-nailed finger, prodded between her golden-haired lips. 'Even my pubic hair is golden.' Just so that she could study herself better, she put her foot up on a chair, and tilted her pelvis towards the full-length mirror.

Strawberry-pink flesh parted her golden pubes. Cupping her breast, she let her finger roll over and around the nerve centre of her sex, that sweet, illicit spot that can easily ache and leap with longing.

Scissor-like, she closed two fingers over her inner lips and left her thumb to press and play with her clitoris. The action of her fingers brought the feathery folds of her inner labia together. It was enticingly painful, exquisitely pleasant.

Pinching one nipple between finger and thumb sent a delicious rhapsody of tingles throughout her body, and yet it was not enough. Her hand left her bosom, and she reached for the silver-handled hairbrush that lay on the dressing table.

'Too pale,' she said in an oddly cruel voice as she eyed the pinkness of her sex, her fingers still holding her outer lips apart.

A strange look entered her eyes as she viewed her open flesh. She looked at it coldly, almost accusingly, as if it were the cause of everything bad that had ever happened to her.

With an air of menace, Andrea began to wave the hairbrush about, her pouting lips melting into a narrow, straight line. 'I'll teach you,' she said, as though she and her sex were entirely different things.

She tilted her pelvis as far as she could towards the mirror and, still holding her lips wide, she began to beat the stiff-bristled brush against her sex.

She groaned as she did it, her body tensing with each blow, her sex reddening as the brush beat and beat again. Even the curled back lips reddened under the firmness of her fingers, and her clitoris blushed like an unseen flower.

Tasting her own tears, and totally at the mercy of her burning flesh, Andrea stopped the abuse of her body. With both hands, she turned the brush around so that

160

the bristles were in her hand, and the wide, silver handle hanging down.

Over pink cheeks, she looked at the mirror. Her body was moving, yet only gently; softly undulating on the hardness of the hairbrush.

Murmuring low, she tucked her buttocks beneath her and saw the silver handle of the brush slide cold and hard into her aching portal.

Once it was completely inserted, she began to mew and jerk her hips, tantalised by the feel of the brush head against her red-hot clitoris.

Breasts bunched before her, she used the brush to pleasure herself, to prolong or hasten her climax as she, and she alone, saw fit.

Seeing and feeling what she was receiving pushed her higher and higher up the dizzy mountain of desire. At its highest apex, it burst into starry brilliance and, like the last explosion of a supernova, she caught the climax, and then fell willingly to earth.

Now, she decided, she would shower and in the warmth of the water; she would wash away her concerns and her annoyance with Venetia Salvatore. In the water, she would run her hands over her body, enjoy her own touch, tantalise her own tingling flesh so it would be ready for when Philippe came back.

Both brothers, she thought to herself; I have had both brothers. The thought satisfied her. There was always triumph in knowing something no one else knew – except of course for Conway. She would keep that triumph and that knowledge to herself, for now.

Forget now, she told herself. Forget *Sea Witch*, forget the red-haired girl. Think of tonight. Think of Philippe and his hard straight body, his untiring sexuality and spine-tingling sensuality. And thinking of that on her way to the shower, she began to sing.

Venetia Salvatore had been put ashore on her own island, so now *Sea Witch* was on her way home. White caps formed then divided as her prow sliced them apart, leaving them to tumble into the deep green water.

Toni, refreshed and invigorated, was now at the helm, her uniform as sharply white as the rest of the crew. There was a dewiness to her skin and she felt a certain pride in the way her wristbands and necklet caught the sun and sent beams of light reflecting off the sea.

Emira was beside her. 'Mister Salvatore owns this island,' explained Emira. One long arm reached out, and a long finger pointed across the bay to where another golden mound rose like a woman's breast from the sparkling sea.

Toni shielded her eyes from the sun with one hand. 'What about that one over there?' she asked, pointing to where another island swelled up from the sea.

'That one does not belong to Mister Salvatore. It belongs to his brother.'

'I see. And do they ever see each other?' she asked.

'Only to fight,' replied Emira.

'Fight? Each other?'

'Sometimes. Most of the time they try to avoid each other. It is very bad when they come together. Each tries to outdo the other, take what the other has. It can be very violent at times.'

Emira rested his arms on the wheel. Beneath them throbbed the engine that would take them out of the harbour. New sails had recently been fitted, and Emira wanted to try them out, and to do that, they would have to go further out to sea.

Unconventional as the initial stages of her interview might have been, Toni prided herself that she had so far passed with flying colours.

Now with the wind in her hair, elation touched her cheeks with a glossy healthiness and her lips with a hint of rose pink.

Once away from the quay, the sails were unfurled and the engine beneath them died. Wind ballooned the sails outward and seagulls screamed and wheeled in the blueness of the sky. Surf spat in indeterminate showers across the prow and left a white ribbon of churning wake behind them.

'Take the wheel,' ordered Emira.

Toni obeyed.

The wheel jolted slightly and the sails lost a hint of the blow as Toni glanced swiftly at Emira.

'Sorry about that.'

Emira grinned. 'You will be. We do not tolerate mistakes, you know. Not from anybody. Mister Salvatore does not like mistakes. Neither does Madame Salvatore.'

Playfully, Emira's hand ran down over her back and cupped first one rounded buttock, then the other before smacking each in turn.

She knew what he was implying, but couldn't quite get to grips with how she felt about it. Being nude and having sex in front of a room full of people had not held the threat she might have thought it would. In fact, she had behaved lasciviously in the gold-carpeted saloon. She had been taken, whipped and, even though her behind was still bright red, just the tingle of it aroused new desires, new arousal.

How much leeway will I get, she wondered, before I feel the cat again?

Emira might have been clairvoyant, but there was no real way of finding out. Anyway, he did answer what was in Toni's mind.

'Madame, or Mister Salvatore gives little leeway before handing out punishment. They both like things done their way. In fact, Madame has already given instructions. She says you are to be called Antonia. She likes the name Antonia. There was someone else here of that name before. She too had red hair and green eyes.'

'And is that why I am here?' asked Toni.

Up until then, Emira had been pretty free and easy with what he had to say. Now he paused before answering.

'There is a similarity. You might evoke old memories, help heal old wounds.'

Toni could have asked more questions, but something in Emira's face and voice told her that no answers would be forthcoming, and she might even come up against downright hostility.

She had no wish to jeopardise her chance of this job and, besides, she was steering and the yacht was principally her responsibility. Another time, she might push it. But not now. 'Shall I keep going on this course?' Toni asked.

Emira studied the blue haze of low-lying islands, the green of the sea and the bulging sails before looking back at her.

'No need to. Mister Salvatore will not be back for another four hours. It's a beautiful day. I think we have enough time for diversion. Set a course for 180 degrees magnetic.'

Toni set her compass three degrees off due south. The sails slackened as they tacked round into the wind before billowing out again and making way.

Before long, the yellow of the main island and quay were behind them. Ahead were a myriad bays boasting the temptation of calm and very blue waters.

'I will take the wheel now,' said Emira. 'You go below and get lunch.'

Toni slid to one side so Emira could take the wheel from her. The wind tossed her hair and threw it across her face before she got down below and made her way along to the galley.

She cut hunks of fresh bread, cheese and crisp salad and, preoccupied with her own thoughts, she didn't hear Mark enter until his hands were on her shoulders.

His lips kissed where her neck curved into her shoulder. A hunger for something other than food accumulated between her legs. The hardness of his bare chest was warm against her back and through the crisp

164

whiteness of her uniform. His cheek was warm against hers, his hair slightly damp, his smell of salt and sex.

'It's good to feel you,' he said, his words lost in his kisses. 'I've been waiting to get you alone for ages. I've been waiting to do this,' he said, eclipsing one breast with his hand. 'And this,' he added.

Her eyes half-closed, a deep purr of pleasure filtered through her lips as his other hand sought the deep division between her legs.

'It feels good,' she murmured and, pushing the butter and bread to one side, let her sexual hunger take over her body.

The tangled sensations centred on her sex began to unravel and creep out over her body. Warmth tempered her skin with a pleasant pinkness. Like the sea and the tide, she eddied against him, aware of his shoulders behind and above hers, his pectorals hard against her back. Against the rounded curve of her buttocks, she felt a familiar hardness tapping gently at her deep cleft. With purpose and with pleasure, she tilted her bottom towards it, and felt his intake of breath against her ear.

Her own breathing quickened and her love juice began to flow. Ripples of pleasure followed the passage of his lips which were hot and moist against her neck, his breath humid to her ear.

Lost in such sweeping sensations, she did not turn to him. His fingers trailed deliciously up over her clothed breasts, then ran down over her stomach and dived over her mound to that secret cleft between her thighs.

She moved slightly. Her legs opened to give him that bit of extra room to manoeuvre his hand and fingers.

Her zip growled as he slid it downwards. His fingers travelled down over her belly and journeyed on through the silky pubic hair and the velvety folds of her softly rolling labia.

His touch was light, gentle against her, and made her want to expose her rosebud to his fingertips.

165

In an act of pure provocation, she pushed her buttocks back against him and rubbed them enticingly against his hardening member. In response, it leapt like a caged animal, aching to get out, to savage her, invade her.

Moaning into the softness of her hair which had come loose and now lay around her shoulders, she gathered his hands to her, and pressed them hard against her breasts. Drowning in her own desires, she closed her eyes and imagined his hardness invading her hidden portal, dividing it like the prow of a boat slicing through a wave.

Now the bread, the cheese and the salad were no longer of any consequence. Her concentration was gone. She turned to face him, barely noticing the brownness of his eyes, the weather-tempered ruggedness of his face, before his lips were on hers. She placed both hands flat on the well-defined contours of his chest and trembled with delight as her palms appreciated the polished texture of his skin, and her fingers the iron prominence of his nipples.

'Where's your uniform?' she asked him, surprised that he wore only shorts.

He smiled, and as he bent his head a shock of blonde hair fell over his eyes.

'I'm off-duty,' he said. 'But I've been watching for the chance to get you alone. I knew I would eventually.'

She was quick to take in the bronzed hardness of his body, the pronounced curve of his thigh muscles.

'You make me feel overdressed,' she said and, furtively, looked beyond him to the galley door which was presently closed.

'Then do something about it.' A laugh caught in Mark's voice as he said it, and he raised his eyebrows in a comical manner, looking down at her open zip.

His look and his body were irresistible.

Toni smiled. 'I think I will,' she said with hesitation. 'My trousers at least.'

She pulled off her ankle boots which had soft bottoms that would not damage the decks. Then she pulled off her trousers. She wore no panties. The sheer elasticity of the trousers was soft against her skin, so underwear was not needed.

Mark's penis expanded in circumference and length as his eyes homed in on her creamy thighs and clutch of crisply curling pubic hair.

She kept her top on. In some strange and indescribable way, being naked from the waist down felt more vulnerable, more shameful than being completely naked. On top of that of course, it increased her desire. She was half-naked and exposed to the cool blast of the air-conditioning, yet the hot desire of Mark's eyes made her feel as though she was on fire.

Firm and demanding, her tongue sought his, and as it sought, her hand dropped to his zip. Soon, it was undone, and there it was, sensual, hot and throbbing in her hand. Like a primeval animal, it seemed to have a mind of its own, knew what it wanted, where it was going, and was impatient to be there.

Mark pulled his shorts to his ankles.

Her eyes met his. He did not waver – not once. Not to gasp, not to blink or look away. The emerald green of her eyes met his as his fingers divided her nether lips.

All her senses seemed to swoop and gather in that one spot nestling so secretively, yet now rising so brazenly, beneath the touch of his fingers. She moaned, oblivious to what she should be doing, and only interested in what she actually was doing.

With strong hands, he lifted her on to the table so that her buttocks sat among the wetness of the lettuce. It was not an unpleasant sensation. After all, her flesh was warm and the stainless steel work surface was cool as well as wet.

How pleasurable, she thought to herself, and how very delightful.

Automatically, she spread her legs, looked down and saw her own pink rosebud peering out from amidst her bush of Titian-red pubic hair.

Mark, his breathing laboured, his eyes narrowed, looked at it too. Then gingerly, as if it were a tabby cat lying full stretch before a fire, he ran his fingers through it.

But there was no fire burning for her pussy, just a flaming stick of passion heading towards it that reared in anticipation.

Unable to resist its steady dance, she tapped at the glistening head with her fingers, stroked its velvet length and, almost with reverent protectiveness, curled her fingers around it and squeezed tightly. Mad with desire, it swelled against her palm, and leapt to her fingers' rhythmic touch as if it were swaying to some secret tune.

She saw it, felt it, but more so, felt her own pleasure as he stroked her pussy, tickled it, spread her lips and sauntered with a care for her pleasure, for her responses as well as for his own curiosity.

He teased the soft pink folds, tapped gently with his thumb at the thrusting clitoris that opened like a rose in summer.

Beneath the swell of her breasts, she could smell the sweet and salty mix of his hair as he bent low before her. For some unknown reason, she wondered what colour his hair would be in some northern clime where the sun could not bleach it and ripen it to something near silver. But her wondering was short-lived. This was the here and now, and the sun was hot. The galley would be as hot as an oven were it not for the air-conditioning. As it was, it was hot enough. Her body was on fire, and it was he who had lit the flame.

His head was between her legs, and his eyes were level with the pert form of her pink clitoris standing proud of the creamy flesh and crown of pubic hair.

She felt the kiss of her hair against her spine as she

threw her head back and exposed the whiteness of her throat.

His mouth kissed her flesh, sucking her in, his tongue licking slowly, tickling the sensitive head of her delight, encouraging her legs to open wider, to spill her love juice and prepare for his intrusion, his onslaught.

She threw her head back further, barely able to control her slide to sheer abandonment. No matter who came in or what they wanted, there was no way she would let him stop or him release her until she was finished.

With undue firmness, she held his head in her hands, moaning with pleasure as his nose nudged at her sensitive nub and his tongue burrowed into her vagina.

Just as she thought her time was drawing nigh, he got up. Again, her eyes met his.

Holding his penis in one hand, he guided it in, two fingers of his other hand holding her lips apart to give him plenty of room for entry. Deftly, almost as an afterthought, but a very necessary one, he lifted his balls on to the smooth steel of the work surface.

Gently his member entered her. His intrusion was welcomed and encouraged by the wetness around her entrance as he thrust and withdrew again and again, quickening on each stroke until he knew she was ready, knew her climax would not be denied.

Muffling her cry of ecstasy with his lips, he thrust mightily, his balls making a swishing sound as they passed back and forth over the smooth steel and wet lettuce. His hand clutched her buttocks to him as if he would bury himself in her entirely and never withdraw again.

He grunted his release in a low moan of pleasure. Within her, his penis jerked with a primitive and indescribable beat. She held him to her as his rapid breathing returned to normal and the last echoes of his orgasm trembled down his stem and over his tense loins. At last, muscles relaxed and bodies gleaming with moisture, their lips parted along with their flesh.

Although Toni had tidied herself up and smoothed her hands over the more rumpled parts of her uniform, Emira gave her a knowing look when she went back up top with the bread, the cheese, and a well-cooled bottle of Chardonnay.

The dark eyes that had seen her naked now on so many occasions raked her up and down. 'You should be saving yourself, Antonia.'

'For what?' Toni's voice was calm, but it was impossible not to think of what had happened with Mark and not to colour up.

Emira studied her closely, but did not answer for a moment.

'For this evening. For the barbecue.'

Somehow, Toni did not believe that was what Emira had had in mind to say.

'Is Madame Salvatore going to be present?'

'Of course.'

'And Mister Salvatore?'

'Yes. Tonight you will meet him for the first time.'

'What about his brother?'

Emira sighed and a dark frown appeared. 'Mister Patterson? Yes. Mister Conway Patterson will be there.'

Emira fell silent as though she were considering the different characteristics of the two brothers – or their similarities.

'I shall look forward to it. Is it a uniform do?' asked Toni, wishing like mad that it wasn't.

'No. No, it is not,' said Emira. 'But I will choose your clothes for you.'

Toni had a sudden and momentous urge to study Emira's face. As usual, his extraordinary beauty almost took her breath away. Also, as usual, it was immobile and yet there was something in the dark velvet eyes that made Toni wonder exactly what might be in store this evening.

She had an urge to know something about the nature of the barbecue, so she leapt in and asked a guarded question. 'Let me presume I will be wearing no underwear.'

'You presume correctly,' answered Emira with a smile.

'Ah!' exclaimed Toni. Tonight, she told herself, there was much more to look forward to.

Chapter Eleven

Garnished with the glow from the bonfire on the beach, *Sea Witch* bobbed about in the bay. Waves ran in hushed gasps to the beach and the sea glowed like silver in the moonlight.

On the beach, the barbecue was in full swing, food plentiful, wine flowing. Tonight held a magic that Toni could almost taste. She tingled with anticipation, her mind as fresh and sparkling as her body and her eyes.

Earlier, and with Emira's help, she had showered. Emira's hands had been incredibly slow yet undeniably efficient as the long fingers creamed the lather over her breasts, down the sweeping curve of her back and into the crease between her buttocks.

She had murmured with a mixture of surprise and delight as Emira had knelt naked before her and licked the soap suds from her drenched pubes, sucking the lathered hair into his mouth while her tongue teased at her most sensitive flesh.

In the shower, with water and lather pouring over and between them, Emira had slid one strong arm under one leg and raised it so the very tips of Toni's toes were nuzzling the cool wetness of the tiles. Bending his knees

172

slightly, he had held her to him as his mighty member slid between her legs and nudged aside her tingling lips.

Melting with sensation, she had groaned and held on to his shoulders which glistened like old mahogany, shiny, rich and very hard.

Firmly, he had grasped her, and held her balanced on one leg, her sex wide and blooming like an open flower.

As rivulets of water mingled between their bodies, the head of his penis had pressed hot and hard against her flesh and, as their lips met, he had entered her.

Like black coffee and rich cream, they had clung to each other, a writhing of bodies and limbs overcome by sweet sensations that erupted from the epicentre of their coupling.

It had been good, she thought, very good, and she trembled as the last memory of their climax coursed again through her veins.

After that, Emira had helped her dress or rather, advised her on what to wear.

'Beach wear,' he had said.

'Bikini?' Toni had asked innocently, though she suspected tonight would be nothing like innocent.

'No. Not at night. Something pretty, but not too formal. What about this?'

The item he had held up for scrutiny was a white thigh-length tunic with long sleeves.

'With no underwear?' Toni asked.

Emira looked from it to her. 'It is very fine,' he said, his dark fingers separating under the hem which was easily the thickest part of the whole thing. He looked thoughtful for a moment.

Still naked, he was gone, but was also quickly back again.

'This,' he had said in the sort of voice that told her he would entertain no protests, 'is just the thing.'

So here she was. She had on her white tunic that was so sheer, her nipples pouted through its fineness.

Beneath it she wore an all-in-one catsuit; not something stretchy and solid, but one made entirely of white fishnet that covered her from head to toe and held her flesh almost as if it were imprisoned within.

Not that it hid much. When the breeze caught at her tunic, her bottom and her thighs were exposed, though not entirely bare. Their form and outline still apparent, they were criss-crossed with diamonds of white fishnet. Between her legs, the tight confines of the fishnet exaggerating the lips of her sex, appeared to be a deeper cleft than it actually was.

Emira had been pleased.

Other eyes, that caught a glimpse of her exposed body when the breeze blew, also looked impressed.

She turned her face to the breeze. The air was cool because it was blowing in from off the sea. It would not stay that way for too much longer. In time, the heat of the Sahara would drift northwards, depositing dust on doorsteps and in nostrils. In time, it would be unbearably hot. For now, it was warm and pleasant.

A voice broke into her thoughts. 'How about a dip?'

The intrusion was sudden, and Toni was surprised to see who had spoken. Marie's voice and smile seemed more friendly than usual.

'Well,' said Toni, patting the heat of her cheeks as her eyes fixed on the ample form of the brown-eyed Marie. 'It certainly is getting warmer. I don't mind at all.'

Marie was enough to make anyone hot. A brimming bosom and bright red nipples were peering over a red silk strapless tunic that seemed to fall just to the top of her thighs. Vaguely, Toni was aware of a frizz of pubic hair curling up over it in copious disarray.

'All right,' Toni replied, putting her wine-glass down and discarding the chicken drumstick she'd been eating.

The softness of sand turned to shingle as Toni followed Marie around an outcrop of rock where a strip of spangled moonlight played upon the water.

They were going away from the barbecue. The smoke

of the bonfire and the rich aroma of cooking food and charcoal were fading. Toni began to wonder.

'Where are we going?'

Marie did not turn round. 'Along here. It's more private.'

Black shadows fell from the rigid escarpment of rock. Here, in a small alcove between high boulders, there was no light except that of the moon, no sound except for that of the sea.

'This looks nice,' said Toni as she took off her tunic and eyed the tumbling waves.

Something bobbed just beyond an outcrop of boulders. She caught its movement, and was about to ask what it was when two sets of hands grabbed hold of her.

She struggled and shouted, and for a moment escaped, leaving only her tunic hanging in their hands, which they immediately threw to one side. But her freedom was short-lived, and although she struggled again, this time she did not escape.

'Let me go,' she shouted, surprised at the strength of her assailants who were both women. Marie had big breasts and big buttocks that slapped together when she walked, and she was definitely beefier than she should be for someone of her height. The other woman was taller, blonde-haired, long-legged. The blonde was also beautiful, though her eyes were chill and her mouth turned down at its corners.

'What are you doing?' Toni shouted again before a hand – possibly the blonde's – clamped tightly over her mouth.

There was a fierce ripping sound as the shoulders of her fishnet catsuit were torn from her. Bits hung in shreds like floating string and, like string, they were used to restrain her. Bouncing naked and free, her breasts seemed blatantly vulnerable as the strips of fishnet were taken behind her and used to bind her arms and tie her hands.

Toni's eyes opened wide and unbidden sensations

rushed through her blood as Marie squeezed one of her breasts.

'Marie! What are you doing?' asked the tall blonde, her voice low but urgent against Toni's ear.

The French girl's face came close. 'Taking care of *numero uno*,' she said, then bit neatly and quickly at Toni's chin.

There was a sneer on her mouth and triumph in her eyes.

'What are you talking about, you silly bitch?' rasped the blonde whose fingernails now dug into Toni's cheek.

Marie gave no reply. Instead, she twisted the shards of fishnet that so tightly bound her wrists behind her.

Toni squirmed, her back arching, her breasts thrusting forwards. In one short, sharp movement, she turned her head and freed her mouth. 'What are you doing?' she cried. 'Who are you?'

Strong but softly scented arms reclaimed her. The hand clamped over her mouth again before a piece of torn-off fishnet was used to gag her.

A knowing smile appeared on the blonde's face. There was a cold, calculating look about it, which reminded Toni of the North Sea in November. The blonde jerked her head at her colleague. 'Like her, I'm taking care of number one!'

Toni shook her head and tried to speak. It wasn't the tying up and her nakedness that worried her. It was the knowledge that this incident looked like it had been coolly planned. A trap had been set and she had walked into it.

This wasn't the Red Tower, where the reasons for her bondage had been explained in terms of sex and sensuality. These women were not only sensuous, they had a goal in mind and looked deadly serious.

'Another ten minutes, and the current will be with us.' The blonde was looking at the sea when she said it.

Marie also looked, sighed, then lasciviously eyed Toni from head to toe. Speculation entered her eyes and turned their blueness to cold steel. As if in anticipation of how Toni's body might taste, her tongue rolled slowly over her lips. Unable to control her own reactions, Toni shivered. Marie, on seeing her flesh quiver so exquisitely, looked pleased.

'Then we will have to find something to occupy ourselves, won't we?' Her voice was as hushed yet as guttural as the shifting of the shingle in the tide.

'But Marie,' Andrea protested. 'We don't have much time. We don't want to be caught.'

'Shut up, you fool. Of course there's time. Just look at her,' she murmured with obvious admiration. 'Just look at those firm, pretty breasts and those hard little nubs. Don't you think we could at least enjoy her body while we wait? Don't you want to try her out? Look at her. She's at our mercy, and yet she is unafraid. In fact I do believe she is enjoying it. Look!'

Although dazed and confused at what was happening to her, Toni glanced down at her own body. Due in part to the breeze and night air, her breasts were firm and lightly touched with goose bumps. Hard as pebbles, her nipples thrust rigidly forward.

A fall of golden blonde hair impaired Toni's vision and she groaned as one nipple was sucked into Andrea's mouth. Andrea's lips were hot and firm, her tongue quizzical as it circumnavigated the plush halo of pink around Toni's nipple.

Unable to ignore the subtle messages that her breast was sending to the rest of her body, Toni arched her back so that her breast was hard against Andrea's mouth and face.

The French girl laughed. Not for one moment did she loosen her grip on Toni's wrists.

'How does it taste?' she asked, the melody of her laugh still lingering in her voice.

Andrea eased her mouth about an inch or two away from the glistening tip of Toni's fruit. 'Hmmm, very good,' she murmured, as though it was some morsel that could be swallowed. 'Like a plump cherry. Taste one yourself.' With that, her mouth refastened over Toni's nipple.

Wide-eyed, Toni just stared into Marie's wickedly grinning face before she too dipped and took a teat into her mouth. Another message of pure delirium raced from the right breast as well as the left. Now each breast was being tasted, being licked, nipped and fiercely sucked.

Toni staggered slightly as both mouths sucked at her, pressed against her. Teeth nipped, then nibbled, and the messages that ran from them to her vulva in the heat of her bloodstream intensified and cried out for more.

Panic was replaced by delight in Toni's mind as the sucking lips and seeking tongues teased her most sensitive nerve-ends. Unable to stop herself, she cried out and threw her head back. So intense was the expression of what she was feeling, that the bit of net was shrugged away from her mouth, and her moans grew stronger.

'Shut up!' growled Marie, and slapped her face.

Andrea raised her head and pushed Marie's shoulder. 'Shut her up, for goodness sake!' she said, anxiety registering in her hushed words. 'The noise will bring someone running before we're ready to shove off.'

Marie sniffed, her eyes still eyeing Toni's nipples, and her tongue still running over her lips. 'Do not panic so much, Andrea. There is no need of it, but just to ease your mind, I will shut her up with this.'

In one easy movement, Marie whipped off the bikini top she was wearing. Large and soft, her breasts fell free, and brushed against Toni's own breasts as Andrea gagged her mouth.

'Lie her down,' added Marie. 'We can do many things to her if she is lying down.'

Hands tied behind her back, her mouth gagged, they tripped her backwards and lay her upon the sand, which was still warm from the day's sun but slightly gritty against her back.

The fishnet that was torn to her waist felt surprisingly protective from there downwards. It was her breasts that were vulnerable, trembling before avid mouths covered each nipple.

Now their hands were free, too.

Andrea and Marie each ran their hands down over her hips, between her legs and, pressing her inner thighs, opened them wide.

Their free hands went beneath her and each grabbed a portion of bottom, squeezing her flesh as their other hands pinched and slapped at her thighs.

As they sucked and nibbled her bosoms, they murmured low groans of pleasure, oblivious, or perhaps uncaring, of her own moans and strangled cries.

Their hands travelled up from her thighs and poked through the fishnet that covered her sex. They opened her labia and used the diamond skeins to hold them open. Through another opening, they teased her clitoris and by twisting the fishnet held it outwards, trapped by the strangling threads so that their fingers could torture and tease as they pleased.

Eyes closed, Toni sought her own remedy for dealing with this situation. She did not need to look far. What she found was fresh and fascinating, still new and intoxicating. Just recently she had enjoyed and endured at the hands of Venetia Salvatore in the Red Tower.

With both mental and physical determination, she resummoned those strengths that had surfaced then. Her groans were really nothing more than murmurs of pleasure but, because of her gag, it was difficult for those listening and tormenting her to determine their true nature.

Beneath the probing fingers that now poked through the fishnet and into her vagina, she writhed just as she had when they had teased her clitoris through the strangling threads. But this time, her movements were in tune with her sensuality. She welcomed their probings, their treatment of her and rode with them, her

179

hips rising to meet the tapping of their thumbs against her clitoris, and their delving fingers within her vagina.

Her buttocks clenched as other fingers explored the tight pink ring of her anus and the slippery wetness of her hallowed haven. With determined persistence, they pushed through the holes in the net with no regard for gentleness or sensual response from her. Only their own quest mattered, and only their own satisfaction.

But those tentative messages, that had increased with their treatment of her, now buzzed throughout her body and subdued any fears she might have had. As selfish in her own enjoyment as they were in theirs, she arched her back so their lips and teeth might better feed on her nipples.

In the recesses of her mind, a quiet triumph had been born. Whatever pleasure they were getting from her, she was getting ten times as much from them. No matter what they did to her, her body was responding, reacting with dizzying currents of pure sensation, pure sexuality.

Lost in their own delight, they delved harder and faster as her hips bucked on to their hands, their fingers taking her higher and higher towards a shattering climax that wetted their hands and the sand beneath her.

Drifting within their own selfish endeavours, it took a while before they realised what was happening. Once she had surged on the highest wave, realisation began to dawn.

'She's come!' exclaimed Andrea, her fingers relaxing and her mouth, red and flushed from its ministrations to Toni's breast, hung open with surprise.

Marie raised her head too and stared at Andrea, then down at Toni. 'Dirty little bitch!' she muttered and, although angry, she also looked jealous.

'Cow! I could beat her for that!' growled Andrea.

Marie looked towards the sea and the bobbing object just beyond the rock. 'Then, why don't you? You do not have very long, mind you. The current is about to turn.'

'Long enough,' growled Andrea. 'Turn her over.'

Toni struggled as much as she could as their hands rolled her over in the sand. Now the grittiness she had felt on her back was ground into her breasts.

'There's rope on the boat,' shouted Maria, her bare bush against Toni's bound hands as she sat astride her. 'I'll sit on her till you get back.'

Showers of sand kicked back over both Toni and Marie until they were out of range of Andrea's long-legged run.

She wasn't long coming back.

'Aren't you using it to tie her ankles?' asked Marie as Andrea looped the rope around Toni's neck and passed the end of it to her.

'No. There's no need to. That's already provided.'

With that, Toni felt Andrea's fingers ripping at the fishnet that still clothed her legs. It seemed to gather at her ankles along with Andrea's fingers. Bound by the torn fishnet, her ankles were tied together. She was helpless.

Marie slid off her, the rope end taut in her hand and tight around Toni's neck.

Their standing shadows fell across her, and she heard both of them sigh. Approvingly, they smiled at her helpless form lying there on the sand.

A hand, she guessed Andrea's, tapped at her bottom which her fishnet outfit still covered; though not, she thought, for long.

There was a ripping sound and, just as she had guessed, the fishnet was ripped away from her behind, though scraps of it still spanned her waist and her thighs.

The same hand caressed her bottom, and two fingers pushed between her cheeks.

'Are you going to get on with it?' she heard Marie say.

'Patience,' returned Andrea. 'Let's get it right.'

'What more do you want?'

'I want her bottom higher than the rest of her – there. Help me get her over that rock.'

They half-carried, half-dragged her to the rock that

Andrea had selected. It was small and round, no more than three feet off the ground. Once she was draped over it, her face and feet were in the sand. Her bottom was inordinately high and staring at the moon.

'Lovely,' she heard Andrea say.

'*C'est belle*,' echoed Marie. 'But you will get a very sore hand.'

'No, I won't,' returned Andrea.

'A paddle!' exclaimed Marie. '*Voilà*! I did not know you had fetched that, too.'

Toni didn't need to look to know what it was Andrea had brought back. Obviously, beyond the rocks was a dinghy just waiting for the tide. In the dinghy would be a set of paddles – at least one long set, and perhaps one short. Panic gripped her for the barest of moments before she again dipped within herself and stirred her sensuality to come to her aid.

Despite what she knew was about to happen, an oozing wetness seeped from her vagina and bathed her inner thighs with a creeping warmth.

Mindful of what she was about to receive, she flattened her belly against the rock and her bottom wriggled then quivered as the first blow struck home. Her bottom stung, then burned, as Andrea landed blow after blow on it.

As the slow burn became a fire, she groaned and writhed. No one – certainly not those handing out this treatment – could know just how she was dealing with it.

Her bottom burned; and her sex, which was pressed hard against the rock. Dependable as ever, the epicentre of her being had recovered from its recent climax, and rose to demand another.

Six beats of the paddle landed on her willing bottom before Andrea took a break.

'There,' she said, not without conceited satisfaction. 'See how pink it is? Even in the light of the moon it's gained colour.'

'It looks very warm,' said Marie. 'May I touch it?'

'Of course. Warm your hands on it as much as you like. Once your hands have taken its warmth, I will make it warm again.'

With slow deliberation, Marie's cool palms and fingers felt the warmth of Toni's behind.

Toni shivered under that touch, her flesh quivering and erupting with pinpricks of chillness as though touched by ice. She felt Marie's fingers part her buttocks, as if any warmth had gone there. But such a thing was done for sheer devilment rather than to trace any travelling heat.

'Have you quite finished?' she heard Andrea say. 'Her bottom's cooling. It's not as pink as it was. Let me give her six more.'

'No,' returned Marie petulantly. 'Let *me*.'

Toni heard Andrea sigh loudly before agreeing and handing the paddle to Marie. Somehow, she knew that Marie's blows would be harder than those of her colleague.

Tightly closing her eyes, she braced herself for the onslaught.

As the first blow landed, her whole body stiffened. From deep within, just like before, she summoned her whole resolve, her whole reservoir of sexual arousal.

The residue of the first six blows was still there. Now, it mingled with the sharp smacks of the new blows that seemed to dive from a great height and land with a harsh thwack on her uplifted behind.

Time after time the blows fell. It might have been six as promised, but it could just as well have been eight.

During this time, her breasts swung as she wriggled and, with single-minded concentration, she transferred the centre of the sensations she was feeling from her bottom to her clitoris, which rubbed so confidently against the rock beneath her.

Sweat now covering her body in a fine and silvery film, she trembled as her bottom bucked beneath the paddle and against the rock. Like a huge wave breaking over the bow of a speeding yacht, a rush of orgasm rushed through her body and enveloped the last sting of the paddle, the last hard protrusion of the rock.

'There!' exclaimed Marie. 'All done.'

'Good,' said Andrea. 'I thoroughly enjoyed that. It made me feel a lot better, though I would have felt even better if Venetia Salvatore hadn't brought her here in the first place. Still, I suppose we'd better be going.'

'Yes,' replied Marie. 'The tide should be with us now. We have to go. And so does she. We'd better get to the boat.'

They got Toni to her feet. She staggered slightly, having been in that position for so long. Her behind smarted, and she had two orgasms behind her from these two alone. Tiredness, she realised, was fast catching up with her.

'Come on, you,' Andrea tugged on the rope that still encircled her neck.

'I suppose he doesn't mind what she looks like,' said Marie as she tucked the paddle under her arm and looked Toni up and down.

Toni wondered who 'he' was, but couldn't ask, what with Marie's bikini top still being around her mouth. Her eyes darted from one to the other. Andrea was looking her up and down like Marie, and she didn't care for the tone of it. Andrea, she guessed, had a reason for all this, and would stop at nothing to get rid of her.

'I suppose we could untie her feet, but I've got a better idea. After all, *I* went hunting for her. It's up to me how she should be packaged. Give me that paddle. I'll take it back to the dinghy and get one of the oars.'

Marie frowned, but passed over the paddle, which was fairly lightweight and useful only for short hauls in calm waters.

Andrea pushed at Toni so she fell back on to the sand, then marched off to the boat, and back again. 'Bring her hands to the front,' she ordered. 'I'll help you.'

Two pairs of hands grasped hold of Toni's, brought them round from her back, and held and retied them above her belly.

Andrea lifted the oar and lay it full length on top of her, then, as though she were some creature caught in the jungle, their busy fingers bound her wrists and ankles to the paddle.

'Ready?' asked Andrea who stood at Toni's head.

'I am ready,' returned Marie from down by her feet.

With that, the oar was hoisted on to their shoulders, and Toni hung there, captured, bound and gagged, the rope from her neck also tying her to the length of the oar.

A sea breeze cooled her hot bottom as they carried her towards the water. Her head hung down, but she could see the stars as she jolted down the beach.

This night had not been the night she had thought it would be, yet she had survived it. In her mind, she had triumphed. Having taken this night in her stride, she could take anything.

But then, she told herself guardedly, she didn't know what else was to come.

Chapter Twelve

'You should have kept a closer eye on her! You've been careless, my dear man, very careless!'

Venetia Salvatore paced up and down the stone floor in the cool darkness of the Red Tower. She was angry, and at her age did not like getting angry. It sent the blood rushing to her face, and was very bad for her complexion. She patted at her face with her palms as if to hide the pinkness, and as she moved her jewellery clinked like angry chains.

'I'm sorry, Madame. I am extremely sorry. I will accept any punishment you care to give me. Any at all.'

Usually tall, and usually regal, Emira now looked like a creature of shame, of defeat. Already, he knelt before her, naked and head bowed. Knowing she would be angry, he had taken his clothes off outside. He knew he would be punished, knew the gleaming glow of his dark brown body would be subjected to all sorts of abuse before she had got her anger out of her system.

His beautiful manhood, generous in size, and as black as ebony, already stood in quiet anticipation of punishment, his heavy balls hanging like rich, dark fruit between his lithe yet powerful thighs. Her voice rang about his head, shrill, but strong.

'Oh you will be punished all right! You certainly will be.'

Her eyes were full of fire, her fists tightly clenched. The love for her sons and anger at her plans being thwarted were fierce within her.

Punishment for him who had failed was uppermost in her mind. Yet she allowed her eyes to run over him, to enjoy his nakedness, his submission to her will. In response to the sheer masculinity of his body, the sublime femininity of his face, her mouth opened, and her hands left her face, cupped her breasts, then ran over the trimness of her waist to the swelling of her hips. By proxy, her hands were his hands. Her arousal was also his.

Emira hung his head and kept his eyes on the floor and Venetia's pacing feet. The pacing stopped. Her feet, so neat, so well cared for, were now still before him. He had always marvelled at how perfectly proportioned his mistress was, and her feet were no exception. Her exquisite and well-tended toenails were before his eyes, so neat yet electric with sexuality.

He sighed a great sigh, then dropped forward, naked and gleaming buttocks high in the air, head to the ground. In each wide palm, he cupped one of her beautiful feet, then kissed each of her beautiful toes which protruded from beneath the strap of her sandals.

Between each breathless and adoring kiss, he explained as best he could.

'Madame ... I can only say I was not prepared for this. I don't know where she is gone. I know a fishing boat put in at the village around the next cove and went again – I must presume she is on that. It is being checked – Martin and Mark have taken the speedboat to catch up with it and will see if she is on there.'

His mouth lingered on her smallest toe.

Venetia looked down on him. 'Most annoying, my dear man, most annoying! Everything was ready, was it not? My son would have seen her last night, would have seen what she could do. In time, my second son would have seen her too and the kernel of my plan would have been set in motion. Now, it has all been undone. She has vanished. It is not good enough. Not good enough at all.'

'I'm sorry, Madame. Very sorry. I apologise most profusely. I am your slave. I have always been and will always be your slave. Do with me as you will. Punish me in whatever way you think fit. My body is yours.'

His actions echoing his words, he lay outstretched, his dark frame like a fallen shadow on the red stone floor.

He closed his eyes as her sandalled feet came nearer. He heard a slight clatter as she removed her footwear, then felt the sharpness of her painted toenails as her foot kicked at his side.

'Damn you! Damn you, Emira!'

He winced at each kick of her light and pretty foot, not so much for its scratching on his skin, but more so because with each connection, his penis became terribly engorged with blood, yet was trapped between his body and the floor.

'Madame . . .'

She had moved. He heard the swish of her wrap as she moved, smelt the vibrant mix of perfume and body above him.

He gasped as he felt the ball of her foot upon his muscular shoulders. It was followed by her sole, then the other foot. Although she was not heavy, her weight pressed him to the cold stone floor. He groaned, but not with pain – only pleasure. Her feet were cold on his back, yet her perfume filled his head, and her presence electrified him as it always had.

Silently, she walked over his hard muscles to that sweeping incline that divided the breadth of his back from the rising mounds of his tight buttocks, brown and shiny as conkers.

Her weight light upon him, she stepped, one foot at a

time, from his back to his buttocks, one dainty foot upon each.

He groaned but remained perfectly still as her toe traced the cleft between the two. He groaned again, but remained still when the same toe thrust into the tightness of his anus.

Light Venetia might be, but she was strong, and that included her toe. It burrowed firmly into the tightness of the hole. He did not clench his muscles around it; rather, he relaxed them and let her enter his most sacrosanct altar. With each thrust of her toe, his cock grew in size and hardness against the cold stone. He spread his fingers, palms flat on the floor. His eyes remained closed and his mouth open.

Venetia did not let up with the probing of her toe. This was her punishment for failure. She wanted to abuse him, wanted to kick someone and that, in her mind, was what she was doing. In strict tempo, aware that his cock was hot with blood and arousal, and yet trapped beneath his body, her toe continued its task.

Gently, so as not to disturb his most pleasurable passenger, Emira began to rock gently against the floor. He also began to moan as his climax came nearer.

Venetia, eyes blazing almost hissed as she spoke. 'Not yet, my dear man. Not yet. Prolonging your climax is part of your punishment.' Her toe retreated. 'Open your legs.'

He obeyed. Firmly, she buried her toes in the warmth of his scrotum.

Anguished, he cried out, then moaned as she wriggled those toes against the hotness of his genitals which sat in a purple heap between his legs.

'You will not be coming yet, will you, Emira?'

'No Madame,' he replied, his voice strangled by restraint.

'Your erection has diminished?'

'Yes, Madame, but not disappeared.'

'Good,' she said. 'Good. I'm glad of that.'

189

Smiling with satisfaction, Venetia immersed each set of toes in his scrotal sac, relishing their warmth, and although her toenails lightly scratched his most delicate flesh, she did not inflict pain or injury.

When she was satisfied that she had adequately curbed his desires, she again thrust her toe into his anus.

This time she did not give him any leeway to prepare himself for its entrance. She thrust it in, forced him to take it as any man might force a woman. Shoulders and head raised from the ground, he yelled out, but she gave him no quarter.

Again and again she drove it into him. Again, he rocked against the floor, yet gently so as not to dislodge her either from off his body or from within it. She was cruel to him, she inflicted pain as well as pleasure, and yet she was his mistress, his divine benefactor, his idol.

Muscles tensing, jaw immobile, he whimpered into the floor, and curled his fingers into the palms of his hands. She had used him, abused him, taken out all the frustration she was feeling on him and him alone. In that, there was honour, he counselled himself. In that, there was love.

Just as it always had, his body reacted to her very closeness and the cruelty of her actions. His body was hers to do with as she pleased, and Venetia pleased herself. But in pleasing herself, she also pleased him. He was putty in her hands, clay beneath her feet, and his desire to be her slave was as powerful as ever.

That desire was rising in him, taking shape, spiralling upwards in some dizzy and heightening cone that spun round and round like a spool of thread, taking him with it, higher and higher until he could climb no more. He reached the summit and convulsed into climax, shudders of release rushing over him before at last shivering into tranquillity.

Toe still active and embedded in his anus, Venetia watched his shiverings, his tremblings, with sublime satisfaction. Only once she was sure that his last tremor had been spent did she get off his back.

'Get to your knees,' she ordered.

This he did, his eyes fixed on the expelled white and warm foam that was so quickly being cooled by the stone it ran over.

He was aware of her adjusting her clothes before standing in front of him.

She had on a long mauve silk wrap that opened at the front. Her breasts thrust each edge to one side, her nipples dark and large, her belly firm and white. Her bush which was thicker and darker than many younger women, was but inches from his face. She smelt of musk, she smelt of perfume, but mostly she smelt of woman.

'My dear man,' she said, in that light and airy way she had at times, 'that mess must be cleaned up. I suppose I must do something about it.'

'I'm sorry, Madame.'

'Yes. So am I,' she went on. 'But there, we will have to make the best of it.'

She opened her legs, held up the violet-coloured folds of her wrap, and stood astride the white liquid. Sighing as though with relief, she let a shower of yellow water fall from her thick bush and watched it as it steamed up from the same spot where he had left the liquid of his release.

At last, she finished. 'There,' she said. 'That should do the trick. Now dry me, then take me off.'

His face beaming with undiminished adoration, he looked up at her, murmured his gratitude, then ran his hands up over her legs, her thighs. His eyes and willing mouth travelled to her pussy.

Soft, yet strong, passionate yet powerful, his lips drew in her flesh. As his mouth sucked in her smell, her hair and her flesh, she purred with delight. His hands – palms as soft as rose petals – caressed her thighs from knees to hips.

As he divided her sex with his tongue, his hands

191

cupped her behind, and his fingers gently pulled one buttock away from its sister.

His tongue darted like a slim fish among the folds of her humid flesh, licked at her rosebud and invaded her vagina which tasted of honey and salt.

He knew that, above him, she would be playing with her own breasts, pleasuring her own nipples, using them as though they were buttons by which she could experience further excess, further excitement. Venetia was unusual like that. Her nipples were extraordinarily sensitive. With those alone, she could take herself to the heights of ecstasy.

Like a hot sea, she shimmered above him, her hips undulating towards his mouth, encompassing his nose as his tongue dived more deeply into her humid portal.

Her hands left her breasts and began to run through his hair. As her climax approached, her fingers gripped more tightly, her nails dug in more deeply.

With a burst of exclamation that fell over her like a veil, she trembled, her thighs quivering as his tongue sucked the last of her orgasm from her.

At last, the clawing fingers released him.

He looked up at her. She wasn't smiling, but she wasn't as angry as she had been. She looked only thoughtful.

'We have to find her again, my dear man. You know that, don't you?'

'Yes,' he replied. 'I know that.'

Later that day, Emira awaited the return of Mark and Martin.

Their faces betrayed their failure.

'Not on the fishing boat?'

'No,' said Mark.

'No,' echoed Martin.

Emira tossed the handful of prayer beads that he held in one hand. He looked at the moving beads as their colour shot through the air. He was not happy; he had his suspicions, and he was not entirely sure what he should do about them.

He turned his eyes to the far horizon and the other islands beyond the three belonging to the Salvatore family. Strange, he thought, that they should appear clustered like bunches of grapes, despite the distance between them.

Perhaps, he thought to himself, she had not gone that far at all.

'Emira.'

He looked behind him to the terrace of the white villa that was now turning to pink in the dying glow of the setting sun.

Philippe, wine-glass in one hand and Andrea draped over his free arm, was looking down at him.

Philippe smiled, his happiness no doubt assisted by the wine. Andrea's smile was far more open, almost triumphant. There was a look in her eye that stabbed at Emira's heart and firmed up the suspicions he already had.

Andrea was beautiful, but possessive, jealous and extremely deadly. But Emira kept his own counsel: that of himself and his female benefactor. He would not betray his suspicions and with them the intentions of his mistress. So he smiled, rested his hand in a languid and lazy way on the sweeping haze of his purple skirt, and tapped suggestively at his hidden cock with the other. 'I'll be right there,' he called.

He knew more or less what they had in mind; what Andrea had suggested to Philippe. There would be just the three of them; Philippe, Andrea and him. A trio of good looks, a trio of colour and vigorous sexual Olympics. A pleasant evening would be had by all.

His long skirt held in place by a *diamanté* brooch at his hip, Emira thanked Mark and Martin, then started to climb the steps.

Chapter Thirteen

Conway Patterson did not live in any plush villa on the rugged but scented island that he called his own. Leaving his sea legs behind him, he merely ranged it and climbed up through its tree-spattered cliffs to bathe naked in its cascading pools and to lounge in its lush green grass.

The classic and beguiling ketch, *Enchantress*, was always his home, always swaying or plunging beneath him like some overly passionate woman who could not get enough of either him or the sea.

He'd left the crew to take delivery of the merchandise the delicious Andrea had promised him. Even once she was aboard, he couldn't get up the nerve to go along and see her.

Andrea would not have known it, and neither would anyone else, but he was nearly as haunted by the spectre of the green-eyed redhead as Philippe was – except that he didn't lose any sleep over it. But that didn't mean to say she wasn't there, drifting in dreamy isolation somewhere at the back of his mind.

So he held off seeing this woman who looked so much like her. Instead, he left *Enchantress* and walked the narrow path that climbed up through the jagged rocks.

The higher he climbed, the more the sea breeze whipped his hair across his face and cleared his mind.

Now he had this woman, what would he do with her?

Many things, he told himself. Many things. She had a lot to answer for. It had been a woman with red hair and green eyes who had initiated him and his brother in the ways that delighted both men and women. It had also been she who had hurt them and caused them to quarrel.

Oh yes, this woman had much to answer for. Not that *this* woman was that actual woman. She couldn't look that much like her, surely. Perhaps, once he saw her, he would change his mind about punishing her by proxy for what she, or one like her, had done. But for now, he envisaged what revenge he could take, imagined her naked flesh stretched out to do with as he saw fit.

The thought made him breathless. At the top of the cliff, he paused, took many deep breaths and laughed into the wind as his hardened cock beat against the rough denim of his shorts which were tight over his buttocks and sharp cut to his hips.

What had his mother been thinking of to bring this woman here? How had she expected him to react when he found out about her? There were no answers to his questions. None he could think of, except, of course, that both brothers had been initiated by such a woman as she, and both brothers had loved her, been besotted by her looks, her scent and her overwhelming passion.

He remembered his youth, his initiation from boyhood to manhood in her arms. He remembered her lying on him, her body rubbing gently up and down against his, her hair like a curtain around them, her breasts and belly warm and pleasantly soft against him.

Even now, just thinking about the way her back swept in a gracious curve to her waist, made his heart beat faster. He thought of the rise of her bottom, pert, firm and deliciously round. Her skin, he remembered, had glowed as though lightly touched with a sheen of gold.

Just thinking of her brought desire to his mind and his groin. That desire would not go, would not dissipate.

Closing his eyes, he threw back his head, undid his zip, and let his erection break free.

With one light touch of his fingers, his cock jerked once, twice, then spurted its load in one long jet to be taken by the wind. This was one satisfaction the woman he remembered would not take from him.

Once it was gone, he did up his zip. He was happier now, more at ease and called himself a fool for not having gone to look at this girl his mother had procured for his brother. He smiled, then began to laugh.

His thigh muscles tensed and stood out in stark relief as he braced his legs and stood there laughing on the rocky outcrop, for all the world like some young Hercules.

Below him, *Enchantress* lay, a rich reddish brown against the turquoise mirror that was Marelda Bay. It was beautiful, an enchanted spot that belonged to him and him alone.

Down there also was a woman with green eyes like the sea, and red hair. She was also his. Though, of course, she did not know that yet.

Toni wriggled, but could do little else. She was near-naked, bound, and knew she'd been pushed into a cupboard. It was as dark as the night she had arrived on. The gag that still covered her mouth prevented her from crying out, not that she supposed crying out would do much good.

By judging the feel of the boat as she rose on the swell, she estimated her approximate position; she remembered the cabin the cupboard was in, but only vaguely. Everything that had happened the night before had been furtive and rushed, except for the episode on the beach. Judging by the muttered orders and the use of muffled oars rather than outboard engine, it was obvious that Marie and the other woman had not wanted to draw any attention from those on the land especially those at the beach barbecue.

Silently, she tried to evaluate why Andrea and Marie had been so keen to get rid of her. She didn't doubt that they had enjoyed the little scenario on the beach as much as she had. But perhaps, she thought, they did not know that she had enjoyed it. Perhaps her capacity for sexual enjoyment was far greater and far more varied than theirs.

At this moment, it shouldn't have mattered, but it did, acting like a strong and purposeful barrier between her and any fear she might have felt.

Methodically, she weighed up the reasons why she'd been brought here. But, apart from the hint of jealousy in Marie's eyes when she had first arrived on the island with Emira, there was nothing she could be sure about. So she sighed, relaxed, and waited for whatever might befall.

Beyond the door of the cupboard, she heard another door open and then close.

She felt no fear – only apprehension and perhaps a little excitement. Whatever might happen to her would be a vast improvement on being locked in a closet like something rarely or never used.

She heard footsteps pacing up and down outside; stopping and then pacing again.

Why didn't whoever it was open the blasted door?

Her patience ran out. Now a sense of panic came to her. Intent on knowing, resolved to leave the cupboard, she knocked the door with her shoulder. Again and again she did it so that it shuddered and rattled on its hinges.

Without warning, it opened wide. Still heaving with her shoulder, she fell out sideways. Her head connected with a pair of bare feet; the feet parted, and her head was on the floor between them.

Her hair cascaded around her in a red and vibrant haze, and even though her impression of him was brief, she knew he was staring, knew he looked amazed at what he had found.

'It is you!' He spoke in one sudden hush as though something had broken at the back of his throat.

Me? she said to herself. Of course it's me.

At first she wriggled violently, then caught her breath and became still. Her eyes glowed like emeralds as she surveyed the view above her. He had strong calves, this man; strong thighs, too. And nestling between those thighs like rich and over-large fruit hung a heavy pair of balls. From that fruit, his rod rose hard and proud, growing before her very eyes. Above his rampant cock, he looked at her, eyes wide, mouth hanging open.

'I don't believe it,' he said. 'I don't believe it.'

Neither do I, she thought to herself, though it wasn't her predicament that filled her mind now so much as the view she had of the ripe fruit hanging between his thighs. She had a yearning to kiss them, to lick and suck at the softly downed flesh.

How ripe they looked, how succulent and extraordinarily appetising. As she looked, she thought of what Emira had said to her when she had first arrived on the island – about developing tastes, about becoming a gourmet of everything set before her.

Well these were most certainly set before her – or rather, above her – and she most certainly wanted to taste them. Yearning gave motion to her thighs. With slow deliberation, she rubbed one against the other, aware of sexual secretions rising warm and wet between her legs. Her breasts rose and fell more quickly as her senses responded to what she was seeing and what she was hoping for.

He didn't move. Slowly, his expression, or as much of it as she could see, came under control. His erection did not. It seemed beyond him, as though it had a mind of its own and would go its own way.

She gazed up its iron hardness, as mesmerized with it as he was with her.

'Well now,' he said at last, though his amazement was still apparent, 'what have we here?'

She tried to tell him, tried to say something against her gag. Nothing came out but a mumble. She saw him smile and bend his knees so that his scrotum hung heavy and hot above her forehead.

Now she could see it well; the dark thick vein that divided the right side from the left. She could smell him too and, despite her bonds, found herself writhing and murmuring beneath him, unrepentant in her desire to take the heat of his flesh into her mouth.

His fingers hooked into the bikini top that had served as a gag. He pulled it from her mouth. The tip of his cock tapped gently against her forehead. It was warm, moist to the very end.

She gasped, took deep breaths of air and looked up into his eyes which looked back at her above his cock – blue eyes, as sharp as a sky in April. 'What am I doing here?'

He raised his eyebrows, looked surprised. 'Is that all you want to know?'

'No. It's not. Who are you?'

He smiled. 'You don't know me?'

'Of course I don't know you.'

He shifted above her. She couldn't see his eyes now. Again, his heavy sac hung full and hot above her nose and her mouth.

'No. Perhaps you don't,' she heard him say, and strangely enough, she felt sorry for him. 'Of course you don't. You're not her. But you look like her. Too much like her.' A cloud seemed to cross his face, and she wondered what had caused it. 'How unfortunate for you.' He said it slowly, precisely and, in its delivery, all trace of his accent seemed to disappear.

'Why?' she cried out. 'Why is it unfortunate for me, and who is "she"?'

Her cry was lost against the soft heat of his flesh. His

balls, their touch as soft as velvet, were very hot and suffocatingly heavy against her mouth.

'You've got what you want,' she heard him say. 'You've got what you always wanted. Now I want you to lick it. It's been a long time since you did that. Go on. Lick it, suck it and see if you like the taste, see if you remember it.'

If the smell and sight of him hadn't already aroused her, and if his scrotum hadn't been hanging directly against her lips, she would have shouted out to him that he was mixing her up with someone else. But in her position to shout was impossible, and his hardware was irresistible.

As the weight of his sac pressed against her nose, the hairs of his testes lightly brushing her face, she opened her mouth. Despite any misgivings she might have had, she poked out her tongue and licked at his pliant flesh before it descended on her and filtered between her lips.

She sucked on his skin, the soft flesh gentle and warm upon her tongue.

As she sucked, she used her tongue to prod at him, to push his sack of skin around in her mouth. The more she did of both, the more she wanted to do: the more she wanted him to touch her and for her hands to touch him.

He did not touch her and, being still bound with her torn and tattered fishnet outfit, she could not curve her own fingers around his penis which she judged, by the position of his scrotum, to be rearing in splendid isolation above her breasts.

She arched her back so that her breasts would quiver and entice his attention. Desire was rushing through her veins like a mountain torrent, and her writhing body was gyrating before his gaze. But still he did not touch her.

Abandoned to her submissive position, she sucked more of him into her mouth. As his body began to rock near her face, he moaned, high above her.

Her tongue prodded, worked and licked at him as her

teeth nibbled and lips sucked him in, her mouth accommodating as much of him as she could.

Flicking gently over his flesh, her tongue encountered the pulsing duct that would take his release to the head of his member.

Engorged with its hot cargo, the duct became rigid. Inch by inch, she felt that hardening travel until it had left the vicinity of her exploring tongue to journey up his stiff cock and ejaculate to the outside world.

With one knee against each of her cheeks, he held her firm as he jerked more violently against her face, then, sitting more firmly on her, pressed more of his sac into her mouth.

He jerked vigorously and his knees tightened against her face. One more powerful thrust of his loins then, as a warm wetness cascaded over her breasts, he cried out loud and long like a suffering beast that has at last been set free.

He didn't move for a while. He stayed there, rocking gently above her. It was almost as though, by sitting on her face, he was avoiding having to look at her, having to see who she was or what she was.

It was only the sparse hairs around his balls causing her to sneeze and bring her mouth down too tight on his own flesh that finally made him move.

'Are you going to untie me?' she asked him.

He had sat himself in a chair, and from there he looked at her thoughtfully. He rested his elbows on the chair arms and intertwined his fingers beneath his chin. For some reason, he needed time to answer that question.

His manner and tone of voice were stern. 'In time. When I want to. Not when you want it.'

He tossed his hair away from his face. It was very light brown and fell from his crown like a lion's mane. Here and there, the sun had bleached it almost to white.

His eyes studied her, running over her body. Lashes as golden as September corn made her think of his eyes as cornflowers, bright blue and shining with independence. His lips moved one against the other as if he were tasting her, licking her flesh and devouring her most sensitive parts.

'Why does it have to be when you want it?' she asked him.

His sneer was cruel. Instinctively, she knew he wanted to be cruel, that all the things he wanted to do to her could be cruel.

Although he was enjoying her discomfort, she sensed a weakness in him, a hint that the very fact that her hair was red and her eyes green somehow unnerved him. His eyes flitted between each of her features as if he was trying to deny her looks, deny his own memories.

'What's your name?' he asked.

Suddenly, he sounded sincerely interested, as though whatever was lurking behind the blueness of his eyes was nothing but a dream.

'Antonia Yardley,' she replied.

His mouth dropped open. 'I don't believe it! Not only did my mother engage a woman who looked like the one she engaged before, she even got one with the same name! It's uncanny – and fantastic!'

'Does that mean you're going to set me free?' Toni asked, sensing the disbelief in his voice.

His look of wonder fast disappeared.

'No!' he replied adamantly, and shook his head which sent his fair curls flying. 'She engaged you for my brother – not for me. That's the trouble with being a second son: all you get are the leftovers. Well this bloke ain't having that. This bloke ain't having that at all!'

'I don't understand,' she said, faint worry causing her to rush her words. 'I came here to crew a yacht. That's all I know. I wasn't brought here entirely for your brother's benefit. At least, I don't think I was.'

The way he jumped to his feet made her cry out.

'Don't hurt me!' she yelled.

His brown suede boot nudged into her side. 'You'll do

as you're told,' he said with a sneer. 'Just as the first Antonia did.'

He saw the look of surprise on her face and laughed before he spoke. 'Oh, you didn't know that, did you. That the first Antonia had red hair, green eyes and looked like you. Even the name,' he said, and shook his head. 'I can't believe it. I just can't believe it.'

'I don't know what this is all about . . .' she started to say, but he was agitated, looking this way and that as if he was afraid to see her body, her hair, her eyes.

'Come on,' he said, gripping her shoulders with vice-like strength. 'Back into the cupboard until I need you again.'

'But I don't want . . .'

Her words were lost in the gag which he forcefully pulled up over her mouth. Then, with both hands and a push of his foot, he got her back into the cupboard.

This time, she was not left sitting. This time, he lay her down, pulling her legs upright and straight, then wound a rope around her ankles which he fastened to a hook above her.

Toni was aware of him having full view of her breasts, seeing her smooth belly, her triangle of hair. At a right angle, he would also see the cheeks of her neat little bottom and the beginning of the slit that passed between her legs.

He became immobile and stared at her eyes. 'I can't stand looking at them,' he said eventually, and shook his head.

He turned his back on her and pulled open a drawer which he rummaged around in before coming back to her. It was only a narrow silk neckerchief, but it was enough to blindfold her.

She struggled at first, then stopped when she realised it gave him a reason to slap her bottom a few times.

'Stop it! Stop it,' he shouted. 'Or you'll get a good beating.'

She did stop it, though she had half a mind not to. She

detected something bordering on pleading in his voice that urged her to continue. But she could have been wrong. She'd think on it. By the looks of things, she'd have plenty of time to do that.

Now blindfolded as well as gagged, she lay there, knowing that he was looking at her. She also heard the door being closed, and in the lonely darkness she wondered about the other Antonia. Was she right to guess that this man was one of the brothers Emira had told her about?

She lost track of time, but knew more or less when night had come again. Sounds were softer; even the waves lapping against the hull of the boat seemed muffled by the darkness, and there were no sounds of men or of gulls. All was silent and very dark, but not entirely uneventful.

Every so often, the door opened and she felt the warmth of a superior ejaculation splash on her breasts or her belly. Each time, she arched her body towards it, aching with the need to have its warmth in her and not over her.

But time was on her side. Eventually, he would have to untie her, have to take her in the way she wanted. At least, that's what she told herself.

Even though she could not see him, she knew he couldn't resist her, knew that whoever the other woman might have been or whatever she might have done, she had been irresistible.

From what she had gathered, she was very like that woman, and soon, she too would prove irresistible.

Chapter Fourteen

*H*is sleep was snatched between the moments he opened the cupboard door and looked at her.

When he did sleep, his memory lapsed into dreams of when he was younger, when his mother had arranged for the woman with the red hair and green eyes to come to him, just as she had for his brother.

He remembered that rush of fiery hair falling across his chest, and trailing behind her as her mouth pleasured his stomach before enveloping the head of his virgin penis.

Just the thought of her mouth on him caused him to cry out, his body to arch, and the blood to course through his veins and along his stiffening rod.

Sweat lay over him like a damp cobweb when he awoke, and its residual yearnings compelled him to rise from his bed, open the cupboard door and look at her again.

How beautiful she was: how bright, golden and gloriously naked, except for those bits of netting, all that remained of what might have been a seriously seductive outfit. Odd, he thought, how those ragged bits of string criss-crossing her flesh and forcing neat bubbles of it through the openings only made the rest of her body seem more available, more irresistible.

Each time, the dream had evoked a rigid erection, so that when he had opened the cupboard door and only lightly touched the end of his rod, a flow of creamy fluid had spurted from its head and cascaded over her firm breasts.

In the morning, a big man with slanting brown eyes, wide mouth and shaved head came and removed her blindfold and untied her ankles. He had a sculptured face with high cheekbones and skin the colour of coffee that had been lightly laced with cream. He was bare from the waist up, his muscles oiled and bulging, and laced with prominent veins. His trousers were loose and black and his feet were bare. A twist of blue-black hair hung from his shining dome and fell alongside one ear. When he bent to take her from the cupboard and raise her up in his huge arms, a gold earring in the same ear jangled as if celebrating her release.

She blinked against the light and, losing the battle against its glare, let her eyes close as he carried her into the bathroom.

Gently, he set her down on an upholstered seat, untied her gag and released the fibrous bonds that had so securely tied her hands and clung in bits and pieces over her body.

Aching and blinking from her ordeal in the cramped and dark cupboard, she groaned and licked the dryness of her lips.

'What now?' she asked.

'Sssh!' he said, placing one slim finger to his lips. 'No sound, or I will have to punish you.'

As her mouth was dry anyway, Toni almost welcomed the order. Numb arms and legs were an added inducement to obey this man. There was no way she could contemplate being trussed up again like a Christmas turkey and returned to the narrow confines of that cupboard. It had been a dreadful ordeal and one she did not want to repeat. All the same, as the warm fluid had cascaded over her breasts, she had tingled. The image of the heavy balls that had been in her mouth were still in her mind. She had been in no doubt that this particular libation had been from the same source.

He took oil from a cabinet and rubbed at her upper arms. Now this, she concurred, was pleasant and extremely welcome.

Still blinking in the aftermath of the blindfold, she groaned, running her tongue over her dry lips again and again and, taking a deep breath, caught the aroma and sight of the semen that now lay encrusted across her breasts.

Recovering beneath the strong but gentle hands that massaged her arms so well, she tried to voice what was on her mind.

'Who is he?' she asked. 'The man who adorned me with this,' she added, indicating her breasts with a quick nod of her head. 'Is he the brother of Philippe Salvatore?'

The big man with the Oriental eyes sighed and looked around him as if to make sure no one was listening.

His bare muscles stretched and contracted as he rubbed the oil into hers and tore away the last of her fishnet outfit. She sat naked when he answered.

'Mister Patterson, missy.'

'And who is Mister Patterson? Is he Mister Salvatore's brother?'

'Yes, Miss. But his name is not Salvatore. Mister Conway's father was Australian. Mister Philippe's father was Italian. He is Mister Conway Patterson. *Enchantress* is his boat – the boat you are on. Now, enough questions.'

'What's our position; I mean, the position of the boat?'

'We are at Mister Patterson's island, missy. He owns that, too.'

She remembered Emira pointing the other islands out to her and telling her who they belonged to.

'You mean, Mister Patterson has his own island?'

'Yes, missy. I do.' The man didn't look too happy about talking so freely about his employer.

'And they also have separate boats. That's not very brotherly, is it?'

'That, missy, is not my business.'

She was prying, but did feel she was getting somewhere. She pressed her chance. 'I hear they don't get on. Is that true?'

Dark eyes regarded her with more than just wariness. There was something resembling awe within that look, but also something slightly cautious.

Snake-like, his tongue flicked over his bottom lip and he swallowed hard before he answered. 'They don't get on none too well, missy. Never have. Their mother always trying to get them closer. Not work though.'

'Why?'

The warm hands that had been so pleasurably rubbing her arms, stopped. 'I don't think I should say – and you should not be asking.'

Somehow, she got the distinct impression that the reason the brothers had quarrelled had something to do with her. But how could it? Until she had come here for a job, she had never known either of them.

She caught at the coffee-coloured hand before the man could resume the massage. He started.

'What's it got to do with me?' she asked him.

'I don't know.' His voice suddenly hardened. 'And if you keep on questioning me, I will have no option but to punish you. I have my orders.'

Curiosity swiftly overrode caution. Toni was determined. Punishment or not, she pressed on. 'But it does have something to do with me?'

This, apparently, was one question too much. He covered her mouth with his hand, his fingers pressing tightly against her cheek. 'Enough! You are a bad and disobedient girl. I will now have to punish you.'

He released her mouth. But a churning of fear was already in her stomach, and her heart beat faster.

'Not the cupboard,' she pleaded, already regretting her words. 'Please, not the cupboard.'

He smiled at that, and his dark eyes that appeared to be outlined in kohl seemed to lengthen along with his mouth. 'No,' he replied, his smile gone in an instant, his voice stern. 'I will not put you back in the cupboard as long as you take your punishment without question.'

She glanced from him through to where the cupboard door swung open on its hinges in time with the swelling of the sea. Grateful for his leniency, and despite anything else he might do, she breathed a sigh of relief.

'I will,' she said, and shuddered. For the second time, she adopted a demureness she did not usually adhere to. She bent her head, looked at her bare toes, and waited for what was to come.

'Good,' he said. 'Now you are learning about obedience. Lie down,' he ordered, and pointed to the floor.

She did as he asked and lay down, resting her head upon her hands. The floor was sleek and shiny and very cool against her naked flesh. She shivered, closed her eyes and waited for whatever was to come.

The first thing she felt was his foot upon her, pressing her tight against the floor.

The second thing was the bundle of towels he forced under her hips so her bare bottom was pushed upwards, pert and incredibly vulnerable.

With obvious apprehension, she clenched her cheeks and closed her eyes more tightly.

Calm, she told herself, be calm. Again she remembered what Emira had told her about relishing everything set before her, and Madame Salvatore with her urging to endure and enjoy.

Just the words circulating in her mind helped her to relax. She opened her eyes, released the hold on her buttocks, and with her torso pinned to the floor by this man's heavy foot, she heard the hush of a whip as it sang through the air, then felt it burning and stinging her upturned bottom.

Instinctively, she bit her lip to stifle her cry. The whip had stung and there was possibly a red stripe where only a creamy whiteness had been before.

Endure, she told herself. The word filled her mind. Such a small word. Such an incredible response. Warm traces of heat spread from where the whip had laced her flesh. Even before another blow fell, she raised her bottom to meet it.

Defiantly, she kept her eyes open and stopped biting her lip. She would take what came, ride it, and even turn it to pleasure.

'I will give you six more,' the big man said. 'You will count them with me. Each time I lay one on your very nice bottom, you will hold up one finger, then two, then three, and so on and so forth. Do you understand that?'

'Yes,' she replied.

'Sir!' said the man suddenly. 'When I am punishing you, it is always "Sir". When anyone is punishing or using you, it is "Sir". Do you understand that?'

'Yes, sir.' Her bottom lip trembled when she answered. Was the cupboard really any more terrible than this?

'Good,' he said. 'But just to make sure you have understood me, I will lay on an extra one for your ignorance in not calling me that in the first place. You will now receive seven strokes. Is that clear?'

'Yes, sir.'

She managed not to tremble, not to bite her lip, and not to close her eyes. But she did clench her fists. Adding humiliation to her punishment only made her more determined to take what pleasure she could from what was happening to her.

Still tightly pressed to the floor by his foot on her back, she heard the whip hiss again before stinging her behind. Her buttocks clenched, her hips jerked, but she only hissed what could so easily have been a yelp.

Obediently, she held up one hand, one finger.

'Say, "Thank you, Taras",' said the man.

'Thank you, Taras,' she said dutifully.

The whip hissed again. Again her hips jerked and her buttocks clenched as another blow burned into her flesh.

This time, she held up two fingers.

'Thank me again,' he said as he slowly dragged the whip across her bottom and pushed it through the crevice in between.

She jerked, squealed, but managed to speak. 'Thank you, Taras.'

It was hard to say it and bite her lip at the same time, so she discontinued the latter.

Again and again the whip hissed, and again and again she held up the correct number of fingers and thanked her tormentor. He changed sides when they got to four. 'So that this lovely buttock can receive the same amount of pressure as the other has done,' he explained. 'Otherwise,' he went on, 'one will receive most of the pressure, and the other just the tail-end of each stroke. This is a job that has to be done properly. I am a man who does things properly.'

Tears hovered around each of her eyes. Her flesh burned and she could well imagine how crimson it now was, how warm to anyone who cared to touch it.

Now she was holding both hands up. Number six finger was finally followed by number seven, and for the last time she thanked him for what he had subjected her to.

Although he removed his foot from her back, she had an inkling that she was expected to stay on the floor until he had given her the order to get up. Anyway, she was breathing heavily, and a light layer of perspiration covered her body. She was hot, but her behind was even hotter.

She felt the cool sole of his naked foot take the heat from each of her reddened orbs.

'Ah,' he said, not without enthusiasm. 'Your bottom is nicely warmed, just as a good woman's should be. You are learning fast. That is very good. Very good indeed. There will be many lessons for you to learn here, many

211

trials for you to endure. Will you do your best to endure those trials, I wonder?'

'Yes, Taras,' she said through lips that were no longer dry. 'Yes, I will.'

She meant it. Venetia had had her reasons for bringing her here. There had also been a purpose in her ordeal at the Red Tower and the words she had spoken. For, whatever the true reasons for her employment, she resolved to survive anything they could subject her to.

'The bath,' he said at last. 'It is ready for you.'

His hands were gentle now, his muscles smooth against her bare flesh as he lifted her up and lowered her into the warm and perfumed water. She sank into it and, without her asking, Taras began to wash her hair and soap her body.

His actions were soothing, his touch and the warmth of the water instilling in her a feeling of great well-being, of delicious decadence despite the burning of her behind.

Through half-closed eyes, she viewed the rippling of his bunched back muscles as he lathered her feet, pushed thick suds and sponge between her toes, or slid his hand through the warm water to wash and pamper her aching pussy.

There was a definite exoticism about this man. The Orient and an air of drama emanated from his face, his body and his clothes. Even his actions, those of the doting eunuch, were reminiscent of some Mogul zenana or Thai temple. And he was smooth. There was no hair on his body to detract from his gleaming flesh, his firm biceps and hard, flat stomach: not on his lip, not under his arms, and little upon his head.

Not seeing any hair in those places, she wondered about his penis; whether he really was a eunuch and if his cock rose from such shining and hairless skin as covered the rest of his body.

She let her eyes roam from his face, down his torso and to the front of his trousers. Nothing could be determined from looking there. His trousers were of a loose-fitting cotton that bunched forward when he leaned forward. So today, she could discern nothing. But another time, who knows?

'Are there any clothes here for me?' she asked, once they were back in the opulence of what was surely the master cabin.

'I expect so,' he replied in an offhand manner, grimacing as he gathered up the bits of string that was all that remained of the fishnet catsuit. 'I expect Mister Patterson and Christopher will be along to tell you what you will be wearing. In the meantime, there are plenty of perfumes there for you. Plenty of make-up and things.'

He nodded towards the long ledge where bottles of pink, mauve, sizzling red and wicked black were ranged.

In the split second she glimpsed herself in the mirror, he was gone.

She was alone except for her own reflection. It caught her, held her gaze, and for a moment she stared at it as though it were a stranger. Was this creature, so long, lean and undeniably lovely, really the same girl who had found herself trapped in London in a dull job with a dull man?

There was no denying that some subtle and sexual change had taken place.

A new suppleness seemed apparent in her limbs and her skin shone with the healthy gold of fresh air and warm sun.

She turned her back to the mirror, and over her shoulder eyed the pink stripes that creased her bottom. Gently, she traced one line with her fingers, and winced as she felt its warmth.

Like a badge, a barrier, they separated her old life from the new. Never would she have allowed such things to happen back in London; never would she have had the chance for such things to happen.

But it wasn't just the physical things she could see with her eyes that had changed. There was something else new about her, that only she could perceive. There was a new alertness in the sensual centres of her being, a constant tingling in her nipples and in her sex for incessant pleasure, unending excitement and experiences.

Whatever this Conway Patterson had brought her here for, she was ready for it, but, she wondered, was he ready for her?

She smiled at her own reflection. There was nothing he could do to her that she would not derive pleasure from. On that score, she was determined to succeed.

With a sigh of satisfaction, and a thrill of apprehension tightening her stomach muscles, she sat her nude and pink-striped bottom down on the soft lushness of the blue satin bed covering. It trembled beneath her, and she laughed and pushed at it with both hands.

What a joke! A water-bed inside something that floated on water. The idea was amazing.

She looked around the rest of the cabin: dark wood and sparkling brass and crystal combined to form a richness that was as old as Victorian brandy.

Brass hooks and anchor chains decorated the walls, and there was a heavy chart table against one bulkhead complete with brass anglepoise light. A row of brass hooks and more chains ranged along the back of it, and the top of the chart table was made of clear perspex. Beneath that, she knew would be a light that would illuminate the perspex and make charts easier to read.

Through one large porthole of coloured glass, the sun shone and threw dappled patches of red, green and blue upon the whiteness of the carpet. There was a smell of rich oils in the air, of the sea and of a man. Closing her eyes, she breathed in his smell, and in her loins that old familiar feeling began to make itself felt.

The bed was opposite the mirror and, on opening her eyes, she again exchanged looks with herself, naked, wanton and not caring who knew it.

Her nipples, dark red and pouting, pointed at her

reflection. There was something enticing about it, and something that made her open her legs and admire the pinkness of her flesh and the redness of her pubic hair. She smiled at the mirror. Her own face and sex smiled back at her.

It was not enough to look at her own body. Her body was made to be used and she had a yen to use it. She had been waiting a while; now she was getting impatient, and almost of their own accord, her fingers curled over her breast, and one finger and one thumb took hold of one proud nipple.

She kind of hummed her pleasure, opened her mouth and held her head slightly higher. Through half-closed eyes, she viewed herself: the swelling nipple, her thrusting breast and the glistening gleam of her open thoroughfare.

No matter that her bottom stung. The fingers of her other hand had run down over her belly and even now were playing with her fleshy folds as a harpist would play with his or her instrument. As though she were listening to some unheard melody or some unseen musician, she began to sway.

Faster and faster her fingers worked, and quicker and quicker her breathing increased. The fingers that plied her nipple pinched more fiercely, and in the confines of her mind behind her closed eyelids, they were not her fingers; not those plying her sex, nor those tweaking her nipples. They were someone else's, someone whose scrotum had hovered above her head then descended into her mouth and on to her tongue.

Wet juices lubricated her fingers, slurped around her fleshy folds. Rising like a playing fountain, her orgasm gushed upwards from her loins, tingled in her breasts, and burst like a song on the murmurs from her mouth.

She was satisfied – for the moment.

Removing her fingers, she opened her eyes to meet those of her reflection. Now when she stood up and looked over her shoulder, the cheeks of her face as well as those of her bottom were very flushed and very well-matched.

She sat back down then, and just when she thought she might go looking for someone, the door opened and the sea green of her eyes met the cornflower blue of his.

He entered: the man from last night with the strong thighs and ripe scrotum. She recognised the hair, the accusing look in the eyes. The rest of his body was not on display. This time, he was dressed – crisp shirt, ragged edged denim shorts that clung to the thickness of his thighs which shimmered with fine golden hair.

All the same, he begged attention. This, she now knew, was Conway Patterson, half-brother of Philippe Salvatore.

Despite having just brought herself to a happy conclusion, looking at him brought renewed wetness trickling around her inner lips and into the crevice between her buttocks. Her nipples were pert and ready for action.

The man beside him was the man she guessed to be Christopher. Something about his presence brought on a very different reaction. She shuddered.

He was tall, long-limbed and long-bodied. He was dressed entirely in black, including gloves. There was something undeniably sinister about him, yet at the same time compelling. He made her shiver; perhaps with fear, perhaps with delight.

Vaguely, she was aware of a tremor passing through Conway as he stared at her. She was also aware of a burgeoning power in his loins. He did not smile as he looked. There was a thoughtfulness about him as though he was remembering something from far back and far away. Perhaps it was hatred she saw, or perhaps it was fear, but whichever it was, she judged it deep-seated and told herself to be careful with him. 'These are the clothes I wish you to wear,' Conway said.

The man in black stepped forward and, from over his arm, took items of clothing which he lay beside her on the bed. His eyes boldly ran over her body as he did so.

Under his gaze, her flesh trembled before she turned to look down at the items of clothing he had laid there.

Lightly, her fingers touched the short skirt, the tight top. Both items were black and fine to the touch.

She looked back up at Conway, her eyes a blaze of vibrant green. 'Why am I here?' she asked.

For a moment, he seemed at a loss for an answer. It was as though he had been drowning in her eyes, the flow of her hair as she had tossed her head. He regained his equilibrium, but there was a haughtiness, a hardness about him.

'Because I wish you to be here. It is where you belong.'

She frowned. The original reason she had come here was ostensibly for a job, but just the way he said those last words sowed doubt and a hint of fear in her mind.

'Do I belong here?' she asked thoughtfully and still frowning.

'Yes,' said the man in black. 'And in time, you will find out that you truly belong here, and then you will know.'

Know? Know what?

By the looks of them, it was no use asking questions, no use letting confusion reign in her brain. Only by experiencing would she find out the truth of what they were saying to her.

Conway Patterson stepped back and leaned one elbow upon a high fitted shelf. He watched as the man in black took over the proceedings. But he never ceased to stare at her. He held her with his eyes, and began to speak as Christopher busied himself with the clothes.

'I understand Taras had reason to punish you. Is that right?'

Toni let her eyes fall and hung her head. Her cheeks reddened, this time from embarrassment. 'Yes.'

'Bend over. Let me see your stripes.'

Despite her determination to take everything handed to her, she flushed more brightly as she raised her head. Defiance threatened to override demureness.

'Do as you're told, girl!' Christopher took a handful of her hair in one hand and pulled her to her feet, swung her round, then bent her head down to the bed.

She squealed. The fine links that hung from her neck collar and her bracelets tinkled lightly.

'Shut up!' Christopher snapped, and smacked her behind with the flat of one gloved palm.

'Open your legs,' Conway ordered. 'I want to see your quim peering out from beneath those stripes. I want to see which is redder, your hair or your behind.'

Before she could obey, Christopher got his own leg between hers, and with his foot pushed one of her feet away from the other. Then he stepped back so Conway could view her behind.

There was silence for a moment. She could feel their eyes upon her, burning into her flesh as much as the whip had done.

'Are they warm?' Conway asked.

Was she supposed to answer that?

She wasn't given the chance. Christopher's leather-gloved hand ran over the surface of her bottom.

'Yes. Taras has done a very good job. I can feel the heat of her dear little bottom even with my glove on.'

He chuckled. Conway chuckled too and seemed pleased.

But how was Conway taking it? Toni wondered. What was he feeling while he was looking at her? Would he now do more than he had done while she'd been in the cupboard? Would he take her and ram his hard rod into her most plush portal?

She heard movement, knew Conway had moved, then felt the coolness of his hand run over each of her buttocks in turn.

She moaned, wriggling beneath the warmth of his palm and the feather-light touch of his fingers. There was no stopping arousal returning to her loins.

'Is the little bitch wet?' Conway asked Christopher.

Christopher's fingers were still tangled in her hair.

Now, she endured his other hand running through her legs, and his thickest gloved finger pushing into her wet portal. There was a slurping of juices, a slick running of wetness down the inside of her thighs.

'Very!' Christopher exclaimed. 'Shall I bring her off?'

'Yes. Now.' Conway's words sounded drunk with power. He was in charge of her sexual needs, and there was nothing she could do about it.

She moaned, writhed against her tangled hair, and jerked against the prying thumb and invading finger of the gloved hand.

As she writhed, Conway stood behind her, studying her striped behind which undulated unashamedly on Christopher's delving fingers.

She rode Christopher's fingers, lost in the throes of her own pleasure, breasts slapping gently back and forth as her climax rushed from that pivotal point and all over her body.

Just as she reached that pinnacle of ecstasy, she felt the bare hand of Conway slap against her bucking behind. She cried out, partly in delight, and partly in confusion. Again and again his hand rose and fell on her bare behind. But she could not stop herself bucking against Christopher's intruding finger and thumb, could not stop crying out in delight until a climax had been achieved, one that held at its heart both pleasure and pain.

Breathless and satisfied, she smiled beneath the mass of her tumbling hair that fell to either side of her face like opulent curtains. She had endured, and she had enjoyed – just as Venetia had instructed her.

Christopher, whose fingers were still entangled in her hair, spun her round so that once again she sat on the bed. At last, he let her hair go.

Toni looked up at his cold yet enticing eyes that appeared to be colourless, though they might have once been blue. She shivered and lowered her gaze as he took a blunt-ended black whip from his black belt.

Not another whipping; not so soon after the other, she thought to herself.

'Put on the clothes,' he said.

Tap, tap, tap went the whip against his gloved hand as he stood before her.

She shuddered, rose, and began to do as ordered.

The skirt was even shorter than she had thought. The now pink cheeks of her bottom were clearly visible at the back. A vestige of fiery pubic hair was just as visible at the front.

She looked from one man to the other: Conway was regarding her in a contemplative and rather far-off kind of way; Christopher watched her coldly, his mouth tight, his whip incessantly tapping the palm of his hand.

'And the top, girl. Now!'

The whip whacked more sharply against his palm.

She speeded up her movements, well aware that there was more than a fair chance of that whip beating against her own flesh, which was still uncovered and entirely vulnerable.

The top had no sleeves and the neckline was low-slung so that it passed beneath her breasts rather than covered them. She looked down at them, so perfectly formed, obscenely available, and so delightfully desirous.

Her breathing increased. Incensed with her own arousal, she watched as her breasts rose and fell more quickly.

Unwilling or unable to recoil, she saw the black-gloved fingers reach for her nipples and tweak each in turn.

'There,' said Christopher with obvious satisfaction. 'Now they are proud. They are without shame before our eyes and beneath our touch.'

She trembled and her eyes glittered. What was the purpose of all this?

Conway answered her question. 'We have been invited to dinner, my dear girl. My mother commands. I – and my brother – obey. I will take you there dressed like this, dressed as I want you dressed. I will show you off as being mine, not my brother's. I will show him your red bottom and tell him how much you enjoy the rough treatment, just as she did, that other Antonia – the woman who was the first woman for both of us. I will tell him that I was right and you preferred the rough ways, just as she did. That will make him mad, and I will enjoy that very much.'

He sneered as he said it and, partly due to the picture he had painted, and partly to the way he had said it, it sent shivers down her spine. Now, she was in no doubt of the situation between the two brothers. Something in her reminded them of someone else with whom she shared her name as well as her looks. But she couldn't really understand all the undercurrents involved.

'Come on,' said Christopher as he clipped a chain lead into the link of her neck collar. 'You're wanted on deck.'

Conway followed on behind.

Up on deck, the afternoon was fading into evening. The sun was blood-red and diving into the horizon, and the moon was faint but ready to take over.

'Make ready!' shouted Conway.

Christopher tugged her forward to the pulpit, the narrow platform which stands forward above the bow of the boat.

'Kneel down,' he ordered.

She knelt on the criss-cross fretwork of the pulpit and braced her hands on the wooden rails to her side. There was little between her and the sea.

Christopher fixed the chain from her necklet to the very apex of the 'V' shape. He did the same to her bracelets so that her hands held the rail at each side of her. To all intents and purposes, she was their figurehead, their fair maid before the mast.

Then, as the engine came into life and the crew let go of the lines, *Enchantress* began to move away from the quay.

Wind in her hair, Toni took deep breaths and fought

221 at bottom center

to allay her fears. In this position, she was the prow head of the ship, the figure of fortune up front who divided the waves before the boat did.

As the engine died and the sails cracked loose, she flexed her fingers against the smoothness of the wood. Her eyes scanned the sea and sky. Hopefully, both would stay kind and calm. As it was, the spray was already kissing her breasts as they turned into the wind. She would get wet. If the sea got rougher, she could get a lot wetter.

With the coming of the moon, the sea turned from green to silver. Her flesh, too, took on the soft glow of its kind light. Sea spray sprinkled her with a myriad drops of trembling moisture. Each drop was kissed by the iridescence of the moon. She must look, she thought, as if she were covered with a coating of seed pearls.

The ketch lunged more energetically as they reached the widest expanse of exposed sea between the two islands.

The prow dived more deeply into the waves. She gasped as she was dipped to waist level, then gasped again as the yacht's course was adjusted, the prow reared upwards, and her nipples responded to the coolness of the breeze.

Soon, the worst expanse of water had been travelled. The harbour lights of Venetia's island were right ahead. Up on the hill, the Red Tower stood proud against the night sky.

Somehow, just seeing it there gave Toni a surge of relief and excitement. It wasn't that she was afraid of Conway; it was just that she knew what to expect from Venetia and Emira. Conway and his brother were unknown quantities.

She also knew that there were questions to be answered and, up at the Red Tower, she just might get them.

Chapter Fifteen

*U*nable to settle to the fact that he was to face his brother at his mother's dinner table, Philippe had walked off into the darkness of the island.

He took off his jacket as he walked, hooked his finger beneath its collar, and slung it over his shoulder. By itself, it was not enough to ease his discomfort. Impatiently, he tugged at his tie, loosened it, then undid the top button of his shirt.

He was hot. Not because the night was hot, but because just the thought of his half-brother made him so.

The road was dusty, and although he knew he was heading back to his boat, he didn't really want to go there. The walk was a long one, but he needed the sea and its stinging air to clear his mind.

Behind him, he heard the soft sound of tyres turning on dust.

'Do you need the car, sir?'

Philippe wasn't going to stop. He was being urged on by his own anxiety. And yet, the quicker he got to the sea, the better.

He reached for the door handle. 'Take me down to the jetty, Emilio.'

'Yes, sir.'

The car purred off and, as the night shapes raced gently past them, Philippe began to calm down. Via the rear-view mirror, his eyes met those of his driver.

'I could do with some fresh air and I could well do without seeing my brother tonight.'

He turned his attention back to the passing scene. If he hadn't, he might have seen the flicker in his driver's eyes, then perhaps he would have asked him what was wrong. But he didn't.

Emilio, who had worked for the family for a long time, didn't like to see him overwrought. He had to say something. First, he licked his lips as he considered how to say it and the consequences of saying it. It was no good. No matter what Venetia might say, he had to go ahead.

'Your mother's not very pleased with your brother. He's taken something that was destined for you.'

Philippe stopped staring out at the sleeping island, and turned his eyes back to his driver. Quizzically, he frowned. 'What are you talking about?'

Emilio cleared his throat before he spoke. Venetia could well punish him for this. But he was used to that and, anyway, he enjoyed the sting of the whip across his rear.

'Antonia Yardley. Your mother engaged her as crew on *Sea Witch* while you were away in Padua. She thought she would be good for you. Your brother stole her away – or at least, your friend Andrea stole her and handed her over to your brother.'

Philippe leaned forward. He'd taken in what Emilio had told him, yet he knew instinctively that there had to be a reason for his mother procuring the girl and for his brother stealing her.

'What's she like?' His voice trembled as he said it. His fingernails dug into the back of Emilio's seat.

'Quite beautiful. Yes,' said Emilio as though he were calling her to mind, bit by delicious bit. 'Quite beautiful.

Unusually so. She's about twenty-three or so, and she has red hair and green eyes.'

Emilio's eyes flitted from the road to Philippe's reflection. He was aware that Philippe's classically handsome features had become frozen. 'Mister Philippe? Are you all right?'

Philippe did not reply.

'Take me to where my brother moors *Enchantress*.'

'Yes sir. I will.'

The rest of the journey was silent. Philippe continued to stare out of the car window, but he did not see the dark shadows, the bright moon or the alternate patterns of silver and black thrown by rows of dark green cypresses. He only saw the woman of his dreams and of his past. The green eyes were bright as chips of uncut emeralds. Her hair was as rich and red as an English autumn. On top of that, her name was Antonia. The coincidence seemed too contrived to be true. Had his mother orchestrated all this entirely for him, or was she truly a double for the woman who had led him from adolescence to manhood?

Only when he saw her and got to know her would he know for sure. But Conway had intervened. Conway always intervened, and always goaded Philippe. That's what he had done when Philippe had been careless enough to say what a gentle lover Antonia had been. Conway had laughed and made fun of him, had told him that she was decadent, utterly depraved. What's more, he had made a point of proving it.

Conway had led him through the depths of the Red Tower and into the dungeon. There his brother had bound him and forced him to watch as that first Antonia had lowered herself on a thick male member of some rough peasant from the village. On Conway's instructions, another had divided the rounded cheeks of her behind and pushed his mighty member into her tightest entrance.

Even now, he could remember the priapic proportions

225

of the man, and the obscene swaying of his drooping balls as he thrust in and out of her.

Conway provided the last action to the tableau. Philippe remembered him smiling down at Antonia, and her smiling back up at him, her eyes glazed as she beheld Conway's own magnificent penis. How red and luscious her lips had been, and how much more when her tongue had licked them, then flicked out at the bulbous crown of the youthful rod.

He had wanted to scream – he remembered that clearly. But he couldn't. His half-brother had gagged him and tied him firmly so that he could see all that went on, though those taking part could not see him.

With painful clarity, he remembered her taking Conway in, and although he felt angry at what Conway was subjecting him to, he could not turn his gaze away.

But his own personal picture of the woman had been shattered. Like an icon broken into many bits of glass, his view of her was shattered and yet she continued to haunt his dreams.

Enchantress was about a mile out when they got to the quay.

Philippe got out of the car and, with the water lapping just a foot or two below him, stood at the edge of the quay and looked out to sea. Gradually, the tang of the sea cleared his head, but did not wipe out his bitter memories.

The white of the masthead light rose and fell with the swell of the sea. The red and green of the port and starboard lights bobbed up and down depending on which side was dipping and which rising.

Mesmerised by his thoughts as much as by what he was seeing, Philippe continued to stare at the triangle of moving lights. Aided by the light of the moon, he saw the sails being reefed in around the quarter-mile mark, then heard the engine spring into life. No good skipper came in on sails to a mooring and, if he was nothing else, his half-brother was most definitely a good skipper.

As the ketch turned from beam on to face the shore, his jaw tightened. Now it seemed as though his legs had become made of ice. In the light of the moon he saw a face and figure he thought he'd never see again.

He could not move from where he was. His hands hung useless at his side, and so firmly did he clench his jaw that it felt as though his face were made of marble.

Enchantress had its very own figurehead. Not one made of wood and painted in garish colours like those on the prows of high-ended sailing barques in years gone by. Oh no. This one, chosen by his brother, was made of flesh and blood, and the striking form and colouring of that flesh and blood was well-remembered.

His heart beat a hefty tattoo against his ribcage. Touched by the glow of the moon, her skin glistened, almost like glass.

He saw her hair flying around her head, tossed by wind, sprinkled by spray. In the darkness, it looked black. When the wind and the moonlight caught it, it appeared to be on fire. But it was her eyes he wanted to see. Even now, just thinking about them made his penis stand proud of his aching loins. Such sensations had visited him many times in the still of the night when she had come to him in dreams. Now she was here again, and she was with his brother.

He had to see her close up. He had to get her alone. But how?

'Emilio,' he said quietly. 'Go hide yourself and the car.'

Emilio looked from sea to Philippe, but did not argue.

Once the car had rumbled out of sight, Philippe stepped into the shadows. He watched as *Enchantress* was berthed, and from where he watched he saw his dream personified.

She was just as he remembered. Her skin was wet, but translucent. Her hair was red beneath the light thrown by the mooring lights. He saw her toss her head and look towards the interior of the island. It was then that

227

he saw her eyes: they were green, and in that moment his mind was made up.

There was laughter coming from on board his brother's ketch. He could hear members of the crew talking about what Conway would do with the girl later before either Venetia or Philippe could get their hands on her. There were also comments about what they had already done. Philippe could not help but be affected by what he was hearing. His cock rose more proudly.

The laughter was followed by silence as his half-brother went below to get himself ready to present himself at the Red Tower.

The crew also were getting ready for an evening's pleasure, though they weren't likely to be required to wear formal attire for what they had in mind. There was little time to waste. Philippe came out of hiding, and sprinted towards the prow of *Enchantress*.

Toni, who by now was feeling drained of energy, saw him, opened her mouth, then shut it again. Their eyes locked, then gently, his lips coaxing her flesh with welcome warmth, he sucked at each nipple. It was so pleasant and so completely unexpected that Toni moaned, though quietly so as not to disturb her captors. Something about this man told her not to be afraid.

In that one strange moment, she felt like a goddess of the sea receiving adoration from one of her followers.

Restricted as she was, she managed to bend her head to rub her nose in his hair so that his scent filled her mind. Then, as he lovingly sucked at each breast again, she kissed the nape of his neck where dark hair curled over hard flesh.

Noiselessly, his lips still on her breasts, he undid her chains.

She was stiff after being in the same position for so long, but she managed to unbend her limbs and reach down to be taken in his arms. Her bare breasts were crushed against his shirt as she slid to the ground. They were wet, and her nipples were hard from their continuous contact with cold water.

For the briefest of moments, Philippe held her tight against him, then groaned. The warmth of her flesh seemed to diffuse through his clothes and he smelt the captivating mix of woman and sea as he buried his face in her hair. This woman was the real thing. She was no longer a dream or the residue of youthful memories: she was here and her breasts were beautifully naked and pressed tight against his chest.

But there was no time to lose. Tightly, he took her hand. Then, both together, and silently, they ran through the dark shadows until the quay was left behind.

Padding on bare feet, and still with her hand locked in his, she went with him through the lemon grove where the smell of the ripening fruit hung heavy in the air.

Moonlight dappled the grass beneath the trees which rustled as they sped over it. Breathless, they both came to a halt, and Toni, for the first time, had the chance to look into the face of the man who had rescued her.

He was staring down into her eyes, and she was vaguely aware of his hands running up and down her back. She was in no doubt as to who he was.

'I presume you are Philippe Salvatore.'

He nodded, and as he did so, his eyes dropped to her naked bosom which heaved with each breath she took.

'You rescued me.'

He nodded again, his breath quickening, his eyes still on her breasts. His palms were warm and moist against her shoulder-blades, his fingers firm against the long indentation of her spine as his hands travelled to encompass her behind. He covered each buttock with his hands.

'Thank you.' She said it in a gloriously gentle way like a fast-escaping breath.

He raised his gaze from her breasts and looked directly into her eyes. There was adoration in that look. But there was also something else. His voice trembled when he spoke. 'Emilio said your name was Antonia.'

She nodded. 'Yes,' she whispered.

The lemon trees shivered in a momentary breeze. In the space between that breeze and the next, he bent his head and kissed her.

His lips were as warm as his hands. Even his chest was warm against her cool breasts.

They parted breathless, but their parting was only brief.

He brought his hands to her shoulders, then pulled the sleeves of her top down to her elbows, thus pinning them to her sides.

She groaned and moved her body against his. His breath was light against her face as his lips travelled to her neck, then on to the hollow of her throat. From there, it travelled on. Gently, he lowered his head to her breasts and kissed each nipple. As he did so, he pulled her top down to her waist.

He dotted fine kisses over her belly whilst his busy hands pulled both her top and her skirt down to her ankles. Then he straightened up. 'The grass is cool,' he said against her ear, 'but it is soft. Very soft. Would you like to lie down?' His voice seemed to tremble like that of an inexperienced youth as he said it.

She looked down at the grass, then back at him.

He was undoing his shirt. His eyes, which filled her with longing, never left hers.

With a smile, she sank to the ground and, like a reclining de Milo, lay on her side with her elbow bent and her chin resting on her hand.

Slowly, his shirt left his body. Although the moon patterned his bronzed flesh with a mix of silver light and dancing leaves, she could see that his skin was smooth and taut over the hardness of his muscles.

Softly, his zip was undone and his trousers pushed down over his trim hips, firm thighs, and well-defined calves. He was naked. Beautiful. Animal, and completely masculine!

She could smell his nakedness; smell the sweetness of his body, and view its supple texture. He was undeniably beautiful, and she wanted him. Desire rising within her loins made her bring up her knee so that her inner thigh pressed against her pussy.

Philippe was one of the most beautiful men she had ever seen. Her tongue ran over the dryness of her lips as she savoured his body.

There was a noble look to his face, and honed perfection to his body. He was not a heavy man by any means, but there was an athletic pronouncement in each muscle, superb undulation in his arms, thighs and the strength of his calves.

In ripe splendour, his penis rose long and hard against his stomach. 'Show me yourself,' he breathed. 'Just like you used to.'

She frowned. 'But you've never met me before.'

He didn't seem to be listening, or perhaps it was that he didn't want to hear.

It didn't matter. She ran her eyes over him. He was a feast she could not deny herself.

Slowly, she let her own hand follow her curves to her hip. Once it reached that flowing contour, she lifted one leg and exposed her sex to his view.

He groaned, and his penis leapt against her.

She looked down the length of her own body, her narrow waist, her flowing curves. Alternate patterns of light and shade moved incessantly over each flowing contour with the rising of the breeze and the rustling of the leaves.

The scent of lemon added an extra piquancy to the whole scene, and the grass around her lightly tickled her tingling flesh.

Penis rearing with each fresh throb of blood, he knelt between her legs and gazed in rapture at the delicacy so brazenly offered. He rested his hands on the inside of her thighs and breathed in her musk and her arousal. 'It's just as I remember it,' he said in a hushed and honeyed voice. 'So firm, yet so soft. So frightening, and so compelling.'

He reached out. His fingers delved into her pubic hair, then gently, as though tracing vaguely remembered lines from memory, he ran one finger down each favoured lip.

She hummed with pleasure, then mewed and circled her hips as Philippe used both sets of fingers to hold her open so he could gaze more fully on her treasure within.

She threw back her head as his tongue licked the softness of her thighs before running along each of her labia and dabbing gently at her freed clitoris.

One hand still cupping her head, she covered one breast with the other hand. She squeezed it, pinched at her yearning nipple, then squeezed harder as his tongue invaded her warm portal.

She tightened her legs around his head, and felt his hair slightly damp against her thighs. He was trapped there, just as his brother had trapped her. He was pleasuring her, yet she was giving him nothing.

She opened her eyes and looked down at his dark head so willingly trapped between her thighs. His mouth and tongue continued to lick and suck at her as though she were some exotic fruit that is available just once in a lifetime. She groaned as shivers of delight coursed over her skin, then, as the moon fell behind a cloud and the dappled light of the lemon grove gave way to complete darkness, she fell back on the grass.

She relaxed her grip on his head, and as his mouth travelled up from her sex, his tongue explored her body.

With deft and generous licks, he pressed her pubic hair into slick, wet strips. Wet yet avid, his tongue licked over her belly. At her navel, he paused and dipped in the tip of his tongue.

When he at last came to her breasts, he traced their shape with his tongue, then sucked at one of them while his hand fondled the other.

232

At the exact moment of his lips kissing hers, the head of his penis nudged through her divide, and without help from him found its way into her vagina.

She gasped, mewed against him and raised her hips to meet him.

This man who covered her was hard, soft-skinned and gloriously male.

His pubic hair grated against her as he thrust into her, retreated, then thrust again.

Her hips bucked against him, her cries lost in her own hair as she turned her head from side to side, lost in her own delirious delight.

Again and again the whole weight of his body was brought to bear on that one all-devouring rod, that supreme tool that ploughed her furrow, turning her nether lips aside as metal does the earth. Like the earth, her flesh clove to him, then tumbled aside in glorious submission.

As she jerked to meet his body, his hands left her breasts and dived beneath her arching back, then bur-rowed downwards to cover her behind in two easy handfuls.

Now his hands guided her powerful exertions. With each buck, he raised her higher against him. As though her body was purely an extension of his, she followed his lead and let her own hands slide down his back then rest on his buttocks which were hard-muscled and tensed with each thrust he made.

As his hands gripped and raised her against him, hers dug into his bottom, pulling him against her so that he thrust deeply and powerfully into her innermost heart.

Rising with the wind, their cries mingled as the giddy trembles of orgasm overtook them.

Their thrusting one against the other continued until the last vestige of ecstasy was gone. Then they clung together, one body against the other, one mouth against the other's ear. They were spent, but only for the moment. This situation and his cock, Toni told herself, would rise again.

As her breasts continued to rise and fall breathlessly against him, she wondered about the person whom she so resembled, and what kind of powerful event could haunt him as it did.

She stroked his hair as one does a child, and sensed he was dozing off into sleep and also into dreams. 'I knew you would come back,' he murmured.

Somehow, she didn't want to say that she wasn't the woman he was dreaming about. There was a magic in being someone else. It was as though she were living some fantasy that she could enter and exit at will. On the other hand, it wasn't in her to lie.

'I'm very glad to be here,' she said softly, though she wasn't sure he had heard. Nevertheless, she continued, her voice as dreamlike as her eyes. 'Very glad indeed. So much has happened between here and London. So much, that I find it hard to believe at times that I am still me.'

He laughed at that. It was low and gentle and sweet against her ear. The whole night, she decided, had become warm and gentle.

Beyond the canopy of trees, she could see the stars, the moon and the blackness of the sky. Philippe's head was warm and heavy against her breast, and his hair was silky beneath her touch. He slept like a child dreaming some forgotten dream, and murmured loving words in his sleep.

She smiled to herself. Whatever he wanted her to be, she would be. Whoever he wanted her to be, she would be that, too.

A short while ago, she had kicked off the traces of an old life and come seeking adventure. Perhaps, in these islands and with this family, she had found it.

Chapter Sixteen

*S*ituated in what had once been a crusader lookout post, the dining-hall at the Red Tower had vaulted ceilings of immense height. At one end of the hall was a gallery with stone pillars that curved to gracious archways. At each end of the gallery, a set of stairs, the colour of fresh honeycomb, curved down like two relaxing arms.

At the other end of the hall hung a huge tapestry depicting a naked and voluptuous Helen of Troy surrounded by her many admirers, all with bulging biceps, but small appendages.

Suits of armour stood like living sentinels between square buttresses, their stiff and dead hands leaning on upright pikes which, judging by their carved uprights and ornate heads, had been fashioned more for ceremonial use than mortal combat.

Shafts of sunset gave lustre to the stone walls and spangled the stirred air with glinting dust motes.

A long table had been covered in a cloth of Italian lace, and on it were silver candlesticks which were noticeably Baroque and matched the cutlery. The crockery was white Dresden, and the wine goblets were seventeenth-century Venetian glass, hand-blown and clear as ice.

Heavy cedarwood chairs with satin seats and lyre-shaped backs were set in equidistant precision from each other. So were the cutlery, the glassware and the plates. Everything sparkled. Everything was perfect.

Just as perfectly presented, Venetia wore a dress of silver and mauvish grey chiffon that was soft and swirling and kissed her ankles. Its collar was stiff and high, and framed her head like an oyster shell does its pearl. Glittering streaks of raised embroidery ran outwards from its base like the rays of the sun, except that these rays were purple. At its centre was her face, her brown eyes, her high cheekbones and a mouth that had tasted many sensualities over the kind and passionate years.

She was smiling as she held her arms outstretched to her youngest son. 'My darling, darling, Conway. How are you, my dear boy? How are you?'

She crushed him to her breast and her hand stroked his neck.

Drifts of soft material fell away to just above her elbows. A silver bracelet coiled like a snake up one arm.

Courteously, Conway kissed first her turned cheek, then the other.

There was the hint of a ritual in it rather than affection. Perhaps it might appear offhand, even cold, to someone who did not know this family. But Venetia loved her sons very deeply. It was just that at her age she saved physical demonstrations for her darling retainers, Pietro and Carlos, who catered for her every need.

On this particular occasion, she eyed her son with a little more than sheer motherly love. For once, she looked a little annoyed with him, although she still smiled. However, it was a fixed smile, one she used for getting what she wanted.

Her bejewelled hand remained on her son's shoulder, her fingers gripping him more tightly as if she were loath to let him go. 'And what have you been up to?' she asked.

He tensed. His mother's voice was smooth as silk, but he was not fooled. Venetia Salvatore, the name she had retained from her first marriage, was clever.

He countered her deviousness with his own.

Tossing his luxuriant curls, he grinned. His earring jangled merrily, and his white teeth flashed in a sudden smile. And yet, there was a disagreeable glint in his eyes. He was as suspicious of his mother as she was of him. The girl had gone. He had discovered that before he'd left his boat to come here, and the knowledge rankled. His own mother was his chief suspect. Antonia's disappearance must have been her doing but, of course, he wouldn't ask her. Instead, he adopted an air of confidence.

'I went in to see that lawyer fellow just as you ordered, and saw my brother at the same time. But of course, you already know that.'

'Yes. I know that. I instructed Guido myself. It is a mother's duty to get her quarrelling children to make friends.'

She still smiled, but said nothing else. He knew she was waiting for him to continue. Of course he would continue. But he would not tell her *everything*.

He took a deep breath before he spoke. 'I was entertaining. A little something special came my way.'

'A woman?'

'Yes. A woman.'

He wasn't lying. He didn't mention who she was, but it could as easily have been Andrea as Toni.

'I see,' said his mother, whose countenance had remained immobile. 'I have a woman here, too.'

Conway started. Again, all the things he had been going to do to that woman Antonia came back into his mind. His face felt suddenly warm. He knew his cheeks had turned pink, and it wasn't due to the sunset.

'You do? Anyone I know?' He tried to make his question sound casual, disinterested. It didn't seem to work.

Her smile changed to a knowing grin.

He blinked and cleared his throat before he asked again. 'Who is it?'

This time, he sounded more urgent.

Slowly, his mother turned from him. 'Follow me,' she ordered.

As her heels clattered over the smooth stone floor, and the lustrous material of her dress swayed around her, he clenched his fists. But he followed. He had to follow.

She led him under one of the sweeping staircases of the gallery and through a dark wooden door that was studded with iron nails.

She opened it, went through, and he followed.

The change in light was dramatic. The glare of polished glass made him raise his palm before his eyes. The room was octagonal and the walls totally covered with mirrors.

There were no windows, no blood-red glare from a setting sun, and the room was cool because it was situated in the base of the tower.

Sudden movement seemed to bring the mirrored walls to life. And yet, they had no life of their own. The movement was only reflected. In the centre of the room, a lone and naked figure, arms outstretched above her head, hung suspended from iron chains that were fastened to an iron hook hanging from the ceiling.

Conway gasped as he recognised the blue eyes and tumbling blonde hair. He could not help saying her name. 'Andrea!'

He wasn't just surprised to see her there. After all, he had been expecting someone else. But the way she was stretched accentuated the round ripeness of her breasts, the concave dip of her stomach, and the sprouting of her pubic hair.

'Conway!' she called.

'Silence!' Venetia watched the pair closely. Now her suspicions were confirmed, and she was not pleased about it.

238

'I don't deserve this!' shouted Andrea.

'Silence!' repeated Venetia, her cheeks reddening as her voice echoed around the room.

'I did it for you, Conway,' wheedled Andrea. 'Honestly, darling. I did it for you.'

'Liar!' cried Venetia. 'You did it for yourself. You knew how Philippe would react to Antonia, at least, you thought you did. You thought you knew how both my sons would react. You didn't care about them. You were jealous of your own position. You cared only about yourself. Now, tell me who helped you take her from me. Tell me!'

Conway stood helpless, mouth open.

Venetia was suddenly all action.

Andrea was breathing heavily, her eyes following what Venetia was doing as best she could.

From a silver bucket that stood on a black iron tripod, Venetia took a whip. It had a silver handle that shone brightly and a tip that dripped water over the white and silver of the gleaming tiles.

'No!' shouted Andrea, her eyes wide, and her hair cascading down her back.

'Yes!' exclaimed Venetia, and raised her arm.

Conway stood transfixed. He could stop Venetia if he wanted to. But he didn't want to. Andrea looked so lovely, her long, slim body writhing this way and that in an attempt to avoid what was to come. And how her eyes widened as she craned her neck to watch the whip on its descent.

He felt a tightness in his stomach, a rush of blood to his groin, and his heart pounded in his chest.

'Now,' exclaimed Venetia, her diaphanous gown swirling like a rain-filled cloud as she raised the hand that held the silver-handled whip. 'Tell me who helped you take Antonia away.'

'No!' exclaimed Andrea, her eyes staring directly at Conway. 'No, I won't.'

The whip sang through the air to be multiplied many

times by the row of mirrors. It landed with a sharp and stinging sound. As it landed, Andrea cried out and spun on her chain.

Conway's penis surged more strongly as his eyes fastened on the livid red streak that crossed her once-white behind.

Again the whip whispered through the air. The slender body writhed to avoid the stinging kiss, but again the whip caught her proud posterior and another red line joined the first.

Venetia stayed her hand. With taloned fingers, she cupped the girl's face in her free hand. 'Now will you tell me?' she asked.

Andrea, sweat clamping her hair to her face, shook her head.

'Well,' said Venetia. 'Then you'll have to have some more, won't you? And in order that you don't avoid the stroke of the whip, my son will hold you more firmly. Conway!'

Conway, mesmerised by the vision of the glorious Andrea, who was so naked and so stretched that every curve was exaggerated, jumped to immediate attention.

He stepped forward, aware that his penis was fighting against the zip of his neat black trousers that he was wearing purely to please his mother. Briefly, he gazed into Andrea's eyes before he turned his back on her, bent from the waist, and walked backwards until her feet were off the ground and she was spread along his back.

He reached for her waist and, by holding her there, she was trapped. Now she could not avoid Venetia's blows and Conway, for his part, could enjoy the press of her naked body against him.

Twice more he heard the whip rise then land sharply across the recumbent's backside. He felt her twitch above him and heard her moan in his ear.

Venetia asked her the same question again.

Again, Andrea did not answer.

He had the impression that Andrea was becoming

heavier, as though she herself was purposely or deliberately pressing her body against him.

He was also aware of her increasing breathlessness.

For his own part, he could feel his cock becoming painful as it beat against the front of his trousers.

Twice more the whip sang. Andrea yelped like a whipped dog. 'My bottom's getting sore,' she moaned.

Conway managed to look over his shoulder at her. He hid his grin from her and his mother. There was an odd light in Andrea's eyes and, although her cheeks were tear-stained, her moans were of ecstasy rather than anguish.

'Then tell,' whispered Conway.

Andrea did not answer, but she looked at him sideways with deviousness rather than wickedness.

'Will you tell me, girl?' cried Venetia as her own cool hand tested the warmth of Andrea's red behind.

'Not you,' moaned Andrea suddenly. 'I won't tell you. But I will tell Conway.'

Conway was aware of his mother's hesitation. So was Andrea. It was an outside interference which forced the decision.

One of the mirrors – the one that covered the nail-studded door – opened and Emira entered.

His eyes were wide and he looked agitated. Apart from that, his gold lamé evening dress and four-inch heels suited his dark skin very well indeed. Gold and black earrings dangled from each ear, and gold eye-shadow glittered in the wide wings from his eyes.

'Madame! I need to talk to you.'

Venetia frowned. 'Can it not wait?'

'No,' exclaimed Emira, glancing swiftly at the naked girl and her pink bottom that was so well-presented and restrained on Conway's back. 'No, Madame. It cannot wait.'

Venetia sighed, and after tapping the whip against the palm of her hand, passed it to her son.

Slowly, he let Andrea slide from his back and regain her feet.

'Give her three more before she tells you – *if* she tells you. She needs it, the selfish little madam!'

In a haze of grey chiffon, Venetia left the room and Emira followed.

Andrea began to laugh soft and low.

Conway looked at her.

Provocatively, she wriggled her full and feminine bottom which now glowed the same red as the sunset.

'Conway, darling. How pleased I am to see you. Are you going to undo these chains of mine, or are you going to push your beautiful penis into me first?'

She half-closed her eyes and licked her ripe lips as she said it.

He smiled, then came up behind her, his bare chest warm and hard against her back.

She completely closed her eyes and let her hair muffle his face. He kissed the soft hollow between her neck and her shoulder-blades. The hand not holding the whip reached round and covered her breast.

'That feels good,' she said in a low and sensual voice. 'Are you going to give me more?'

'Yes,' he said throatily. 'I am going to. I'm going to give you more of what you had and better. And all the time, you will be chained up and will be able to do nothing about it. Great, don't you think?'

'Marvellous,' she murmured, and Conway knew she really meant it.

'But first,' he said, his fingers fiercely squeezing one nipple so that she cried out, 'I want to know who it was who helped you. Am I right in thinking it was Marie?'

'You might be.'

He squeezed her nipple that much more fiercely. 'Am I right?' he asked.

Andrea winced, but then smiled.

Knowingly, he smiled back. 'So,' he said. 'You like pain, you hot little bitch!'

242

Venetia's laying on of the whip had all been in vain. She wouldn't like knowing that, he thought to himself, she wouldn't like someone not conforming to her rules and personal ideas. Still, he was alone, and this, he decided, was his chance to take advantage of it.

'Fair enough,' he said suddenly, and moved away from her. 'Then I won't bother you any more.'

'But you were going to give me more,' Andrea cried out in panic. 'You were going to give me your cock while I was tied up like this!'

'Then tell me the truth. Now! Otherwise, you get nothing!'

Andrea hesitated for the briefest of moments, then sighed. 'All right,' she said. 'I'll tell you. It was Marie who helped me.'

He nodded, his smile lop-sided and vaguely triumphant. 'Fine. I thought it might be.'

It didn't really matter to him who had taken Antonia and brought her to him. The person that mattered most was the one who had taken her from his boat *Enchantress*. Who was it, and where was the girl now? She wasn't here. Not at the Red Tower. That much at least was obvious.

But he had an immediate and pressing need. His penis was almost painful now, and Andrea was available and more than willing.

Slowly, and with both hands, one still holding the whip, he undid his flies. His rod sprang out, hard, handsome and totally demanding.

Eyes wide and full of wonder, Andrea squealed with delight and obligingly opened her legs. Her breasts began to rise and fall with her quickening breath. 'Oh, please,' she moaned, 'please, please, please.'

It was all she could say.

With a smile on his face and his cock throbbing, Conway approached her. The whip was still in his hand. 'First,' he said with undisguised glee, 'I'm going to give you the three strokes Venetia ordered.'

'Really?' There was enthusiasm in Andrea's voice and in the way she closed her legs and stuck out her bottom. Leaving him in no doubt that she wanted him to whip her, she wriggled her behind. The act was brazen and blatantly exciting. Besides that, her bottom was well-shaped, each rounded buttock kissing gently against its sister as though promising they would never be parted.

Conway was transfixed. The round cheeks were even redder now than before. Tentatively, he reached out and felt the heat of her flesh with his fingertips. She trembled beneath his touch, and his cock rose in response.

He covered one cheek with his whole hand. The heat of her flesh warmed his palm. He did the same to the other, and felt the tightness in his stomach and the hardness of his prick increase.

'Please,' moaned Andrea. 'Oh, please. Don't keep me waiting.'

He didn't answer. He tucked the whip under one arm, and used both hands to prise open her buttocks.

She groaned in delight as he used his finger to test the tightness of her smallest orifice.

Around his finger's intrusion, it expanded and contracted as though it were a living thing that needed feeding.

While still holding open her cheeks, he pushed his finger in that much further without any sympathy for her protest or discomfort.

But Andrea did not protest. She only groaned and seemed to flop on her chain as though she were made of nothing but rags. Her nether mouth tightened around him as though it were sucking him in.

'I will have that, too,' he said in a husky voice.

'Please do,' she replied. 'Oh, please do!'

'But first,' he said, 'you have three more stripes to receive.'

'Yes,' she murmured. 'Yes.'

He took his finger from her, took the whip from under his arm, and laced it three times across her behind.

Each time she cried out, and his eyes grew bright. There was pleasure in those cries as well as pain.

Her bottom was now truly red and extremely enticing.

Conway could wait no longer. Throwing the whip to one side, he grasped her hips and raised her feet from off the ground. Her wrists were still fastened over her head, so he was free to take her in any way he fancied.

As she thrust her bottom towards him, he pushed his member into her anus, bridged its barrier, then felt her muscles close over him and draw him in.

Around them, the mirrors reflected their coupling, the heaving of his behind, the eclipsing of hers. Ahead of him, he could see her face, eyes closed in rapture, mouth open and breasts swinging as she hung on her chain.

And he could see himself, face contorted as he drove himself into her, his hands gripping her hips so tightly that, when he moved them, he left behind livid red marks.

He gave no account to what satisfaction she might have been seeking. From what he'd seen so far, Andrea gained most of her pleasure from other sources. Andrea liked pain, liked being whipped.

With one last fierce thrust, he came.

She cried out, and once it was all over, he released her hips and let her feet back down to the floor.

'That was fantastic,' she said breathlessly.

'Fantastic,' he repeated, though it was not better or worse than anything he had experienced before.

He tidied himself up, zipped up his trousers and smoothed back his hair.

He walked towards the door.

'What about me?' she cried. 'What about satisfying me?'

Andrea looked panic-stricken when he turned back to look at her. He guessed that being left without a climax was an unusual occurrence for her. Actually, he thought, it was probably more than that. After submitting to her pain, her sort had to have the pleasure to make it all worthwhile. To have reached his own climax without allowing her to do so was truly a torment to someone like Andrea. It was something that made him smile and even went some way to making up for Antonia having disappeared.

He decided to play it till the end. 'What about you?' he asked as he stuffed his hands into his pockets. Above the deep V-neck of his shirt, a gold ingot on a gold chain glinted in the surrounding mirrors.

In the mirrors, Andrea looked devastated. 'Aren't you going to undo these chains and set me free?' she demanded.

'No,' he said, shaking his head. 'I can't.'

'You must! You have to!' Her voice was bordering on a scream and he was reminded of the black-frocked women who shouted at their children and screamed at their men in the fishing villages around the Mediterranean.

'I told you,' he said casually. 'I can't. I haven't got a key.' He shrugged his shoulders and looked suitably helpless. Then he blew her a kiss, and as he waved goodbye her mouth was hanging open.

I'll always remember her like that, he thought to himself, and beamed from ear to ear.

Outside the mirrored room, he took a deep breath and took on a deeper frown as he wondered where he might find Antonia.

Chapter Seventeen

*P*hilippe should have gone to the Red Tower and Venetia's dining-hall, but he did not.

Instead, when he awoke with the moon high and bright, he got to his feet, dressed and took Toni by the hand.

'Where are we going?' she asked him as he handed her the black frontless top and bum-skimming skirt.

'To *Sea Witch*, my yacht,' he replied.

With the light of dawn like a mauve veil on the horizon, they sped through the thick grass of the lemon grove and headed for the place where he had moored the *Sea Witch*.

Knowing that his brother would be arriving at the main quay and wanting, as usual, to avoid him, Philippe had berthed his boat at an old jetty that had once been used by a ferry plying between the islands and the mainland.

Pounding waves had ravaged the line of stones that reached away from the land, and green mulch had grown where there once used to be mortar. But the jetty was still usable and, just as he had told her, there was *Sea Witch*, white and sleek and rising up and down on the constant swell of the sea.

'It is so good to see her,' he said as they stopped at the place where rough shingle met uneven stonework.

Toni was breathless. They were standing only inches apart, yet she was aware of the heat of his body. It seemed to reach out to her, wrap round and draw her closer.

She looked up at him, and saw that he was also looking at her. Adoration was in his eyes. Then it was gone as his gaze dropped to her bare breasts, and was replaced by desire.

Just as before, the neckline of the top she was wearing dipped beneath her breasts and left them naked. Already proud and firm, the cold air gave them greater definition, and the stiff breeze teased her nipples into hard and needful nubs that gently caressed the hardness of his chest as she pressed closer to him.

The breeze also caressed her naked pubes, but did nothing to cool the desire that Philippe aroused in her. A softness was in his eyes and face, but a hardness nudged against her belly as he took her in his arms and bent his head to kiss her.

He clasped her tightly to him, and she pressed herself willingly against him. His body was warm. Her breasts were chill and glad of his closeness.

She curved herself against him and murmured with pleasure as his hands smoothed down her back and took each of her buttocks as their own. The skirt hid nothing. His hands were under the skirt and they too were warm upon her flesh.

Perhaps it was the warmth of his hands, or the heat of the moment, but she had to say what was going through her mind. She remembered his mumbled words as he had dozed against her. 'I'll be anyone you want me to be,' she told him. 'Anyone at all. Even the woman you were talking about in your sleep. The one like me with the red hair and green eyes.'

Immediately, she regretted her words. His hands

became still. She felt his body grow rigid against her as though his blood had stopped flowing.

A gap appeared between them and widened as his hands loosened and travelled up to her back. He seemed to be holding her off from him. His look was suddenly harder. 'What do you mean?'

'I don't know,' she said, and shrugged her shoulders. Her heart was racing. 'I don't really know. All that I do know is that I remind you of somebody you once knew. I seem to have the same effect on your brother, too. It was Venetia and Emira who hinted at it, and Venetia who had me brought here because of my red hair and green eyes. I thought it was because I was a good sailor. But it wasn't.'

Philippe's eyes became round and wide. So did his mouth. He seemed dumbstruck.

She didn't like him looking at her like that. 'Philippe?' She reached out to caress his sweet face.

He backed off.

'I'm sorry. I need time to adjust to this. It's just that you mentioning her makes me feel confused. I don't know whether I want you to be her, or not.' He shook his head as though he were trying to shake off the old memories, the old rivalries between him and his brother.

Toni frowned and shook her head, too. 'I know she brought me here for a reason. She's never actually explained that reason to me. All I know is that it's got something to do with healing the rift between you and your brother. But that's all I know. I don't know how I'm supposed to do it. Even my name seems to have some relevance. Everyone back in London called me Toni, except for my mother. She always called me Antonia. Oh,' she said suddenly, 'and Julian. He used to call me Antonia too.'

Philippe's hair fell forward and framed his face as he bent his head and stared at the ground. He seemed to be searching for something in his mind. His hands dropped

249

away from her and hung at his side. 'I don't understand,' he mumbled.

'Neither,' said Toni, her own hands dropping uselessly to her sides, 'do I.'

Suddenly, she had a need to find out. She reached for him again.

He started, but did not pull away from her. His eyes looked darker than they had done, almost bordering on the deep green of her own. If his expression was anything to go by, he was as confused about this as she was.

'First,' she said in her gentlest voice, 'I'll tell you about Julian and London and why I came here. Then you can tell me about this other woman with red hair and green eyes. Is that a deal?'

He stared at her for a moment, and she could quite easily have thrown her arms around him and pulled him close, kissed him and enjoyed his body then and there. But that would have been too simple and would have solved nothing. She had thought she could be that person he had mumbled about if he wanted her to. But somehow, she knew she couldn't. Whoever or whatever it was that was haunting him had to be exorcised. Until then, he could never be free, and neither, she knew, could she. If she could not be herself in this place and had to slip into someone else's shoes, she could not stay here. On the other hand, there was no way she wanted to go back to London.

Even though he had not urged her to do so, she told him about Julian and their affair back in London. There was a quietness about him once she had finished, but his jaw was tight and his eyes unblinking. It was a while before he spoke. 'You look so much like her.'

'The other Antonia?' she asked tentatively.

He nodded.

'Tell me about her.' Her voice was as soft as her fingers as they trailed down his face and along his lips.

Through her fingers, he told her. 'I had finished school and was at home in Rome before going on to university.

My mother, as I am sure you have noticed, is a woman of some charm and much sensuality. In the absence of my father, she felt obliged to organize my initiation from boyhood to manhood. Not that I hadn't had some knowledge of girls, because I did. But she told me those were just the fumblings of amateurs. Only a true woman could make me a true man. So she brought Antonia to my bed one night.

'I don't know where she came from. All I know was that seeing her in the glow of sunset, naked, red-haired and green-eyed, was the most incredible event of my life.

'I must have appeared terrified. But I wasn't. Not really. It was just that she was so beautiful. Perhaps it was also because it was sunset and the redness of the sun was swallowing the green of the sea. I don't know for sure. I'm only surmising. But there she was, red-haired and green-eyed – just like you. And there I was naked in my bed.'

Toni stood spellbound, aware that his eyes were glassy and he was not really seeing her or the boat or the sea at all. He was seeing *her*; remembering his first, true sexual experience. His voice was as vague as the mist rising on the sea.

'Her skin was very creamy,' he said with a sudden glance. 'Just like yours. Her hair was like fire in the sunlight, and for a moment I wondered if she was real or if she'd risen from the sea at my mother's command.

'I remember her hair falling on my chest as she bent over me. Beneath its touch, I felt my flesh burn and my rod rise to her.

'She kissed my mouth and I felt I was drowning. I tangled my hands in her hair and held her face to me.

'She disentangled herself – never spoke. Only smiled and made quiet signs. Her lips kissed and lapped at my neck, my chest, my stomach and my groin. She took my member in her mouth and I filled it. I could not help myself. No one had ever done that before.

251

'But she did not scold me. She was patient, and under her ministrations my erection returned.

'She gestured to me that it was my task, on this occasion, to ride her. Obligingly, she lay on her back and opened her legs. I remember most vividly how red her pubic hairs were, how moist she was and how rich was the colour of her sex. Because I had come in her mouth, I was more relaxed than I would have been. So I took my time. I played with her breasts, kissed and sucked at her nipples and even licked and kissed her pussy. All the time, I was mindful of being as gentle with her as she had been with me.

'When my erection was as fiercely erect as it had been earlier, I pushed it into her. She moaned I remember, and for a moment I panicked as I had no wish to hurt her.

'"Are you all right?" I asked her. "Have I hurt you?"

'She smiled at me. Not just her mouth, but her eyes too. She shook her head, clasped my behind in her hands, and pushed my pelvis down on to hers. At the same time, she arched her back and raised her pelvis to me.

'I came then. It was mind-blowing, a dizzying experience as though all the lights of the world had gone out then come on again in a blaze of glory.

'It was stupendous, the most beautiful moment of my life. I shall never forget it.'

Silently, he stared at the sea and the twinkling lights on one of the other islands.

For a moment, Toni realised, he was back there in his youth. Then he was with her again. She chose that moment to speak. At the same time, she placed her hand on his groin. His penis was hard and bucked suddenly against her touch. 'Did you see her again?'

'Yes,' he replied. 'A few more times. It may sound old-fashioned, but it was a tradition in my family – as in a lot of old Italian families – that a young man is initiated by an experienced woman. My mother, although she is

252

American, was insistent that my father's dying wish would be strictly adhered to.'

'Was sex with her just as good on those other occasions?' She asked this as her fingers found the slim head of his zip and pulled it down.

'Yes,' he answered, his voice growing more husky as she pulled his penis from its lair and led it warm and hot into the night air.

He gasped and threw back his head. Every sinew in his neck, every vein, was accentuated. He closed his eyes, but his lips stayed slightly open.

'Did she look very much like me?' Toni asked as she encircled his stem with her fingers and tapped at his glans with her thumb.

'Very much!' he exclaimed, his words rapid on his breath.

Toni began to move her fingers up and down his stem. With her free hand, she undid the buttons of his shirt and caressed the fine hair of his chest. Not too much hair, but just enough to accentuate the curve of his chest muscles. 'Is my hair the same?'

'Yes.'

'And my eyes.'

'Yes!'

Lost in the sweetness of the moment, he did not see the cunning in her eyes. Clasped tightly in her hand, his penis grew, and she knew exactly what she would be doing with it.

Along with his erection, her plan was growing. She was beginning to understand the trouble between the two brothers.

Her action quickened, and she knew he would not be long in coming. 'And my mouth?' she asked finally.

'Yes!' he answered. 'Yes!'

His voice shivered as much as his body. She was on her knees, and his glans was in her mouth.

Groping through his trouser opening, she found the soft warmth of his balls. As her head began to move up and down his stem, she gripped his velvet sac, and with her free hand tightly clasped his left buttock.

Without interrupting her stroke, she pulled at his trousers until his lower torso was entirely exposed. Then, as she opened her throat to swallow his libation, she plunged her finger into his anus.

Accompanied by a loud shout, he thrust his hips forward. With her throat, she hugged his erection and, as she twisted her finger inside him and clutched tightly at his balls, she felt the warm sweetness of his honey spurt hotly into her throat.

She licked the last trickle of fluid from his cock before getting to her feet.

With a look of surprise on his face, he stared at her. Then he ran his fingers through her hair and held it out as though studying its length and texture. Suddenly, with a contented sigh, he let it fall, cupped her face and kissed her mouth.

'I taste of you,' she said, once their lips had parted.

'I'm glad of that,' he answered. 'I don't want you to taste of anyone else.'

Alarm bells began to ring in her head. This protectiveness was something too reminiscent of Julian, and she thought she'd explained about him.

'I don't know about that,' she said.

The stormy, unsettled look came back to his eyes. 'You are just like her!' he exclaimed. 'You'll let my brother do all the things to you that he did to her. You'll enjoy it like she did. Just like she did!'

'Philippe!' She touched his arm.

He hit her hand away.

Perhaps things might have got worse, or they might have got better if Emira's red car hadn't pulled up at the end of the quay.

Emira's heels clattered as he ran down the jetty to where they were moored. The sea heaved on either side of the slipway and spray reached for the hem of his dress.

Emira did not come right up to them, but spoke from where he stood. His eyes glanced at Toni's breasts and the cluster of red pubic hair peeping from beneath the hem of her black skirt.

He also took in the fact that Philippe was refastening his waistband.

'My mistress, Madame Salvatore, asked me to come for you.'

He said it haltingly, as though his skin was on the line if he went back without them.

'I won't be there,' said Philippe abruptly as his eyes scanned the sky and the sea. 'I'm going to the Calabri Regatta. The long-range weather report forecasts a storm, but I will not allow that to put me off. I will trust to my skill and that of my crew. I have also decided that Antonia is going with me.'

He didn't look at Toni when he said it, but she looked at him. Somehow she knew there was turmoil going on inside him still, but she had a sneaking suspicion that all would be well.

'My mistress will not be pleased,' returned Emira.

To Toni's surprise, Philippe curved his arm around her shoulders and hugged her close. 'I don't care. On this occasion, I will have to let her down. Please take her my regards and my regrets.'

Emira looked stunned.

His heavily made-up eyelashes blinked rapidly.

Philippe's closeness made Toni feel wonderfully secure. His scent and the hardness of his body tantalised her flesh.

Emira looked nervous. As usual, he also looked beautiful. He wore a white dress which flowed, rather than fell, from a circlet of gold around his neck.

Toni remembered seeing an Egyptian queen wearing something like that. Nefertiti was her name. Not so beautiful, she decided. Emira's male hormones gave greater strength to his features, though at the moment he was visibly agitated.

'What shall I tell her if she wishes to contact you?' he asked, his eyes fluttering nervously.

Philippe turned to Toni and gently kissed the sweetness of her hair. His expression was calm again. 'She has my number. I will be at the Regatta. Tell her the clubhouse is very good. She will be most welcome there.'

His eyes as dark as his looks, Emira sighed, then turned and slowly picked his way back through the crumbling stones and spitting spray.

Toni frowned. She liked Emira and couldn't help feeling sorry for him. What fate, she wondered, awaited him back at the Red Tower.

'I hope Venetia won't be too disappointed,' she said softly.

Chapter Eighteen

*F*rom three miles out, they could see the masts of luxury sailing yachts, and the bland whiteness of sleek motor yachts whose engines drank fuel and whose owners had more money than sense.

Not that everyone chose a sailing yacht simply because the wind was free. The yachts lying off the Calabri Regatta were just as expensive as their motorised sisters.

The seas had been high during the night, and the wind had howled around the most minimum of sail. Grey clouds still sat low in the sky, but patches of blue were appearing as the wind veered to the south.

Rolling towards and with each other along with the movement of the sea, Toni had spent a glorious night in the arms of her lover. But he had still mumbled in his sleep. She heard him say her name, but then again, it might not have been hers, but that of the Antonia who had taken him from boyhood to manhood.

Six times he had taken her during the night. Now he lay sleeping, and she was up on deck allowing the early morning mist to freshen her naked body and dissipate the scent of sex that still clung to her.

In an effort to avoid the crowded harbour until they really had to enter, they had anchored three miles out;

though if the wind became much fiercer, they would end up having to motor into the harbour.

Mark waved at her, his golden hair catching the early morning glint of the sun. She waved back. After shouting orders to someone at the stern, he disappeared into the wheel-house.

There was a clanking of chain and a splash as the anchor entered the water. It grated as it left its housing, clanged and rattled some more, then was silent.

Shielding her eyes against the rising sun, she looked to the stern.

A wide figure with broad shoulders was bending over the guard-rail. She knew he was checking that the chain had not fouled its housing.

He glanced over his shoulder, and she saw his coal-black eyes. She recognised him immediately. It was Emilio, the man who had driven her and Emira from the airport on the day she had arrived.

When he saw her, he seemed momentarily to stop dead. Then he was suddenly all action. The task he had been undertaking with such concentration until he had seen her now became rushed. Then he came towards her, his eyes black as chips of burned cinder.

With the sun behind him, he looked even bigger than she remembered him. In her confusion and sudden fear, she forgot she was naked and smelt of spent sex.

Emilio's bulk seemed to surround her. His massive arms grabbed her. His hand clamped across the back of her head so her cry for help was muffled against his chest. Her feet swung off the ground as he carried her to where he had been standing, to where the anchor chain sliced through its housing and down into the sea.

Ample rope hung from the rear boom to gag her mouth and tie her wrists. Once they were secure, he tugged on them so that her arms were hoisted above her head and her breasts thrust forward to his face. The anchor chain lay slack. There was enough to wind around her ankles and weigh her feet to the deck.

A glint of power appeared in the coal-black eyes. The wide and licentious mouth spread over his face. 'Now,' he said, as he admired her. 'Now I will take what you allowed me only to look at when you first arrived here. Emilio will not be teased like that. Emilio will have it all.'

Toni swung on her bonds as she wriggled. The rope gagging her mouth was made of hemp. It was coarse and tasted of dried grass. Those binding her wrists were nylon and became tighter the more she wriggled.

As his massive hands covered her breasts, she shivered, and tried to shout. But it was only a mumble, the murmur of a woman whose fate is assured.

His hands were warm and as rough as sandpaper. She winced as he pinched her nipples. He murmured deep in his throat as he rubbed his nose between her breasts. It was as if he could not get enough of the smell of her, the feel of her.

His head and body smothered her breasts and her senses. He smelt of sweat, of salt and of the rich spices of North African casbahs; of bitter coffee and black tobacco.

He was bare to the waist and only wore a pair of loose black trousers, the sort associated with corsairs or harem eunuchs. His flesh was warm and very soft against her. So big was his body, so hard and firmly pronounced his muscles, that she felt surrounded by him.

As his hands held her back, he sucked gently at each nipple. She moaned. His lips were so soft, so generous of flesh. He sucked her in, and she felt the tip of his tongue poke gently at each sensitive teat. A fuzz of hair on his top lip tantalised her flesh as his teeth nibbled like a sucking lamb.

Despite the fact that Emilio was forcing his attention on her, she could not help but respond. True, Philippe had taken her many times during the night, his technique so gentle, it was almost at times as though she were made of china. That, she reasoned, was why her desire was rising.

Philippe had great passion. She could feel it in him, coursing through his veins just beneath the surface of his skin and his behaviour. He was kind, he was gentle to her, yet she sensed something was missing And this, she thought to herself, seemed to be it.

This massive man who smelt of debauchery and decadence was forcing her to experience the salacious, the sinful.

Breathless, his mouth left her breasts and he looked into her eyes and briefly loosened her gag.

How black his eyes were. How they glinted with the heat of the moment, of desire – no, of sheer lust.

'You kept showing your breasts to that half-man,' he said. 'That man who wears women's clothes. And you forced me to watch, and I did watch. I wanted them. I dreamed of them, and now I have them. I will do everything to them. Philippe will not do such things to you. He will only do such things to other women – not to you. But his brother would. And still would. That's why they hate each other. They need a woman who is all things to them both, to unlock the gentleness in one, and the perversion in the other.' He laughed, this knowledgeable man who had watched each member of the family and knew each better than they knew themselves.

Now at last, Toni understood why she was here. 'But I can be both. I know I can. All I need is the chance to prove it. Couldn't you tell them this, Emilio? Couldn't you go to each in turn and tell them I will be everything they want me to be?'

'Do not try and fool Emilio, woman. Do not try and hoodwink me with such things. Nothing will stop me from doing what I want to do to you. Nothing at all. You can scream if you like. No one will hear you – not yet. It is early. Only Emilio is up and about. Emilio and you.'

'You don't understand, Emilio. But you are right; I cannot stop you from doing what you want to do. I cannot stop you and I will not stop you.'

He laughed at her. 'You are just trying to keep me talking, hoping that I will change my mind. I know women. I know they talk too much and don't always like what Emilio does to them.'

'You're wrong, Emilio. You're dead wrong!'

But Emilio seemed absorbed in his own thoughts, his own intentions. He ducked low beneath a spar, then came back up with more rope in his hands. 'Lovely bits of rope,' he said in a childish yet devilish way. 'Now see what I will do with them.'

Breeze-blown hair flying across her face, she watched, then winced as he bound a piece of rope around each breast. She squirmed, but he gave no heed. Each breast was firmly bound, her flesh bulging, her nipples bright red.

She wriggled her thighs against each other; not because she was protesting, but because her sex was on fire as much as her teats and she wanted his attention.

'No protests!' he exclaimed, and smacked her bottom. His hand was huge and hard. Her bottom stung.

'I wasn't protesting. I just want to know what you're going to do next.'

He grinned and held up his hands. In his fingers, he held two canvas ties. They were thin, fine and dangled like ribbons from his fingers.

His eyes positively sparkled as he tightened the gag once more and there was a wetness around his fat lips. 'I'm going to tie these around your teats,' he said. 'Now what do you think of that?'

Her response was lost on the hemp rope.

He laughed at her inability to tell him what she was feeling. After all, he wasn't really interested in that. What he was doing to her was for his own satisfaction, not hers.

First, he tweaked and sucked at each nipple until its length suited his purpose.

'Now they are ready,' he said with a smile.

He let the first canvas tie wave with the wind before her eyes.

He laughed again, then carefully he wound the first tie around a blood-red and lengthy nipple.

Toni groaned. The nylon rope was already forcing her breasts to swell and bulge in front of it. Now the finer tie dug into one nipple and forced it to maintain its prominence.

He did the same with the other. Then he stood back and surveyed his handiwork. 'Marvellous,' he said, and licked his lips.

She had thought at that point he might force her legs apart and push his penis into her, or bend her over and redden her behind with another length of rope. But he didn't.

To her surprise, he reached above and pulled again on the hanging ropes. this time, she found her arms were loosening, but he only took this operation so far.

Just when she thought she could relax, he forced her to her knees and piled an anchor chain over her legs so that she was weighted to the deck. Again, her arms were stretched high above her. Now, she realised exactly what he intended.

His crotch was level with her breasts. He dropped his trousers, and a demon of a cock sprang towards her.

It was purple, massive and lush with purple veins and a manic mushroom head.

Already, fluid was running from it, and as her mouth was already full, she guessed exactly where it was going.

It tapped hot and sticky on each imprisoned bosom. Emilio placed each of his hands on the side of her breasts and pushed them together.

Toni groaned as the tightened rope and ties gripped her flesh more firmly. Above her, he moaned in ecstasy as he pushed his mighty member into her cleavage.

He prodded at her breast-bone. For all the world, her

breasts had formed a fitting receptacle for what he was about to bestow on her.

Her nipples stung and her breasts felt fit to burst, but all the time he grunted and groaned and pushed and prodded until, in a shower of hot fluid, he gave all he had to give and shouted his triumph to the circling seagulls.

Foaming white covered her breasts. He stood back from her. His look of pleasure was short-lived. Furtively, he looked over his shoulder, then back at her.

She tried to tell him that she wouldn't tell, that everything would be all right.

He paused, not sure of what he should do next. Then, with a sigh, he decided. Gently, he let loose the hemp rope from her mouth.

Toni gasped and caught her breath before she spoke. 'Is that all you wanted?'

He nodded. 'Will you tell?'

She shook her head. 'Not if you don't want me to.'

'But you might.' He looked at the sea.

She shook her head again. The last thing she wanted was to be shoved over the side.

'No,' she said. 'I won't.'

He undid her bonds and, with a look of regret, refrained from undoing the constraints that bound her breasts. His fluid was still upon them: sticky, white and dripping like melting snow from her nipples.

'Don't worry,' she said and smiled at him as reassuringly as she could. She jerked her head towards the sea. 'It'll soon wash off.'

Before he could change his mind and perhaps tie her up and shove her over the side, she made her way to the chromium steps that led to the swimming platform. From there, she dived into the sea.

Emilio stood watching her for just a moment. His mouth hung open and he looked most surprised that she had recovered that quickly from her ordeal and had no intention of telling on him.

Toni ducked beneath the water, determined to enjoy her early morning dip, and just as determined to instil more fire into Philippe's sex drive. And then, of course, there was Conway.

The water was cool at first, but felt warmer as she swam further. She opened and closed her legs to allow the water to wash away all traces of last night's sex.

The water touched her gently and ran with fluid precision into her most secret of places.

It cleansed her pubes, her labia and revitalised her breasts so that her nipples stood out anew. She immersed herself again and again in its salty freshness, then re-emerged some twenty feet further from the yacht than she'd intended.

She looked towards the yacht and frowned. Her heart began to flutter in her breast. Was it her imagination, or was *Sea Witch* drifting on the current? As panic began to take her, she told herself to stay calm. That was easier said than done.

Think, she cried inwardly.

With sudden clarity, she upturned her bottom and dived down into the cool, green water. As she swam submerged, she could see the anchor of the yacht dragging along the sea-bed. At this particular spot, the sea-bed was nothing but rocks and scatterings of shingle. There was no way the anchor could hold. *Sea Witch* was drifting inland. Her presence had diverted Emilio from paying due attention to the fixing of the anchor. Now both the yacht and she were likely to pay the price.

Breathless, she bobbed to the surface. Once she'd caught her breath, she shouted out for help.

No one heard.

She imagined the crew were eating breakfast and taking their time over it before Philippe put in an appearance.

The current was inward-drifting and fast enough. Hopefully, someone would notice that they had a problem long before they reached the shore. Even if they didn't, someone on shore might notice.

But what about her?

There was both a surface current and an undercurrent at this point and, as the yacht drifted inwards, the undercurrent had caught at her legs and she was drifting seawards.

She tried swimming towards the land and the course *Sea Witch* was following. Her arms curved into a perfect crawl and divided the deceitful surface of the sea. Her legs kicked, and she gulped salt-water as well as air. 'I can't!' she gasped. Despite all that effort, she'd moved in the opposite direction to where she wanted to go. She could feel the undercurrent pulling on her limbs, tugging them under and dragging her further out to sea.

Tread water, she said to herself, then spluttered as she swallowed a mouthful of sea. Now, think, she told herself. Bloody think!

What she was going through was subject to textbook theories and textbook answers. Unfortunately, what she had read seemed decidedly glib now she was in the situation for real.

Keep going, she said to herself. Just keep going.

Her eyes were closing and her legs felt as if they were fastened to the sea-bed on strips of strong elastic. She was weakening; she *knew* she was weakening. But still, she kept treading water.

Numbness spread from her fingertips and toes. For some silly reason, she wondered if they looked like white prunes now. Not that she could raise her arms or legs to look at them. Her strength was ebbing, and she was too exhausted to be frightened.

The sea seemed to be swallowing her up. It was lapping against her ears and gradually dragging her downwards. The sun had begun to shine again, before a shadow passed between her and its brightness.

She heard noises, wondered if they were angels and she'd got to heaven.

By the time she was lifted from the water, she was too weary to notice whose arms held her and to see the look of surprise on his face as she softly murmured her thanks.

She didn't see the shock in his eyes.

As she slipped into unconsciousness, she was vaguely aware of the tilt of a deck and the flapping of sails as the yacht that had picked her up now turned seawards.

Then she blacked out and knew nothing until she smelt the crisp cleanliness of starched white pillows and felt the coolness of cotton sheets against her skin.

Vaguely, she was aware of someone being by the door, a very still and very quiet figure.

Slowly, she turned her head and felt the wetness of her own hair against her cheek. Her eyes met those of Conway Patterson, and suddenly she felt hopelessly lost.

She turned away from him and sighed. 'What next?' she said softly.

Vaguely, she remembered what Emilio had said, about Conway needing the gentleness brought out of him. Was it really there? She didn't know, and at this moment in time she was in no fit state to find out.

His shadow fell over her, and if she had had the strength to roll further away from him, she would have. As it was, she only had the strength to wince, and then to close her eyes as if that would make him go away.

She felt his hand upon her head. To her surprise, his fingers were stroking her hair.

'My brother really thought you *were* Antonia,' he said thoughtfully. 'As if the woman was still the same age as she was when we were pimply adolescents.'

He laughed, and yet she sensed it was a different laugh from before. In her weakness, had she touched something deep within him? She didn't know. She only knew that if a small chink had been made in his prickly armour, it was worth encouraging.

It was hard to speak, but she managed it. 'My name is Antonia, but not the one you two seem obsessed with.'

266

His fingers now gently touched her cheek. Almost as if he were drawing her features with a soft pencil, he followed the line of her eyebrows, the straightness of her nose and the curve of her lips.

'Yes, I know. I also know you're not her. He reckons she's been haunting his dreams. Wet, my brother. Silly bugger. Treated her like a bit of bloody glass. Seemed to think she liked it that way.'

'Didn't she?' Toni's voice was not much more than a whisper, but she forced herself to speak.

'No! Not when she was with me!'

The stridency of his voice made Toni wince, although she had the feeling he was trying to convince himself of the fact rather than her.

By now, his fingers were tracing the lines of her collarbone and edging towards the hem of the cotton sheet.

Her strength at low ebb, and her mind none too clear, she could do nothing to escape him. Whatever he wanted to do to her, he could do. There was nothing she could do to stop him. But one thought, one fear, played on her mind.

'Please,' she said in a low whisper. 'Please don't put me back in that cupboard. Don't put me through that again. Anything but that.'

It was hard to keep her eyes open, but she could see his face change. It was the same look he had adopted when she had murmured in his arms earlier, though, of course, she didn't know that.

'You didn't like the cupboard?' He sounded surprised.

'No,' she murmured.

He paused. 'Nor any of the rest of it?'

She managed to smile. 'I didn't say that.'

He paused again as though he were contemplating what she had said alongside some old memory. 'That's strange,' he said suddenly. 'She said that, too. I couldn't ever remember her saying it until you did. Now I do. She didn't like the cupboard either. Well, I'm blowed.'

He lifted the sheet from Toni's breasts and let it fall

around her waist. She took a deep breath as his hands covered her breasts. Tired in body she might be, but her nipples rose as though they had nothing to do with the rest of her.

'He told me about her,' she managed to say. 'Philippe told me how your mother procured her to initiate you into manhood and how you became jealous of each other. He told me how the other Antonia went away and each of you blamed the other for her going.'

Conway had been looking at her nipples, which he was pinching between his fingers and thumbs. Now he looked into her eyes. With effort, she managed to keep them open, and return his mystified gaze. Despite her precarious predicament, Toni could not help but be aroused by the intense blue of his eyes, the sun-kissed length of his curls.

'It was his fault,' he said defensively, pinching more fiercely at her nipples. 'It was his soft and silly ways she didn't like. Women like it a bit rough. They like a man to be a man. Don't you?' he asked suddenly, and dug his thumbnails into her nipples.

She groaned and surprised herself by arching her body away from the bed. 'Not necessarily,' she replied thickly. 'I like both. I like the gentleness in a man, but I also like his darker side. I will play your games, but you must play mine too.'

He became very still. His eyes stared at her in disbelief. 'I can't be both. I just can't!'

She closed her eyes and shook her head. She even managed to smile. 'You don't need to be,' she said quietly as his hands pushed the sheet down to her thighs. 'You are two different men. One is one way, one another, and yet you both embody the same gentleness, the same perversions. Like the Roman god Janus, you look both ways – just as Emira does. Only, in his case, he looks to both genders, not to different facets in a man.'

It was as his fingers began to push between her legs that she tried to raise her arms, but to no avail. Her being half-drowned had not stopped Conway securing her wrists to the sides of the bed. Again, the gold wristbands had come in useful.

She sighed. On this occasion, she need not take any active part in whatever he had in mind. For once, she could lie there and let him do whatever he wanted.

'What are you going to do to me?' she asked him.

'Whatever I want,' he replied. 'Do you mind?'

She shook her head. 'No,' she answered. 'I can cope with Philippe, and I can cope with you.'

She saw him smile. There was a new joy in his eyes as he turned his face to her.

'Good,' he said. 'Because no matter how much you protest, I will do what I like.'

Relaxation spread over her like a warm wave. She closed her eyes. Her pubic lips divided, and her inner petals burst out like a fast-blooming flower as he spread her legs and secured her ankles to the brass uprights at the foot of the bed.

She was vulnerable and helpless to anything he might want to do to her and yet she was not afraid. Conway might not admit it, but something about her had got through to him just the same as it had his brother. If he wanted to be really cruel, he only had to return her to the cupboard. But he had not. His gentleness was coming through.

He left her there for a moment, and went into the bathroom. She heard the sound of running water, but could not detect what he was doing.

With limpid eyes, she watched the steady swing of his bathrobe from a hook on the back of the door. It swayed like a pendulum in time with the rhythm of the sea. By her own estimate, they must now be entering harbour and also sailing before the teeth of another gale.

When he came back out of the bathroom, he had a bowl in one hand, a shaving brush and a razor in the other. She was in no doubt about what he intended to do.

'This will be pleasant,' he said as he kissed her forehead, then her lips, and finally the ripe plumpness of her mons.

She groaned as the warmth of the soap was whisked through her pubic hairs. If she lifted her head, she could see that what had been a thick bush of hair was now flattened, matted over her flesh.

When he had finished soaping her, he held up the razor and twirled it in his fingers. 'It's very sharp, he said with a cruel smile. But his eyes were merry. She convinced herself of that, and told herself not to be afraid.

More gently than his smile could have promised, he drew the steel blade through her soaped and slicked hair. The touch of the blade was cold, yet she felt no sharpness. As her hair began to peel away, her denuded skin felt cooler; as though it had just taken off a jacket.

Her mons was easy to deal with. When it came to her hidden lips, he held each back with his fingers and then gently ran the blade through until all her hair was gone.

He patted her dry and once the towel was removed, he admired his handiwork.

Toni closed her eyes. If she had been naked before, it was nothing to how she felt now. There was a profane nudity about her sex, a coolness over that area of her flesh that had hidden so snugly behind its fleecy red coat. How does it look now? she asked herself.

As though hearing her question, Conway answered. 'See. I have exposed you completely. I know you completely. Philippe would never have done this to you, but I am doing it. How do you feel about it?'

With one hand, he raised her head. With the other, he held a mirror to her shorn sex.

She gasped. How vulnerable she looked. How naked and exposed. It was symbolic somehow, as though he had stripped away all her worldly covers and trappings and could see into her soul.

She could not help but be drawn to the sight of her

270

own naked genitals, so primly white, yet so salaciously red in between.

Like a lush-lipped mouth, her labia seemed to be smiling.

It was difficult not to look, hard not to respond to her own arousal. The heat of desire swept through her body. Conway's fingers burned into her neck like red-hot rods. The twin peaks of her naked breasts rose close to her mouth. From the mirror, her labia filled her gaze, yet she was very aware of her nipples lengthening and hardening as they responded to how she was feeling.

Suddenly, her lips seemed very dry. Slowly, as though she were tasting her own denuded labia, she ran her tongue all around her mouth.

Conway winced – out of character for him. After all, this was the way he liked his sex. But she had not forgotten Emilio's words. Like his brother, Philippe, there were also two sides to Conway.

His jaw seemed to set firmer as he let her head fall back on the pillow, and put the mirror back where it had come from.

She closed her eyes as she lay back. He covered her sex with the warmth of his hand and firmly squeezed it. Her eyes remained closed, but she could not help raising her hips as though asking him for more. Her action did not go unnoticed.

'You are enjoying this?' he asked.

She noticed he sounded surprised. 'Yes,' she replied. Only a one-word answer, yet it was difficult to say, coming as it did on the back of a deep and satisfying purr.

The pressure of his grip lessened. His fingers sprang into renewed agility. They played with her sex, touching and squeezing, exploring her folds of flesh as if she were a toy he had just been given.

She moaned and, though her time in the sea had drained her, she found the strength to respond to him.

271

'I am going to go in there,' he said sternly, and pushed his finger into the humid warmth of her vagina.

Her hips jerked upwards. 'Then do it,' she moaned. 'Do it!'

He removed his hand.

She heard the rustle of hastily removed clothes and remembered a hanging sac and a jetting stream of whiteness from a proud penis.

Without too much effort, she half-opened her eyes. Her breathing increased and the heat that filled her body intensified.

Conway had taken off his black T-shirt and matching trousers.

A silver skull and crossbones hung amid the blond hairs of his chest. Like treasure, she thought; then, as her eyes ran down his body, she changed her mind.

His true treasure rose like a Palladian column from a bushy expanse of golden hair.

As though it were wrapped in silvery cellophane, his glans shone in the half-light of the cabin. A pearl of semen crowned it and trembled precariously each time his penis throbbed.

Proudly erect, his penis pointed at her, and the pearl drop of secretion changed shape before falling to the floor.

Now she found it impossible to close her eyes. There was no way she could tear them away from the virile, purple rod that sprung, so thick in circumference, and so generous in length, from his golden thatch.

Below it, weighty and beguiling, hung his balls. They had, she remembered, a light covering of hair. It was his downy haze that now caught the light and shone like pale gold.

As the memory of their taste came to her mind, her mouth opened.

'You remember?' he asked.

'I remember,' she answered.

'I'm glad,' he responded, his right hand stroking his

272

pulsating rod, his left cupping his golden nuts as if they were too heavy to hang by themselves. 'If you hadn't,' he went on, 'I would have reminded you how they taste.'

'I remember,' she said, and couldn't help but lick her lips. How ripe they looked, how hot, how soft, and yet, how incredibly masculine.

He saw her look and smiled.

Was it his former cruelty she could see in his eyes, or was there something else stirring? Was he, in fact, beginning to see just how much she could enjoy the things he enjoyed?

Her eyes fixed on his vigorous erection, she wriggled against her bonds. Visibly, his stem thickened and hardened before her eyes. Obviously, she concluded, he wanted her to wriggle, wanted her to portray denial when all she was feeling was rampant desire.

His shadow fell over her and she trembled with apprehension. How can it be, she asked herself, that I feel so hot and yet I shiver?

'I'm going to take you just as Philippe would take you,' said Conway, his teeth brazenly white against the sun-bronzed hue of his skin.

'But my hands and feet are bound. Philippe does not do it that way.' Even as she said it, she knew it was a pointless effort. He would not unfasten her finely forged chains, and strangely enough she didn't want him to.

His smile lessened as he shook his head, but it still took her breath away, almost as much as his fingers did as they pinched her upright nipples.

'That's the beauty of it,' he said. 'And that's the difference. I'm going to take you like he does, but with a few little refinements.' His hands left her breasts and ran in hard-palmed caresses down over her ribcage and her hips.

His gaze alighted on her shorn pubes. Deftly, his fingers took her naked lips and curled them away from each other. He smiled at the slippery folds that were so sweetly gathered and so obviously aroused.

She could feel them tingling with all the sensations he had aroused in her, and she imagined what he was seeing: her sex, deep pink, but glistening beneath a silver sheen.

Then his hands left her.

In the warm confines of the cabin, where reflections of sunlight on water danced across the ceiling, Conway Patterson blindfolded her eyes and gagged her mouth.

'With these added refinements, you will fully appreciate what I am going to do to you. And when I am finished, you will know that, not only am I a better man than him, but I am also a more innovative one.'

The gag was in place before she could say anything, and the blindfold not long after.

What happened next both surprised and excited her.

From head to toe, he covered her with his body. Her breasts rose to meet his chest, then were crushed beneath its hardness.

Like a blanket, his warmth and his body lay full length on her and, in her darkness, she more accurately felt the contours of his muscles, the outline of form and the feel of texture against her own.

She breathed his smell, and remembered Emira. How stupid she had been not to have recognised Emira's hidden sex from the very first. Smelling Conway and remembering the dark hardness of Emira's supple body, lent new vigour to her reactions. Her hips rose as his pelvis dug into her belly and his member divided her nether lips.

At first, only the very tip of his penis nudged aside her newly naked lips. Like a giant exploratory tongue, it kissed at her slippery folds, then nudged them aside as it delved further.

Almost as though they were her own, she felt the heat and softness of his velvet sac against the satin smoothness of her inner thighs.

He paused at the entrance to her vagina. The round

smoothness of his glans loitered there, poking like some wild predator at the lair of his prey.

Toni tightened her stomach muscles and lifted her bottom off the bed. The blindfold had taken her sight. She didn't need to see his face close to hers to know how he was feeling. His beautiful, vibrant cock was telling her that. Even now, she knew the pressure inside it must be intensive. His skin would be turning a deeper shade of purple as it stretched to accommodate the totality of his erection. So she rose to meet him, to entice him to plunge his member into her and give her what she needed.

At the same time, the gag that silenced her encouraged her body to lift and entice. That was her only way of communicating with him, and she knew she was doing it well.

Once again she arched her back and heaved her hips towards him. This time, she was irresistible. He had to take her.

As he plunged into her, his hands dived beneath her and cupped the perfect spheres of her behind. One hand and one finger moved more closely to her anal divide than the others. Toni wriggled as she had before, but this time her movements were directed upwards to Conway's pelvis and away from the inquisitive finger.

But her movements were manipulated by him and not by herself. As he completely impaled her on his strident rod, his finger slid uninterrupted into her rectum.

She arched her back more and screamed her protest against the gag that bound her mouth but, despite initial reservations, the muscles of her behind tightened around the intruder as though it were sincerely welcome.

She felt one hand leave her behind and almost fainted with pleasure as one breast gained its undivided attention, the palm pressing, the fingers and thumb squeezing her errant nipple. The finger, embedded so firmly in her behind, stayed where it was.

Symphonies of whirling sensuality flowed in, over and around her body.

Tension gripped her stomach as the first tingles of climax circled her swollen clitoris. There was nothing she could see of this man, nothing she could say, yet she could not deny that he was giving her enormous pleasure.

His enormous erection filled her vagina. It was as if she were engaging in a sumptuous feast, but was too full to partake of any more. And yet, she did have more. The finger in her anus sent spears of electricity throughout her body. It divided her cheeks, and ground against her flesh as he turned it around inside her and pushed it in as far as he possibly could.

'So,' murmured Conway in a rich voice that was faintly touched with tyranny. 'How does it feel to have me invade you, to have my prick in your pussy and my finger up your ass? Eh?'

He jabbed fiercely with his cock and fiercer still with his finger.

Unable to voice her view, Toni's head tilted back, and her throat stretched, as white and as vulnerable as her labia.

'Good,' he said, his voice little more than a long and satisfied sigh. 'Good. I don't want you to like it. I want you to endure it. It's for me to like it, not you.'

She heard him, and yet she knew he was not speaking the truth. She also knew that what she was really feeling might confuse him, but perhaps that was what Venetia was hoping for.

As wave upon wave of exhilaration eddied throughout her body, Toni felt something else sweep over her. A primal realisation born of her own inner energies, her own desires, was flowing through her veins. She was aware of her inner muscles gripping at both intruders as though they were becoming some intrinsic part of her body.

Tension seemed to leave her, and also leave the body of the man who ploughed her sex and speared her behind. Something had changed in him – she just knew it. And that something was to do with her.

Rippling through her body, the first tremors of her climax caused her to stiffen and her head to roll from side to side upon the pillow. The juice of feminine ejaculation flowed down the sides of the invading penis and filtered out to flood her petals of flesh and lie sticky on her thighs.

'You can't climax!' she heard Conway cry. 'You can't!'

But she had done so and, with just as much enthusiasm, the final thrusts of his rod brought him to the same conclusion.

Still blindfolded, she murmured against her gag and her breasts strained against the weight of Conway's body.

He lay there, his lips soft against her neck, his soft voice and warm breath gentle, like feathers. 'You can't have enjoyed it,' he said again, but didn't sound as though he believed it.

He didn't move until the boat lurched angrily to one side and he, and a few navigation instruments, fell on to the floor. Heavy rain began to beat on one of the windows.

'Damn weather!' he grumbled and, clinging on to the side of the bed, got to his feet. 'There's a storm brewing,' he said as another wave ploughed into the side of the boat.

He removed her blindfold and briefly caught the look in her eyes. Her look seemed to hang heavy on him and, for a moment, he glanced at nothing but the floor, the walls and the rolling and sliding items still on the floor. Once he'd gained some semblance of his old air of self-confidence, he removed her gag.

'There's a storm brewing,' he said brusquely, but did not meet her eyes.

'No,' she answered. 'It's not brewing. I think it's already here.'

Chapter Nineteen

*O*ld memories too often recalled and dwelt on can affect judgement and undermine concentration.

It might have been the reason why the course charted by Conway was none too accurate, or it could just have been that the storm was too fierce and the waves too strong to be ignored.

Whatever the reason, sails reefed and, proceeding on engine alone, *Enchantress* ploughed through twenty-foot waves, her prow at times disappearing as the water thundered upon her decks.

Everyone had donned wet suits and life-jackets. Lifelines were clipped to the running rails along the sides, and two helmsmen battled with the wheel.

The wind slewed in squalling gusts as cyclone mixed with anticyclone and produced a mixed stew of wind and rain. Dark clouds made the day look like night and, every so often, ribbons of lightning connected the sea with the sky.

There was no time to shout out who should be doing what. Conway was shouting, but his voice was lost in the wind.

When the boom swung and the two helmsmen got knocked out cold, it was Toni who raced to fill the gap and Conway who came to assist her.

Taras lifted the limp bodies of the other helmsmen under each of his mighty arms and took them below. It was also he who came back up to secure the swaying boom before it could knock Conway and Toni out, too.

Wave after wave crash-landed on the deck as Toni and Conway attempted to keep her on a straight course to the safety of the harbour.

In a lesser wind, or even one that didn't change direction so often, they would have succeeded, but one super-fit gust caught them, spun them like a top, then turned them beam-on. The waves crashed against the port side of the sturdy and classic lines. With all their strength they heaved on the wheel, and through narrowed eyes and wet lashes peered with alarm at the far-off lights of the harbour.

Their efforts were commendable, but as the boat slewed to port once more, a huge wave a little less than mast high pounded and took Conway and Toni over the side.

Once again Toni was in the water, only this time the waves were higher and she was not as fresh as she had been.

Salt-water crashed on her head, and she thought the end could not be far off.

But she hadn't reckoned on Conway. She felt his arms hugging her to him, his voice telling her to cling to him, and not to give up. Body against body, they bobbed like twin corks in the water. His cheek was against hers, and their arms were entwined.

But the sea was strong.

It's hopeless, she thought, but did not have the strength to say it.

All sense of time – and even fear – seemed distorted. They were helpless, and in a hopeless situation, and yet they still clung to each other.

Only when she felt the last of her strength seeping away was she vaguely aware of the yellow beam of a masthead light and the *chug-chug* of powerful diesel engines.

Other arms took her before she fainted away.

Gentle hands stripped off her clothes and rubbed at her body with warm, soft towels.

She was aware of a smell she recognized and adored, but in the haze of her semi-consciousness, she couldn't quite put a name to it.

Red fingernails scattered like falling stars as warm hands massaged her body.

'My darling Antonia,' she heard a voice say. 'You need much warming, and I will have to give it to you.'

In the confines of her mind, and the senses of her body, she was aware of the warmth of soft towels being replaced with white palms that smelt of sandalwood. The hands to which the palms belonged had dark fingers that knew how a woman's body worked and how quickly it could react to sexual arousal.

'Emira?'

Sweet lips kissed her neck, and a gentle hand caressed the dampness of her hair. 'It is indeed Emira,' the dark voice answered. 'Emira knows how to warm you. Emira will get you warm very quickly.'

Inwardly, Toni smiled. She tried to open her eyes, but without success. It didn't matter. Strangely enough, Conway had prepared her for this moment. She didn't need to see to respond to what Emira was doing, and didn't need to say anything either.

His hands brushed over the upper swell of her breasts before covering them with both hands. Toni cooed her appreciation. Not only were Emira's hands warm, but they were also doing the right things; things that made the blood rush through her body and gather, hard and pulsating, around her nipples and in her groin.

Deliciously, the knowing touch followed the form and outline of her ribcage, lay flat over the concavity of her belly, then fanned outwards to encompass the rise of her hips.

280

'I feel better already,' mewed Toni, and her body began to ache with that old familiar feeling.

She smelt perfume and was aware of the splendour of her surroundings. Thick white leather covered the ceiling. The walls seemed to blink with light, and there was a sumptuousness in the cabin that few sailing yachts ever possess. 'Where am I?' she asked through swollen lips.

Emira's lips came near. His voice was low and his breath hinted at Oriental spices and full-bodied wine.

'This is *Adonis*. It is Madame Salvatore's motor yacht. You were almost drowned, you know.'

'Yes,' said Toni weakly. 'I know. Is Conway all right?'

'Yes. Everyone is all right. *Enchantress* lost her mast, but a fishing boat threw her a line and towed her in.'

'Good, I'm glad of that. I wouldn't like to see such men wasted.'

Emira smiled. 'No. Neither would Madame Salvatore.'

Toni managed another smile. She knew exactly what Emira meant. Venetia Salvatore had those young men around her for one reason and one alone. They were there for her own personal – very personal – service.

Behind Emira, and next to Venetia, Philippe stood watching, his eyes staring as Toni writhed decadently beneath the skilled hands of Emira.

Toni's hair was damp, but spread out around her lovely face like a giant halo.

There was a hazy unreality about her body, the creaminess of her skin, the dark arched eyebrows, the long eyelashes that so easily kissed her cheeks.

Her lips were parted slightly, and she was purring like a contented cat.

To him, she was his dream, a dream that had erupted from his first sexual experience. No, he thought to himself, that isn't quite right. She isn't the other Antonia. The dream did not erupt from her. This Antonia is real.

Venetia stood between her two sons. With interest, she watched the naked girl who was responding with such abandon to the dark and experienced hands of the big black man. Hope teetered in her heart. How she hated animosity, especially between her sons. In a way, she blamed herself for that enmity. It had been her own loyalty to Philippe's father that had caused all this. She had promised him that Philippe would be initiated into carnal love in the same way as his father and all his ancestors had been. She had made that promise to him when he was on his deathbed, and she had ensured that it was carried out.

Of course, she hadn't needed to do the same for Conway. His father had been Australian. But no matter what she gave to one son, she had to give to the other. Her sons were the joy of her life, but on reflection, perhaps she should have found a different woman for each one. Using the same woman was where the trouble had arisen.

The old Antonia of the red hair and green eyes had been good at her job. Yet probably, because Philippe and Conway had been young, she had only enticed one side of each of their natures – at least – when it came to redheads. Now, with the new Antonia, both sides of their characters would become whole again in each man. The new Antonia, Venetia told herself, would do this.

Conway's mouth was slightly open as he watched Emira use the palms of his hands to press Toni's thighs open. Already he was seeing Toni differently than before. When she had arrived, it had been Andrea who had fuelled his anger and said she had been employed purely for his brother's pleasure. Now, he knew otherwise.

Warmth and desire were twin partners now in Toni's body. She murmured and moved more freely as her arousal increased, her nipples flame red and rigid, her bracelets tinkling as she gripped at the bedding.

Emira's dark fingers and red fingernails were lingering on her plush white lips. Positively glowing with slippery juices, the pinkness of her clustered flesh came into view as Emira turned back the folds of her labia.

Venetia heard both of her sons catch their breath.

Quietly, satisfied that her task was done, she left their sides and made her way back to her own cabin where Pietro and Carlos were naked and awaiting her.

Wild with desire, Toni opened her eyes.

Never in her most erotic dream had she contemplated an adventure like this.

Three male faces looked down at her face and body.

One was Philippe, his brow and facial outline as Roman and classic as the head on any ancient coin. His eyes glittered like sapphires, and he smiled at her.

Next to him was Conway. There was a sweet boyishness about him that most definitely appealed. The ogre in him had disappeared; in fact, he still looked as surprised as when they'd been together earlier in the cabin on *Enchantress*.

The deep and dark eyes of Emira only glanced at her, but the loving and wide mouth continued to smile.

'Perhaps,' said Toni hesitantly, 'you can now explain to me in full exactly what the job is really all about.'

Emira looked to Philippe and Conway. In turn, they looked at each other, then to Emira.

'You tell her. You can explain it far better than I can,' said Philippe in his clipped, patrician manner.

'Yeah,' added Conway. 'It's better coming from a ...' He stopped and laughed. 'Sorry, I was going to say "a woman".'

For the briefest of moments, a deeper darkness stirred in Emira's eyes.

Toni noticed it. Somehow, it touched her deepest senses. Gently, she reached for one of the glossy dark hands that were both gentle and strong. With warm affection, her fingers folded over Emira's fingers, then squeezed them.

The handsome transsexual, his cheeks rouged with a hint of deep purple, smiled.

'I think,' said Emira in a slow and measured tone, 'they mean that I encompass both sexes, so I understand

283

the needs of both. As for your job interview, you have passed with flying colours. All you need to be is everything to both these young men. To Philippe, you must be the lover of his body; the one who will lie with him and endure the more disciplined side of his nature infrequently. In Conway's case, he prefers a submissive subject rather than a sexual partner, though from what I can gather, for you he might very well make an exception. If you accept the position, you also accept both men and bring both brothers back together.' Emira paused and took a quick breath as he studied the flaming redness of Toni's hair, the deep green of her eyes. 'Well,' he said, a worried frown playing over his eyes. 'Do you accept the position? Will you be of service to both brothers just as the first Antonia was?'

Toni stretched and reached her arms above her head. Her hair felt soft and drier than it had been. Perhaps, she thought, it's because I am hot, and I want to be hotter.

At last, she smiled. 'Both brothers,' she said, then added, 'and a third man – of my own choosing.'

Neither man said anything to the other. They just stared, and as the engines of the magnificent cruiser sprang into life, three men disrobed, and three glorious erections filled her eyes. All three were pointing at her.

NO LADY – Saskia Hope
ISBN 0 352 32857 6

WEB OF DESIRE – Sophie Danson
ISBN 0 352 32856 8

BLUE HOTEL – Cherri Pickford
ISBN 0 352 32858 4

CASSANDRA'S CONFLICT – Fredrica Alleyn
ISBN 0 352 32859 2

THE CAPTIVE FLESH – Cleo Cordell
ISBN 0 352 32872 X

PLEASURE HUNT – Sophie Danson
ISBN 0 352 32880 0

OUTLANDIA – Georgia Angelis
ISBN 0 352 32883 5

BLACK ORCHID – Roxanne Carr
ISBN 0 352 32888 6

ODALISQUE – Fleur Reynolds
ISBN 0 352 32887 8

OUTLAW LOVER – Saskia Hope
ISBN 0 352 32909 2

THE SENSES BEJEWELLED – Cleo Cordell
ISBN 0 352 32904 1

GEMINI HEAT – Portia Da Costa
ISBN 0 352 32912 2

VIRTUOSO – Katrina Vincenzi
ISBN 0 352 32907 6

MOON OF DESIRE – Sophie Danson
ISBN 0 352 32911 4

FIONA'S FATE – Fredrica Alleyn
ISBN 0 352 32913 0

HANDMAIDEN OF PALMYRA – Fleur Reynolds
ISBN 0 352 32919 X

OUTLAW FANTASY – Saskia Hope
ISBN 0 352 32920 3

THE SILKEN CAGE – Sophie Danson
ISBN 0 352 32928 9

RIVER OF SECRETS – Saskia Hope & Georgia Angelis
ISBN 0 352 32925 4

VELVET CLAWS – Cleo Cordell
ISBN 0 352 32926 2

THE GIFT OF SHAME – Sarah Hope-Walker
ISBN 0 352 32935 1

SUMMER OF ENLIGHTENMENT – Cheryl Mildenhall
ISBN 0 352 32937 8

A BOUQUET OF BLACK ORCHIDS – Roxanne Carr
ISBN 0 352 32939 4

JULIET RISING – Cleo Cordell
ISBN 0 352 32938 6

DEBORAH'S DISCOVERY – Fredrica Alleyn
ISBN 0 352 32945 9

THE TUTOR – Portia Da Costa
ISBN 0 352 32946 7

THE HOUSE IN NEW ORLEANS – Fleur Reynolds
ISBN 0 352 32951 3

ELENA'S CONQUEST – Lisette Allen
ISBN 0 352 32950 5

CASSANDRA'S CHATEAU – Fredrica Alleyn
ISBN 0 352 32955 6

WICKED WORK – Pamela Kyle
ISBN 0 352 32958 0

DREAM LOVER – Katrina Vincenzi
ISBN 0 352 32956 4

PATH OF THE TIGER – Cleo Cordell
ISBN 0 352 32959 9

BELLA'S BLADE – Georgia Angelis
ISBN 0 352 32965 3

THE DEVIL AND THE DEEP BLUE SEA – Cheryl
Mildenhall
ISBN 0 352 32966 1

WESTERN STAR – Roxanne Carr
ISBN 0 352 32969 6

A PRIVATE COLLECTION – Sarah Fisher
ISBN 0 352 32970 X

NICOLE'S REVENGE – Lisette Allen
ISBN 0 352 32984 X

UNFINISHED BUSINESS – Sarah Hope-Walker
ISBN 0 352 32983 1

CRIMSON BUCCANEER – Cleo Cordell
ISBN 0 352 32987 4

LA BASQUAISE – Angel Strand
ISBN 0 352 329888 2

THE LURE OF SATYRIA – Cheryl Mildenhall
ISBN 0 352 32994 7

THE DEVIL INSIDE – Portia Da Costa
ISBN 0 352 32993 9

HEALING PASSION – Sylvie Ouellette
ISBN 0 352 32998 X

THE SEDUCTRESS – Vivienne LaFay
ISBN 0 352 32997 1

THE STALLION – Georgina Brown
ISBN 0 352 33005 8

CRASH COURSE – Juliet Hastings
ISBN 0 352 33018 X

THE INTIMATE EYE – Georgia Angelis
ISBN 0 352 33004 X

THE AMULET – Lisette Allen
ISBN 0 352 33019 8

CONQUERED – Fleur Reynolds
ISBN 0 352 33025 2

DARK OBSESSION – Fredrica Alleyn
ISBN 0 352 33026 0

Published in October

LED ON BY COMPULSION
Leila James

When Karen shelters from the rain at a country pub, an extraordinary series of events begins to unfold. The attractive owner of the pub wastes no time in seducing her into his world of fast living and luxury. Whisked away to his exclusive retreat, Karen meets his female partner in perversity, and together they introduce her to a new way of life.

ISBN 0 352 33032 5

OPAL DARKNESS
Cleo Cordell

Another piece of darkly erotic writing from the author whom *Today* newspaper dubbed 'the queen of suburban erotica'. This tells the story of beautiful twins Sidonie and Francis, trapped in the strict confines of nineteenth-century British morals. Their unique fondness for each other and their newly-awakened sexuality alarms their father, who packs them off on the grand tour of Europe. But they swiftly turn cultural exploration into something illicit, exciting and indulgent.

ISBN 0 352 33033 3

Published in November

JEWEL OF XANADU
Roxanne Carr

In the land of the Tartar warriors lies the pleasure palace of the Kublai Khan. But Cirina has grown up knowing only the harsh life of the caravanserai. When she is captured and taken to the palace, she meets Venetian artist Antonio Balleri, who is making his way across the Gobi desert to reclaim a priceless Byzantine jewel. Together, they embark on an erotically-charged mission to recover the jewel together.

ISBN 0 352 33037 6

RUDE AWAKENING
Pamela Kyle

Alison is a control freak. She loves giving orders to her wealthy, masochistic husband and spending her time shopping and relaxing. But when she and her friend Belinda are kidnapped and held to ransom in less than salubrious surroundings, they have to come to terms with their most secret selves and draw on reserves of inner strength and cunning.

ISBN 0 352 33036 8

To be published in December

GOLD FEVER
Louisa Francis

The Australian outback is a harsh place by anyone's judgement. But in the 1860s, things were especially tough for women. The feisty Ginny Leigh is caught in a stifling marriage and yearns for fun and adventure. Dan Berrigan is on the run, accused of a crime he didn't commit. When they meet up in Wattle Creek, their lust for each other is immediate. There's gold in the hills and their happiness seems certain. But can Ginny outwit those determined to ruin her with scandal?

ISBN 0 352 33043 0

EYE OF THE STORM
Georgina Brown

Antonia thought she was in a long-term relationship with a globe-trotting bachelor. She was not. His wife told her so. Seething with anger, Toni decides to run away to sea. She gets a job on a yacht but her new employers turn out to be far from normal. The owner of the craft is in a constant state of bitter rivalry with his half-brother and the arrival of their outrageous mother throws everyone into a spin. But the one thing they all have in common is a love of bizarre sex.

ISBN 0 352 330044 9

If you would like a complete list of plot summaries of Black Lace titles, please fill out the questionnaire overleaf or send a stamped addressed envelope to:-

Black Lace
332 Ladbroke Grove
London W10 5AH

BLACK
lace

WE NEED YOUR HELP . . .
to plan the future of women's erotic fiction –

– and no stamp required!

Yours are the only opinions that matter.

Black Lace is the first series of books devoted to erotic fiction by women for women.

We intend to keep providing the best-written, sexiest books you can buy. And we'd appreciate your help and valued opinion of the books so far. Tell us what you want to read.

THE BLACK LACE QUESTIONNAIRE

SECTION ONE: ABOUT YOU

1.1 Sex (*we presume you are female, but so as not to discriminate*)
Are you?
Male ☐
Female ☐

1.2 Age
under 21 ☐   21–30 ☐
31–40 ☐   41–50 ☐
51–60 ☐   over 60 ☐

1.3 At what age did you leave full-time education?
still in education ☐   16 or younger ☐
17–19 ☐   20 or older ☐

1.4 Occupation _____

1.5 Annual household income

    under £10,000 ☐   £10–£20,000 ☐

    £20–£30,000 ☐   £30–£40,000 ☐

    over £40,000 ☐

1.6 We are perfectly happy for you to remain anonymous; but if you would like to receive information on other publications available, please insert your name and address

_____

_____

_____

_____

SECTION TWO: ABOUT BUYING BLACK LACE BOOKS

2.1 How did you acquire this copy of *Eye of the Storm*?

    I bought it myself ☐   My partner bought it ☐

    I borrowed/found it ☐

2.2 How did you find out about Black Lace books?

    I saw them in a shop ☐

    I saw them advertised in a magazine ☐

    I saw the London Underground posters ☐

    I read about them in _____

    Other _____

2.3 Please tick the following statements you agree with:

    I would be less embarrassed about buying Black Lace books if the cover pictures were less explicit ☐

    I think that in general the pictures on Black Lace books are about right ☐

    I think Black Lace cover pictures should be as explicit as possible ☐

2.4 Would you read a Black Lace book in a public place – on a train for instance?

    Yes ☐   No ☐

SECTION THREE: ABOUT THIS BLACK LACE BOOK

3.1 Do you think the sex content in this book is:
Too much ☐ About right ☐
Not enough ☐

3.2 Do you think the writing style in this book is:
Too unreal/escapist ☐ About right ☐
Too down to earth ☐

3.3 Do you think the story in this book is:
Too complicated ☐ About right ☐
Too boring/simple ☐

3.4 Do you think the cover of this book is:
Too explicit ☐ About right ☐
Not explicit enough ☐

Here's a space for any other comments:

SECTION FOUR: ABOUT OTHER BLACK LACE BOOKS

4.1 How many Black Lace books have you read? ☐

4.2 If more than one, which one did you prefer?

4.3 Why?

SECTION FIVE: ABOUT YOUR IDEAL EROTIC NOVEL

We want to publish the books you want to read – so this is your chance to tell us exactly what your ideal erotic novel would be like.

5.1 Using a scale of 1 to 5 (1 = no interest at all, 5 = your ideal), please rate the following possible settings for an erotic novel:

Medieval/barbarian/sword 'n' sorcery ☐
Renaissance/Elizabethan/Restoration ☐
Victorian/Edwardian ☐
1920s & 1930s – the Jazz Age ☐
Present day ☐
Future/Science Fiction ☐

5.2 Using the same scale of 1 to 5, please rate the following themes you may find in an erotic novel:

Submissive male/dominant female ☐
Submissive female/dominant male ☐
Lesbianism ☐
Bondage/fetishism ☐
Romantic love ☐
Experimental sex e.g. anal/watersports/sex toys ☐
Gay male sex ☐
Group sex ☐

Using the same scale of 1 to 5, please rate the following styles in which an erotic novel could be written:

Realistic, down to earth, set in real life ☐
Escapist fantasy, but just about believable ☐
Completely unreal, impressionistic, dreamlike ☐

5.3 Would you prefer your ideal erotic novel to be written from the viewpoint of the main male characters or the main female characters?

Male ☐   Female ☐
Both ☐

5.4 What would your ideal Black Lace heroine be like? Tick as many as you like:

Dominant	☐	Glamorous	☐
Extroverted	☐	Contemporary	☐
Independent	☐	Bisexual	☐
Adventurous	☐	Naive	☐
Intellectual	☐	Introverted	☐
Professional	☐	Kinky	☐
Submissive	☐	Anything else?	☐
Ordinary	☐	_____	

5.5 What would your ideal male lead character be like? Again, tick as many as you like:

Rugged	☐		
Athletic	☐	Caring	☐
Sophisticated	☐	Cruel	☐
Retiring	☐	Debonair	☐
Outdoor-type	☐	Naive	☐
Executive-type	☐	Intellectual	☐
Ordinary	☐	Professional	☐
Kinky	☐	Romantic	☐
Hunky	☐		
Sexually dominant	☐	Anything else?	☐
Sexually submissive	☐	_____	

5.6 Is there one particular setting or subject matter that your ideal erotic novel would contain?

_____

SECTION SIX: LAST WORDS

6.1 What do you like best about Black Lace books?

_____

6.2 What do you most dislike about Black Lace books?

_____

6.3 In what way, if any, would you like to change Black Lace covers?

_____

6.4 Here's a space for any other comments:

_____

_____

_____

_____

Thank you for completing this questionnaire. Now tear it out of the book – carefully! – put it in an envelope and send it to:

Black Lace
FREEPOST
London
W10 5BR

No stamp is required if you are resident in the U.K.